DEMO

VIA DAEMONIA MOTORCYCLE CLUB
BOOK SIX

ELISE GEDICKE

Kim Gedicke

Cover design by: Elise Gedicke
Editor: Sarah DeLong
ISBN: 979-8-9921222-0-6
EMG Publishing

DEMO'S SPOTIFY PLAYLIST

Demo's Spotify Playlist

VDMC CHARACTER LIST

STEEL–PRESIDENT

- Real Name: Jack Duncan
- Branch of Military: Marines (20yrs)
- Ol' lady: Jenna Duncan
- Kids: Carter, Jordan, & Melanie
- Foster Kid: Oliver "Ollie"
- Grandkid: Andrew "Drew"
- Job: Owns *Little Shoes* consignment store

LUCKY–VICE PRESIDENT

- Real Name: Russell McCoy
- Branch of Military: Marines (4yrs)
- Ol' lady: Harper McCoy (formerly Hannigan)
- Kids: Scotty, Charlotte "Sissy", Conner
- Job: Art Welder

BULLDOG–SERGEANT AT ARMS

- Real Name: José Santiago
- Branch of Military: Army
- Ol' lady: Abigail "Abby" Santiago (formerly Knight)
- Kids: Cassandra "Cassie", Lila, Caleb, Georgianna "Georgie"
- Family: Mom-Louisa, Brother-Carlos
- Job: Author

JUMPER–SECRETARY

- Real Name: Marshall Sager
- Branch of Military: Navy SEAL (medically discharged)
- Ol' lady: Jasmine Sharpe, DVM
- Pet: Aerial (service dog)
- Family: Brother-Pirate
- Job: part-time at garage due to severe PTSD

DEMO–TREASURER

- Real Name: Ron Snyder
- Branch of Military: Air Force
- Ol' lady: Paige Hannigan
- Kids: Nelson "Nelly Bean" & Michael "Mikey"
- Job: CPA & Club accountant/business manager

BEAR–ROAD CAPTAIN

- Real Name: Terrance Collins
- Branch of Military: Marines (10yr)
- Ol' lady: Dr. Tessa Collins (formerly Fisher)

- Kid: Margaret "Maggie"
- Job: Hospice Nurse

GHOST—ENFORCER

- Branch of Military: Navy SEAL
- Job: Co-manages *Demon on the Rocks*

KEYS—MEMBER

- Branch of Military: Navy Intelligence
- Job: Cyber Security

ANGEL—MEMBER

- Real Name: Selene Matthews
- Branch of Military: Army
- Ol' man: Vasileios "Cage" Georgiou
- Kid: Brianne "Bree" (formerly Brianna Faux)
- Job: Tattoo Artist, owns *Inked Ya*

GRUMPY—MEMBER

- Branch of Military: Army
- Job: Manages garage/mechanic

CAGE—MEMBER

- Real Name: Vasileios Georgiou
- Branch of Military: Navy Submariner
- Ol' lady: Selene "Angel" Matthews

- Kids: Aaron & Bree
- Job: Manages construction company

PUMPKIN–MEMBER

- Real Name: Seth Andrich
- Branch of Military: Marines
- Kid: Seth Jr. "SJ"
- Job: Mechanic/tow truck driver

RANGER–MEMBER

- Branch of Military: Army Ranger
- Job: Co-manages *Demon on the Rocks*

BONES–MEMBER

- Branch of Military: Army
- Job: Electrician for construction company

LIONHEART—MEMBER (DECEASED)

- Real Name: Conner
- Branch of Military: Marine
- Family: Owen (twin)

PIRATE—MEMBER

- Real Name: Gus Sager
- Branch of Military: Marine (medically discharged)
- Family: Brother-Jumper

- Job: Security Guard at High School

STARBUCKS "STAR"—MEMBER

- Real Name: Quinten "Q"
- Branch of the Military: Marine Raider

SCAR—FORMER MEMBER

PROSPECTS

- Sara
- William "Will"
- Mitch

VDMC EMPLOYEES

- Frankie (Nanny)
- Yelizaveta (Housekeeper)

FORMER HONEYS

- Ginger
- Cheryl (deceased)
- Gracie
- Monica
- Evette (deceased)
- Lacy

COPS

- Carlos Santiago–Sheriff
- Ronald Hannigan–Sheriff (former)
- Mark Connelly–Deputy (deceased)
- Bert Anderson–Deputy
- Daniel Weiss–Deputy
- Jeffery Miller–Deputy
- Scott Pan–Deputy
- Carl Kostrab–Deputy

MOUNT GROVE TOWNSFOLK

- Mable Weiss–owns *Loafin' Around*
- Tony–owns *Bella Pizzeria*
- Penny—waitress at *Bella Pizzeria*
- Kelly–waitress at *Groveton Diner*
- Frank Rockland—High School Principal
- Coach Wallace—High School Football Coach
- Mrs. Crape—High School Secretary
- Juliana—Bree & Lila's Therapist
- Dr. Rutenberg—Jumper's Therapist
- Dr. Skurja—Abby & Cassie's Therapist

TRIGGER WARNING

This book contains references to blackmail, assault, torture,
bankruptcy, and foot fetish/podophilia.
Please be aware. Your mental health matters.

PROLOGUE

$\mathcal{R}$on "Demo" Snyder stood between two of his club brothers, Jumper and Bear. The night air was heavy with tension and anticipation of what was about to happen. They were all gathered around the moonlit, snow-covered field. Every patched member and prospect of the *Via Daemonia* Motorcycle Club was present. The club's hands were not as clean as they had been for the first five years of their existence. Blood now stained them red. One could argue the justification of their actions, but it did not change their new color.

And now? Their red hands were about to become even darker. The club had never had an execution like this before.

Though none of the ol' ladies or club kids were present, they knew something was amiss from the tension around the clubhouse.

Demo looked over at his club brother, Pumpkin, and did not envy the man. His son had been born less than four hours ago yet here he was, stuck in the snow with the rest of them. Though Pumpkin's face was devoid of any emotion, Demo knew his friend and brother well enough to know how badly he was hurting. His son's birthday would forever be tainted. He would never be able to celebrate without having this moment stuck in his head.

As much as Demo knew that Pumpkin didn't deserve that, he also knew that Steel had to make a point. That point was simple: *do not betray your club.* If the Honeys hadn't already been dismissed of their duties, Demo had to wonder if Steel would have made them be present too. After all, it was one of them who had betrayed the VDMC.

Cheryl knelt in the snow. For all that she had just given birth four hours before, she didn't look sleepy. Pale, certainly, and shaky with nerves. Silent tears streamed down her makeup-less cheeks. Steel had allowed her one final meal and a shower before escorting her out to the field himself. She wore a pair of medical scrubs but no jacket or shoes.

The club's President stood stoically behind her. Demo knew Steel's only reservation about what was to happen was because Cheryl was a woman. It went against the grain, but Steel would never ask someone to do a job he wasn't willing to do himself.

Which was why he was standing behind Cheryl with a gun and a silencer as she said her final prayers. Angel had offered to do it. As the only female member, she knew how the rest of them felt about executing a woman. She'd taken care of Evette, Cheryl's partner in crime. The only reason Cheryl was still alive was because she'd been carrying Pumpkin's son up until four hours before.

Steel, however, had declined Angel's offer. Perhaps Steel did not want to put another death on Angel or perhaps he wanted to make an example of Cheryl. Regardless, he would be the one to pull the trigger today.

Pumpkin and Bulldog flanked him. The only reason Pumpkin was there instead of Lucky, the club's VP, was because he'd asked. He expressed time and time again that he did not have feelings for Cheryl. That she'd been nothing more than a convenient fuck. But Demo had to wonder if Pumpkin was as detached from what was about to happen as he claimed. He had spent a lot of time with Cheryl over the past three months. He said it was taking care of his son, which he couldn't do without also taking care of Cheryl.

Demo hadn't held the baby or seen him yet. He'd gotten the message that the baby had been born and then to come outside. They all had known this was coming. In the past, the club had circled around the pregnant ol' lady, protecting and helping her as much as they could as they all impatiently waited for the new club baby to make his or her appearance. This time, it had felt more like a *guillotine watch*. Demo wasn't even sure where the baby was, though he was certain he hadn't been left alone. Most likely Tessa, Bear's wife and ol' lady who had helped deliver the baby, was caring for him until Pumpkin could get back.

The number of club kids had exploded in the past year. Steel and Lucky used to be the only ones with kids, and then suddenly Bear, Bulldog, Angel, Cage, and now Pumpkin had joined the ranks of parenthood. Demo loved his club nieces and nephews, but there was no doubt he was closer to Sissy, Lucky's adult daughter, than he was Lila, Bulldog's six-year-old daughter. Kids? Well, they terrified him.

When the question of paternity had come up for Cheryl's unborn child, Demo had nearly shit a brick as Bear had come towards him with a mouth swab. All of the unattached members had been tested with the exceptions of Angel, who was a woman and *couldn't* have fathered a child, and Jumper, who had been celibate prior to pairing up with his ol' lady, Jasmine, due to his severe PTSD.

Demo knew that he would have stepped up to care for the baby had it been his. He *would* have—at least, that's what he kept telling himself. But he also knew he had been praying with every fiber of his being that he was *not* the father. Kids were observant and loud and needed constant protection.

The idea of holding a small little person that was solely

3

dependent on him? That wasn't the terrifying part. No, Demo knew down to the marrow of his bones that he would do *anything* for his child. That *unknown future* was what terrified him.

His own mom had made the ultimate sacrifice for him. He'd been raised by a single father who loved him, but also blamed him for his wife's death. None of it was Demo's fault—his father knew that—but it didn't stop the looks, the *pain*. Demo had joined the military in hopes of finally proving to his father that he wasn't selfish. He wanted to honor his mother's sacrifice by making something of his life.

Though his relationship with his dad had gotten better over the years, it wasn't the greatest. They talked on holidays and birthdays. Demo went out to Wyoming to visit him two times a year. His dad had never come to Pennsylvania to visit him.

He didn't remember much about his mom. Since he was five years old, it had been just his dad and him…and the guilt. It was hard to imagine ever blaming his child for something that was entirely not his fault. Demo knew that nothing short of unconditional love would be how he would raise his children. No sacrifice would be too great. He would give his child *everything* he was and *everything* he had to ensure they had a bright and happy future.

And *that* terrified him.

Not the idea of dying for his child as his mom had. He'd gotten past the fear of death while in the military. But not knowing what he would do for his kid. How far he would go to protect them.

Pumpkin's son was four hours old and now Pumpkin was about to watch his club's President execute the mother of his child.

All the times he'd pushed off the idea of having his own kid, Demo had never paused to wonder about that kid's mother. Of course, he or she would have to have a mother. That was biology. But Demo had never pictured her before.

He liked women. Hell, he *loved* women. He loved their shapes and their laughter, their hips and their lips, their sassiness and their coyness... He loved the challenge of the chase and the thrill of the win once they made it to a bed, or a wall, or a cage, or a closet.

But come morning, Demo never had the desire to stick around for seconds. The game was won, the chase was over. There was nothing left to discover. He didn't even have it in him to say he would call, knowing he never would. It was just a quick goodbye, the occasional 'thank you', and off he went. The only repeats in his history had been the club Honeys and that was because they had known the score. There had never been the concept of 'more' with them.

Now that the Honeys were a thing of the past, there were some changes to Demo's routine. Getting shot hadn't helped that either. He'd needed time to recover too. Sex hadn't been a priority when he'd been worried about dying.

Nearly dying had given him some perspective though. He saw the relationships of those around him and had to wonder if that was in his future. Hell, if *Cage*, the biggest man-whore the club had, could be tamed and domesticated by love, there had to be hope for Demo too.

Right?

Steel stepped forward. He placed a hand on Cheryl's shoulder. Though her back was to the club members there to bear witness to her execution, Demo saw her wince.

He wondered what was going through her mind. Was she worried about going to Heaven or Hell? Was she concerned about her son and how he would be raised? Maybe the fact that he would never know her? Perhaps, she was contemplating how she'd lived her life. Did she have regrets or was she satisfied with the life she led?

"Any last words?"

Demo's head snapped up at Steel's words. His face was emotionless, giving meaning to his moniker. His eyes and face were 'hard as steel'.

Whether from nerves or the cold, Cheryl's body trembled as she shook her head.

Steel raised his handgun. The silver gleamed in the moonlight. The muzzle of the silencer was aimed at her brain stem. Despite what he was about to do, Steel was not a cruel man. He had no desire to have Cheryl suffer needlessly. Had she been a man and did what she did, Demo had no doubt that her life would be ending far differently. Steel was not the sort of man to treat a woman so heartlessly regardless of transgressions. Aiming the bullet for her brain stem would be an instant and painless death.

Demo saw Steel's finger start to squeeze on the trigger when Cheryl suddenly shouted, "Wait!" and spun around. Steel lowered the gun without firing. On her hands and knees in the snow, she looked up at Pumpkin with tear-filled eyes. "His name. Just... please... I want to know his name."

Pumpkin didn't owe her anything. He could also have lied to her, but this was practically her dying request. Almost like a last cigarette.

Still, there was enough hesitation where Demo wondered if Pumpkin was going to answer or not. Then he said, "Seth. I'm giving him my name and will call him 'Junior' or 'SJ'."

Cheryl's chin trembled. "Seth," she muttered softly. "Please..." She wiped at her wet cheeks. "When he's old enough, tell him I'm sorry that I couldn't be there for him. And... And that I don't blame you." Her eyes never wavered from Pumpkin's, making Demo believe she meant him specifically and not the club as a whole.

After another moment of hesitation, Cheryl nodded to Steel. "I'm ready." Her chin wobbled as she turned back around.

She tipped her chin up towards the moon. Steel once more raised the muzzle of his gun.

When Demo had been shot, it had been a reflex. Jasmine had been in danger and he'd placed himself between that danger and her. He would have done so for any of the ol' ladies, the club kids, and even his brothers. Demo had been in many firefights, though his time in the military was generally spent disarming or building various demolitions. Due to the lack of fingers on his left dominant hand, he'd had to work through years of therapy to force his right hand to become his new dominant hand. His aim was just as true now as it had been prior to his injury.

Even bleeding out with two bullets in him, Demo had fought to protect Jasmine. His returning fire had taken out the tire of the van. The possibility of death had occurred to him, but his primary emotion had been concern for Jasmine. He'd failed to protect her from being kidnapped.

One had to wonder what went through someone's mind as they were being executed. When Demo had been shot and thought he was going to die, he realized he had regrets. One of the first things he'd done upon waking up after surgery was to call his dad. Even though it had just turned into another one of their disjointed conversations, he'd made the effort. With Christmas coming up, Demo planned to fly out to see him. He did not want his relationship with his father to be a regret at the end of either of their lives.

His other regret was harder to explain. He didn't see a specific woman, merely the silhouette of one. Demo had no idea who she was and thought perhaps it was merely the absence of a woman in his life. Unlike Bulldog, he wasn't secretly pining for a lost love or like Jumper, fearful he wasn't worthy of love. There literally was no woman who had ever caught his eye as the ol' ladies had with his club brothers.

It made him wonder if perhaps he was destined to be alone. The lack of kids didn't bother him, but the lack of a woman made him feel like he was missing a limb. Even now, it was like there was a faceless phantom standing behind him.

In the silence of the night, Steel pulled the trigger. The sharp *thwick* of the bullet was followed immediately by the *thud* of Cheryl's body crumpling in the snow. No one moved for several long minutes. Crimson stained the white blanketing the frozen ground beneath their boots.

Finally Bear moved forward. Squatting down, he verified Cheryl's death with a single nod up to Steel.

Demo took several steps forward. He didn't touch or say anything to Pumpkin. The two men were nearly the same height at six feet. Though Demo was a few years younger, the two had become fast friends upon Pumpkin joining the club. He'd been one of their first prospects, serving only six months instead of the required year.

Others eventually left. The prospects took the body. And still Pumpkin stared at the stained ground.

Demo's shoulder throbbed from the cold, but he didn't want to leave his friend. He wasn't sure what Pumpkin was thinking or feeling. Steel remained behind too. Demo knew there was no animosity between the two. Pumpkin would never blame Steel for doing what he had to do.

"I don't feel bad about her," Pumpkin finally said. His voice held little emotion. "I'm worried about my son who is now motherless. What if he turns into some sort of psycho serial killer because he didn't grow up with a mother's love?"

Demo gave his friend a sidelong glance. "I think he's more likely to grow up to become an asshole with you as his dad."

Pumpkin snorted.

"He might not have a mother," Steel said quietly from behind them, "but he'll have family. You think the ol' ladies are going to allow him to grow up not knowing how to treat a woman with respect or to protect those weaker than him? He'll have plenty of maternal input in his life."

"Plus," Demo added, "I hear that DILFs are totally in right now."

Pumpkin chuckled. He ran a hand down his tired face. "You know, those fuckers who told us in Sex Ed that abstinence is the best form of birth control lied. Having a baby is. I don't think my dick's worked right since Bear told me the baby was mine."

Demo wanted to laugh at his friend's joke, but a sharp pain in his shoulder distracted him. He flinched, his right hand going automatically to his left shoulder.

"SJ's going to be just fine," Steel said. He stepped up beside them. Though his words were for Pumpkin, his sharp eyes that seemed to miss nothing were on Demo. "He's *Via Daemonia*. There's more to his legacy than having you for his father or who his mother was."

Slowly, Pumpkin nodded. He turned his back on the crimson snow. "My kid's hours old and I'm already worried about so much. Like, his first date and explaining girls to him. What if he has an allergy? What do I do if he gets sick?"

Steel let out a very rare chuckle and clasped Pumpkin on his shoulder. "Welcome to fatherhood, brother. And just a word of warning, those fears will never go away—no matter how old your son gets."

That said, Steel headed back towards the clubhouse. Throwing his head over his shoulder, the President added, "And Demo? Get yourself to the fucking doctor!"

Demo grimaced. He was a fucking adult, yet he felt like he'd just been scolded by the principal. "How does he fucking do that?"

Pumpkin shrugged. "I have no clue." His eyes narrowed on Demo's hand on his shoulder. "What's going on?"

Demo tried to push it off. "It's just being out in the cold."

"Bullshit," Pumpkin snapped. "What's going on?"

Rubbing the healed wound, Demo tried to alleviate the stabbing pain. "You have a baby to take care of," he reminded his friend. "You don't need to be worrying about me too."

"Having a kid doesn't change the fact that you're my friend and are hurting. Tell me what the fuck is going on."

"It's phantom pains," Demo explained. "The nerves were damaged by the bullet. The doctors repaired what they could, but it will likely always be there."

"Meaning what?"

"Meaning that the body is a remarkable thing," Demo mocked the doctor's explanation. "It can remember an injury long after it's healed."

"Can they do anything, give you anything?"

"I'm not getting hooked on drugs," Demo snapped. He pulled his hand away from his shoulder, even though he hadn't actually stopped the pain. Sometimes, when it got too bad, he would ram his shoulder into a door frame. It would hurt like hell, but it made the throbbing go away faster.

'Remarkable thing', my ass, Demo thought cynically.

"Come on," Demo encouraged, starting to follow behind Steel. "Let's get you back to your kid."

He heard Pumpkin's footfalls in the snow trailing after him. "I'm only letting you change the subject because I do want to get back to my kid. But I still want to know what's going on with you."

Demo said nothing. The doctors said the pain would eventually go away. His body just had to remember he wasn't *currently* shot. The nerves would settle. At least, that's what the doctors claimed anyway. Until then, he just needed to grin and bear it.

He could handle the pain.

CHAPTER 1

*D*emo sat at the bar with a beer in his hand, watching the chaos around him. He was never so grateful to be single in his entire life as he was in this moment.

When Demo had first joined the club, he'd seen it as a way to reconnect with society after the military and his medical discharge. The explosion that had taken the pointer, middle, and ring fingers on his left hand forced him back into a civilian lifestyle he was no longer used to. He had seen the club as a way to have that camaraderie with fellow veterans without the illegal shit most motorcycle clubs were known for.

And he was also willing to admit, he saw it as a way to get a lot of convenient pussy.

In the nearly eight years since the club had been formed, they had gone from keeping their hands clean to dirtying them for the right reasons. Demo did not have issues with breaking the law, so long as it was to protect and not to harm the innocent.

The club had grown a lot, especially in recent years. Jenna had been the only ol' lady for five years before Harper came around, followed closely by Tessa and Abby, then Jasmine. Though not an ol' lady, Jasmine brought her best friend, Sophia, with her. The sassy minx was anywhere Jasmine was and had somehow become a fixture amongst the club's ol' ladies. She might not be claimed, but Demo wasn't blind to the looks a certain club brother gave the other single men if they got too close to her.

Not only was there now a distinct feminine touch to the club, but the club kids seemed to be multiplying. In the nearly five months since the club Honey position had been dissolved, the clubhouse had become more of a family hangout center.

Demo didn't mind, per se, but his blue balls raised the occasional argument. There was something nostalgic about once being able to just curl his finger at a Honey from across the room and know he was about to get blown.

Now, Demo was watching the chaos unfold and just prayed that, if he ever did find his woman, she was on the best birth control on the market.

Following the December holidays, Lucky and Bear had made the announcements that their ol' ladies were pregnant—*again*. Shortly after that, Harper had been found in the clubhouse reorganizing the bar and putting laundry away inside the refrigerator. Shortly after *that*, Tessa had been discovered on the kitchen floor surrounded by half-eaten tubs of ice cream, a bottle of maple syrup, salt and vinegar chips, *Skittles*, and a jug of orange juice while crying and watching a *Titanic* documentary on her phone.

Nearly a week after those instances, Tessa came storming up into their Church meeting to demand where Maggie was because she'd forgotten her daughter was at her in-laws' house. After Bear had calmed her down, he'd taken her back to their house to rest. The meeting had gone on for another hour or so until Sara, one of their prospects due to be patched over in another month, had come up to get Lucky.

Harper was down in the clubhouse in a panic because her car wouldn't unlock and she had to get Conner, their son, to a doctor's appointment. Lucky had to calmly explain that she wasn't holding her car keys, but the television remote. Then he had to remind her that Conner's checkup appointment wasn't until the next day and that Lucky would be going with her.

These instances seemed to be just the tip of the iceberg for this round of pregnancies.

Around mid-January, both Tessa and Harper were reaching the halfway mark of their pregnancies. While they were over their morning sickness, they were overheard in the clubhouse one afternoon complaining about their lack of bladder control, swollen ankles, cracked nipples, hemorrhoids, the sharp pains of their baby moving around inside them, and the one-eighty mood swings.

To which Starbucks, because he was an utter dumbass, made the very loud statement, "Please. If pregnancies were that difficult no woman would willingly *get* pregnant. Personally, I think you guys are just saying all that to butter up your men. Pregnancy, periods, labor..." He waved it off. "Annoying, sure, but they're probably not painful at all." Then he rolled up his sleeve to show a round-ish scar. "Now *this* was painful."

This suggestion then prompted an all-out gender war between the couples. Even Angel and Cage were taking sides.

Like many of the single members, Demo was staying safely on the sidelines. There was absolutely no doubt in his mind that the women would win though—mostly because their men couldn't stand to see them upset and Harper at least seemed seconds away from bursting into tears.

Then DeeDee, Bear's mother, and Louisa, Bulldog's mother, came storming through the clubhouse doors, followed closely by Lawrence, Bear's father. The man stood at six and a half feet tall, yet it was his pixie of a wife whom everyone moved out of the way for.

DeeDee walked right up to Tessa and handed her a box. "Finally! I've been waiting years for this."

Which was how Lucky, Bear, Bulldog, Cage, Starbucks, and Lawrence found themselves hooked up to electrical stimulators that mimicked period pains and cramps. In a surprisingly short amount of time, the women created an obstacle course of sorts that the men had to complete to, quote, *win the Gender War.*

Lucky went first. He moaned, groaned, whined, and cried his way through doing fifty jumping jacks, moving the clubhouse couch and lounge chairs around, balancing a serving tray of plastic glasses of water—of which he dropped four—and then finally had to carry his wife twenty feet between two pieces of masking tape that had been placed on the floor.

Harper was laughing so hard at Lucky's pain and torture that she had to be let down halfway to Lucky's finish line to run to the bathroom to pee. As soon as his wife was out of sight, Lucky curled up into the fetal position on the floor and let out the most pitiful whimper.

It was not looking good for Demo's gender.

Angel, Jasmine, Sophia, DeeDee, and Louisa were representing Team Vagina. They were doing the exact same challenges with the stimulators on even higher settings with such ease that Demo was ashamed for the first time in his life to be a man. Since Harper and Tessa were pregnant, they couldn't put the stimulators on and, while Bulldog was completely on Team Penis, he adamantly refused to allow Abby to participate. Bulldog claimed she was already subjected to her biological symptoms once a month and he would not see her uncomfortable just for a "stupid fucking bet".

Jenna and Steel were the only couple not participating since, per Steel, he already knew his wife was better than him in every way.

When Team Vagina prevailed, Team Penis would be paying for a kid-free spa weekend at a fancy resort. Demo saw Keys already researching the closest five-star places that they could take the women to. It would seem none of the observing men had *any* faith in Team Penis. It wasn't until the challenge had started that Demo realized that Team Penis didn't have faith in themselves either, because no victory prize had been named should Team Penis win.

Abby cheered for her man from her seat next to Demo on the bar stool. Bulldog was sweating bullets and looked ready to puke —even though Tessa only had the stimulator on level five out of ten.

A small hand on his arm startled him, making Demo look over at the redhead. Her bright green eyes held concern. "What's wrong?"

Demo's eyebrows drew down. "What do you mean?"

"You're pressing your elbow into the bar, almost like you're trying to push your shoulder further into the socket," Abby explained.

Demo glanced down at his left arm. He hadn't even realized he'd been pushing so hard. In recent months, he'd been trying more subtle ways of relieving the pain. None were working that well. He was sleeping like crap because every time he twitched slightly in bed, pain would radiate like someone had jammed a hot poker into his shoulder.

He forced himself to sit up, trying hard not to flinch as he did. "Just tired."

Her eyes narrowed, not believing his lie. "Did you ever go see Paige?"

Paige Hannigan was Harper's sister-in-law. He knew *of* Paige, as she was around the clubhouse often with her two boys, Michael and Nelson, but he'd never spoken to her. In truth, he knew more about her finances than he did of *her*. As Treasurer, it had been Demo's job to work with Keys to fake a life insurance policy and deliver monthly checks to help her out. Her husband, Richard, had been Harper's brother—and a complete dickwad. The club didn't want to see Paige and her boys suffer for the man's sins.

Richard was dead, but no one who wasn't a patched member knew that fact. Harper and her parents suspected, because they weren't stupid. There was no proof, though, no body. As far as the world knew, Richard Hannigan was just another missing person. Keys faked the insurance policy to make it look like it was a preemptive stipend to hold Paige over while missing the family's primary income. Such a policy didn't exist, nor did any life insurance policy in Richard Hannigan's name, but the club had wanted to do something to help Paige out without delivering a suspiciously large wad of cash to her.

Harper and her parents knew Richard's sins. As far as Demo knew, his wife and young sons did not.

Paige owned an acupuncture clinic in town. She'd opened it just under a year ago. Abby had been one of her first clients, seeing her for pain and stress management. Demo didn't know much about the practice of acupuncture, but Abby swore by it. Bulldog still took her weekly for a session.

Before Demo could think of something to say to Abby, whether the truth or a white lie, Lucky's phone rang.

After releasing the Honeys from their positions, the club had voted to hire two housekeepers who were *actually* housekeepers. Yelizaveta, a wife to a local plumber and the mom of one of Harper's students, and Frankie, a college friend of Sissy's, were hired on. However, Frankie soon became more of a nanny to the club kids than a housekeeper. She lived in one of the trailers the club kept on the property too, since she needed a place to live when she had moved to town.

While Ollie, Aaron, Bree, and Scotty attended high school and Lila attended the local elementary school, Cassie was home-schooled due to her agoraphobia. Frankie helped out with Cassie's lessons, though her primary job was to take care of Conner, Maggie, Georgie, Caleb, and, most recently, SJ. With two other babies on the way, Demo wouldn't be surprised if Frankie was going to be getting an assistant or two soon. The club kept joking about opening up a daycare.

With it being a Saturday, Lila and Scotty were hanging out with Frankie and the infants at Bulldog and Abby's house. Since they had the biggest house, that tended to be the residence where the club kids were babysat.

Demo saw Tessa turn off the stimulators attached to Lucky's abdomen and groin area as he pulled out his phone. No matter a bet or challenge or adult antics, the club kids came first. Demo assumed Lila and Scotty had gotten into some mischief and the caller was Frankie until he saw Lucky's scowl when he looked at the Caller ID on his phone screen.

"It's Mitch," he said to no one in particular.

Mitch was the prospect on the front gate. He was in his sixties, a former Marine and POW, and a recent widower. His prospect year would be up towards the end of March, almost two months after Sara's and Will's year. The club was going to need to start recruiting again.

Lucky answered the phone with a short, "Yeah?" He listened for a moment, his eyes landing across the room on Harper. His ol' lady hurried over to his side, their opposite teams forgotten. Lucky pressed his lips to Harper's raven hair before instructing, "Give us ten minutes and then let him in. We're at the clubhouse."

After disconnecting the call and pocketing his phone, he turned to Steel. "Game's over. Officers need to stay."

Steel's eyes narrowed but he trusted his VP without needing further explanation at this time. "You heard him. Everyone clear out." More gently to his wife, he said, "Ollie is at Angel and Cage's with Aaron and Bree. Why don't you go with them?"

Demo exchanged worried looks with some of his brothers. Though no one had said anything, it was becoming rather obvious that Jenna wasn't well. She'd lost a lot of weight recently, looked tired and rundown, and her complexion was paler than usual. Demo knew Bear was keeping an eye on her, but neither

Steel nor Jenna had offered up an explanation as of yet. Demo had a sinking feeling whatever was going on, it wasn't good.

The fact that Jenna didn't argue with Steel practically handing her over to Angel and Cage to babysit also sent up a lot of red flags.

Everyone cleared out. Husbands kissed their wives, helping them don their jackets and escorting them to the door. Tessa and Harper walked on either side of Abby, almost like bodyguards. They would see to it that she got back to her house okay. Demo heard Pirate offer to take Jazz and Sophia out for pizza since Jumper had to stay behind. They were trailed behind by three nearly grown Pitbull puppies, Enola Bones, Winnie the Pooch, and Kidd. Aerial, Jumper's service dog, remained with him.

Though Keys was not an officer, he remained behind too. More often than not, when a problem arose, Keys' computer expertise was needed anyway. It had been mentioned more than once to call for a vote to make Keys an officer with the title of IT Specialist or as a second Enforcer. However, in doing so, it would create eight officer positions, which would mean there was no longer a tie breaker. Bear's position as Road Captain did not qualify him as a voting officer unless there was a tie or another officer needed to pass their vote onto him for whatever reason.

While the others understood Keys' value as a computer genius to the officers, Demo could also understand how unfair it was that Keys was privy to officer-only information when he wasn't an officer.

Steel turned to Lucky. "Who's at the gate?"

"Hannigan," Lucky told him. Ronald Hannigan was Harper's father, Lucky's father-in-law, and Mount Grove's former (dirty) sheriff. "And he's alone."

Steel's eyes narrowed. While Hannigan had been on property before to visit with Harper and his grandson, it generally was with his wife, Cindy, *and* with knowledge he was coming. The club did not trust him, even though he'd been tortured and nearly died for his part in his son's sins. The fact that he was dropping by unannounced did not sit well with any of them.

As SAA, Bulldog was in charge of security. Ghost, as Bulldog's Enforcer, followed his lead and command when it came to club protection. While Jumper was the club's Secretary, Demo generally ended up taking the minutes for the meetings. Demo didn't mind. As Treasurer, he took notes anyway and sometimes Jumper spaced when his anxiety was high, though that had been happening less and less since falling in love with Jazz.

There was a running joke around the club about Demo and his obsession with yellow legal pads. Even in the age of computers and how often Demo had to use his accounting programs to keep the club's finances and businesses running appropriately, he still preferred to write everything down using a pad and pencil.

"Did Mitch say why he's here?" Steel inquired.

Despite his relation to the former sheriff, Lucky had no love for the man. None of them were going to forget the time Hannigan pointed his loaded gun at Scotty after he'd crashed Lucky's fortieth birthday party with a search warrant. The *only* reason Hannigan was alive and not six feet under with his son was because of Harper. Demo knew the man was trying to make amends, but some things were just unforgivable. Even though Cindy had chosen not to divorce him, she was no longer the submissive, docile wife she'd been for most of their marriage. Per Lucky, the man's life was miserable and he got a kick out of seeing Hannigan's guilty conscience torture him on a daily basis.

"Just that he wants to speak with you."

Steel's hard expression did not change. The look exchanged between President and VP was understood by all. If Hannigan was here alone and wanted to speak with Steel, it was not a family matter. Lucky was right to send the others away, especially if Lucky did not want to stress out his pregnant wife with whatever news her father was bringing.

Keys was already typing away on his laptop behind the front bar. There was a good possibility he would find out what was going on before Hannigan even parked his cage.

Several minutes later, they heard the rough echo of tires and the groan of an engine in the parking lot. There were enough cameras around the property that they didn't need to have a prospect escort him in. Bulldog was watching Hannigan's progress from the app on his phone.

Like his daughter, Hannigan was tall and endomorphic. In the years since the entire Hannigan clan had come to Mount Grove, Demo had seen many different sides of the former Detroit detective. When he first arrived, he'd been stern, cocky, and vindictive. After the truth had come out about his involvement in Richard's crimes, he'd been remorseful but still arrogant. It hadn't been until after Mateo Castillo had captured, tortured, and nearly killed him that Hannigan had shown any signs of true regret and sorrow for his actions.

Since resigning in August, Hannigan had lost a lot of muscle. The man had been fit, taking pride in his body and appearance. Not so much anymore.

Hannigan looked *old*. His once salt and pepper hair was now completely salt, and his skin had a sagginess Demo had never noticed before. The dark circles under his eyes indicated that he hadn't been sleeping much or well.

Lucky hadn't been kidding when he'd said the guy was miserable.

Steel gave the man a once over, clearly picking up on the same things Demo was. Lucky stood directly behind Steel with his body slightly turned, as if he wanted to give Hannigan his back but his instincts wouldn't allow him to.

"Hannigan. This is unexpected." Steel's voice was not welcoming. The fact that Steel did not offer Hannigan a seat or indicate they should take this meeting upstairs to their Chapel also hinted at a disrespect towards the man. Carlos was not a member of the

MC but he'd been up in the Chapel several times in the past two years.

"Steel, thank you for seeing me." Hannigan's eyes danced around the room, taking in the unfriendly gazes. He cleared his throat. "Is there somewhere we can talk in private?"

"No," Steel said shortly. "My officers stay. Say what you came to say or leave. The choice is yours."

Silence fell. Hannigan looked to Lucky, but his face was just as cold as Steel's. Finally, he nodded slowly. "Very well. It's my daughter-in-law."

Lucky unfroze. He dropped his arms from their crossed position over his chest. He shifted to face Hannigan fully. "Paige?" Lucky couldn't give a crap about his father-in-law, but he certainly cared about his sister-in-law and young nephews. "What's wrong? Did something happen?"

"She just left our house." Hannigan looked sheepish as he admitted, "She needs help. Financially, I mean. Her clinic is not bringing in enough revenue. She's swimming in debt Richard left behind." He swallowed hard, cheeks reddening. "Cindy and I are barely getting by ourselves. As much as I want to help her, I can't. I offered for them to sell the house and move in with us, but her house has negative equity with the second mortgage. Selling it wouldn't help her. Plus, our house is small. We have a very small guest room. It would be doable only in the short term."

Demo didn't look away from Hannigan but heard Keys' fingers on his laptop's keyboard behind him. He schooled his features to give nothing away, though inside he was deeply confused. Keys and Demo had set up a recurring monthly system for Paige Hannigan to be receiving a couple thousand dollars. She was depositing the checks, because it would have flagged Keys' system if she didn't. But if she was taking the money, why was she in such debt? Where was that money going?

Hopefully Keys would be able to answer some of those questions once Hannigan left. No one in the club wanted Hannigan to know Paige was getting money from them. While Hannigan had selflessly given up his life savings to help get his son out of debt with a cartel loan shark, no one believed he had a right to any of the money the club had stolen back to help the victims of the cartel's human trafficking scheme or the two rape victims of Deputy Mark Connelly. Recently, Keys had taken funds belonging to a one-percenter motorcycle club in Pittsburgh, the Black Pythons. That money also helped their victims, as well as a large donation to a rehab center in Alexandria for the club women who had been hooked on drugs.

Steel's face betrayed none of his knowledge about Paige's situation. "I fail to see what Mrs. Hannigan's finances have to do with us."

"You have pull in this community. Help her get some business to her clinic." Hannigan's voice was turning frantic, almost pleading. Demo saw Lucky's concern increase, though he continued to allow Steel to take the lead. "Maybe host a fundraiser for her. Anything to help out is better than nothing."

Demo tried to think back to the last time he'd seen Paige. Over the summer, she'd been around during some of the women's ol' lady get-togethers. The patched members would take the kids for the day or afternoon while the women had a carefree day to do as they wished—most of that time included wine, snacks, and a lot of giggling. Lucky would occasionally bring his nephews, Nelson and Michael, which meant Paige was with the ol' ladies. Despite the name of their gathering, it was for more than just the ol' ladies of the club members. Female family and friends of the ol' ladies were also included.

Hell, even *Cage* called himself Angel's ol' lady and would hang out with the women while Angel went off with her club brothers and the club kids. He originally did it as a joke, but now was an honorary ol' lady despite being a patched member. Demo had a feeling he also did it because calling himself her ol' lady never failed to bring a smile to Angel's face.

Love had a funny way of changing a man. Not that Demo knew from experience, but he'd seen it enough times in his life to know the truth of the statement. Some men thought that love made them weaker—and it did. But Demo had also seen the strength the love of a good woman gave a man. Looking around the clubhouse, his eyes fell on Steel, Lucky, Bulldog, Bear, and Jumper. Men who would do, *had done*, anything for their wives.

Demo had witnessed the pain and the suffering Bulldog had endured when his Abby had returned to him broken and abused. At first, Demo had pitied him, thinking that his intense love for Abby made him seem wounded. How could loving a woman so much be a good thing? If Bulldog lost Abby a second time, it would have destroyed him.

Like it had Demo's dad.

Demo quickly pushed that train of thought away. Bulldog hadn't lost Abby. She was alive and healing, getting stronger every day. There was nothing *weak* about Bulldog. His love for his wife and children had only made him a better man.

But was that love worth the risk of losing it?

Steel started speaking again, and Demo forced himself to concentrate on his President's words rather than his childhood memories. "I feel for Mrs. Hannigan, but I still do not understand what this has to do with us—"

"Her parents are threatening to take the boys!" the former sheriff shouted. There was a desperation in Hannigan's voice that did not match his words.

Clearly, Steel picked up on it too. "Why would her parents do that?"

Hannigan shook his head. "You don't know her parents or the havoc they bring with them." Hannigan ran a hand down his haggard face. "I've fucked up a lot in my life. Richard is dead because of me, I know that. You'll never understand the pain that knowledge inflicts on me daily. But I have to make this right, Steel. I have to protect my grandsons. If they... If the boys are taken... There's a reason Paige went no-contact with her family years ago. You don't know what they're like. You don't understand what they'll do to the boys, what they'll turn them into."

Steel's eyes flew to Keys behind Demo. Out of the corner of his eye, Demo saw Keys lift his chin to Steel in acknowledgement before returning his attention to his computer.

Through all their dealings with cleaning up Richard Hannigan's crimes, Demo could not recall seeing anything about Paige Hannigan's side of the family. But above the anxiety and shame Hannigan was portraying, his biggest emotion was fear. Something about Paige's family made the former sheriff *afraid*.

Demo shifted in his seat. His arm tapped the side of the bar and pain shot up to his shoulder. He had to bite back a hiss of pain, as well as keep his right hand from going to the healed wound. His eyes met Bulldog's from across the room and he saw his SAA's eyes narrow on his shoulder.

Demo forced himself to look away, ignoring Bulldog's concern. He was *fine*.

"What do you mean?" Steel asked Hannigan without drawing any more attention to Keys. His voice deepened in anger. If there was one thing Steel would not stand for, it was women and children being threatened or harmed.

"They're awful people. Paige hated growing up in that house. Her birth father died when she was three and her mom remarried. I don't know all of the details but she told Cindy that her stepdad and stepbrother were horrible to her growing up. Not physically abusive, but mentally. Always putting her down. She was never good enough, never smart enough." Hannigan shook his head. "I know what you think of me, Steel. Believe me, it's no worse than I think of myself. I failed my son, but I refuse to fail my grandsons. Which is why I'm here, begging for your help. I no longer have the means to do so myself."

Steel was silent for a long time. Then, finally, he nodded. "We'll see what we can do."

Though his answer was noncommittal, Demo knew his President would not allow anything to happen to Paige or her sons.

* * *

THE VDMC OFFICERS sat around the long conference table. Keys set up his laptops and various equipment in front of him while Demo placed his trusty pad and pen before him. As soon as Hannigan had left, Steel ordered them upstairs.

Steel wasted no time getting to the point. "I thought we were sending her money each month?"

"We are," Demo and Keys said together. Demo nodded for Keys to continue, since he was the one with the more accurate information in front of him. "She's depositing the checks each month," Keys informed them without looking away from his computer screens. His eyes were squinted as they darted around between devices, his fingers dancing across the keyboard like spider legs. "However, about four months ago, she started putting the funds into a savings account instead of her checking account. Once the checks are deposited, she never withdraws the funds. I don't understand why. She has close to fifteen-thousand dollars just sitting there."

Steel looked to Lucky on his right. "Has she said anything to you or Harper?"

Lucky shook his head. "We haven't seen them since before the holidays. She was invited to dinner here with us on Christmas Day but chose to remain at home. I think Harper said something about wanting a day with the boys without the 'festive hubbub.'"

Demo could understand that. The holidays were certainly a time for stress and not relaxation. He did not understand why so much time and effort were put into them when the end result was always too much exhaustion and a lot of holiday weight. Maybe he would feel differently if he had a wife and kids to spend the time with, but those were his current opinions.

Jumper spoke up, making Demo glance up in surprise. Generally, Jumper did not speak during Church meetings. He preferred to sit back and listen. "She donated to the community Angel Tree. I know because I happen to be the one who logged her donated gifts."

"She has one credit card that isn't maxed out," Keys informed them. "It was in her name only so Richard would not have had access to it. However, she's nearly to her credit limit on it and has only been paying the minimum due each month. She manages to pay her ridiculously high mortgage on time each month but she dropped her homeowners insurance to the bare minimum. The three credit cards she shared with Richard are all maxed out with interest eating away at the payments she provides. Her savings accounts for the boys have not been touched. They're both 529 Accounts. She's only adding the occasional dollar or two to both, but she *is* adding to them. The savings account she shared with Richard was practically emptied with only thirty-two dollars and forty-three cents left in it. Her checking account only has a few hundred.

"The business account she set up when she created her acupuncture clinic is in the red. She is behind on her rent payment by two months and received another Past Due notice this morning. Her utility bills on both the house and the business are past due as well. I just paid her electric bill for her house as it was on the schedule to be turned off tomorrow if payment wasn't made. She owns the title on her car, so that's something going for her at least."

"If she has the money we're sending her, why isn't she using that to pay off her overdue bills?" Lucky asked Keys.

Keys shrugged. "I don't know. It's not like she wrote an email explaining her decision."

Bulldog scratched his long beard. "I saw Paige last Tuesday for Abby's appointment. She said her receptionist called out that day."

Keys shook his head. "I can already tell you that's a lie. She let her receptionist go before the holidays to help save on payroll costs. With her lack of customers, a receptionist probably wasn't worth the payroll anyway. Besides Abby, she only has five other regular clients and the occasional walk-in."

"She's an outsider," Bear said with a shrug. "It's not surprising to me that the townspeople aren't being receptive to her new business. They're a small town and generally only trust those whom they've known since birth." He made a gesture around the table. "Only reason the club was accepted as we were was because you had three of us born and raised here sign on as officers. They would not have been so open to the idea of a motorcycle club if they didn't know that Lucky, Bulldog, and I would never stand for the guns, drugs, and general mayhem that motorcycle clubs usually bring to small communities."

"With Carlos and Sheriff Longhill welcoming us, it backed our credibility even more," Bulldog added, referencing his brother Carlos's mentor and the town's beloved sheriff prior to Hannigan.

"We should have backed her clinic as soon as she opened," Steel said with recrimination. "She's family," he indicated his head towards Lucky, "regardless of who her husband was. But I don't understand why she's not using the money we're providing for her."

"She might be saving for something," Demo murmured. "Trying to pay something off. Not everyone knows how to effectively 'rob Peter to pay Paul'." It was an accounting term used to indicate transferring funds to pay current balances that are actually allocated for other future balances.

"I'm wondering if that money is meant for something else." Lucky's tone brooked darkness. "What if someone from Castillo's organization is squeezing her for money? When was the last time we checked on Juan Castillo and what he was up to?"

"Nearly every day," Keys said as Bulldog said, "Probably not since Abby returned."

Everyone looked towards Keys. The man continued to study his monitors as he typed away until he picked up on the silence of the room. Looking up, he straightened when he saw his brothers staring at him. "What?"

Steel was the one who spoke. "You check on Castillo's organization nearly every day?"

Keys looked a little nervous, like he wasn't sure if he messed up by his admission, but still nodded. "I wanted to make sure he was keeping his word. We had enough going on with the Heaven Haven community, Scar going rogue, and then the Pythons. I didn't want Castillo to go back on his word and it come back to bite us in the ass."

Sometimes Keys' young face misled the quick brain it housed. The kid was the youngest VDMC member, but they would truly be lost without him and his skills. Only those in this room knew that he was the exception to their bylaw that they only allowed veterans who were honorably discharged from the military to prospect for them. As a teenager, Keys had been recruited to become an analyst for Navy Intelligence due to his incredible computer skills. He was the closest thing to being a spy without joining the CIA. Ghost, a former SEAL, had vouched for Keys when he'd been relieved of duty with a OTH discharge. Keys had disobeyed orders that would have cost civilian lives if he hadn't. Though his superiors had chosen to punish him for his disobedience, Steel had not. Ghost knew of Keys' situation and had tracked him down once he'd become a civilian. As far as Ghost was concerned, Keys' Other Than Honorable discharge was bullshit.

Demo knew Steel was too big a person to allow someone else's opinion of the kid to influence his decision. Keys had been with the club for nearly four years, having prospected for a year. Now at twenty-three, Keys was running the club security alongside Bulldog as well as his own cyber security business.

"Is he?" Steel asked, referring to Juan Castillo.

Keys nodded, seeming to relax when he didn't get into trouble. "He's sticking to the west coast as promised. He even abolished the Detroit syndicate completely. As far as I can tell, he's gone above and beyond to honor his word to you."

Demo turned his gaze back to Steel in time to see his slow nod. "Good," the VDMC President said. "Things are finally settling down after September. I do not want to see that sort of drama start back up again." Though he wasn't superstitious, Steel reached forward and rapped his knuckles against the wood table. "Tell me about her parents. I did not like Hannigan's reaction to them or that they're threatening to take the kids away."

Neither had Demo.

Keys reached into his bag at his feet and pulled out a pile of tablets. He passed them to Bear on his right, who started to distribute them around. Demo put his pen down on his yellow pad to accept the tablet handed to him. He ran his finger across the bottom lock screen that held a black and white image of their skull and rifles logo. He didn't need to open an app or webpage, though, because Keys had all the tablets mirror his own screen.

The images of two men came up. They were clearly related with similar cheekbones, stern gazes, and hair coloring, though one was obviously older. Father and son, Demo would guess.

"Meet Thaddeus 'Thad' Barrington and his son Clifton," Keys told them, confirming Demo's suspicions.

Bear snorted. "Clifton Barrington? Guy sounds like a douche already."

Others chuckled. Demo's laugh was cut short by a sharp pain radiating from his left shoulder as his body shook with his amusement. *Fuck!* Demo snapped his eyes and jaw shut, clenching his arm against his side to hide the tremor overtaking it.

As Keys continued speaking, Demo forced his eyes back open to make it look like he was paying attention. The image on the screen changed to that of a woman in her late forties. Despite the obvious Botox on her face as well as what Demo could only assume to be a boob job to increase her size, the woman was no longer beautiful. Demo thought she could have been once, if she'd allowed her body to age naturally, but the cosmetics procedures done had given her a plastic, stiff look. "This is Velma Barrington, Paige's biological mother. She married Thad when Paige was four years old."

The screen changed to a posed family picture. Demo's eyes landed on Paige's wild brunette curls he would have recognized anywhere, even on the little girl that was maybe six or seven years old in this photo. A white mansion stood behind the family. Velma and Thad sat ramrod straight in white wooden chairs. Paige was in a white dress with a pink bow around her waist and in her curls. Despite what was probably professional effort, her curls would not be tamed, resulting in two corkscrew strands falling down her left cheek. Though she was smiling, the expression did not meet her eyes.

"Clifton is Thad's son by his third wife. He has other children, but they are all older and most will have nothing to do with him. Clifton is eight years older than Paige. Velma is Thad's fourth wife and I was able to confirm he's keeping at least two mistresses on the side."

Demo tried to recall how old Paige was from his research on her. She was thirty-three to his thirty-one, which would place Clifton at forty-one.

"The Barringtons come from old money. They're like Detroit Royalty, but the cost of living in the city as well as some recent bad investments has significantly depleted their funds in recent generations. They tried to buy into the pharmaceutical industry and gambled on the wrong drug to back. When it did not get FDA approval and was rejected, the Barringtons lost millions.

Their business is buying and selling Fortune 500 companies, rebranding and remarketing them, and then selling them for profit. They're like professional house flippers but with mega companies."

Pictures of different company logos and buildings came across their tablet screens as Keys spoke.

"As a stepdaughter, Paige was not welcomed into the family business or fold. Unlike her stepbrother, Paige did not go to private schools or an Ivy League college. Thad paid the bare minimum for her nearly her entire childhood. The exceptions were, of course, to appease the public eye. When Paige married Richard Hannigan, Thad would only pay for the wedding if he controlled everything, from her dress to the guest list."

A picture of Paige and Richard Hannigan's wedding appeared on the screen. Demo rubbed his shoulder as he stared at the picture. She looked happier in this one than she had in the family photo, her hair just as unruly as ever. A teenage Harper, dressed in a long burgundy gown, stood in line with Paige's seven bridesmaids. Richard Hannigan, the bastard, looked like he'd just won the lottery with his chest out and a smug smile on his face. The only groomsman Demo recognized was a younger Clifton immediately to Richard's left, indicating he had stood up as best man.

"Richard Hannigan's first job out of college was at *Barrington Holdings*, which is where he met Clifton. The two men became friends and, years later, he married Paige. Richard was on the fast track to becoming CFO of *Barrington Holdings* until his gambling habits became a problem. Actually, we can thank Clifton Barrington for introducing Richard Hannigan to Mateo Castillo, who owned and operated out of Clifton's favorite casino. About eighteen months before the Hannigan clan moved from Detroit to our fair town, Richard was let go due to an accusation of mishandling funds. No charges were brought against him, nor was anything proven, but the accusation was enough for Thad Barrington to let his stepson-in-law go."

The tablet screen switched to what looked like an internal email from *Barrington Holdings* informing the company staff that Richard Hannigan was taking an extended leave of absence to spend time with his family. It did not say anything regarding misappropriation of company funds, which made Demo wonder how Keys knew the real reason behind Richard's termination.

"Sounds like the Barringtons are rich assholes," Bulldog said in a bored voice. "What does any of this have to do with Paige or Hannigan's fear of them?"

"Patience, grasshopper," Keys scolded with an eye roll.

Their tablets went black but for a silver arrow in the middle of the screen. However, when Keys pressed play, the recording did not come from their multitude of tablets but the surround sound speakers throughout the room.

"...listen here, bitch. If your fucked-up husband does not return the money he owes, I will call every lawyer at my disposal and have them take those fucking brats from you. Have them work off their loser of a father's debt on their hands and knees scrubbing my floors like the fucking servant *you were..."*

There was a small *click* followed by another recording.

"...you think a measly thousand dollars *even comes close to paying off your debt?! I wipe my ass with that after taking a shit. You have six months, bitch. Your husband might be able to run from his problems, but I will hunt you down to the ends of the earth. GET ME MY FUCKING MONEY!..."*

The tablets went blank after that.

"Was that the father or the son?" Steel's voice held a dangerous tone that said no matter what, he would stand between Paige and the Barringtons. From the faces on the men around the table, he would not be the only one.

"Father," Keys replied. "There are others from the son, though. Just as nasty and just as threatening."

"How much does Hannigan owe them?" Demo asked the computer nerd, trying to keep a leash on his own anger. There was no way in hell Demo would stand back and allow her step-family to take her sons away from Paige and force them into servitude to pay off their father's debt. He'd pay it back himself if he had to.

Keys' jaw was tight as he admitted, "Over seven hundred thousand."

Jaws dropped at the number. With Hannigan's debt of three hundred thousand to the cartel, the man owed a million dollars in gambling debts.

"We killed him too quickly," Lucky growled.

Demo agreed. So much for his thought of paying it back himself to clear Paige's debt. He had savings, but not that sort of savings.

"Even with the checks she's saving, she'll never get the amount she needs to pay off the debt because *we* don't have that sort of money," Demo reminded the room. Clearly, Paige was using the money she thought was coming from the insurance company to help pay her debt by the six month deadline.

Steel demanded. "When's the deadline? The message said six months, but how long ago was it sent?"

Keys did not look happy as he said, "She has less than two months." Meaning, she needed seven hundred thousand by the end of March and she only had fifteen thousand.

"Like fuck am I going to allow that dirtbag take her kids away," Steel snapped. "We failed Paige by not taking her under our wing more. She's family," he repeated, nodding to Lucky, "and we failed her."

Turning to the table at large, Steel said louder, "From this moment on, I don't care if you need treatment or not, you are going to make an appointment at her clinic. Buy your friends, family, anyone you can think of gift certificates for her clinic. Most of all, though, you spread the word: Paige is *ours*."

"We can offer discounts at the dealership if they provide a receipt from her clinic," Demo suggested.

Steel nodded. "Speaking of which, you're going to be her first *Via Daemonia* customer." His eyes narrowed as he added, "Get your fucking shoulder looked at."

Demo swallowed audibly. "I'm fi—"

"You are not fucking *fine*," Steel snapped, speaking over him. "You're slouched over in pain. You think I can't see it? You're not that good an actor. Get your ass to her clinic first thing on Monday or I will drag you there by your ear myself."

Knowing Steel wasn't bluffing, Demo nodded.

"I added you to her schedule for nine Monday morning," Keys told him from across the table.

Demo glared at Keys, the fucking traitor.

"We're *all* going," Bulldog reminded Demo. "Abby has her appointment on Tuesday. I'll go with her and see if she can see me too."

"According to *Google*," Bear said while looking down at his phone, "acupuncture can work wonders for pregnant women. We'll take the girls."

Lucky nodded his agreement, but then said, "Even if everyone in town makes an appointment, it won't be enough to pay them back. Even with the money we took from the Pythons, we don't have that sort of scratch."

Jumper cleared his throat. "We might not, but the Grovetons would."

The Grovetons were like Mount Grove Royalty. They came from old money and claimed to be the founding family of their small town. Some were skeptics on that fact, but no one questioned it more than a passing wonder. The Grovetons were good people and did not allow their money to rule their town as so many other families would have. Sophia, Jasmine's best friend, was the only daughter of Beatrice and Darnell Groveton and she, along with her two older brothers, were the heirs to the Groveton fortune.

Steel, though, shook his head. "I don't want *us* to be in debt to the Grovetons. A family like the Barringtons? They have to have skeletons in their closets." To Keys, he said, "Find them. Find all of them. CPS won't take her kids once they've heard that voicemail. Let's see how easy it will be to go after Paige and her sons when they're putting out their own fires." After catching the eye of everyone at the table, Steel slammed his gavel down and then pointed the hammer end at Demo, "Get your ass to the fucking clinic."

CHAPTER 2

*P*aige Hannigan closed her bedroom door quietly, not wanting to wake her boys. Her chin trembled as her stomach growled painfully. How was this her life? Skipping meals so her boys could eat? Wondering what the hell she was going to do tomorrow when her electricity got turned off for nonpayment?

She'd already sold everything she could possibly sell. From all of the electronics in the house to the toys the boys didn't use as much anymore. She also took all of Richard's belongings that he'd left behind to a consignment store. Some of his Italian suits had gotten her a couple hundred, but they were custom fit so they were not worth the value Richard had paid for them. She had sold every piece of jewelry she owned, including her wedding band and engagement ring. Her bastard of a husband had left her with his debt, what was the point of holding onto the symbols of their commitment to each other when he obviously didn't care about her or their sons?

Turning so her back was to the door, Paige slid down the painted white wood. Her house was filled with expensive equipment and custom designed features, but it wasn't worth anything.

Richard had insisted on this house when they'd moved to Mount Grove two years ago. He'd told her their house in Detroit would pay it off once that sold, so the mortgage wouldn't be an issue. Except, that money had gone towards paying off other debts when they'd received it. Not a penny had gone towards their ridiculously high mortgage with a ridiculously high interest rate. If she lived alone, she might consider taking in a roommate to help with the growing pile of bills, but she couldn't risk that with her sons living here too.

Clutching her knees to her chest, Paige wrapped her arms around her legs. Tears fell silently down her cheeks. Despair, worry, fear, and shame swirled in her gut, but were unfortunately unable to stave off her growing hunger.

She'd reached a new low today. She'd gone to her in-laws, Richard's parents, to beg for money. They were suffering too, but their sorrows were emotional from the sudden absence of their son. Hers were very much physical if she didn't figure out a way to pay some of these bills. Her emotions, her anger, her rage, could wait until her boys were properly fed and the threat of bankruptcy wasn't looming over her head.

She'd swallowed her pride for the sake of her sons. If Paige had needed to, she would have begged on bended knee, but it hadn't come to that. Her father-in-law, Ronald, had been beyond apologetic. With his medical bills, their move to Mount Grove, and his retirement, they did not have anything extra to give her. Ronald and Cindy offered for Paige and the boys to move in with them, but she couldn't sell her house due to the second mortgage she hadn't even realized Richard had taken out on their home. Potentially, they could still move in with Ronald and Cindy and rent her house, but no one would rent the house for the amount she needed each month.

For months following Richard's disappearance, neither Cindy nor Ronald would talk to her. She'd gone to Ronald over and over again to demand answers. He was the *sheriff* after all. He had to know what was going on, even if there was some rule about him not being allowed near the case because the missing person was his own son. Over and over again, Paige's concerns were dismissed. No one but her sister-in-law Harper would tell her anything—and Harper hadn't had much information as it was.

Finally, she'd snapped. She was not the type to mope around the house waiting for the breadwinner to come home. She had her degree in acupuncture but hadn't practiced since Mikey was born. It had taken her almost six months to transfer her licenses, get her business permit and Pennsylvania business license, and find an appropriate business location. Opening her clinic *Serenity Springs* was supposed to be her step towards independence.

Then the true extent of Richard's debt had come to light. Creditors had come collecting for credit cards she hadn't even known Richard owned, either on his own or with her. The second mortgage that had been taken out on their home needed to be paid back before she could sell. And then her goddamn stepfather.

Her *stepfather*.

How could he? Richard *knew* how she had felt about her step-family. He *knew* she hated how controlling, demeaning, and demanding Thad had been. He *knew* she did not trust her family. She understood that Richard was loyal to her stepfamily to an extent—he worked for their company—but that didn't mean he didn't know how she personally felt too.

How could he be so heartless? What gave him the right to go to *her* stepfamily to ask them for money? She understood that her stepfamily had means that his did not, but still... Richard had *known* how they treated her. How much she hated being a part of that family.

As if potential bankruptcy wasn't bad enough, she was under threat of having her boys taken away from her. Child Protective Services would not hesitate to come and take away her babies if they received a call from *the* Barringtons that their grandchildren were being mistreated or neglected. Even if there was no proof, knowing her stepfather, he would resort to less reputable means of swaying their minds. Like bribery.

Paige had thought she'd left that manipulation behind. It had been one of the reasons she'd agreed to Richard's suggestion to move to Mount Grove. Their marriage wasn't perfect, but she hoped it would improve once they were away from the city life and her family.

Little did she know that Richard had brought her family to Mount Grove with them—in a manner of speaking.

Her phone let out a sharp *ding*.

Paige didn't want to look. The only electronic device she'd kept was her phone. All of the tablets, televisions, laptops, and Richard's desktop had been pawned. She'd even sold the laptop from her clinic because she could schedule her measly amount of appointments from her phone and she needed every penny she could get. Without having devices in the house, she'd been able to cut her internet and cable bills too.

The last message she'd received had been from her step-brother, Clifton, with a not-so-gentle reminder to pay back their money by her deadline.

Taking her phone out of her pocket with a shaky hand, Paige unlocked the device. There was a bit of relief when she saw it wasn't her stepbrother. That meager relief was short-lived though. The app's notification announced a private request for a total of five hundred dollars.

Since these requests were first-come, first-serve, Paige quickly opened the app to accept the offer prior to reading the description. She was not about to pass up the chance to earn five hundred dollars, no matter how degrading the request might be.

Thankfully, it was fairly mild for the amount of money offered.

Sighing, Paige forced herself to her feet. She had ten minutes to get ready before the offer would expire and open to others again. Walking over to her closet, Paige pulled out the ring light and selfie stand she'd gotten for pennies on the dollar at the pawnshop. Setting up the tripod, Paige looked around her to ensure there was nothing identifying in the shot. Live videos could be disastrous since she didn't have a chance to review them before they were posted. If one of her sons woke up during the video, it would be even worse. She prayed they would remain asleep, because she desperately needed that five-hundred dollars.

Her stomach growled again as she toed off her shoes. After a quick wash in the bathroom sink, she pulled out her assortment of nail polish. She'd learned quickly to always remove the polish after a video so she could grab new requests without having to take the time to clean any old polish off her toenails.

Swallowing her pride, Paige placed her foot on the over-turned crate with a bathroom rug covering it, put on a pedicure toe separator, and started the recording.

Five hundred dollars, she reminded herself with each new coat of red paint. She pictured her sleeping boys in the next room and continued her video. She would suffer through any humiliation to ensure her boys had a roof over their heads and food in their bellies. Even if it meant becoming a foot fetish model.

Thank God this request was mild in comparison to some of the others she'd done. In her current state of mind, she probably would not have been able to stomach some of the more unusual requests.

Like the time she'd had to put little hot dogs between her toes and cover her feet in ketchup, mustard, and relish.

Five hundred dollars...

Five hundred dollars...

* * *

THE NEXT DAY turned out to be a good day. Her electricity did not get turned off. With her new five hundred dollar income—which was actually closer to four hundred and eighty after the fetish site's fee was deducted and she'd paid the percentage for an instant transfer of funds—Paige had called the electric company to pay her outstanding bill. It was then that she was informed there had been an error in the system and she'd been overpaying her bill for months. Once the error had been corrected, she actually had a credit on her account that should cover the next month's bill too.

Which meant she could put that five hundred dollars towards her outstanding bill for her clinic's lease. If she hadn't signed a two year lease, she would have closed her doors permanently for lack of business. She honestly wasn't even sure why she tried to stay open with only five to ten clients per week. This small town was not open to having a Chinese medicine clinic in their midst.

No sooner had that thought come through did she get two notifications from her website's scheduling system that she had new client appointments for the upcoming week.

Harper and Lucky came over to pick up her boys to take them to the park for a snowball fight. With a couple of hours kid-free, Paige started cleaning the house and did several loads of laundry. Thank God her water was from a well and not city water or she would have had to pay that bill too.

Another request came in from the foot fetish website. She quickly grabbed it, even though it was only for a hundred and fifty dollars. They wanted to watch her wash her feet in a bubble bath. Paige had to empty one of her dead potted plants she had yet to throw out all over her feet to get them *filthy* per the request first and then drew a bubble bath. She wore a bathing suit despite the instructions for her to be naked. With the tripod set up over her bathtub, Paige took a bath with her dirt-covered feet.

The next request that came in had a different timeframe than the others. Thank God for that, because she was able to text Harper to ask her to pick up a cake from the bakery on her way home. Paige came up with some PMS craving excuse that hopefully her sister-in-law would not question. As soon as the boys went to bed that night, she would bring her tripod out to the kitchen and walk in the requested red velvet cake for three hundred dollars. The only instruction was that she had to *squish* the cake between her toes for five or more minutes.

She could do that. Though she'd have to add red velvet cake to her list of ruined food items. Hot dogs and gelatin were also on that list.

By the time she laid her head on her pillow Sunday night, she'd earned another four hundred and fifty dollars. Not to mention some of her photos had sold on the fetish site *and* she had two new clients on the schedule for her week. Hopefully, it was a sign that things were looking up.

DEMO GRIMACED as he pulled into the parking spot on Main Street. He was a couple doors down from Paige's clinic, *Serenity Springs.* Normally, he didn't mind the winter months that prevented the club from riding their bikes. Shortly before he'd been shot, Demo had purchased a new *Ford* Bronco Raptor. The off-roading vehicle had been his birthday present to himself and an encouragement to start going on more outdoor adventures. Despite his job as an accountant, Demo enjoyed the outdoors and exploring nature. However, since his injury, he'd been unable to take his kayak out or hike any length of time that required a supply backpack or to go rock climbing. He hadn't even been able to finish out the club's season with them since his doctor had prohibited him from riding his *Harley-Davidson* Heritage Classic.

Demo did not want to admit to himself or anyone else how badly driving still pained him. The way he drove with his shoulder rolled back, his elbow tucked in, and his hand sticking out from his chest, he honestly thought he looked like a demented chicken or a T-rex. Reaching with his right hand to unlock the cage's door, he slid out into the slush-covered road.

Flinching, Demo worked his left arm through his cut before sliding it up his arm. The pull of the action sent fire shooting down his limb and up the side of his neck. Fucking Steel *might* have had a point that his pain was getting out of hand. The cold weather of January certainly was not helping.

On the back of Demo's cut were five large patches that were all identical, regardless of one's position in the club. In the center was a horned demon skull with crossing rifles behind it. The skull was missing its lower jaw. *Via Daemonia*, which was Latin for *Road Demon*, was on the top downward curved rocker. The lower upward curved rocker said *Mount Grove, PA*. Two rectangular patches paralleled the skull with the Latin phrases *Cum Honore Ministravimus* and *Cum Honore Equitamus*, which translated to *With Honor We Served* and *With Honor We Ride*, respectively. The embroidery on the rockers was white with a black background.

Last winter, Jenna had ordered winter coats with the club cuts sewn into the material so the members didn't have to bother with having their jacket *and* cut. Demo thought the action was sweet and he did appreciate the forethought. However, the leather jacket had a tricky zipper and Demo had discovered he'd been unable to get his shoulder to cooperate long enough for him to zip it up two-handed. His current jacket was older with a worn zipper that was fairly loose.

Trudging up onto the sidewalk, his shitkickers protected his feet from the snow and slush on the ground. Tying shoelaces was another issue he'd come across in recent months. Unfortunately, he could no longer get away with summer sandals without drawing negative attention to his situation. Thankfully, he wasn't planning on running any miles today. He'd figured out that he could tie his boots loosely before putting them on and then tighten them by pulling on the knot. It still left them loose, and they would continuously get looser the more he walked, but at least he was able to get them on and his plight wasn't obvious.

Paige's clinic had an LED lotus sign in the window. Above the door on the brick was a cute swinging wooden sign that said her business name and had an etching of a curved human back with three needles sticking out like porcupine spikes.

Demo let out an involuntary shudder that had nothing to do with his shoulder pain or the cold morning. He didn't have a fear of needles, per se, but he was not looking forward to getting poked and prodded by a multitude of them at once or seeing them sticking out of his skin.

He was no coward, though, and he knew Steel would hogtie and deliver him to Paige himself if he did not suck it up and get this over with on his own. Letting out a puff of visible air, Demo squared his shoulders and entered the clinic.

PAIGE'S MONEY problems were apparent as soon as he walked through the door. The entry was small with a four foot reception desk facing the door attached to the left wall. No computer or electronics littered the empty reception desk. The waiting chairs immediately to Demo's right upon entering had a layer of dust on the cushions. No bell or chime signaled his entry into the clinic—which he did not like. Though the smell of disinfectant was in the air, there weren't any aromas or scents that Demo would have thought an acupuncture clinic would have like lavender or peppermint.

Only some of the overhead lights were on. One might be able to argue that she was keeping the lights low for aesthetics or even that a lightbulb or two were out, but something told Demo that wasn't the case. More likely, she was trying to keep her electric bill low.

The room was not unclean. In fact, other than the dust on the chairs, it was extremely tidy. Demo could see the pride in the place, from the flowers in the vase on the reception desk to the freshly cleaned windows behind him. Lack of clients had not diminished Paige's obvious love for the place.

A small fishbowl sat on the counter, filled halfway, with something floating in it. It wasn't a fish, dead or alive. Demo took a step forward, lowering his nose to the glass. It was a lily pad and lotus spinning around on the water. The center of the lotus was empty. Based on the shape, though, Demo assumed it wasn't supposed to be. Maybe it was missing a candle? The bowl definitely wasn't for anything living.

Beyond the reception desk were empty shelves. Demo wondered if it was supposed to be a mini store or if it was supposed to maybe hold patient files? Like Angel's tattoo studio, the clinic had a door leading back to, he assumed, the patient rooms. Angel's tattoo studio was parallel to Paige's across the street. Additionally, her studio's entry was bigger in square footage. Given that, Demo could only assume that Paige's clinic also had a smaller number of rooms than Angel's tattoo studio.

If she had a full docket, how many patients could she see at once? Demo would assume only one, but then why would she need more than one patient room? It would have made more sense to find an office space with only one privacy room and maybe a small office. From other layouts on Main Street, Demo estimated two or three patient rooms in the back of Paige's clinic. Unless the need called for an additional practitioner, why would she get a clinic this size?

Footsteps approached and Demo straightened in time to see Paige walking out from the back area. She wore dress pants with sensible shoes, a nice blouse that hung loosely, and a white lab coat. Her unruly brown curls were thrown up in a messy bun atop her head. She wore little to no makeup, but Demo honestly preferred that on women anyway.

But what brought a smile to his face was the number of pens

in her hair. He'd seen the style before in the Asian culture with decorative chopsticks, but that was usually with one or two sticks. Paige had a total of seven pens of various styles and colors sticking haphazardly out of her mass of curls. It reminded Demo of when he'd seen someone absentmindedly leaving multiple pairs of reading glasses on their person.

She paused in the doorway, her shoes letting out a sharp *squeak* at her abrupt halt. Paige blinked, looking for a moment like a deer in the headlights.

Then she shook her head slightly. "Demo, right?"

Demo nodded sharply. While the two of them knew of each other, Demo could not recall a time when they'd ever spoken to each other before. He'd always seen her at a distance.

As she completed her journey to the reception desk, Demo really took her in. Like him, she had a lean look to her. He was more height than muscle, built for speed over brute force. He'd been told more than once in his life that he had a swimmer's body.

Like her shirt, her lab coat and pants seemed too big for her. Paige's lean frame was almost *too* thin. Unhealthily so. Her loose shirt hung awkwardly, not accentuating her breasts or hips. She had a belt around her waist that was tightened more than necessary and bunched her pants, which were clearly a size too big. With her feet now hidden by the reception desk, Demo couldn't comment on her shoes, though he had a feeling they would be worn and not an expensive brand.

Demo thought back to the last time he'd seen Nelson and Michael. Lucky and Harper brought them around the clubhouse at times. His son, Scotty, was over the moon about not only having a new little brother, but also another baby on the way as well as new cousins. Per Scotty, bigger families were the best.

Even with Paige's obvious money problems, he could not recall seeing the boys in clothes that didn't fit or looking hungry. With how attentive many of his club brothers were towards children, Demo had a feeling that was something they would have noticed and brought to question long before Hannigan had shown up on their doorstep Saturday afternoon.

She was barely making ends meet, but the boys weren't showing a lack of care or necessities.

Demo's eyes narrowed on her too big shirt. Trailing up her slender frame, he spotted the edges of her collarbones just under her long neck to the sharpness of her jawline. Her skin looked naturally tanned but also pale in a way. There was no natural flush to her cheeks. Dark circles accentuated her eyes.

When was the last time she'd eaten a full meal or slept the entire night?

Here he was mentally complaining about his damn shoulder pain when *she* likely hadn't eaten yet that day.

"If you're here to pick up Abby, I'm sorry to inform you but you've got the wrong day. Her appointment isn't until tomorrow."

Demo blinked. "What?"

Paige raised an eyebrow. "Abby? Her appointment's tomorrow."

She thought he was here to pick up Abby? Hadn't Keys made him an appointment? If it had been a bluff, maybe he could still get out of this without getting pricked like a pincushion. "I have an appointment," he informed her.

Surprised, Paige reached into her pocket and pulled out her cellphone. Was she doing all of her appointments and work from that small device? Why didn't she have a laptop at least, even if she shared it between her personal and work uses?

"Are you Ron Snyder?"

He probably should have thought of that. Keys wouldn't have made the appointment under *Demo*. He wasn't Sonny or Cher after all and *Demo Snyder* was just weird. Other than his dad and doctors, he was so used to being called 'Demo' that hearing his legal name from her lips sounded wrong. He didn't like it, almost as if it lacked intimacy.

He blinked and internally huffed. Where had *that* thought come from?

Not wanting her to feel uneasy, Demo gave her a crooked smile. "Only if you promise to go easy on the needles."

Glancing up from her phone, her chocolate eyes held a depth of amusement—and maybe even a bit of cockiness. "Don't tell me the big, bad soldier boy has a fear of needles?"

It didn't surprise him that she knew he was a veteran. Everyone in town knew that the *Via Daemonia* were all former military. She was around them and Lucky enough to have picked up on that, even if the town still considered her an outsider.

Demo dramatically puffed up his chest. "This *air* boy doesn't *like* needles but tolerates them just fine."

Paige's eyes lit with interest. "Airman? I don't think I've met anyone who was in the Air Force before. I know Lucky and Bear were Marines and Abby's Bulldog was Army. Angel was Army too, right?"

Demo nodded, finding it interesting that she referred to Bulldog as *Abby's* rather than just using his name. Somehow, though, it suited their relationship.

"So you're my first airman," she said with a wide smile.

The unintentional innuendo was not lost on him. "I was Enlisted, EOD."

"Elephants Over Donkeys?" she inquired with a sassy twinkle in her eye. "No! No, wait, I got it!" Paige waved her hands in front of her. She snapped her left hand, indicating she was a fellow leftie. "Eggos On Donuts?"

A laugh escaped Demo before he could stop it. She was the perfect blend of cute and feminine, he noted. Her smile was infectious. Demo couldn't help but react to her. In more ways than one too: not only were his eyes taking notice of her, but so was his dick.

"Explosive Ordnance Disposal," he corrected good naturedly. "We located, recovered, and disarmed dangerous weapons." He held up his left hand to show her he was not over-exaggerating the description of his former AFSC.

In the past, women had reacted differently to his hand. The two most popular reactions were to either be awed by his missing fingers or to be disgusted. What remained of his ring and middle fingers were melted together to make one large stump between his scarred pinky finger and what remained of his pointer finger. Scotty, bless him, called Demo's mangled hand his 'surfer hand', because it permanently formed the 'hang loose' hand sign Scotty had seen on an episode of his favorite TV show *Monk*. Even Demo could admit to it not being the prettiest of sights.

Paige, however, had an entirely different reaction than the typical ones he'd come to expect. She leaned over the counter as if to get a better look at his missing digits—then she made a *tsk* sound with her tongue like a mother scolding her child and said, "You weren't very good at your job, were you?"

There was utter silence in the room before they both burst out laughing.

CHAPTER 3

*P*aige had no idea what had come over her. When she'd seen 'Ron Snyder' on her schedule that morning, she had no idea who he was. The few people from town she was on a first name basis with were mostly women and none of the few men she knew were named Ron. Actually, since moving to Mount Grove, the only 'Ron' she knew was her father-in-law, who, like her husband, did not go by common nickname versions of their names. They were Richard and Ronald, not Rick or Ron.

She'd seen Demo at a distance several times while on club property. Many of the members she knew by their name but not their face; or she would recognize their face but would have to cheat and look at their cut to know their name. There were just too many of them when she didn't know them personally. If she didn't trust Lucky as much as she did, she never would have accepted Abby's invitation to have the club men take her boys on their outings with the other club kids while she socialized with the ladies.

But the truth was, even at a distance, she knew Demo. The first time she'd seen him, at Harper and Lucky's wedding last May, her entire body had reacted on a molecular level. Since hanging out with the club women, Paige had heard some things about the men's reputations. Prior to Angel domesticating him last year, Cage had been the club's biggest womanizer. Many of the women had called him an Adonis for his striking Greek looks. And, while Paige could not deny that Cage was ruggedly beautiful, Demo was *hot*.

If she was twenty years younger, she might even have the nerve to call him *h-a-w-t hot*. Sadly, though, she was not. While there was no love for Richard still in her heart for his deception and desertion, it did not change the fact that she was still legally married. A status which she couldn't even afford to change because she was too busy trying to keep her boys fed with a roof over their heads.

Wherever the hell Richard was, she hoped he was miserable. Downright miserable. Like living on the streets with fleas and mice and cockroaches miserable. Living in squalor and having to sell his body for mere scraps of food miserable. Following the first pictures she'd taken to be posted on the foot fetish website, she'd even prayed for Richard to contract genital warts, chlamydia, and gonorrhea all at the same time. Just to even out their suffering.

If she was free of Richard, though, she might have pursued Demo. Or at least, introduced herself. Learned his legal name. Made sure he knew she existed.

But she wasn't free...

Based on the information he provided when he had made his appointment online, she knew he was two years younger than she was. Two years wasn't *that* big of a deal. It wasn't like she was a cougar. Hell, Lucky and Harper had a fourteen year age difference and they seemed to make it work. More than work. Lucky looked at Harper like she was his entire universe.

Richard had never done that. Paige had been an ornament, a prize to be won. Hell, if one of her stepbrother's nastier messages could be believed, she'd been a *bet*. Clifton claimed that he'd bet

Richard a hundred grand that he couldn't fuck his stepsister by the end of the summer before her last year of college.

"...*who knew my little sister was so big a slut that she kept on fucking him for free...*"

Paige internally winced at the memory of listening to that message, drawing her shared laughter with Demo up short.

She was aware enough of herself to admit she'd been flirting with him. As soon as she realized he was here for her—or rather, for her services—she hadn't been able to help herself. To finally be able to talk to him...

But it couldn't go anywhere. She was still married.

She had to get her head on straight. Ring or no ring, hot guy or no hot guy, she was still married. Richard might not take that seriously, but she did. Her inability to even consider becoming intimate with another man had nothing to do with loyalty to Richard but her own personal morals. She'd made a promise, a vow, and *she* would not be the one to break that vow. Despite her suspicions, she had no proof of Richard's affairs. When he returned—*if* he returned—she would not give him any fuel to potentially take her children away from her.

Everything she did was for her sons. She would not do anything that could risk them or their future.

Paige found herself blushing as she recalled her comment about his hand. Covering her mouth with her fingers to hide her smile, she shrugged, "I'm sorry, I couldn't resist."

He thankfully did not seem offended. Even with the laughter, he could have taken her comment very differently. "You should have seen the other guy."

"Is that what you're here for?" Paige asked, wanting to steer the conversation to a more professional level. "Is your hand causing you pain?"

Normally she wouldn't speak about a patient's private reasons for seeking her experience out in the main room, but it wasn't like she had a receptionist or other patients around to overhear.

A swell of depression at her empty clinic tried to take hold of her heart until she pushed it away.

She'd actually gotten to eat the day before *and* she had plans to go grocery shopping after she was done at the clinic—which, unfortunately, was whenever Demo's appointment ended. In an effort to cut back utility costs, she'd only been coming in for scheduled appointment times. If she had a higher walk-in clientele, she might have stayed open. There were only so many times she could clean the clinic from top to bottom before the reality that no one else was coming in would come crashing down on her.

Demo shook his head. "That's an old injury. Other than the occasional phantom pains, the only issue with missing my fingers is my inability to count higher than seven." He held up his right hand with all five fingers and his left hand with his two remaining fingers, wiggling the digits individually like a child learning to count.

Paige stifled a laugh.

Demo's good mood soured as he admitted, "It's my shoulder. I have nerve damage from an injury about six months ago."

Paige came around the reception counter, her eyes fixed on his shoulder. She knew immediately which one he meant from how stiff he was holding the arm. Even with his cut and jacket on, she could tell.

"Can you remove your jacket for me please?" Paige indicated to the coat tree by the front door as she reached into the pocket of her lab coat for a pair of latex gloves. Some acupuncturists looked down on her for using them, claiming that they took away from the transference of energy, but Paige was too conscious of illnesses and diseases she could potentially bring around her sons to not wear the gloves. Additionally, the shower in the back was why she had chosen this building for her lease even though it was bigger than her requirements. She always made sure to sanitize and shower before returning home to her sons.

When Demo returned to her without his jacket but still wearing his cut, she fought to roll her eyes. Even Lucky treated the garment like it was sewn with pure gold thread. There was even a rule about the cuts not being able to touch the ground, like there were for American Flags. A part of her wanted to ask if they had to burn the cuts too if they touched the floor.

"What happened?" she inquired, putting on one glove.

"Bullet," he said shortly.

Paige froze with her second glove only halfway on her hand. She looked up at him. He was about six inches taller than her five-foot-six frame. Richard was only two inches taller at five-eight. It had always been a point of contention for him that he hadn't been taller like his father and was the same height as his little sister.

Is, she corrected herself. Richard might be in her past, but until she was able to serve him divorce papers, he was still a part of her life.

The moment Demo said 'bullet', though, Paige knew exactly how he'd gotten injured. "You're the one who got shot protecting Jasmine."

"Poorly protecting Jasmine," he amended. There was definitely self-contempt in his voice. Like he hadn't done *enough* when he'd gotten shot.

Paige knew the story. Jasmine and Sophia had been kidnapped after stumbling across an illegal dog-fighting ring just outside of town. Harper had told her that one of the club brothers had been shot protecting Jasmine, but she hadn't said who. Paige wasn't close enough to any of the brothers other than Lucky and Bulldog for 'who' to have mattered. It would have been nothing more than a faceless name. *However*, what had stuck with her was the sacrifice of that member. He could have *died* protecting Jasmine. Who does that? Besides the Secret Service?

Apparently, Demo did. Paige recalled Harper saying he had taken two bullets, but Demo had used the singular definition.

"I wouldn't call taking a bullet for someone 'poor protection,'" Paige told him sternly, making sure her voice portrayed her disagreement with his word choice.

"Taking a bullet also didn't stop her from being taken," he asserted.

Paige finished putting on the second glove. Her hesitation at her next question wasn't as a practitioner but as a woman. She needed to know the answer, but she didn't *want* to know either. "Harper told me about it. If I recall correctly, she'd said you were shot with...two bullets." Her voice cracked on the word 'two'.

He nodded. Demo untucked his shirt from his belted pants to reveal his right abdomen. A few inches to the right of his belly button was a vertical scar, about an inch and a half long.

Paige swallowed hard. *Wow.* Every female part of her body woke up and took notice of his firmly muscled stomach. Richard had paid an ungodly amount of money over the years for gym memberships and personal trainers to not even get a single pack, let alone six of them. Demo's middle was firm and cut. The hard ridges of his body were as defined as a marble sculpture.

Paige had to bite the interior of her bottom lip to keep from licking her lips—or worse: asking if she could lick *him*. Her nipples sharpened to tight peaks against her bra and there was an embarrassing damp spot forming on her panties that reminded her she hadn't had sex since before her three-year-old son was born. In fact, the last time she'd had sex might have been when she'd conceived him.

Richard had not been a generous lover. Nor had he been an understanding one. Her period had been 'gross' and he refused to even sleep in the same bed as her when she was menstruating. Her cramps had been a figment of her imagination. Pregnancy had been a means to an end, one that he did not partake in. Despite her assurances that it was safe to have pregnancy sex, Richard had refused. Something about the baby being able to see his penis from inside the womb. To this day, Paige still did not know if he was joking.

Even though she was a mother of two, she probably had only had sex with her husband a dozen or so times over the course of their seven-year marriage. He'd refused to touch her after Mikey had been born due to the baby weight she'd gained.

When they'd been dating, they'd been unable to keep their hands off of each other. It was one of the reasons Paige had suspected him of having an affair or multiple affairs, because she knew he wasn't satisfying himself with her. It was like putting a ring on her finger had turned her unattractive and unappealing to him.

Needing to hide her reaction to Demo's body, Paige bent forward as if she was examining the healed wound closer. Her heart was beating like a drum line in her chest, she was surprised her boobs weren't visibly dancing to the tune. She felt flushed and a little lightheaded.

Unfortunately, getting closer to him was a mistake. His scent enveloped her like a cloud, seeping into her pores. The perfect mixture of *Old Spice*, leather, and manly musk.

Paige rose slowly, knowing she couldn't remain bent over and staring at his abs for too long without drawing suspicion. After all, his abs were not his problem area.

Their eyes met. His sea green to her chocolate brown. Demo had a unique shade of caramel brown hair that made her wonder if he dyed it to achieve that color. The sides of his head were shorn close to his skin with a burst fade mohawk, the longer strands falling backward versus standing straight up in the air. The look did not appear juvenile or unprofessional on him. If anything, it gave him an aura of confidence and masculine strength.

There was nothing *youthful* about him, despite being two years her junior.

His pupils dilated and his nostrils flared. There was something powerful, almost possessive in his gaze on her. For a moment, Paige thought he might kiss her. God, she wanted him to.

Paige forced herself to step back. It had been a long time since she'd been this attracted to a man. Beyond that, he was her patient. It was entirely unprofessional and unethical to even consider kissing him.

"Um," she cleared her throat, "follow me back to the therapy room please. Let me take a look at your shoulder."

She turned her back on him, needing to put distance between them but also clear him out of her vision. He was about to take off his shirt *and* pants. It was going to be hard enough when he did so—God, she hoped that statement did not turn into a pun.

This is not a porno! Get your head out of the gutter! He's a patient, not a porn star you can ravage!

As Demo followed her back into the room, though, she caught a whiff of his scent again and, damn, she was screwed. And definitely not in the fun way.

* * *

"Please remove your shirt, boots, socks, and pants. I'll step out a moment to give you some privacy. I don't know if you're familiar with acupuncture or acupressure practices but I will need access to your entire body."

The air in the small therapy room practically crackled at her words. Demo was not a shy man, but he did not have the sort of control over his body that he needed to remove his pants in front of her and not embarrass either one of them.

The room housed a sheeted massage bed, a heat lamp with a bendable arm, a rolling stand with cotton balls, needles, lotions, a flat looking green rock, glass bowls, and a lounge chair. Though there was a step stool to aid patients up and down from the bed, Demo would not be requiring such assistance.

Despite her offer of privacy, Demo stripped off his shirt and started to toe off his boots while her back was still to him. Thankfully his boots were loose enough that he didn't need to struggle with the laces. How fucked up that he couldn't even wear boots without needing to make accommodations for his shoulder?

Paige turned from what she was doing at the rolling tray, saw his naked chest, flushed a bright red, and spun back around.

Demo immediately regretted starting to undress already. He hadn't meant to make her uncomfortable. Sometimes getting his shirt on and off was a challenge. It just made sense to have her here in case he needed assistance. He did not want to be Winnie the Pooh-ing it when she walked back into the room because he was unable to get his shirt off on his own.

"Sorry." His voice came out a bit deeper than normal. He was aware of the effect he had on her. What she didn't seem to be grasping was that she had just as much, if not more, of an effect on him.

"It's fine." Her words came out quickly. "I, uh, I usually just step out to give my patients privacy."

"Never understood that." Demo was desperate to make her smile again. He did not like seeing her flushed and anxious—even if it derived from arousal. "Why do doctors step outside to give us privacy to undress when they see us naked when they come back into the room anyway?"

There was a heavy second before he saw her shoulders start to shake. "Honestly," she giggled, "I have no idea. I guess it's just something that's expected or it signifies privacy..." Paige shrugged and slowly turned back around. "Some people would feel uncomfortable undressing in front of their doctor, even if that doctor isn't watching."

Demo held her gaze as he flicked open the button of his dark blue jeans. His shirt and cut were lying on the massage table at his hip. "I take it you don't watch then?"

Her cheeks blushed but she held her head up high this time. "Not generally, no."

That didn't mean she didn't plan on watching now.

Demo lowered the zipper of his jeans. "What if a patient needed assistance out of his or her clothes? Would you help them undress?"

Her chocolate eyes seemed to darken and her breath hitched. "So far that hasn't happened yet. Most of my patients know to wear loose clothing so they don't have to disrobe. Because you're wearing jeans, I need you to remove them completely."

"Not sure I own any loose clothing."

"I'll buy you a pair of gray sweatpants," she offered with a twitch of her lips that said the sweats were for her as much as they were for him. Her eyes trailed down his naked torso to his hand still on his fly.

Demo tipped his head to the side. There was no way she couldn't see his erection, even with his hand where it was. He was a shower, not a grower. He didn't need to be fully erect for his long cock to be noticeable. Like his body, his cock lacked width, but he was long. Very long. With her eyes on him, there was little chance of him *not* getting an erection regardless.

"I'll take you up on that."

His voice seemed to snap her out of her staring. Paige's head rose so fast, he was surprised she didn't lose her balance.

"What? Oh, um, just..." She looked around, her eyes landing on his shirt and cut. "I'll just bring these over to the chair while you remove your pants."

Still amused by her fluster, Demo dropped his pants down his long legs. His boxer briefs did nothing to hide his own arousal.

As Paige bent over to grab his boots, his eyes landed on her ass. Fuck. His cock was *not* going to behave during this session. Even the throbbing in his shoulder couldn't seem to quell his libido.

"Sit up on the table please." Demo did as instructed. Moving forward, Paige removed his white crew socks from his feet.

She paused at the sight before her. Glancing up, Demo shrugged his right shoulder unapologetically. "Lila likes to paint our nails." He wiggled his painted toes for emphasis. "According to her, yellow is my color."

He saw Paige bite her lips between her teeth in an effort to not laugh as she folded his socks together and then placed them on top of his other folded clothing.

Approaching the table, she came just short of touching her hips to his knees. "Stick out your tongue please."

Demo blinked in confusion. Despite the tension in the room, he did not think Paige meant that request sexually. "Excuse me?"

"I need to look at your tongue," she told him, her eyes sparkling with amusement. There was no doubt she knew *exactly* what had caused his confusion. "Your tongue can tell me a lot about you and your lifestyle. From the coloring and coating to the cracks along it."

That did not clear up his confusion at all. But he silently stuck out his tongue at her. Why did it feel like he was in third grade again, sticking his tongue out at the girl he liked across the classroom?

Paige leaned in to study his tongue. She even put a hand on his scruff-covered chin to adjust his face to the angle of her choosing. Demo sat still with his hands laced on his lap to help cover his erection.

"You're slightly QI deficient," Paige said as she dropped her gloved hand and took a step back. "Fatigue, poor appetite, shortness of breath, and I'm guessing spontaneous sweating. I can attribute most of that to the pain in your shoulder, but some of it is coming from your liver. We'll take care of that today too."

Demo stared at her in amazement. "Are you a witch?"

She laughed. "No."

"Mutant?"

"No."

"Alien?"

She shook her head. "*No!*" she laughed. "I can tell all of that from the shading of your tongue and the thin white coating on it. You have a couple of red spots too."

Demo stuck out his tongue and nearly went cross eyed trying to look down his face at it. He knew damn well that he wasn't going to be able to see his tongue, but he loved hearing her laugh. Even if it meant making a fool of himself.

Paige reached into her lab coat and pulled out a compact mirror. "Here."

Demo accepted the mirror. She didn't seem like a vain person to be carrying around a compact mirror so readily.

"You're not the first person to question the tongue exam," she explained without him having to ask. "I learned a long time ago to carry the mirror in my pocket for the skeptics."

That did make more sense. Demo looked at his tongue in the mirror and, sure enough, everything she said was true. His pale tongue did have a thin, white coating over it and very small red spots.

Demo closed the mirror and handed it back to her. "You know, when they say 'don't tongue on the first date', I don't think this is what they meant."

That delightful blush reappeared on her cheeks. "It's a good thing we're not on a date then." Demo was very tempted to take the opening and ask her out on one for that afternoon, but she instructed, "Lie back please. I want to take a look at your shoulder before we get started. I know you're nervous about the needles, but rest assured, I'll be gentle and talk you through your first time."

"You mean you're not going to tell me to just lie back and take it? I do appreciate your tenderness as you pop my cherry, Doc." Demo was fairly certain he was going to hell—but it would be worth it.

* * *

HOLY FUCK. Was there something in the air in this place? Demo could not remember the last time he'd felt such a pull towards a woman. Paige was girl-next-door beautiful, but it was her sense of humor and tenacity that caught and held his heart.

There were a lot of men who did not see the appeal in strong women. They thought it lessened their masculinity. Demo had never been one of those men. For him, strength had less to do with what you could offer someone and more to do with what you would *do* for someone.

Paige was trying to do it all. Her struggles weren't attributed to her failing but to her resilience.

As he laid back on the exam table, Demo knew several things were about to happen. First, he was going to order her some damn lunch to be delivered from the diner down the street. It might be too early for traditional lunch, but he'd bet every dollar that he owned that she hadn't eaten yet today. Second, he was ordering her a damn computer and paying off the lease on this place for the next several months. She did not need to be working in a low light environment to save on electricity bills. Third, he was getting her some clientele. She hadn't even worked on him yet and he knew she was good at what she did. The amount of pride she took in this clinic when she barely had any paying patients made that obvious.

And finally, he was taking Paige Hannigan on a fucking date. It was time for her to catch a fucking break in life. Demo had every intention of being the provider of that break.

* * *

RELAX, she said... *Find your inner peace,* she said.

Not exactly an easy feat, that. Paige had left Demo in the dimmed room with a variety of needles sticking out of his body and soothing harp music playing low in the background. It *should* have been relaxing, but his damn dick would not behave.

The fun part about having a long dick was that he could enter or remain inside a woman while still partly or fully flaccid. The downfall was the fact that there was no hiding his dick while laying back just in his underwear, despite his efforts to think only of the erotic furry magazine one of his fellow EOD specialists had given him for a gag gift for his twentieth birthday instead of the luscious single mom rubbing her hands all over him. On a dare, Demo had once tried tucking, but he hadn't even lasted ten minutes with his balls hidden and his dick pulled back between his legs. There was a possibility that Demo had done it wrong, but he also had no desire to try it again until Paige had her face inches from his groin while putting needles in his thigh to help increase blood circulation.

"Generally, this point is used on women to help with PMS or menstrual cramps, but I'm doing it for you now because we need to stimulate your blood flow to help your shoulder pain."

Demo really wanted to tell her that lack of blood flow was not a current problem for him but did not want to draw further attention to his dilemma. If she was anyone else, he would have, but this was *Paige*. Lucky would castrate him if he did anything to disrespect or upset her. Hell, Demo would sit back and let him if he did too.

Paige was refreshing and funny. He'd never met a woman like her before and wondered how she could have been under his nose for so long without him knowing about her.

True to her word, Paige was very gentle with him. She talked him through the different points and why she was placing needles in his feet to help his headaches and his calves to help his liver spots. He was still pretty sure she practiced witchcraft. There was no way she could know based on feeling the *energy of his body* that he was sleep deprived due to pain.

And why were there needles in his ears? Demo couldn't remember her reasoning.

Demo was definitely going to do some research once he was out of here. He truly didn't doubt Paige or her profession, but it was a bit freaky to watch her work her magic after being subjected to thirty-one years of modern 'Big Pharma' medicine. He found acupuncture and her practice of it utterly fascinating. He'd heard of acupuncture before, seen it in movies and such, but he'd never experienced it himself. It was in his nature to learn everything he could about something that caught his attention like Paige had. Acupuncture was a big part of her life, so it was about to become a big part of his.

That knowledge still didn't help him relax though. By the time Paige came back into the room, he was trying to think of the time he'd accidentally walked in on his grandparents doing it to get his libido under control. *Fuck.* Watching her approach him in the low light, seeing her stand over him, her loose shirt gaping just enough for him to see she was wearing a lavender bra beneath...

Fuck! Demo slammed his eyes closed. Careful of the needles, he slid his fingertips beneath his ass to force his hands to behave when they wanted nothing more than to pull her down on top of him. Christ, the things he wanted to do to her body... Nope. Fuck. Demo wondered if one of her magic needles could divert blood flow. *That's* the needle he needed right then.

"How are you feeling?" Her voice was slow, soothing. Like she didn't want to wake him. Jesus, he wanted to hear what she sounded like first thing in the morning just before he plunged inside her...

"Fine," he forced out. His own voice sounded tight and restrained. Demo cleared his throat and retried, "Fine." At least that time he didn't sound like he had swallowed a dog's squeaker toy.

Her eyes narrowed slightly, like she didn't believe him. She journeyed down towards his feet. "I'm going to remove the needles and then we'll get started on your shoulder."

Demo couldn't take his eyes off of her. Looking longways down his body, his eyes tracked every minute movement. He pictured taking all of those pens out of her hair, one by one, and then grabbing her elastic hairband that must have the strength of Superman and easing it out of her curly locks... Letting her mass of curls fall down to her shoulders, brushing them out of her face, holding them bunched on top of her head as she sank to her knees before him...

"Demo?"

He jumped. Blinked. Paige was standing by his left hip now. Fuck, when had she moved up from his feet? So much for watching her every move. "Yes?"

He didn't bother to hide the heat in his eyes or his body's obvious desire for her. It wouldn't have mattered anyway. Nothing was working to quash his need and he had every intention of making her just as hot as he was later on.

"You know I'm married, right?"

And just like that, a bucket of ice water was thrown on top of him. The fire extinguished, sizzled down to burnt embers.

HE'D FORGOTTEN. It was his only excuse. He certainly hadn't forgotten who her husband was or what he had done or how his decisions were still affecting Paige now, but he'd forgotten she didn't know Richard was dead.

Two years ago in April. Two years since the club had secured Richard Hannigan naked to their cellar ceiling and tortured him for abducting women for Mateo Castillo's human trafficking ring. Two years since Lucky had burned the man's feet like they were rotisserie chickens as payback for Richard throwing several Molotov cocktails through Lucky's living room window while

Lucky, Harper, Scotty, Steel, and Jenna slept peacefully inside. Two years since Steel had ordered Scar to remove Richard's cock and balls as punishment for raping a woman to prove his loyalty to the cartel. Two years since Scar had delivered his broken, dead body to Mateo Castillo as proof that he was no longer alive to pay back his debt of three hundred and fifty thousand dollars and as an example of what would happen to Castillo if he came to Mount Grove seeking that money from Richard's widow or sister.

Four months later, Bulldog had shot Castillo in the head as he hung from the same chains Richard once had.

Paige knew none of it. As far as she knew, her husband was a missing person. Did she think he'd been kidnapped or joined the ranks of deadbeat dads who ran off with their secretaries? What did Paige think of her husband? Had she known about the depths of his sins? Even if she didn't know everything, did she know anything?

Did she still love him?

Demo's stomach soured at the thought. Clearly, she was still loyal to him at the very least. She didn't wear her wedding rings, but that might have been because she was at work and wore gloves.

He had the strongest urge to tell her the truth, that she was a widow and free of any obligations she might feel towards her husband. But what the hell was he supposed to say? Why would *he* know her husband's fate when the police didn't? Demo knew from Carlos's last report that Paige was still making inquiries with the sheriff's department about her husband's disappearance.

Didn't that show she was still concerned about him? How fast does one fall out of love? Especially if she didn't think Richard did anything wrong? What if she thought he was the victim? Her money troubles meant she knew at least some of his gambling habits. Was she still praying and hoping he would return home? *To her?*

Paige was a single mom. She had two young sons who were also missing their father.

Demo needed to talk to Lucky. He needed to know how much Paige knew and what she believed. At the very least, he needed to know if she still loved her husband. The argument could be presented that she did. After all, if she didn't, she wouldn't have reminded Demo of her marriage when he was so openly aroused by her.

"I know," he told her solemnly. "Ignore me. My body's a total flirt when it comes to beautiful women. Curse of being a good-looking bachelor."

Her cheeks flushed again—but this time it wasn't from her own arousal. She was close enough to the club to know about the Honeys. Even if they were no longer a filled position within the club, it was a known fact around town that two of them now worked as waitresses for the club's bar, *Demon on the Rocks*, and that many of the single club members still frequently visited them after work hours. Ghost would not hear of anything happening during business hours, refusing to allow his bar to become a brothel.

Was it wrong of Demo to remind Paige that he was single and that women found him attractive? Probably. The words tasted like acid coming out of his mouth. But what could he say? That he wanted to flirt with her because she was enticing and she was free to flirt back because her husband was actually dead? That she deserved to have a stress-free life filled with nothing but love, happiness, and more babies?

Demo's brain faltered at those words. *More* babies? What the fuck? He was not in the breeding or fatherhood business. He was *not* like his club brothers who had taken children under their wings so readily, regardless of biology. He was around SJ recently because he and Pumpkin were friends and SJ was wherever Pumpkin was. There'd been a few floundering moments and first-time panics, but Pumpkin had taken to fatherhood like a fish to water. Additionally, the club had bombarded Pumpkin with pumpkin baby toys, clothing, and accessories. A few weeks ago, when Pumpkin had been out with the ol' ladies shopping at *Costco*, the brothers, Scotty, and Lila had completely redecorated SJ's nursery with pumpkin-themed bedding, pillows, and a tummy time rug. If they had the time, Demo was sure they would have painted the nursery to look like a pumpkin patch. One drunken mistake over six years ago and Pumpkin was still paying the price.

Despite his love for his son, Demo wondered if Pumpkin also considered his time with Cheryl a mistake. Demo didn't think so. Lord knows, Cheryl had spent time with a lot of brothers, including Demo.

Even with the sudden depression and guilt swarming inside him at the reminder that *Paige* did not know she was a widow, Demo couldn't shake the fantasy of Paige, the desire for her. God forbid—the *need* to claim her.

The only adult female who had ever ridden on the back of his hog with him was Sissy. As Lucky's daughter, she was welcome to all club events, including the runs. She had a club kid denim cut, even though she was an adult. She was also very much off-limits. Recently, she'd come out as bisexual and was dating the club's female prospect, Sara. Her sexuality aside, Demo had never looked at Sissy as anything more than his niece. He'd spent a lot of time with her in her late teenage years to help her prepare financially for college. There'd been nothing *extra* about their time together, and not just because she'd been jailbait age. Sissy had always been *family*, like a little sister. Having her ride as his backpack had been fun and pleasurable, but in a completely platonic way.

Besides, until Sissy had told the club at Christmas that she was dating Sara, most of them had been under the impression something had been going on between her and Scar. *That* idea had taken some brainpower to process. Scar was... Well, he was

Scar. There was nothing normal or typical about him. Since everyone knew that Scar did not like to be touched, it hadn't been that far of a stretch to assume Sissy would need to ride with another club member on the club runs, even if there was something romantic between the two. No matter how many times Sissy insisted they were 'just friends', there was no getting past the fact that, for years, Sissy was the only person Scar would hang out with at gatherings or have a conversation—though silent on his part—with.

Demo saw it though. He saw Paige on the back of his hog, her thighs spread around his hips, her breasts flush against his back. The clearest part of the vision, though, was the cut on *her* back.

The one that said *Property of Demo.*

It floored him. Completely threw him for a loop. Was this some aftereffect of nearly dying? Of the regret he'd felt at never having had a permanent woman in his life? Or was this something more profound, more life altering?

Was this how it had been for Lucky when he'd met Harper? Bear and Tessa? Bulldog had once described meeting Abby as shifting his life's focus. Mind, he was six years old, but it had been intense enough for a six-year-old to notice. Demo knew little about Steel and Jenna's history, though recently it had become known that Jenna's father had hated Steel and tried to pay him to break up with Jenna. Steel had taken her father's check—but then he used it to pay for his and Jenna's wedding.

Demo knew very little about Paige's life. He didn't even know which of her sons was Nelson and which was Michael. But there was something…*possessive* about his desire for her.

Her cheeks were flushed and she wouldn't meet his eyes. It was like her confidence had been sifted from her. "It's a perfectly normal reaction for men," she explained in a very demure voice. Professional. There was nothing familial or sassy about it or her expression. Demo found his jaw tightening in dislike at the sight. "It's common and you are not my first patient to react so."

The fuck, went through Demo's mind. He did *not* like the idea of other men sprouting erections during her treatment. Not at all.

"Acupuncture and massage therapy increase blood flow and release toxins from your system. It is normal for male genitalia to react to that and the stimulation. It's nothing to be embarrassed about," she added quickly, though the color in her cheeks darkened. "I just need you to know that nothing can come of it. I'm sure you know about my marriage from Lucky or Bulldog, but please know that I am not..." Her voice trailed off. Still staring down, she continued in a sterner voice, "I am still married. I hope you will respect that."

Demo stared at her for a long, silent moment. Lying on his back on the massage table, he had a good view of her, despite her shy posture. In one regard, she did have a point. Despite his apprehensions about being pinpricked by hundreds of needles— yes, he was aware of the exaggeration—the treatment had felt good. He probably wasn't as relaxed as she'd been hoping when she left him alone for twenty minutes, but he couldn't argue the fact that his muscles felt less stiff and the pain in his shoulder seemed less intense. It wasn't gone, not like an instant cure or anything, but more spread out with less sharpness to the pain. He felt like he could at least move his shoulder without the risk of agony.

But his 'bodily reaction' as she put it? That was all *her* and not the treatment. He'd been fighting with his dick against 'reacting' since before they'd walked into the therapy room. *That* reaction was all Paige's fault.

However, he didn't think she'd be happy knowing that fact.

Which brought him to his second realization: Paige did *not* love her husband. There was no longing or desire in her voice when she spoke of her marriage. It was more like a fact of life that she couldn't change, like saying she had curly hair. She was married. Period.

"I apologize for making you uncomfortable." That was entirely true and not a line. Regardless of her reasons to claim her marriage, he was sorry he'd caused her embarrassment by his obvious arousal and flirting. "That was never my intention. In all honesty, yes, I know about your husband. I assumed with your ring gone that you were legally separated or divorcing him."—Fuck, he hated to lie to her. But what else could he say?—"You're a beautiful woman, Paige. Flirting aside, I *do* wish to get to know you better. Even if it is only as friends. You're a part of my club, even if only by marriage. The very last thing I want to do is disrespect you or cause you anxiety."

Slowly, her chocolate brown eyes lifted to meet his. In the low light of the room, they shone with unshed tears. "Thank you," her voice was moist, like she was holding back a sob. "That means a lot to me."

Conscious of the needles still protruding from his body, Demo sat up. His shoulder let out a protest, which he dutifully ignored.

"What are you doing?" she gasped out, putting her hands up as if to stop him.

Demo swung his long legs over the side of the massage table. When she stepped up closer, either to help him or stop him, Demo snagged her hips with his hands and drew her between his knees. He kept a distance between them. Christ, he wanted to drag her flush against his body, to grind their hips together.

Her breath hitched but she did not protest. "You shouldn't be moving with the needles still—"

"Look at me, Paige."

"Demo, I—"

"*Please* look at me." His tone was gentle and coaxing. She swallowed hard and then met his eyes. Demo lowered his hands from her hips. His grip on her only proved what he already suspected; she was too thin. He could feel her hip bones protruding under her dress pants. Regardless of how this conversation ended, he was ordering her a large lunch from the diner, enough for her and the boys to have the leftovers tonight for dinner. "While I hold no respect for your husband who ran out on you, I *do* respect you and your marriage. If you are not emotionally available to date, that's perfectly fine. I'm not mad or angry. Did I have the intention of asking you out once you finished trying to pop me like a balloon? Fuck. Yes," he said with emphasis. "But I'm not going to force you."

He gave her a half smile, to which he saw her lips twitch in response. "I like you, Paige. You're funny and sweet and drop-dead gorgeous." He lifted a needle-pricked hand to touch the corkscrewed curls at the side of her face. He gently pulled one straight and then watched it bounce back into place upon releasing it. Fuck, he could spend hours playing with her hair. "You could use a solid meal but needing some meat on your bones doesn't take away from your beauty."

Her eyes widened and her cheeks reddened again. When she opened her mouth to say something, Demo put a finger over her lips. "I'm not saying that to embarrass you or make you feel less. I would bet my last dollar that, while you haven't eaten a full meal in some time, your boys are well-fed and not wanting for anything." He lowered his hand. "I understand that times are hard. Moving to a new town is challenging enough, and then dealing with your husband walking out on you? It only complicates matters. How about instead of asking you out on a date, I ask you for friendship. We can start off slow, get to know each other. When you feel comfortable, you can introduce me to your sons." Then he added, "Or re-introduce me. I've already met the older one. What's his name?"

"Michael," she answered automatically. "We call him 'Mikey.'"

"Mikey," he repeated with a grin. "I knew they were Michael and Nelson but wasn't sure which was which."

"Mikey's five and a half. Nelly Bean's my baby and almost four."

"They're good boys. I've seen them with Lucky and Scotty. You've done really well with them, even on your own for the last two years."

Her cheeks flushed. "They're everything to me. Which is why, as flattered as I am, Demo, I *can't* go on a date with you. I can't risk giving Richard any ammunition to potentially take away my boys in the divorce."

Demo had to school his features. Fuck. There would be no divorce, but she didn't know that. What the hell was he supposed to say in response to that?

"If you recall, I never actually asked you on a date," he pointed out. "It's actually a bit presumptuous of you to decline when I haven't asked you."

Paige blinked at him and then let out a long giggle. She rubbed her fingers against her forehead. "You are such a flirt."

He couldn't deny that. With his knee, he gently bumped her right hip. "I want to get to know you, Paige. Even if nothing comes of it, I'd like to be your friend. Lucky can vouch for me, if needed."

He didn't offer to financially help her. Her pride would automatically decline and he didn't want her to make the assumption he was trying to help her in return for sexual favors. He had every intention of helping her, regardless of her accepting his hand of friendship or not.

Paige licked her lips. Fuck, she had no idea how enticing that action was. He wanted to pull her closer and taste those lips but forced himself to refrain. "Steel wouldn't have allowed you into the club if you weren't trustworthy."

Demo cocked his head to the side. Her relationship with Lucky was obvious, she was Harper's sister-in-law, and she saw Bulldog weekly for Abby's appointments. For some reason, though, it hadn't occurred to him that she would know Steel too. "You know Steel?"

Paige nodded. "The boys are growing like I'm adding *Miracle*

Gro to their milk. Jenna suggested stopping by her consignment shop a few months ago. Both Steel and Jenna have been a godsend, even putting clothing or shoes aside for me that they knew were my boys' sizes until I could get there. I'm pretty sure they don't charge me for half of it," she said with a trace of shame. "My bill never seems high enough for the amount of clothes and toys I take home." Her statement didn't surprise Demo in the least. Half the town's kids were provided clothing at discounted rates or no charge by Jenna's good heart. "Steel's often at the store with her and I've gotten to know him well too. They're both exceptionally good people."

They were. Even with Steel's outward hardness, his moral compass always pointed north. It was what made him such a good leader. He saw the entire picture, not just the individual aspects. His first and last priority was the protection and safety of his family, which included the club he ruled over with an iron fist. Or, rather, a *steel* fist.

"But even knowing what a good man you are, Demo, I'm not ready or able to date anyone. Pennsylvania's separation laws are stricter than Michigan's. Until my divorce is finalized, meaning Richard agrees to the divorce and signs his rights away, my priority has to be my boys."

Demo had to bite his tongue. "I respect that. So, no dating. Everything we do is in public or with your boys. That way no one can claim you were the one being unfaithful."

God, he was such a bastard. He was dirt. He was lower than dirt. He was the sludge worms pooped out that mixed with dirt. He could so easily set her free of her worries and stress, but he couldn't. Telling her the truth would endanger not only himself but his club. Regardless of Richard's crimes, his club had murdered him. Scar might have been the one to do the physical deed, but the rest of them were complicit. Even Carlos could be connected to Richard's death. Former Sheriff Hannigan too—not that Demo was holding back his tongue to protect *him*. He would just be collateral damage.

The law saw what the club had done as wrong. They had not killed Richard in self-defense. In fact, they'd tortured him before they'd killed him.

Paige could not know the truth. Harper couldn't either. If they knew, they could be implicated too. He wasn't just protecting his club brothers, but the women too. What was the saying? *Two can keep a secret if one of them is dead.*

Paige was struggling enough in her life. She didn't need the burden of her husband's crimes and murder weighing her down too.

Demo had never looked into the marital laws of Pennsylvania before. It wasn't something that had ever come up before. "Do you have a lawyer?"

She let out a dry chuckle. "Lawyers cost money. No, I don't have a lawyer. Everything I know has been from *Google* searches. I have grounds to seek a divorce but not the ability to. Every penny I have goes towards keeping the lights on and food." Demo knew that statement to be false but did not call her out on it. "What I do know, though, is that I have to *find* Richard to serve him papers."

Which she couldn't do because his body was wherever Mateo Castillo had dumped it. Which was unfortunate. If there was a way to find his body, Paige would know she wouldn't have to seek a divorce without Demo or the club admitting to anything.

"It's been two years. You haven't heard anything?"

Paige opened her mouth to answer, closed it, and then put her hand over her mouth to stop her giggles. "I'm sorry, it's hard to take you seriously when you have a needle sticking out of your E-12 point."

Demo had honestly forgotten he was littered with needles. "Probably not the most appropriate questions to be asking my doctor either."

She nodded. "Another reason for me to turn down your not-asked question of a date. It wouldn't be ethical of me to."

Demo let out a long sigh. She stepped back and he once more positioned himself on the massage bed. "Just for the sake of my curiosity, if I had asked, and you *were* divorced and not my doctor, would you have said 'yes'?"

Paige leaned over him and started to remove the needles from his forehead, nose, and ears. She clicked her tongue against her front teeth. "Probably."

He smiled widely up at her. Masculine pride swelled in his chest. "It's because I'm naked, right? No woman can resist this body."

Paige let out a loud laugh. "I've seen many naked men, good sir. Yours, while remarkable, is nothing extraordinary."

Demo clutched his chest as if he was suffering from a heart attack. "Oh, the pain! Doc, the pain! It hurts."

Her laugh was soon becoming one of his favorite sounds in the world. "Stop, you're going to knock out your needles." She moved down his arms and hands, removing needles as she went. He continued to fake the heart pain until she conceded, "Fine! You have an amazing body. I *would* go out with you because of it."

Then she leaned close to his face and added in a sultry voice, "But just know that after I've had my hands all over it today, you're going to be the one chasing after *me*. I know erogenous zones western culture doesn't know about."

Demo swallowed hard. His goddamn cock twitched as if trying to stand up to be her first volunteer. They both glanced down his body at what was concealed in his boxer briefs. Paige slowly turned back up to face him. She smiled wickedly at him—and Demo was pretty sure that was the moment he fell for Paige Hannigan.

CHAPTER 4

*P*aige was sorry to see Demo leave. She couldn't remember the last time she'd had such fun. Their flirting certainly wasn't ethical on her part but was a relief all the same. Demo had been a distraction to the worries and shame of her current life.

She looked down at her phone where the notification on the fetish site still stood open. She'd seen it come in while letting Demo rest and it had immediately soured her mood. Frankly, she was a bit surprised it hadn't been snatched up yet. She hadn't looked to see what the private request was. Demo's cash and tip were still sitting on her counter. She did not like the idea of accepting a fetish modeling gig after the time they'd just spent together.

But she had to feed her babies. Demo's treatment bill had been her standard rate of one-twenty-five and he'd given her a generous tip of fifty dollars on top of that. One-hundred and seventy-five dollars should not be the saving grace it was. But it still wasn't enough. She was over a thousand short this month between her mortgage and insurance payments, paying back rent, and utilities. The electric company's error helped, but it would only give her a break for maybe the next month.

Paige glanced at her phone. She shouldn't be so ashamed of becoming a foot model. The site was anonymous, so it wasn't like there was a glaring sign that stated she was *Paige Hannigan of Mount Grove, Pennsylvania.* No one knew they were her feet in those pictures and videos. She knew that some models, both men and women, did foot fetish posts for a living. She had nothing against those people. That was their choice and she did not shame them for it.

But there was a difference between choosing to become a foot model because she *wanted* to and becoming a foot model because she *had* to.

Paige had a Doctorate of Acupuncture and Chinese Medicine. She'd spent four years of her life studying at Michigan State University with over twenty-one hundred lab hours and eleven-hundred training clinical hours. She was proud of her profession.

Perhaps part of her guilt derived from allowing Richard to talk her into quitting her job when she became pregnant with Mikey. She hadn't wanted to quit. She'd argued against it for months, but Richard had been insistent. She knew his words were meant to hurt now. They'd been manipulative and made her already emotional state worse. He hadn't told her she *was* a bad mother by staying at work. Instead, he'd said, *"You don't want to be a bad mother, do you?"* She'd taken his words as genuine concern for their child.

Stupid and foolish.

After Mikey had been born, she'd discussed going back, but Richard had convinced her she would only have to quit again once she got pregnant with their next baby. *"You want more kids, don't you?"*

And she did—she *still* did.

The difference was, she refused to bring another child into this world without knowing she could financially take care of him or her. She was barely taking care of the two she had. If she didn't have Cindy willing to watch them for free and had to pay a daycare to do so, she had no idea where she would be or how much deeper into financial debt she would be. Cindy might not be able to help her out with physical cash, but she was able to help her out in other ways.

Would CPS see her inability to pay for a daycare as a bad thing? Would they hold that against her?

Her anxiety spiking, replacing the joy Demo's visit had given her, Paige turned her phone over on the reception counter. Even if the money was worth it, she was not in a good frame of mind to answer a private request. She needed to go clean the therapy room she'd just been in with Demo. After that, if her mood had improved and the request was still open, she would consider it.

She needed to find a way to better stomach those requests. She knew it *shouldn't* be shameful, but it was.

* * *

"Um, Paige?"

Paige jumped at the voice coming from the front of her clinic. She quickly put down the disinfectant spray, took off her gloves, stood, and donned her lab coat. Rushing out of the therapy room, she found Kelly, the waitress from the diner, standing in her lobby.

Kelly was one of the few locals who had welcomed Paige and Richard when they'd first come to town with a smile instead of a sneer. Then, after Richard had walked out on her, Kelly had whispered to Paige that her boys could stay at the diner with her while Paige looked for work. It had been one of the sweetest conversations she'd ever had with a complete stranger. Paige had never taken her up on it but had nevertheless appreciated the offer. At the time, neither Cindy nor Ronald were speaking to her much and Paige had felt extremely alienated in an unknown town by everyone except Harper.

To this day, it made Paige wonder if Cindy or Ronald knew something about Richard walking out on her, even though they swore they didn't. Their four-month silence suggested otherwise. But Paige was too desperate for help to argue with them. At the very least, she knew her kids were safe with their paternal grandparents. Richard might be an asshole, but his parents loved her boys.

"Kelly, hi." Paige walked forward with a gentle smile. "What can I do for you?"

Kelly held up a white plastic bag filled with *Styrofoam* to-go containers. "I got your lunch order."

Paige blinked, confused. "My lunch order?"

"Yeah." Kelly placed the bag on the counter and then lifted a second bag with even smaller containers inside. It was just as full as the first. "Demo said you wanted your usual. I put in your garden salad with grilled chicken order and he practically balked. Told me to tell you to stop eating like a 'fucking rabbit'. He added on an order of chicken parmesan and an order of a BLT, not knowing which one you would prefer. I also have the boys' chicken nuggets and fruit cups here." She put her hand on the bag with the smaller containers and said, "I hope you have a fridge or freezer in here. If not, I can hold this one at the diner for you until you're ready to go home. I've got three slices of apple pie, three cups of vanilla ice cream, and three cups of caramel drizzle for you guys to pig out on later. Demo said it wasn't a part of your order but he wanted to do something to say thank you for helping him."

Paige's jaw dropped. "I don't... I didn't..." The diner was a relatively cheap place for her to take the boys to eat. Their portions were generally big enough where she had leftovers for one or two of them for a later meal. But this order was going to take a good chunk out of what Demo had just paid her.

"Here's your receipt." Kelly passed over a long thermal piece of paper.

Paige took it and looked down in shock. In big red letters *Paid in Full* was scrawled at the top. There was even a spot at the bottom where the tip was filled in and Kelly had crossed out the delivery fee of five dollars and ninety-nine cents.

She hadn't ordered this food and she certainly hadn't paid for it. Obviously, Demo had. But for some reason, he made it sound like *Paige* had placed the order. Why? He'd made a comment before about her not eating enough, but that didn't mean *this*. Who goes out and buys a massive amount of food for someone they, technically, just met? Their doctor, no less.

"So I have a question," Kelly went on, either ignoring or completely oblivious to Paige's shock and confusion. "I have an old knee injury from when I slipped and fell in the diner. Mrs. Groveton keeps begging me to go into Pitts to see an Orthopedic there, but I keep putting it off." She shrugged, a little self-consciously. "I don't really have the extra time or money for something like that. The Grovetons are great with their employee benefits, but it's still a small-business insurance policy and the injury is old enough that insurance might not cover it. Anyway, I was wondering if you could take a look. Demo said you worked wonders on his shoulder in only one session."

Paige felt like someone had taken an AED to her brain. "What?"

"Do you have time now?" Kelly asked hopefully. She pulled her phone out of the pocket of her white apron around her waist. "I have a little more than forty-five minutes left of my lunch break before I have to be back."

For some reason, her statement stuck Paige as odd. "You brought me food on your lunch break?"

Kelly nodded. "Demo offered but I said I'd take it to see if you had an appointment available."

The dead silence of the clinic should have told her that Paige had *no* appointments at the moment—or for the rest of the day.

"Um, yeah. Let me..." Paige glanced over her shoulder at the therapy room she'd been in with Demo. Since her clientele numbers were so low, she rarely used the second room and hadn't cleaned it in a very long time. "I was just wiping down from my last appointment. Let me finish and I'll be right with you."

"Thanks!" Kelly said appreciatively.

She turned and headed towards the door. After a glance at the waiting room chairs, Kelly pulled a rag from her apron and wiped the dust from the faux-leather cushion. Paige's cheeks flamed at the amount of dust on the chairs. How could she have forgotten to wipe those down too?

Quickly, so Kelly didn't see her blush, Paige headed back into the first therapy room. It took her just over five minutes to finish up and get her embarrassment under control. Taking her cleaning caddy out of the room with her, Paige walked it to the lockable storage cabinet across the hall between the two therapy rooms. Then she walked down the hallway to the waiting area.

Kelly still sat there patiently. "This place is adorable," she commented when she saw Paige enter. "I can't believe it's taken me over a year to come here."

* * *

PAIGE WALKED Kelly back out to the lobby following her treatment. "Let me find you that company for the shoes you need to help with your knee pain," she was saying. Not paying attention, she didn't realize her lobby had another person in it.

Paige nearly skidded to a halt before she recognized Steel. The VDMC President stood with his back to them, hands clasped behind him, as he stared out the lobby window onto snowy Main Street. He turned upon hearing them enter the waiting area.

"Steel," Paige smiled. "It's good to see you. Give me a minute to check Kelly out."

Kelly walked around the reception desk and did a full three-sixty spin. "Did you put the food away when you left me to relax earlier?"

Paige shook her head. She'd been so perplexed by having a second patient that day she'd optimistically gone into the other therapy room and started cleaning it up while trying to hold back tears of excitement that *maybe* she could get some more clients. Kelly worked at the diner and was a gossip. If *she* recommended Paige's clinic, there was no doubt in Paige's mind that she would have more clients soon.

"I saw it sitting on the counter and put it in your fridge in the back," Steel offered. "I hope you don't mind. I didn't want the food to spoil."

Had it been anyone else, Paige *would* have minded. If she had employees, she would call the back room a break room, but since it was just her, it was the junk room. The fridge had come with the lease and housed some of her cups for cold therapy. Unfortunately, there wasn't much else in it most of the time. Paige had stopped packing lunches for herself and didn't have enough clientele to warrant the expense of the water machine she'd wanted to have when she first opened the clinic.

She hoped it didn't smell, she thought offhandedly. Out loud, she said, "Thank you, Steel."

"Yes, thank you," Kelly echoed. She turned back to Paige behind the counter. "So, as I was saying, my mom makes scented candles and soaps. She sells them on *Etsy* but not enough to have her own brick and mortar store. If you don't mind, I'm going to send her over here to talk to you. I think it would be beneficial to both of you if you could sell her products in your store. Plus, it would keep her from having to lug orders to church every Sunday."

Paige's heartbeat picked up with her excitement. "I would love that! Thank you, Kelly." Paige picked up her phone to open the Point of Sale app to ring Kelly up. The waitress had already told her that Mrs. Groveton had given her cash to pay for the treatment, but Paige wondered uncomfortably if Mrs. Groveton knew how much the standard acupuncture treatment was. What if Kelly didn't have enough cash on her or claimed the treatment was too expensive and told others in town not to come?

Paige nervously glanced at her price chart to her right on the wall. It clearly stated what an individual treatment was as well as what it would be if they bought a multi-treatment package. Should she offer Kelly a discount?

Glancing up, she caught Steel's eye over Kelly's shoulder. It was like the man radiated enough strength to transfer some to her. Paige straightened and squared her shoulders. She stood behind her treatment and her prices. Some of the chain clinics could offer sixty-five, seventy-five dollar treatments because they had the backing of a corporation. She had the backing of her years of experience and the small-town hospitality. Her rates might be more expensive, but she was worth that cost.

As if Steel knew the thoughts running through her head, he tipped his head slightly in approval.

Paige unlocked her phone and paused when she saw she had multiple text messages from an unknown number.

> Unknown number: A salad is not lunch, Doc.

> Unknown number: I still think you're a witch. What the fuck did you do to my shoulder? I haven't had this much range of motion in MONTHS!

> Unknown number: Just in case it wasn't obvious, this is Demo.

> Unknown number: My headache is gone too. Did you dance naked in the moonlight to get your powers?

> Unknown number: If you did, can I be there the next time you have to get naked?

> Unknown number: Under the moonlight, of course. Don't worry; I'll join you so we can say we're just naked friends worshiping the universe for our witchy powers.

Paige nearly laughed. She had to stifle it with a hand over her mouth. Shaking her head, she exited out of the messages app and pulled up her POS app.

"I know that look," Kelly said with a sassy voice. "Who's the lucky guy?"

Paige's eyes flew to Steel and then back again. She couldn't admit it was Demo because that would be extremely inappropriate. Kelly knew that Demo had just had a session with her. What would Steel say if he knew how flirty that session had gotten?

"It's nothing," she insisted. *Danced naked in the moonlight?* She shook her head again at the thought. "Your total today comes to one-twenty-five."

"Worth it," Kelly exclaimed. Paige let out an internal sigh of relief that she hadn't balked at the cost. She handed over two one-hundred dollar bills. Thankfully, Paige had the ability to make change from the cash Demo had just paid with. She hadn't been keeping much cash on hand. "This was excellent, Paige. Thank you for squeezing me in."

Kelly's treatment had taken longer than the forty-five minutes of her break, but she'd texted another waitress who agreed to cover her until she came back.

"Thank *you* for coming in," Paige emphasized. "I've got you on the schedule for two weeks and here's my card to take to your mom." She offered the small piece of thick paper along with Kelly's change.

Kelly waved to both Paige and Steel before heading out into the cold, her pink fluffy jacket going around her shoulders.

Thankfully, it wasn't bitter cold out today and the wind was manageable. Some days, the wind off of the mountain felt like splinters of ice against her skin.

As soon as the door closed behind Kelly, Paige turned her attention to Steel. "All right, what did you do?"

Steel was the ideal silver fox. His silver hair was thick and he'd had a closely cropped beard around his mouth for as long as Paige had known him. He stood tall at six-two and was caked with muscle. Twenty years with the Marines had given him a natural confidence Paige had always lacked. He wore all black from his long sleeve shirt under his cut down to his jeans and biker boots. Paige did not see a jacket on the wall behind him and had to question his sanity for going out in this weather without a coat on.

Steel raised an eyebrow, his face an emotionless mask. "Me? What makes you think I did anything?"

"I haven't had this many people in my clinic since my Grand Opening when I offered a day of free services. Spill."

"I only came by to make sure Demo came in for his treatment."

Paige's eyes narrowed. "I call bullshit. You did something," she pointed at him. "Demo, Kelly, Kelly's mom..." She held up her phone to show him her schedule. "Abby has been the only person on my Tuesday schedule *for months*. Now I have six people on the schedule for tomorrow?" She'd seen the notifications when she'd opened the app to ring up Kelly's bill. "What did you do, Steel?"

"While I am flattered you think I have that sort of power over this town, I can assure you that I do not. However, I do know that Abby has been singing your praises recently. Perhaps the town is finally taking notice of your unique talent."

His voice was too smooth, too even. But she also highly doubted that she was ever going to get a straight answer from him. She knew Steel was a straight shooter and did not bullshit his way through life like Richard did, but there was an honor about him that was rare in today's society. He would never admit that he helped her because it would be a bruise to *her* pride.

Paige lowered the phone and made sure her appreciation showed through. *"Thank you,"* she emphasized. "Whatever it is you didn't do, thank you."

Steel's lips twitched but he didn't offer her one of his rare smiles. He stepped closer to the reception desk. "I owe you an apology, actually. It was an oversight on my part that you've been struggling for as long as you have."

Paige felt her stomach do a little flip flop. "I don't understand. My," she cleared her throat, "struggles are my own. You didn't cause them and you aren't responsible for them."

"There lies the second apology I owe to you." His eyes held emotion that his face did not, Paige realized. She saw sorrow there, regret. For a man like Steel, she had to wonder how often he felt those sorts of emotions. "You're family, Paige. The moment Lucky put a cut on Harper, you became family. Your boys too. I offered Cindy a hand of friendship a long time ago, but somehow you slipped through the cracks. I am incredibly sorry for that oversight."

Paige's mouth flopped open and closed for several seconds like a fish out of water. Her brain was having trouble processing the gravity of his words. He spoke as if he was royalty or nobility accepting her into his ranks or offering her the protection of his title. That might also be because Paige had a proclivity for historic romance novels full of scandal, passion, and forbidden love.

"Steel, I—"

"You and your boys are welcome at the clubhouse at any time for any reason. Neither Lucky nor Harper has to be there. If you need something, *you call me.* Day or night, rain or shine. I don't care if it's because you need a lightbulb changed in your house or if you hear something creepy downstairs. *You call me,* Paige.

You're *Via Daemonia*. You have been and I'm sorry it took me this long to acknowledge it."

He looked around her clinic. "Same goes for here. You've got Angel immediately across the street. Lucky's studio and Jenna's shop are on this strip too. There are many of us around at all times. Do not hesitate to reach out if you need something."

Steel tipped his head towards the right. "We're also looking to add a daycare on club property. As long as everything goes to plan, we'll have it built and furnished by the spring. This would not be a community daycare center and only available to club kids—which yours are." There was a hardness to his eyes that brooked no argument at his statement. "I know Cindy has been helping you out with childcare. It's your choice whether you choose to continue with that, of course, but your sons are always welcome with the club. Also doesn't have to be an all-or-nothing schedule. Cindy can have them part of the time and you can bring them to the club at other times. Completely up to you," he added.

Then he leaned forward, placing his hands on the raised portion of the desk between them. "I heard about your parents' threat to take your boys away, Paige." Her eyes widened as she let out a gasp, her blood running cold at his admission. The only people who could have told him were Cindy and/or Ronald. They were the only ones who knew about the threatening voice-mail. "I'm here to tell you that I will never let that happen. You're a good mom, Paige, and your family sounds like a bunch of assholes."

Paige couldn't help but let out a snort at his words. He was *not* wrong.

"If they do more than verbal threats, if they make a formal complaint about you or show up in person to take the boys, you call me. I hope this isn't too forward of me but I contacted our attorney, Susan Black. Her specialty is business law. However, she told me to tell you to call her if anything progresses more with your parents. In the meantime, if you have anything you can use against them, text messages, voicemails, instances with witnesses, where you can prove they are not safe guardians for your boys, contact Susan and she can start the process to get a restraining order against them. Even if a complaint is made, CPS cannot place them with your parents if there's a restraining order against them. And she said to remind you that CPS will *only* take the boys immediately if there's obvious signs of abuse. Otherwise, it is a long investigation that involves multiple court hearings. Pennsylvania also does have a history of allotting grandparents rights to their grandchild, but your parents are out of state, so that should work in your favor."

Steel pulled a business card out of the inside of his leather cut and handed it to Paige over the desk. She hadn't realized she'd sat down until she had to stand to take it. Her hand shook as she accepted the card.

"Susan also said to not worry about your husband or a divorce. Richard lost his parental rights to your sons after six months of no-contact with them. Even if he came back today to demand custody, he would not even make it inside a courtroom."

Paige gasped, her eyes flying up from the lawyer's business card to Steel. "Seriously?"

"Seriously," he parroted.

A shiver ran through her body, tears of relief filling her eyes. "Thank you." Even with Richard being the cause of her current debt, she feared his return would mean having to split custody of her boys with him. Paige quickly wiped at her eyes. "Thank you," she repeated. "You have no idea what a relief it is to hear that."

"I can't help you with the divorce. Pennsylvania doesn't acknowledge a legal separation or divorce without the signature of both spouses." Paige nodded; unfortunately, she already knew that. "However, I can hire a private investigator to help find him. I know of a few in the area who might be able to help."

Paige immediately shook her head. "I can't afford that—"

"I don't think you heard me." Steel's voice was stern but held no irritation. "*I* can hire a private investigator to help find him. You would not have to pay a penny."

"No," Paige insisted. She tried to keep her voice steady, but it wavered. "Steel, no. I can't have you do that. That could cost thousands—"

"The club has contacts with several PIs," he told her smoothly. "Keys has his license for his security business, though he doesn't do active cases often. Let me do this for you, Paige. Let me help you get the distance and separation you deserve. Let me help you be free of him."

Paige bit the inside of her lip. It was so tempting, but she couldn't allow Steel to take on such a burden. It didn't matter that Steel was 'claiming' her—whatever that meant. Her morals could not let him carry such an expense on her behalf.

"I really appreciate the offer, Steel, but I can't let you do that for me." Even if he never asked for payment, she would still feel obligated to pay him back.

Steel shrugged offhandedly. "Well, it's a good thing you're not doing the hiring then. You see, I have a reason to find Richard myself so I'm doing the hiring and the finding. I'm just offering you the opportunity to serve him divorce papers once he's found."

Paige's eyes narrowed. She'd never heard such a load of horse crap in her life. Steel had never even met Richard. What reason could he possibly have to need to find him?

"Please, Steel, whatever misplaced guilt you feel you have for not 'claiming' me earlier is not worth the money it will cost to find Richard. *He* is not worth it." Steel seemed like the type of man who would argue if she said *she* wasn't worth it. "I can wait for my divorce. I appreciate the additional business. That will definitely go a long way towards helping me. You don't need to do more."

Steel leaned closer. "You're family, Paige Hannigan. There are no limits to my aid, no expense too high, no risk too great. I will guide you and protect you with all that I am. You need to wrap your head around this—preferably sooner rather than later."

She swallowed hard. "Why sooner than later?"

Despite his nearness, there was nothing romantic about his declaration. Steel was a happily married man and loyal to his core. Paige truly believed he meant it with every fiber of his being. Like a vow that went deeper than mere words.

That rare Steel-smile she'd heard the others talk about tipped the side of his lips up. "Demo made another appointment without me having to blackmail, hoodwink, or bully him into returning. As much as I believe that your treatments could and did help him, only one thing would make that man end his stubborn streak and make another appointment to see you." Steel tipped his chin down towards her phone on the desk. "You should probably answer his text messages before he finds a reason to stop by again to ensure you're still alive."

Paige's cheeks flushed. Steel knew those flirty text messages were from Demo!

"I hope you're prepared for his attention, Paige. When my boys fall, they fall hard and fast. Nothing will stop them from protecting and claiming their women. Demo's no different."

At that moment, her phone alerted to another text message. Paige glanced down to see another message from her unknown caller.

> Unknown Caller: Did you eat yet? Don't make me come back and force-feed you. You need to eat, beautiful!

Though his expression did not change, Steel's eyes held a glimmer of arrogance. They seemed to scream *I told you so* at her.

Paige turned her phone over so the screen was down without responding to the text message or the ones from earlier. "Demo and I are just friends."

Steel nodded once. "Keep telling yourself that, Paige. I give it a month before you're wearing his patch." Paige shifted uncomfortably. She liked Demo—she really did—but a month? That was too fast. Harper had told her being an ol' lady was irreversible. There was no *divorce* in the MC world. "Still want me to not hire a PI to find your husband?" Steel asked with a raised eyebrow.

Paige fiddled with her lab coat. "I suppose finding him couldn't be a bad thing," she hedged slowly. Maybe she'd be able to convince him to take on his own debts and relieve her of their burden.

Steel wrapped his knuckles on the desk twice in quick succession. "Great to hear. Now, on a more serious note, what do you know about late onset multiple sclerosis?"

Paige's back stiffened. Her eyes looked up and down, assessing Steel's strong body. The most outwardly signs of MS were fatigue, dizziness, and muscle spasms. She saw none of that with Steel. Which meant he wasn't asking for himself. Was it someone in the club?

"Many with MS seek out alternative medicines, including Chinese medicine. Acupuncture, acupressure, and even daily uses of certain herbs can help with MS symptoms and even slow down flare-ups." The amount of hope on his face made her add, "I've seen acupuncture work miracles, Steel, but there's no evidence that it can slow the progression."

"But it can help relieve her pain?"

Her. Paige got a very sick feeling at the pronoun. There was no doubt in her mind whom he was asking for. Harper had mentioned more than once how rundown and tired Jenna had seemed since the holidays.

Paige nodded. "Yes. I can devise her a schedule and recommend some supplements to also help flare-ups." She was sure he knew this already but felt the need to add. "There is no cure, Steel."

"Do you have any more appointments this afternoon?"

His voice revealed none of the pain in his eyes. Paige couldn't imagine Steel without Jenna or Jenna without Steel. They seemed like the perfect couple with the strength and fortitude every other couple should strive to be.

"I'm free," she told him softly.

He nodded once and then turned to leave her clinic. Paige stood there, cold as stone, for several long minutes. *Jenna?* She knew the statistics, but still... MS was a difficult diagnosis. She had to fight against many odds in the coming years. Even if she did, the disease would eventually claim her life. The average was five years following diagnosis. There were many cases, more in recent years, where the patient lived to ten or twelve years past diagnosis. Treatments and new therapies were being developed each year to help with symptoms.

But no cure.

The door opened. Steel guided Jenna into the clinic, using his body almost like a shield against the elements. Paige noticed immediately why Steel wasn't wearing a jacket—because Jenna was wearing his jacket. She certainly looked more haggard from the last time Paige had seen her before the holidays.

Paige came around the desk. "Hi, Jenna."

Jenna was walking on her own accord, which was a fantastic sign. Paige wondered how long it had been since she'd gotten her diagnosis. She placed Jenna in her late fifties, which put her in the 'late onset' category as Steel had said. Despite wearing two coats, she shivered like she was still cold. "Hi, Paige. How're you?"

"I'm doing well. The bigger question is how are you?"

Jenna shrugged, trying to brush it off but Paige saw pain mixed with fear on her face. "I've had better days. My hands don't seem to want to cooperate today and I can't seem to get warm. Jack left me in the car with the heater running on high and I was still shivering."

For some reason, Jenna referring to Steel as 'Jack' made

Paige's heart clench in her chest. She'd never heard anyone but Jenna call Steel by his legal name.

Paige was glad she'd cleaned up her second therapy room while Kelly had been resting in the first. Jenna's symptoms did not surprise her. "Let's get you back into my room. Steel, can you grab the heat lamp from the first room?"

"Of course."

As they walked back towards the second therapy room, Jenna said in a soft voice. "They don't know. I haven't had the heart to tell them."

Paige knew instantly who she meant. "You're going to need to tell them eventually. You've got a doctor and a nurse living next door to you. They're going to figure it out."

"I know," she said in a sad voice. "Maybe I'm just hoping to keep from burdening them a little longer."

"You're not a burden!" the women heard Steel call out from the other therapy room.

Jenna caught Paige's eye and rolled her own. "Damn his Vulcan hearing." The affection in her voice was accentuated by her smile. Jenna had the most beautiful red-orange hair Paige had ever seen. It always shone like her hair was on fire.

Once getting Jenna settled on the massage bed, Paige said, "Let me go get a new patient chart. I'll be right back." Paige passed by Steel carrying the second heat lamp on her way out. "You can plug that one in over there and get both of them turned on her how she needs."

"Paige?" She turned around in the doorway to face Steel. "Grab some food while you're out there. You still haven't eaten. You don't need to stand on formality with us." When she opened her mouth to protest, he snapped, "Eat your damned lunch, Paige. Demo would never forgive me if I let you starve while sitting here talking to us."

The mention of Demo brought a blush to her cheeks. She

nodded. "Can I get either of you anything? There was some of the diner's pie in the bags?"

Both Jenna and Steel shook their heads. Paige left to get a new chart and the necessary paperwork and then went back into the junk room to get one of the containers of lunch Demo had delivered for her.

Despite the sadness she felt at the knowledge of Jenna's illness, the fact that she had three patients in a row was hopefully a sign that she was going to continue to have a good day.

* * *

DEMO GLANCED down at his phone again. Still nothing from Paige. It was possible she was busy, but too busy to reply? He didn't like the thought of that. Had he talked to too many people today and sent multiple patients over to the clinic where she couldn't handle them and reception herself?

Maybe he should swing by the clinic after he was done at the club's *Harley-Davidson* dealership. Though he had an office at the clubhouse and the club's bar, *Demon on the Rocks*, Demo also kept one at the dealership. It was just easier to keep certain papers and items in certain locations while he, his laptop, and his legal pads traveled to where he needed to go on whichever date.

When the club had first put forth the idea over two years ago to purchase the dealership up for sale, Demo had gone through the old owner's books with a fine-tooth comb. At first, he was fearful that the owner was fudging his sales numbers. How else could he explain selling so many motorcycles in the winter in Pennsylvania? But the man was a bit of a genius. He put forth and marketed such winter sales that people would come from all over the state and even surrounding states just to get a new *Harley-Davidson* that they wouldn't be able to ride for months at a massive discount. He might have sold the occasional bike, but the real sales during the winter were on merchandise. Selling the amount of shirts, helmets, and even offering discounts on maintenance and services kept the dealership running just as smoothly during the cold, unrideable months as it did during the summer. The man never went into the red over the winter.

Steel had put Demo in charge of the books for the dealership. As the club's Treasurer and accountant, that made sense. What Demo had not been expecting was for him to suddenly have to become an expert in retail. *That* had been a bit of a learning curve. Thankfully, the previous owner's records and notes were so meticulous that Demo had been able to catch on fairly quickly. After a couple of bumps and what Scotty would call an *oopsie* mistake, Demo seemed to have found his footing.

The biggest concern when purchasing the dealership was employees. One could not have a sales business without salesmen. The previous ownership had been family-run with only a few non-family members working. When they'd moved, they were taking a good chunk of the workforce with them. The idea had been put forth that the best representation for the club would be if the patched members were the salesman, except every patched member but Jumper already had full-time jobs and careers. Lucky had then suggested that the patched members be put on a rotating schedule. Rather than a couple of them working full-time at the dealership as salesmen, *all* members worked one or two part-time shifts during the week.

It had taken some finagling, and some *Tetris* skills Demo hadn't known he'd possessed, but he'd finally been able to get a potential schedule to present to Steel, showing that Lucky's idea held merit. Since then, the club had lost two members, gained two patched members, and had three new prospects. The ol' ladies even took the occasional shift—so long as they were never left alone in the dealership.

Demo himself had purchased his hog from this dealership when it had been with the previous owner. Unlike Steel, Bulldog, and Jumper, he hadn't come to the VDMC officer table knowing how to ride a motorcycle. Lucky, Bear, and Demo had gone through the classes to get their licenses together. Scar had just shown up one day with a motorcycle and no one had the guts to question him as to whether it was acquired legally or if he even had a license to drive it.

The service department was taken over by the club's auto garage that Grumpy managed. Two of his techs were already certified in motorcycle repairs and one had been interested in getting the certification. Those three moved over to the dealership and Grumpy hired on new mechanics at his garage for the workload there. He'd since lost Jumper as a mechanic due to Jumper's head injury.

Like Demo, Jumper had been severely injured in Jasmine's kidnapping. His head injury had required surgery and resulted in him being unable to drive either his *Indian* or his cage for over six months. In fact, if Demo remembered correctly, he had a driving exam coming up to have his medically suspended driver's license reinstated. While Jumper spent his days with Jasmine at her veterinary clinic and didn't need his license during the winter, Demo knew that Jumper wanted to get it reinstated in time for Jasmine and Jumper's honeymoon in April and May. They were taking their motorcycle with the sidecar for Aerial on a cross country trip to see some of the more famous National Parks, like Yellowstone, Yosemite, and the Grand Canyon. They had other stops both there and back but hell if Demo could remember the long list. Their plan was to be gone approximately six weeks. A vet from Johnstown that Jasmine had worked with before and was considering offering a partnership to would be coming into town for the six weeks to cover Jazz's clinic during her vacation.

Jasmine had taken the necessary lessons and classes to get her motorcycle driver's permit. It meant she couldn't drive a motorcycle without a licensed driver accompanying her, either riding behind her or separately next to her. Pirate, Jumper's brother and Jasmine's soon-to-be brother-in-law, had been helping Jasmine get some of her needed driving hours in prior to them having to put the sleds away for the winter. Once Jumper's license was reinstated, the two of them could take turns driving during their honeymoon. While Jumper appreciated his brother's help, there was also a strict rule in place that Jasmine and Pirate were to practice on *separate* bikes unless there was an emergency. Jumper trusted his brother implicitly, or he wouldn't allow Pirate to be in charge of Jazz's lessons, but that didn't mean Jumper wanted Pirate holding onto Jazz while riding a motorcycle.

Demo certainly wouldn't want Paige riding with any other brother unless absolutely necessary.

Fuck!

Talk about a full circle train of thought. How the hell had he gone from thinking about the dealership's work schedule and inventory to Paige and not liking the idea of her riding as someone else's backpack? Others might call it 'riding bitch' but many in the VDMC had gotten out of that habit due to Scotty and the other club kids. For a long time, Scotty, Jenna, and Sissy had been the only passengers on their club runs. It had seemed so disrespectful to say 'riding bitch' when referring to a child, an ol' lady, and a young lady. The members said it when referring to each other having to double up on a bike for whatever reason, but not in deference to the women and kids.

Plus, Scotty used to run up to random members before club runs and hop onto their back, yelling, "I'm a backpack!" Then he would proceed to be carried around on his uncle's back while everyone was still getting ready for the club run. He'd been a lot smaller back then and there had been less club kids going for rides with them. He'd had his pick of drivers because, per Scotty, Lucky drove like an old granny.

Neither Demo nor any of the other brothers felt right about saying Scotty was 'riding bitch'. In that regard, as well as many others, the VDMC was a tame motorcycle club. They did not traffic guns, drugs, or people. They ran legitimate businesses that were neither a strip club nor a porn company, and they were looked at respectfully by the town they called home. Demo knew that if Steel had propositioned him for a one-percenter club, he would have turned him down. That just wasn't how Demo lived or wanted to live.

He loved that family meant everything to his club and it wasn't just talk. Every decision their club made revolved around protecting the women and the club kids.

The number of club kids had exploded recently. Steel's kids had never really been into the motorcycle life or lifestyle. When they attended functions, they wore their cuts, if only out of respect for their father. Melanie, Steel's daughter, had never even ridden on a motorcycle and would instead drive a cage with a prospect if she was attending a club run. So while Carter, Jordan, and Melanie were 'club kids', they weren't counted on for club run numbers. Sissy had been sixteen when the club had been formed and had gone on most club runs with her dad and brother.

Now there were Bree, Aaron, Ollie, and Lila who rode with them regularly too. Bree was Angel and Cage's paraplegic adopted daughter, Aaron was Cage's biological son, and Ollie was a foster child Steel and Jenna were looking to adopt. All three were teenagers at fifteen, sixteen, and sixteen, respectively. While Bree had a special harness that could allow her to ride on the back of anyone's sled with them, Angel preferred Bree ride on her *Harley-Davidson* Trike. The three-wheeled motorcycle provided Bree with more balance and also meant Bree could remain on the hog while parked without risking falling off or over.

With the number of ol' ladies also increasing, the club members would soon be outnumbered. Only a few of them even rode solo anymore. Sophia wasn't a club kid or an ol' lady and she also had a tendency to join them for club runs.

Demo wondered if Paige would allow Mikey and Nelly Bean

to ride with them. Currently, when the boys joined the guys on their outings while the ol' ladies had their get-together, they rode in one of the cages with a prospect and the other kids too small to ride. Hell, pretty soon Demo was going to need to look into purchasing another SUV or two for the club because they were running out of room with only three eight-seaters.

In Demo's opinion almost four and five were too young to be on a motorcycle. Bulldog allowed Lila to ride. She was almost seven and had gone through a lot of practice runs around the club property before going on her first club run last April. Bulldog also placed her specifically with Ghost, his Enforcer, and made Ranger ride tandem to keep an eye on her. Despite her mischievous nature, Lila had not caused any problems or done anything dangerous while on a motorcycle. It would seem she took Bulldog's warning of "one mistake and you'll be riding in cages for a year!" very seriously.

Tessa and Harper would be out for most of the upcoming season. Neither of their men would allow them to ride while pregnant and neither of them would be in any condition to ride after giving birth. That meant Bear and Lucky were able to take a club kid riding with them. Sophia was almost always riding with Pirate.

Sissy usually rode with Demo. But with her girlfriend, Sara, about to be patched over, it would make sense for Sissy to start riding with her. Which would free Demo up to have Paige—

"Hey, man."

Demo looked up from his desk to see Keys and Pumpkin standing in the doorway. Pumpkin had some cloth wrapping around him that strapped SJ to his front. Though not without some learning curves, the man was thriving as a single dad. Demo knew how freaked out Pumpkin had been about the idea of having a son but was exceedingly proud of his friend for stepping up as he had.

"Hey," Demo responded automatically.

"What're you up to?" Keys asked as they walked into the office. Keys took the chair opposite Demo's while Pumpkin started doing some weird bouncing-walk back and forth across the office parallel to Demo's desk.

Demo's eyes glanced down at his laptop, only to see it had gone dark. How long had he been sitting there lost in his head and not working? "Not much," he said nonchalantly. "Just catching up on some invoices."

Keys glanced at the back of Demo's laptop and then back up at Demo, clearly not believing the line of bullshit Demo had just tried to feed him.

"How did your treatment go this morning?" Pumpkin asked, his big hands rubbing up and down the back of SJ's covered back. He wore a skullcap with the VDMC logo on the rim.

"Better than expected," Demo answered honestly. "I can't remember the last time my shoulder didn't feel like there wasn't a twenty pound weight sitting on it."

Neither Keys nor Pumpkin responded right away. Both were just staring at him. Pumpkin had even stopped pacing.

"What?" Demo demanded.

"Dude, you're smiling." Keys said it like Demo had just walked on water.

Demo felt his cheeks fall and knew that Keys had not been lying. He tried to school his features better. "It's just a relief to not have a stabbing pain every time I move my arm."

Pumpkin's eyes narrowed on him. Even from across the room, Demo felt like his friend was looking at him through a magnifying glass. "No, it's not that. There's something different about you."

"No, there's not," Demo insisted. He was not sure if that was a lie or not.

"Is it Paige? Did you find something out about her parents?" Keys asked.

"No—" Demo started but Pumpkin cut him off with a loud exclamation. "It's Paige! Holy fuck!"

Both Demo and Keys looked at him in surprise. There was an innocence to Keys' expression, almost like confusion, that made Demo take a second look at him. The kid wasn't *that* young. He knew he'd been with the Honeys at parties and such.

Pumpkin continued, pointing an accusatory finger at Demo, "You fell for her! What the hell, man? We were supposed to go down as the last of the club's bachelors!"

Demo knew the vehemence in Pumpkin's voice was feigned. They'd never once said such a thing to each other.

Before Demo could argue Pumpkin's statement, Keys turned back around towards Demo. "You fell for her? How? You said you'd never met her before."

"I hadn't," he told Keys. "And I didn't," he told Pumpkin.

"Oh, please." Pumpkin resumed his pacing. "I know that look. You've got the same look on your face as the others after they met their ol' ladies. You fell." Then he leaned forward and slapped Keys on the shoulder. "Text the women. I need them to know I wasn't the next to fall."

Keys looked both shocked and confused. "Fall for what?"

"Kid, we need to get you out from behind your computer screens more if you're not following along with this conversation," Pumpkin told him with all seriousness.

Demo had to agree with that statement at least. "I didn't fall for her!" he insisted again. "I like her, yes, and I enjoyed my morning with her, and I wanted to ask her out but she reminded me how unethical that would be, plus she still thinks she's married, for Christ's sake, and I don't want to move too fast... I just think it's best for us to be friends."

Both Pumpkin and Keys stared at him for another long moment.

Demo sighed in frustration, "What?"

"Okay," Keys nodded, "now I see it."

Pumpkin let out a loud laugh. His son started to squirm and he quickly cut off the sound. Increasing his bouncing and rubbing his son's back, Pumpkin said in a much lower voice, "Friends, my ass. I'd bet SJ's entire college fund that you were daydreaming about her when we walked in here. You had the goofiest look on your face."

Demo's eyes narrowed on him. "You have, like, ten bucks in his fund." Demo would know; he'd been the one to set up the fund as soon as SJ's social security card and birth certificate had come in the mail.

"Kid's barely three months old. I've got like eighteen years to build it up," Pumpkin said with defense.

Demo chuckled. "Look, yes, I like Paige. But nothing can come of it while she still thinks she's married."

Pumpkin waved that off. "We've faked worse."

Keys snorted. "Yeah, you helped so much with that," he said dryly. "I couldn't have done it without you."

Pumpkin gave the kid a cocky smile before turning back to Demo. "If you like her, go after her." Then he added, "Just make sure the ol' ladies know you were the next to fall. Apparently, they think babies will automatically attract single women like sharks to blood and I was going to be the next to fall." Pumpkin rolled his eyes. "I don't need a woman to raise my son."

Demo had to bite his tongue against reminding Pumpkin he'd been singing a different tune not too long ago. "Are they still placing bets on us? I thought that stopped after Bulldog took the last plot in the Pentagon?"

The Pentagon was the club's name for the five houses that had been built on club property. When the club had purchased the former distillery, there had been the main building, a large garage, an outdoor pavilion area, and a lone rundown house that Steel and Jenna had moved into with their two teenage kids. One of the first projects that the club did together was rebuilding Jenna's new house to her specifications. Nearly five years later,

Lucky had added a modular home next to Steel's house after his had been burned to the ground by Richard Hannigan. Four months after that, Bear and Angel added their homes following Tessa and Bree entering their lives. Angel's house was handicap accessible and designed specifically for a wheelchair user. The four houses had remained there for nearly six months with no club member claiming the fifth and final plot in the pentagon shaped area.

Then Abby had returned to Bulldog's life.

"It did," Pumpkin nodded, "but they recently started it back up again. Something about the next plot of land..." He shrugged. "I don't know about you but I have no desire to move out of the clubhouse anytime soon. Steel even gave me permission to turn my apartment into a double with the one next to mine once SJ gets old enough to need his own room."

Demo was impressed by that news. Steel would have never allowed that if the Honeys were still around. He wondered if it would affect any of the single men living in the clubhouse to have a kid living in there too. Before club kids had only visited the clubhouse, but none lived there.

Then Demo frowned. He hadn't included himself in that wondering.

He was single. Nothing about Paige's and his flirting during his treatment that day had changed that. And yet...

Demo didn't *want* to be single anymore. He hadn't since he'd gotten shot. But he also hadn't been actively looking for a woman. Between healing, therapy, and the nerve damage, finding a woman had been put on the back-burner.

Paige had been right under his nose for nearly two years. He knew a lot about her life from tearing apart Richard's finances with Keys. But today had been the first day he'd spoken with her. If only he'd known...

Known what? It was ridiculous to think he was in love with

her. He didn't believe in love at first sight. Love took time, energy, and commitment.

But hadn't Bear taken one look at Tessa and known? Lucky made it sound like he'd been hit with a sledgehammer rather than Cupid's arrow when he'd laid eyes on Harper for the first time. Jumper had been secretly in love with Jasmine for four years before the two of them got together. Despite his womanizing ways, Cage claimed he knew he wanted Angel from the very beginning but overheard her tell another brother that she would castrate any patched member who tried to hit on her with a dull spoon.

Abby and Bulldog were in a league all their own that transcended the laws of physics, time, and space.

Was it so out of the realm of possibility that Demo had fallen for Paige after just one meeting? His eyes landed on his phone next to his right hand. He'd been checking it all day like a dumbstruck teenager who had given his number out to his first crush and wondering why she hadn't texted him back yet. Hell, he'd just been considering going *back* to her clinic to check on her because she wasn't answering him.

Keys tilted his head. "What's going through your mind?" Demo noticed he'd been squinting his eyes more recently and wondered if the kid needed glasses.

"Contemplating how much stalking I can get away with before it becomes creepy," Demo muttered without thinking. Then felt his cheeks heat when he realized he'd said that out loud.

Pumpkin threw his head back and laughed. "None! Fuck, man, you have it bad."

Sadly, Demo wasn't sure he could argue with his friend.

CHAPTER 5

Paige: Hi. I'm sorry it took me so long to get back to you and to thank you for lunch. That was extremely generous and unnecessary but I do appreciate it. I'll pay you back at your next appointment.

Paige: I can guarantee you that I am not a witch but dancing naked in the moonlight does sound like fun. I miss dancing. I used to go all the time before the boys were born. Though, probably not the type of dancing you're thinking of. [smiley face emoji]

Demo: As long as you're naked, you can do whatever dancing you want and I promise you I'll enjoy the fuck out of it.

Paige: [link to video of Michael Scott's Awkward Dancing from the Office]

Demo: [laughing emoji] [laughing emoji] [laughing emoji]

Demo: So long as you're naked...

Paige: I actually prefer swing dancing.

Paige: Are you still there?

Demo: Yeah. Had to look that one up. I didn't think people did that anymore.

Paige: I joined a club in college and fell in love with it.

Demo: These YouTube videos are wild! You do all the swinging and the dancing like that?

Paige: Well...yeah... It's called Swing. Dancing.

Demo: Smartass.

Demo: I am completely impressed.

Demo: How long has it been since you last went dancing?

Paige: Probably around six years.

Paige: Richard promised he would learn for our wedding dance but got too busy at work.

Paige: Sorry, I didn't mean to bring him up.

Demo: No need to apologize. He was a part of your life and your kids' father. I get it. I don't like it, but I get it. Never be afraid to talk to me about him, your feelings, or your past.

Paige: It feels weird but I appreciate the sentiment.

Demo: Also going to reply to your first text now because your second text distracted me so much...

Demo: If you ever try to pay me back for food I've had delivered to you, it will only make me tip you higher and then go out and buy you more food. You've been warned.

Paige: You're such a guy! I was trying to be nice.

Demo: I appreciate you noticing that I'm a guy. Your "nice" gesture is noted and ignored. You will NEVER have to pay for anything in my presence.

Paige: If I ask you a question, will you be honest with me?

Demo: Depends on the question.

Demo: If you ask me if those pants make you look fat, I will answer 'no' without even looking so I won't know if it's the truth or a lie.

Paige: Ha-ha. You're so funny. (She says sarcastically.)

Demo: I'm hilarious. (He says seriously.)

Demo: What's your question, beautiful?

Paige: Did Steel talk to you? I mean, I know things got a little out of hand with us flirting during your appointment. I'm still sorry about that. That was entirely unprofessional of me. But were you here and then the food afterwards... I mean, was that because Steel told you to?

*P*aige jumped as her phone rang unexpectedly. She was sitting in her car in Cindy and Ronald's driveway texting Demo. It was silly to take advantage of a couple of minutes of kid-free, work-free time when there was so much she had to do, but she felt bad about having not texted him back yet. Especially after he sent all that food over to the clinic with Kelly.

She hesitated slightly before answering her phone. "Hello?"

"Steel came by to see you?" There was something odd in his voice. More so than the fact that he skipped over a greeting entirely.

"Yeah," she said honestly. It wasn't a violation of her doctor-patient confidentiality to ask about Steel. She just wouldn't add about Jenna coming in after their conversation to get treatment. "He came in shortly after you had my lunch delivered. He went on about needing to apologize to me. That family's important and I'm family through Harper. He made it sound like I was this big oversight on his part."

Demo was silent for a long minute. "And you think Steel made me fake shoulder pain to come to the clinic and flirt with you?" There was disapproval but no censure in his voice.

"What?" she gasped out. "No! That's not what I meant at all. I know you weren't faking the pain."

"But you think I was faking the flirting?"

Paige flinched, pinching the bridge of her nose. "No, yes... I don't know. I'm a mess, Demo! As much as my inner goddess was swooning all day at your attention, my stupid, logical brain has to question it. I'm not a catch. I don't have riches or a young woman's body. I have stretch marks from my pregnancies. I just... I appreciate you flirting with me. I appreciate the food. I just... I guess I don't understand it."

"You know, it's a shame you don't know where your husband is."

Her eyes flew open and she sat up straight in the driver's seat of her car. "What?" she demanded harshly.

"If you knew where your husband was, I'd hunt him down and kick his ass. What the fuck did he say to you, *do* to you, to make you question your beauty, Paige? Could you put some meat on your bones? Fuck yes—but *you are beautiful just as you are.* You think *riches* make a woman desirable? I would take an honest woman who lived in a travel trailer and earned minimum wage over some rich skank who only cares about how she looks to others any day. Did I flirt with you because *Steel* told me to? Fuck. No. I wouldn't even if he had. I'm not that kind of man, nor is Steel. Did he recommend I go to the clinic to see you for my shoulder? Yes. Abby and Bulldog have been pushing for me to go see you too. Feel free to ask them. It wasn't until Steel *threatened* to drag me there by my ear that I manned up and went. I'll admit to that. They had the influence to get me to your door. But everything afterwards? They had *nothing* to do with it."

Paige's heart hammered in her chest as she tried to process everything he just said, declared, and admitted. She had no idea how to accept the fact that he thought she was beautiful. Richard hadn't given her such a compliment since before she'd gotten pregnant with Mikey. Looking back on it, it was a wonder she'd ever gotten pregnant with Nelly Bean. It was a wonder she ever let Richard touch her at all after he casually mentioned to her that pregnant women were ugly to him. She'd made so many mistakes with Richard. Believing his lies and hidden insults.

Was it so impossible that Demo could *actually* like her? She'd seen his body's reaction to their flirting and her nearness. She recalled the feel of his hands on her hips and how he'd stared into her eyes like he was searching for her soul.

"Paige?"

"Yeah?" she managed to get out. It sounded like a toad croak.

"I meant every word that I said, but I can also understand your dilemma. I'm your patient. You're technically still married. I've laid out my intentions. I want you in my life. I want to get to know you as no one else does. I want to be your confidant and your supporter. I'll be your biggest cheerleader if you'll let me. I will stand between you and all the bad in the world. Not because I don't believe you're not strong or can't fight your own battles, but because you deserve no less.

"I can be your white knight if you let me.

"Why don't you take some time? Think it over. I don't want to stop treatment on my shoulder. You're actually the first doctor I've seen that was able to help me without turning my medicine cabinet into a pharmacy. But I will gladly take myself off your schedule if it will ease any guilt you may possess about dating me too. And if it turns out that all you want is friendship, well, I'll be the best friend you ever had, Paige Hannigan."

Her breath hitched in her throat. "What I want and what I should do are two entirely different things, Demo," she admitted softly.

"Yeah," he drawled, "but only one of those lets us go dancing naked in the moonlight."

Paige let out a loud laugh in spite of the tears in her eyes. "I need to go pick up my boys."

"Go," he encouraged. "I'm here when you need me. And Paige?"

"Yeah?" she answered. She quickly wiped the unshed tears from her eyes.

"I meant what I said. Don't try to pay me back for any food I buy you. With how busy your work schedule sounds tomorrow, don't be surprised if you get another delivery."

She bit her lip before asking, "Can I request you as my delivery driver?"

His low laugh was husky and held the promise of shared passion. "Absolutely. I'll even let you tip me in kisses."

Her heart swelled to dangerous proportions at the fact that the sexy as hell man on the phone with her just said 'kisses' with a straight face. Or, rather, *voice*.

"Good night, Paige. Drive home safe."

"Good night, Demo. And thank you."

"I'm going to take a page out of Bulldog's book and tell you something I've heard him say a million times to Abby but never fully understood until just now: you *never* have to thank me for helping you."

She couldn't have prevented the adoring smile on her lips if she tried. "I'm going to thank you anyway. I truly do appreciate it."

"You're welcome, Paige. Will you at least text me that you got home okay or would that be a bit out of line?"

"I'll text you," she promised.

"Text me when you're locked inside your house. Not from your driveway," he ordered.

It was odd. The order should have upset her or gotten her defensive. Instead, it only made the decision she had to make harder. "I promise."

"Good night, Paige," he said again.

She repeated, "Good night, Demo."

* * *

PAIGE FROWNED as she pulled up outside her clinic Tuesday morning. It had snowed a little overnight. She'd dropped the boys off at Cindy's earlier than her usual time because she assumed she needed to come shovel and salt the sidewalk outside her clinic.

But it had already been done.

Not all of the shops, she noted. Just the ones connected to the club. Hers, Angel's tattoo shop, the bakery, Mrs. Bunu's antique store, Lucky's studio... The bakery was owned by Mabel Weiss, Deputy Danny's mom and a friend of the club's. Mrs. Bunu was a widower and Paige had noticed more than one person wearing a prospect badge helping her out around her antique store throughout the year. The parking spots outside each of the storefronts were also shoveled and cleared.

After her talk with Steel the day before and then her conversation with Demo later in the evening, Paige shouldn't have been surprised that a club member or prospect had shoveled and salted in front of her clinic. But she was. Maybe seeing and believing were two very different things after all.

Richard had promised her all sorts of things when they were dating that never came to pass after they'd been married. He'd cared about appearances at the country clubs, how prestigious their home looked when people came to visit, how expensive a car he drove... Richard's priorities had been far different than her own.

Paige exited her car, her snow boots hitting salted asphalt rather than white fluff. Making her way over to her clinic, she saw that there was a bunch of boxes sitting outside the door. She frowned. She hadn't ordered anything. She *needed* to order supplies, but she'd been holding off doing so with as few regular clients as she'd had before yesterday.

She recalled the conversation she had with Kelly about her mom's candles and soaps, but these boxes *couldn't* contain that. She hadn't even had a chance to talk to Kelly's mom yet about an arrangement. It would be completely unorthodox and rude to just pile up her mom's products outside her clinic door unattended anyway.

Upon closer inspection, she saw a note taped to the top box.

Paige,
I'll be back before you open at 8. Needed more coffee.
Keys

Keys had been here? *Keys* as in the computer tech guy who worked for the motorcycle club? If she recalled correctly, Harper had said he was twenty-two, but that conversation had been almost a year ago. Regardless, why was *Keys* going to go get more coffee and then be back before she opened? What did her opening have to do with his being here anyway? And what was in the boxes?

There was one large box at the bottom with three medium

sized boxes and several small boxes. Plus what looked like a plastic bag of tied-off wires. What the hell was going on?

"Oh good, you're early."

Paige spun around. She had her hands in her pockets because she'd given Mikey her gloves against the brisk wind that morning and forgotten to get them back after dropping the boys off with Cindy. Her scarf was pulled up over her ears, muffling his voice. "Are you Keys?"

Like Demo, she hadn't actually met him in person before. Only knew stories from Harper, Abby, or Lucky. He was lanky and not very muscular. He had on a winter coat with the club's logo and his info on the front pockets. If the club had winter coats, why had Demo been wearing a different coat and his leather cut?

"That's me. If you'll unlock your door, I can get started." He really was so young. Bright blue eyes, a dusting of freckles across his nose, bright smile, rosy cheeks, and onyx hair that shined in the winter sunlight.

"Get started with what?" A sharp wind wracked them and Paige realized she was not going to have this conversation outside. "Wait a second."

She rushed over to her door. Using her keys, she undid the deadbolt and lock. Shuffling inside, Paige flipped on the light switches. The heat was on low, so it wasn't that much warmer inside than out, but at least there was no wind. She stepped back to hold the door open for Keys. He was holding all of the small boxes and the plastic bag of wires when he came in.

Paige took off her scarf so she could hear him correctly. "Okay. What is going on? Why are you here?"

"I'm here to set up your security system and new computer."

She blinked at him. He just stood there smiling at her. "I didn't order a security system or a new computer." There was no way she could afford any of that.

"Steel did," Keys informed her. He walked past her to put the boxes on her reception desk. Then he walked outside, picked up the medium boxes, and used his butt to push his way back inside her clinic. One more trip brought in the big box that he struggled with. Eventually, he had to put it down and push it across her hardwood flooring to the reception desk. "Don't mind me. I'll be out of here in no time. Just show me where your router is and I'll take care of everything."

Paige shifted uncomfortably. "I don't have a router." Well, she did, but it stopped working due to nonpayment.

Keys frowned. He removed his coat to reveal a brown leather messenger bag slung over his shoulder. He looked like he was on his way to college classes. It was hard to believe he owned his own security company at his age.

He pulled a tablet out of his bag. After several taps one-handed, he scratched his smooth cheek. It was mean of her to wonder if he was even old enough to shave. Compared to the others in the club though, he really was just a kid. Which made his life all the more impressive. He had to be some sort of prodigy. What branch of the military would he have served? Maybe he hadn't served and he was the exception to the rule because the club wanted his computer expertise? Harper made it sound like he was able to accomplish anything as long as he had a keyboard. It also begged the question why a motorcycle club needed someone like Keys amongst their membership.

Harper swore to her that the club members were not criminals. Paige would not have allowed her boys around the club otherwise, even if Lucky *was* her brother-in-law.

"You signed up for service when you signed your lease," Keys informed her. "Did they never set it up for you... Oh." Keys' eyes flew up to her and his cheeks darkened. This time it wasn't from the wind.

Paige swallowed hard. "It just became too expensive for how little I use it." That was *partly* true at least.

His young face looking back down at his tablet, Keys said in a flustered rush, "Don't worry. I'll take care of it."

Paige didn't know what it was he planned on taking care of. She had a feeling, though, if she refused, Steel would be on her doorstep in less than an hour and not taking no for an answer. She had to get the clinic opened and ready for her first appointment at eight-thirty. Abby had her standard appointment at ten and Paige had seen Bulldog's name on her schedule too. That was a first. The only reason Paige even knew 'José Santiago' was Bulldog's legal name was because Abby called him 'José' and not 'Bulldog'. No one called Demo 'Ron' so it was completely understandable that she wouldn't have known who he was.

If Abby called Bulldog 'José', did that mean Harper called Lucky 'Russell' when they were alone and 'Lucky' when they were in public? Paige had picked up on certain protocols around the club. Things they did and did not do based on tradition or rule. Abby seemed to be in a category all her own, so Paige could believe she wasn't supposed to call Bulldog 'José' but did anyway and Bulldog just stood between her and any ridicule for it.

One thing she knew for certain, though, was that Steel was in charge. Like a monarchy and he was king. There was no arguing or disobeying him. If Steel ordered Keys to come to her clinic and set up a security system, Keys would do it regardless of Paige's wishes.

She scratched her forehead. "How much is this going to cost?" Steel meant well, he really did, and she did want a security system, but it would increase her electric bill and add an internet bill back to her ever-growing pile.

"Don't worry about it," Keys said offhandedly.

Unfortunately, that wasn't an option. "Keys, I need to know what it is I am expected to pay—"

He shook his head, still not looking at her. "Like I said, don't worry about it. It's covered."

"What's covered?" He couldn't possibly mean her bills.

"Look, I'm just here to do the set up. I don't know about the bills or anything like that. You'll need to talk to Steel or Demo. He runs the books."

Paige's eyes narrowed. "I'll do that," she told him. But first she had to get ready for her day. She couldn't have clients come in when the clinic wasn't warmed up yet.

As she walked towards the backroom, Keys flipped on the rest of the lights out front. Paige winced. She absolutely hated that she had to pinch pennies so tightly and really hoped the few clients she did see regularly thought the low lighting was for the ambiance.

* * *

PAIGE ESCORTED her first client out to the waiting room. Her jaw dropped. Holy fuckeroni! A large *Mac* desktop computer sat on her reception desk. Along with a pristine white keyboard and mouse. Her logo was even on the wallpaper of the computer.

Mrs. Guthrie paid in cash. She didn't like computers or credit cards and had originally tried to pay via check. It wasn't that Paige didn't trust the older woman to give her a good check, but she couldn't risk the possibility of it bouncing and having to fight charges at the bank. She also hadn't charged Mrs. Guthrie full price because she only wanted her hands worked on for their arthritis. Paige would have liked to have helped with her varicose veins or her balance, but Mrs. Guthrie refused.

"Just my hands, dear," she'd said. She'd even questioned Paige's knowledge of anatomy when Paige had asked her to take off her shoes. *"Dear, do you know where the hands are?"*

It had been an interesting appointment to say the least.

Keys hopped up from underneath the receptionist desk to escort Mrs. Guthrie out to her car. He gave Paige a smile on his way out.

She gaped in dreadfulness at the changes done to her lobby.

She saw three cameras attached to her ceiling. From the last security system they had at their home in Detroit, she knew the white rectangles on her front door were to detect when the door opened and closed. She did not know what the white squares on the two, large bay windows were for. There was one on each window.

Her eyes landed on the desktop and she felt tears start to well up. She could *not* afford this. She supposed she could pull from the account where she had been collecting the insurance money but she needed to use that in less than two months to prove to her stepfather she was seriously trying to pay back Richard's debt. It was hopefully enough for him to not file that bogus complaint with CPS that could result in her boys being taken away.

A bell sounded, causing Paige to look up. When had a bell been installed above her door? That was when she realized, it was electronic with a very good mimic of an actual bell. It sounded behind her, which meant Keys had somehow added a speaker in the back too.

A very bundled up Abby came shuffling into the clinic. From the fresh flakes on top of her bright ginger head, it had started to snow again. Paige hadn't had a chance to check her weather app since arriving and really hoped it was only going to be a light flurry. She didn't have chains on her tires or an all-wheel drive car. Even though she was from Detroit, Richard had cared more about appearances than safety. Thankfully, her car was paid off and she had the title. It was one less bill to have to worry about, but she couldn't trade it in with how bad her credit score was and hope to get a decent monthly payment on a more appropriate car.

Bulldog was covered in even more snow than Abby was, making Paige believe he'd literally held himself over Abby to protect her from the falling snow. *Snow!* It wasn't like it was acid snow, but regular snow. It might seem ridiculous and overbearing to some, but Paige's inner goddess swooned and she was pretty sure her ovaries fluttered.

She wanted *that*. She wanted a man who would love her so fiercely he would protect her even from harmless snowflakes.

"I want you in my life. I want to get to know you as no one else does. I want to be your confidant and your supporter. I'll be your biggest cheerleader if you'll let me. I will stand between you and all the bad in the world. Not because I don't believe you're not strong or can't fight your own battles, but because you deserve no less.

"I can be your white knight if you let me..."

Her heart longed for Demo in that moment. It was so foolish of her. They barely knew each other, but she felt a desire and a connection with him that she never had before. Not even when she'd been dating Richard. Demo had the ability to take her breath away with just a crooked smile.

The door hadn't even closed fully yet before Bulldog started to wipe snowflakes out of Abby's hair, neck, and shoulders. She unzipped her jacket and he slid it down her arms. It was like a very intimate dance, Paige realized. They moved in a synchrony that was so perfect it had to be choreographed.

Bulldog was a big guy, in height and in muscle. He had a long graying beard and a bald head. Paige knew he shaved it in solidarity with his mom, who was a two-time Breast Cancer survivor. Following so much radiation and chemotherapy, her hair had never grown back right, so she kept her head shaved and wore wigs. Both her sons, Carlos and Bulldog, took very good care of their mother, even though she'd been cancer free for over eight years.

Abby in comparison was petite. She had certainly gained weight from the malnourished woman Paige had first met, but she was still little. At five-six with bright red hair, Abby looked like she could turn sideways and disappear. When she'd first met the couple, Paige had thought it a bit—for lack of a better word—*misogynistic* how Bulldog did everything for Abby. He hovered, and Paige had once wondered if he chewed up her food and transferred it into her mouth like a mama bird did to her babies.

But Paige had been wrong in her judging.

Abby was fragile, but Bulldog didn't treat her like glass. He treated her like she was the most precious and rare diamond in the world. Like her very existence was the key to his survival. Protecting her from snowflakes might seem extreme, but it was also a testament to his declaration that he would protect her from *anything*.

In the near year since Abby had returned to Mount Grove, she'd started to come out of her shell. As her doctor, Paige knew some of the horrors Abby had survived during her sixteen-year captivity in the religious cult her parents had joined when she was seventeen. Paige also knew she did not know *all* the details.

Abby had told her how she had been repeatedly raped by a man who had *bought* her within the community. How sick and fucked up was that? Paige's stomach turned every time she thought about it too much. While it wasn't common knowledge around town, Paige knew that Abby and Bulldog's two youngest children, Caleb and Georgie, were results of that rape. She did not know how Lila and Cassie, the older two children, were related to Abby or Bulldog, if at all. Not that it was any of her business, nor did it matter in the long run. Abby and Bulldog loved their four children, regardless of the circumstances of their conceptions.

And Paige loved that for them.

She wasn't even convinced Richard loved either of his sons. He only ever seemed to show affection towards them around others, like his sister and parents.

Her phone let out a sharp *ding* from her lab coat pocket. Paige pulled it out, under the romantic delusion that it was Demo somehow sensing her want and longing for him.

But it wasn't.

It was from her stepbrother. Another message, reminding her of her deadline to pay back money she didn't have.

Shame washed over her. Dousing the fire that had been brewing and wiping out her fantasies of Demo like a flash flood. Embarrassment replaced the fire inside.

"Hi, Paige," Abby smiled brightly.

Paige shoved her phone back in her pocket. Not responding nor deleting the message. She tried to smile, but her shock and anxiety prevented it from forming fully. "Hi, Abby."

Bulldog's eyes narrowed on her. "What's wrong?" He took off his coat. Like Keys, his had the club symbol on it. He hung both his and Abby's coats on the rack by the door.

The bell above the door rang again as Keys hurried back inside. He made a show of shivering and then bent over to shake out his hair on Abby like he was a dog. Abby giggled and squirmed from the cold flakes hitting her. Rather than running behind Bulldog for protection, even in jest, Abby reached into her pocket and took out a reusable pink water bottle. With Keys' head bent over to shake out the snowflakes, he didn't see Abby open the bottle and pour some onto his hair.

"Hey!" the younger man shouted, stepping back. "Eh! Cold, cold, cold!" This caused him to shake his head out more, splattering water all over.

Bulldog stepped between a shaking Keys and a laughing Abby, keeping her from getting wet from the water bottle. He had a look on his face as he stared down at his wife that was a mixture of adoration and admiration. Despite that his back was currently getting wet from Keys' attempts to get the water out of his hair, he was proud of Abby for her actions.

Paige loved that. Their bond and connection was so powerful, it felt like they were always in an intimate bubble.

"That was mean, Abby!" Keys scolded as he took his jacket off to try to dry his hair even more.

Abby leaned around Bulldog's thick arm and smiled. "Don't start something you can't finish, Keys!"

Keys looked like he wanted to retaliate again, but his eyes flicked to Bulldog and he clearly thought better of it. Instead, he made a gallant bow. "I concede to the victor."

Abby's smile looked like it could have been seen from space.

Bulldog gave Abby her moment of victory before he turned his attention back to Paige. "What's wrong?" he repeated.

Both Abby and Keys turned towards her too.

Paige tried to stand up straighter, appear more confident. This was her place of *business* after all. They were her *clients*...plus Keys. She was supposed to be professional. "Nothing," she told them. "Therapy room two is ready for you if you want to come back."

Bulldog wasn't having it. "Not until you tell me what's wrong." His eyes scanned around the room and outside her windows. Like he was looking for danger.

"Nothing," Paige insisted again. Her eyes flicked to the computer equipment.

Bulldog must have caught the move. "Don't play poker, Paige. You'll lose." He gestured towards the computer. "This is a gift from the club to you. If you're worried about the expenses, don't. It's covered."

"I even contacted your internet provider and squared away your account," Keys added as he stepped around Bulldog. More like sidestepped, in case there was any retaliation on Bulldog's part for Keys shaking snow onto Abby. When Bulldog did nothing, Keys' posture straightened and he walked more confidently to the reception desk. "I need to give you your new password, but you have Wi-Fi again. I even created a guest network for you to advertise. It's a great amenity to have at really no additional cost to you. People specifically go places with free Wi-Fi over businesses without."

Paige's jaw dropped. "You... You... How... You..."

Abby approached her. She was wearing a cute little dress with flannel leggings. Bulldog carried a small drawstring bag that had a change of clothes that were a much looser fit. Looser clothing meant they weren't as warm, so Abby changed once she got to the clinic during the winter months and Paige could put the heat lamps on her.

Paige always ignored the fact that Bulldog would go into the therapy room with her to 'help' Abby change. She once walked past the closed therapy room door to overhear Bulldog's deep baritone tell Abby it was too bad he didn't have any handcuffs with them because Abby looked sexy enough to eat. Given what she knew of Abby's history, it was difficult for Paige to wrap her mind around Bulldog tying Abby up for sexy-kinky fun but she tried not to judge. They were consenting adults and there was no way Paige would ever believe Bulldog would do anything to harm Abby.

And good for Abby for working to get past her trauma enough to be intimate with her husband. But it was also difficult to get that image out of her head after that, so from then on, Paige stayed away from the therapy room until Abby said she was ready to start her treatment.

"This is what they do," Abby told her as if that was explanation enough. "Welcome to the club."

Paige looked between Bulldog, Keys, and Abby. "I am not a part of your club!" she finally shouted. "I don't need you guys coming in here with your fancy computers and cameras," she waved her hands around at the offending objects, "and making my life more complicated. I don't care if Steel thinks he 'overlooked' me or feels guilty about not including me. That's *his* problem. I," she tapped her chest, "need to be able to run my own business and live my life without you guys bulldozing your way through it. I didn't ask for all of this! I don't want it and I don't need it." Paige rounded on Keys. "And you 'squared away' my account? How the hell do you even have access to it? There's a reason I let the account close! It's too expensive for just me to run the clinic."

Keys shifted, guilt radiating off of him like sunbeams. "I thought it would be easier for you. I set you up with social media accounts too. I was just trying to help. And with you being Demo's, he said—"

"Demo's?!" Paige shouted. For as much as she longed for a relationship like Bulldog and Abby's and as much as she thought perhaps she might find something like it with Demo, she was not the sort of woman to allow a man to come crashing into her world and take over for her. *She* had the right to choose her own path. Paige thought Demo understood that after offering her time to figure out what she wanted from a relationship between the two of them. "I am not 'Demo's'! What is it Demo said, Keys?" Paige demanded. "Did he tell you to come here with all of this equipment? Did he pay for all of this and expect me to be grateful for it? To fall on my back with my legs spread wide with gratitude?"

Keys' face turned redder than a tomato. She hadn't meant to embarrass the kid, but she had also been expecting him to argue and defend Demo. To say that *Steel*, not Demo, had been the one to order all of this equipment and upgrades.

But he didn't. Even flustered as he was, he didn't argue that all of this wasn't Demo's idea.

Paige felt her nostrils flare. She didn't know if she was more pissed or hurt. She *wanted* Demo to want her. He claimed he did. But for him to come barging into her life like this? And he wasn't even here himself to explain things to her? Food was one thing, but this was thousands of dollars of electronics.

She turned towards Bulldog. He was a straight shooter. He would tell her as it was. "What is going on? Was all of this Steel's or Demo's idea? Who is paying for all of this?"

"Demo is," he told her without preamble. "He wants you to be safe while you're here. We already had one shop attacked," he indicated out the windows towards where Angel's tattoo shop was across the street, "and he wanted to ensure you were safe since you work here alone."

Paige's eyes also looked to Angel's studio. She'd heard about her attack by a rival MC and it had scared the crap out of Paige to think she'd been so close that night. What if she'd had her boys here at the clinic too that evening? She was beyond grateful Angel and Bree had gotten away unscathed, but the proximity still shook Paige for a long time following the attack.

She'd even looked into a security system afterwards, but the costs had been too high. That was how she knew how much a setup like what Keys was installing was worth.

"I can appreciate that," Paige begrudgingly admitted. "But it doesn't explain the computer equipment or Keys paying my internet bill."

"You'd have to talk to him about that part." Paige did not appreciate the amusement in Bulldog's voice. "But, if it were me," he looped his arm around Abby's waist, pulling her back against him, "I'd be doing everything in my power to ensure your life is *easier*. Not by taking over," he pressed when Paige opened her mouth to argue. "But by providing the needs to help you along to your success."

Paige rubbed her forehead. "Why would Demo do that?" she asked through gritted teeth. "We're not dating. We're not... *anything*." Phone call the night before aside, she hadn't made any decisions yet regarding their relationship, whether platonic or romantic.

"You're not?"

Paige lowered her hand to look at Keys, who was standing by the reception desk like a deer in the headlights. "*No*," she said, almost breathlessly. Paige closed her eyes and took a deep breath. When she opened them, they were all staring at her with different levels of sympathy. "Look, I can't deal with this right now. Abby, please, head into the therapy room to get ready. I'll be next door cleaning up, so take your time." Before she turned to leave, she faced Keys. "Can you go, please? I just... I can't deal with this right now."

Then she walked into the first therapy room and closed the door.

* * *

"Dude, your lady is really pissed off." Keys' voice came over the speakers of his Bronco as Demo headed towards Main Street.

"What are you talking about?"

"Paige," Keys said like Demo was an utter moron. "She's really pissed off."

Demo tried not to let out a frustrated sigh. He'd known who Keys meant with 'your lady' and he honestly liked the way that sounded. Not just the 'your lady' part but that it was *Paige* who was his lady. That hadn't been what he was questioning. "That wasn't what I meant," he snapped. "*Why* is she pissed off?"

"Um... Well, there might have been a talk about her being yours and then you bulldozing your way through her life and, um, her not being able to afford the new equipment and not wanting to be a part of the club."

Demo jerked the wheel to the right, grateful no other cages were on the road, as he skidded to a halt on the snow-covered shoulder. He was maybe ten minutes from Main Street and the clinic, but he needed a moment to process what Keys had just said. He threw his gear shift into Park.

"The fuck did you just say?"

Keys stammered out in a ramble, "Look, man, I am not a people person! I deal with software, not soft women! I tried to give the line that everything was a gift from Steel and the club, but then she started on about how she's not a member of the club. I thought calling her your woman would calm her down."

Demo pinched the bridge of his nose. "Let me guess, it didn't."

"Yeah, not so much." At least Keys sounded sympathetic.

"She's not my woman," Demo told him emphatically. "I *want* her to be, but she's not. Paige needs *time*, man. I was trying to give that to her."

"Well, how was I supposed to know that?"

"Why was I even brought into the conversation at all?" Demo asked, though it was more rhetorical than anything. "Where are you now?"

"In my cage outside the clinic. I wasn't sure if I was supposed to stick around or not."

"Go home," Demo sighed. He straightened up and put the Bronco back into Drive. "I'll be there shortly. Just…"

"I know, man," Keys said when Demo paused. "I *am* sorry."

Demo nodded, though Keys couldn't see it. "She doesn't even know she's a widow," he finally said. "She wants to go on a date with me, I know she does, but she thinks she can't or shouldn't because she believes she's still married."

"I'm working on that," Keys told him with a bit of hope in his voice. "Steel's got me figuring out if we can either bring Richard back to life virtually or fake his death."

That was something at least. Demo winced as his shoulder reacted to his body's stiffness. He felt looser since his treatment the day before and the pain was more distributed instead of localized to one part of his shoulder. In a weird way, it felt like his shoulder blade was flexing without him consciously doing so.

"Also, you should know she got another threatening text from her stepbrother."

Demo's jaw tightened. "Bulldog's at the clinic with Abby?"

"Yeah."

Good. He needed to speak with his SAA. Demo thought Clifton Barrington would make a particularly good hanging ornament in the club's cellar. *No one* threatened his Paige and got away with it.

"I'm pulling in now," Demo told Keys. He didn't see Keys' cage as he parked in front of the clinic. "Have you found any of the Barringtons' skeletons yet?"

"Too many to count," Keys drawled. "I'm on my way to show Steel. Between what I found and Paige getting a restraining order, there's no way they can take the boys."

That was really good news. Demo turned off his Bronco. "Has Paige filed the restraining order yet?"

"No, and frankly, she might not have to with what I found. But I still think it's a good idea."

Demo agreed. "I'll talk to her." The snow had stopped coming down. Based on the forecast, they weren't due to get anymore until that night.

"Sorry again, man, if I made your life more difficult. If she agrees, I can come by any time to finish the installs."

If being the opportune word. Demo had a feeling the next few hours of his life were going to involve a lot of groveling and maybe even some begging. Bottom line, despite her pride, Demo needed to know Paige was safe. She didn't have a secretary anymore and worked alone in an insecure office building. After what nearly happened to Angel and Bree, Demo hoped and prayed she at least agreed to keep the security measures. He could see how the computer equipment *might* have been a bit too much too soon.

But he wanted her to have everything she needed.

She'd been on her own for too long. She deserved to have someone by her side, in her corner, and dare he hope, in her bed.

CHAPTER 6

*a*n electronic bell sounded as Demo entered the clinic. Good, at least Keys had been able to finish that before Paige had kicked him out. He had *not* liked it when he'd come into the clinic the day before and there'd been no signal to her. Demo didn't think she would have taken away a device like that. The electricity used would have been minimal enough where it wouldn't have affected her electricity bill. Not like turning off overhead lights—which he now noticed were all on—and taking away computer equipment would have. No, Demo suspected she hadn't had a bell or anything over the door because she'd had a receptionist up until recently.

Bulldog sat in one of the waiting chairs. His large body was spread out with his elbows on the arm rests, his hands gripping the corners, and his booted feet planted on the floor. He looked tense as if he was getting ready to be shot out of a circus cannon. It was the agony in his eyes that held Demo's attention, like Bulldog was burning from the inside out.

Without looking up at Demo, Bulldog confessed, "I don't want her to know. Abby loves coming here and I will do anything to make her happy."

Demo glanced between his SAA and the hallway that led to where Abby was getting her treatment and then back to Bulldog. "You don't like being away from her," he concluded. "It's killing you to not be in that room with her."

Bulldog nodded stiffly. "I don't want her to know," he repeated.

"She's right back there," Demo argued, unsure he understood Bulldog's current torment. "She's fine. You know she is. Paige would never harm her."

Demo moved to sit in the chair next to him as Bulldog stared longingly down the hallway.

"We were separated for sixteen years. During that time, unspeakable things happened to her while I was living my life, fucking around, and trying my damndest to forget about her. Having her back in my life is a miracle beyond measure. I will never take her or her love for granted. Her unwavering love is what brought her back to me after all these years. *But*," he added with a hint of self-deprecation, "I can't shake the feeling that I'm going to lose her again. You guys make fun of the two of us for being glued at the hip. You call it sappy or being whipped or romantic, but I don't think it's occurred to any of you that I *can't* let her out of my sight. And the few times that I have to is agony."

Demo looked at his friend in a new light. He'd always thought Bulldog was so strong, admired him for the way he took in Abby's biological children as well as Lila and Cassie. But he hadn't considered the toll it had taken on him. "Have you talked to your therapist about this?"

Abby, Bulldog, and Cassie telecommunicated with a therapist from Philadelphia. Demo had met her once at Abby and Bulldog's wedding, but damn if he could remember her name. Lila saw a child therapist here in town, the same one that Bree also saw. Her name was Joanna and she shared an office space above the local bookstore with Jumper's therapist, Dr. Rutenberg. Demo wasn't sure if Bulldog still saw his therapist regularly or on his own, though he knew Bulldog joined Abby on some of her sessions when they wanted to discuss something with him.

"Oh, she's aware. Dr. Skurja says my anxiety derives from a fear of losing her and guilt from not being able to protect her in the past."

Demo wondered at the derision in his friend's voice. "So you sit out here in pain while Abby's only a few yards away behind a closed door because you want Abby to be happy and don't care what that costs you?"

"Pretty much," Bulldog nodded minutely. He glanced at Demo out of the corner of his eye. "I know what you have with Paige is new. I can't give you advice about being in this stage of a relationship because I was never *in* this stage of a relationship. Abby was mine from the moment I laid eyes on her. There wasn't a question of *if*. Hell, I'm not even sure I gave her an option." He let out a humorless chuckle. "But I can tell you this: figure out what makes *her* happy and give that to her. Not what you *think* will make her happy."

He indicated with his chin towards the expensive computer on the reception desk.

Demo scratched the back of his neck self-consciously as he admitted, "I thought it would make her happy."

Bulldog raised an eyebrow at him. "You thought she'd open up the computer box, jump up and down with joy, and then fall madly in love with you? Hate to break it to you, brother, but that's cheating."

Demo glared at him. "That's not exactly how I saw it in my head," he grumbled. Though it was so damn close, it was embarrassing.

Bulldog chuckled. "Relationships are hard work. It's a give and take, almost like a dance. You need to listen to what it is she *actually* needs. Not what *you* think she needs, which is actually about what *you* need."

Demo felt a headache coming on. His shoulder twitched

uncomfortably. "You make it look so easy. All of you do. Hell, I've never seen any of you fight or have a disagreement. Angel and Cage are in this weird honeymoon phase where they seem to sense the other one before they even walk into a room. Jasmine and Jumper are busy planning their wedding. Lucky and Bear have knocked up their women *again*. And you and Abby have, like, merged into this single organism that defies the laws of physics." He shrugged. "I think... Or maybe I *hoped* I'd found my happily ever after with Paige. She's amazing, Bulldog." Demo couldn't keep the smile off of his face. "I swear, I'm kicking myself for her being right under my nose this whole time."

"You didn't see the behind the scenes of all of us," Bulldog told him. "You didn't see the struggles each of us faced to get our women. You saw the glamor shots, the final cut. I guarantee you, Abby and I fight."

Demo's jaw dropped. "What? You do?"

Bulldog nodded. Demo saw his beard twitch with a smile. "It's not big, shouting matches that result in blood being spilled, but we have our disagreements. Every couple does. Those who don't probably have underlying problems that they aren't dealing with. Most recently, Abby and I argued about whether we should push Cassie into going outside more. She does well the few times she's been off property and Abby thinks we should continue to encourage that. I think we should wait until *Cassie* says she's ready."

Cassie had agoraphobia and often had difficulty leaving her own house to walk to the clubhouse down the path. She'd attended Bulldog and Abby's wedding at the beach last October, but she'd struggled. Aside from the wedding itself, she had remained in her hotel room most of the weekend.

"Don't look so surprised. Abby's fierce when it counts," Bulldog said with a level of love Demo could only hope to one day have. Maybe with Paige. "My point is, relationships, even the ones with an instant connection, are hard work. They take *time* and you have to be willing to put aside your pride and preconceived notions to figure out what your partner needs."

Demo glanced down the hallway. He didn't hear or see Paige or Abby. Still, he lowered his voice to barely a whisper. "Even if Paige feels for me what I feel for her, she won't do anything about it so long as she still thinks she's married."

Bulldog nodded thoughtfully. "We're working on that. But that actually might be a good thing," he added.

Demo's eyebrows drew down. "How so?"

"It gives you time to lay a foundation, Demo. Take romance out of the equation, *build something* sturdy, unbreakable. Make her fall for you *before* you get physical."

As much as Demo's cock disapproved of Bulldog's suggestion, his mind couldn't argue the logic in it. "Be her friend first."

"Be her friend *always*," Bulldog corrected. "You can have the best sex in the world with a woman, but it's not a relationship without that friendship." He let out a small snort. "You have to actually like her before you can love her."

Demo scratched his forehead. His eyes roamed around the waiting room. He let out a long sigh. "You're making too much sense. Can we change the subject?"

Bulldog laughed, his eyes still never straying from the hallway for more than a second or two. He clasped Demo on the knee once before letting go. "Sex is the easiest part of a relationship, brother. It's when it's removed that couples tend to see what their relationship really is made of." He nodded down the hall. "Be with Paige. Be everything to her. Give her everything she needs and desires. If the two of you decide to add sex into the mix, that's your business and no one but you needs to know those details. But a true relationship? A partnership? It needs more."

"I couldn't have said it better myself."

Demo's head whipped up. Paige stood in the doorway. Her

unruly curls were thrown up into a messy bun that had just as many writing utensils in it as the day before. She had on a loose turtleneck sweater and dress pants under her lab coat.

And fuck if the sight of her didn't make Demo's heart expand. She was a vision.

Paige indicated behind herself to Bulldog. "Abby's done. She's getting changed now."

Bulldog shot out of his chair like the cannonball Demo had equated him to earlier. He rushed past Paige and down the hall to the second therapy room door.

Paige stepped further into the waiting room. Demo stood but didn't approach her. He wasn't sure what to say or even how much she'd overheard.

With the reception desk almost as a barrier between them, Paige said, "I was going to yell at you when I saw you. Scold you for being too much and trying to take over my life when we aren't even dating. But Bulldog has a point that I can't ignore. Bottom line, I *do* want to build something with you. I want to have a relationship like theirs that is stronger than sex."

She waved her hand towards the computer equipment. "I don't need money or trinkets or *things*. I've had that relationship and look where it's gotten me. I don't need a white knight, Demo. I can fight my own battles. What I need is a partner who will face the bad and the good with me. Who will be my support and my guide as much as I am his. I want someone who is proud to be out in public with me on his arm but just as content holding me on the couch while we watch movies in our pajamas with the boys. I want a *partner*."

Demo walked around the desk. Paige stood still, allowing him to approach her. He carefully lifted his right hand to one of the curls that had fallen around her face. He twined the corkscrew around his finger. Her chocolate eyes stared up at him with such longing, it took everything in Demo not to pull her against him.

"I will absolutely be your support and your guide. It would be my honor to show you off and dance the night away with you. Lounging on your couch with you and the boys for movie nights? Hell, yeah!" He shook his head slowly, "But I'm afraid I can't be your equal partner, Paige. Because I will always stand between you and the bad, always lift you up and cherish you like the *queen* you are."

Her pupils widened, almost making the browns of her eyes disappear. "You shouldn't say things like that. It makes me want..." Her words caught in her throat. "It makes me forget I shouldn't..."

Demo leaned in, breathing her in. She had a unique scent of lavender, lemon, and peppermint. His nose trailed a path across her right cheek, tilting her face up towards him. Two steps forward pressed her back against the wall next to the door frame that led to the hallway. Demo released her hair, letting it go like a coiled spring, and cupped her left cheek with his right hand. He placed his left on the wall next to her ear.

"I don't want you to forget," he murmured against her skin. "You can't change your past, Paige, but you *can* decide your future. I want a future with you. The question is, do you want one with me?"

Their chests were pressed so close together that he could feel the rapid beat of her heart against his own.

"Yes," she breathed out.

"Thank fuck," he said before he kissed her.

* * *

WHAT AM I DOING...? Though the query was at the forefront of her mind, Paige could not stop herself from kissing Demo back. His touch was like a balm to her soul, healing and nurturing. Oh, it turned her on all right. Paige struggled to get close enough to

135

him, completely forgetting the fact that Bulldog and Abby were inside her clinic too. But there was also a sense of peace that accompanied the fiery kiss that gripped her to him.

She wasn't so prideful that she wasn't grateful for his efforts to help her. Unlike Richard or her stepfamily, Paige knew he hadn't bought everything and had Keys come set it up for her to flaunt wealth and status over her or to assert dominance. He truly had just wanted to help her. It meant a lot to her that he was willing to own his error and apologize. Not many—men or women—would so readily admit a mistake.

He would never know how much that meant to her.

Demo gripped her face between his calloused hands. His tongue stroked her lips, begging for entry. All thoughts of protest left her mind as their tongues tangoed.

A throat cleared.

Demo and Paige froze. Her eyes flew open to see Bulldog and Abby standing in the doorway just to the left of her.

Demo, though, didn't move to step back. Instead, he pressed his body *closer* to hers. "Go away," he said against her lips and then returned to kissing her.

Heat suffused Paige. She'd never been big on PDA, but she wasn't against it either. It had just been a long time since she had the opportunity or the desire to kiss a partner without caring who was around to witness.

Demo's touch was such a distraction that she feared she might become addicted to it. He was passionate, yet gentle. The evidence of his own arousal pressed against her stomach. Paige imagined him lifting her up so she could wrap her legs around his hips and—

The throat cleared again.

Demo let out a sound that could only be described as a growl. He tore his mouth away from hers and rounded on Bulldog. "What the fuck do you want?"

"Other than to spare Paige any embarrassment should

someone walk in off of the street into her place of business?" Bulldog inquired with a glance to the door.

Paige's eyes went wide as she gasped, "Oh fuck."

Bulldog sent her a gentle smile, indicating that he was neither angry nor disappointed in her by her wanton actions. "I also have an appointment," he added.

Paige's cheeks blazed so hot, she was surprised steam did not come out of her ears. "Oh God! I am so sorry." She pressed against Demo's chest, but he wouldn't budge. "Demo, move!" she ordered. "I am so sorry, Bulldog. This is completely unprofessional. I don't know what came over me. I am so sorry. Of course, I'll comp your treatment."

"The fuck you will," Demo snapped. He glared at his friend. "Take your wife to get something to eat at the diner. I need to speak with Paige alone."

"Demo, no," she argued, but Bulldog nodded.

"You available in half an hour?" he asked her.

"No," she said and then backtracked, "I mean, yes. I mean, my next appointment isn't until one. But you don't have to go. Demo, please—"

"It's all right," Bulldog told her. He moved forward and Paige's eyes went wide as she saw Abby had been standing behind him. Her friend looked happy despite witnessing Paige's lewd behavior. Bulldog took Abby's hand, guiding her towards the door. "You two might want to lock your door."

Paige covered her face with her hands. She could not remember ever being so embarrassed in her life.

As soon as the clinic door closed after Bulldog and Abby, Paige pushed harder against Demo's chest. "Move, damn you!"

Demo took three steps back. Unlike her, he did not look embarrassed or ashamed by their public behavior.

She glared at him. "Why would you do that? This is my place of *business*."

Demo waved that off with a flick of his hand. "Trust me.

Neither of them cared. Did you see Abby's face? She's happy for us."

"I don't care!" Despite her embarrassment, Paige was grateful for the interruption. It made her see sense. "We shouldn't have done that. It was inappropriate."

Demo crossed his arms over his toned chest. "Because of where we are or because of your marriage?"

Paige couldn't stop the guilt that filled her at his question. It had nothing to do with betraying Richard and everything to do with her own morals. "I *am* still—"

"That man doesn't deserve you!"

Paige jumped at the harshness in Demo's raised voice. There was a hidden anger in his eyes that she'd never seen before. The only reason *she* didn't fear him was because that rage was not directed at her. "I agree," she said evenly, hoping to calm him down too. "But it doesn't change the fact that I *am* still married."

Demo's nostrils flared. "I thought I respected the sanctity of marriage before I met you. Never once have I ever gone after or knowingly dallied with a married woman. Never wanted the drama. Never felt it was worth it." He stepped back up to her. "You're worth it, Paige. I don't care that you're married. I don't. If Richard walked through that door right now," he pointed at the clinic door, "I'd tell him to fuck off. Well," he corrected, "I'd punch him first but then I'd tell him to fuck off."

Paige had to suppress a laugh. She shouldn't have found his violent statement hilarious.

Approaching her again, he cupped her face between his warm hands. "You're worth any battle, any fight, to make you mine, Paige Hannigan. You've already said you want a future with me. I think the better question isn't if you want it, but if you're willing to fight for it with me."

He leaned forward, pressing his lips against her forehead.

Paige's entire body trembled. She gripped his forearms with

all her might. "It might not be easy. My kids have to come first, Demo. No matter what."

"Agreed," he said against her skin.

She took a moment to breathe in his scent of leather and aftershave. Then, slowly, she nodded. "On one condition," she told him.

"What's that?" he asked seriously.

"If Richard does come back, I get to punch him first."

Demo barked out a laugh and pulled her tighter against him. His warm breath caressed her hair and forehead. "Deal."

* * *

Demo: I didn't like not seeing you today.

Paige: I know what you mean. This week has been crazy busy. You'll never convince me the club didn't have a hand in all my additional appointments. I am extremely grateful, but it also means less time with you and the boys.

Demo: How about I pick up the boys from Cindy's tomorrow and we join you for lunch at the clinic? What time do you have free?

Paige: Really? You would do that? Oh, it's so tempting, Demo! It's not that I don't trust you with them, but they don't really know you. I'm not sure how they would handle being in the car with you like that.

Demo: I do mean to change that soon. I want the boys to get to know me. But you're right. They don't know me like they do Lucky. So how about LUCKY picks them up from Cindy's and brings them to the clinic to have lunch with us? If you and they are fine with it after the meal, I'll take them back to Cindy's or we have Lucky come back to pick them up.

Paige: That sounds amazing, Demo, but I don't want to put Lucky out. He has his own job and responsibilities.

Demo: I'm sure he won't have an issue with it. If you want, I can text him or you can.

Paige: Let me think about it. I love the idea, but I think maybe we should put a pin in it until after the boys get to know you better.

Demo: How about we take them out this weekend? There's plenty to do around town or we can take them out of town and get a hotel room for the night. Don't worry—I promise not to ravage their mother. If you're not comfortable sharing a hotel room, I'll get an adjoining room to you guys.

Paige: [heart emoji] I love that idea. Why don't we stay here this weekend and plan for an overnight trip in the future?

Demo: Sounds like a plan! Anything specific you want to do? I think Mabel is offering cookie decorating this weekend. That would be fun to do with the boys. If I remember correctly, it's $10/cookie kit. We could do dinner afterwards.

Demo: It's either this weekend or next. I need to double check.

Demo: I overheard some of the others wanting to take the club kids to it.

Demo: Paige?

Paige: I'm here. It sounds really fun, Demo, but I'm not sure I can do that right now. It might not sound like much to you but $30 is a lot for me right now. No doubt the boys are going to want drinks too. Plus dinner afterwards? Maybe if we did just one of those.

Demo: Slow down, beautiful. I asked you and the boys out. I'll be paying. You never have to question about who is going to be paying the bill with me. I told you this. When you're with me, you're covered.

Paige: I wasn't sure if that included the boys. It really shouldn't. They're my responsibility.

Paige: I appreciate the offer. I just don't think it's feasible right now.

Demo: What's going on? Tell me what changed in the last 10 minutes to have you questioning who would be paying on our date?

Paige: Nothing. I just don't want you to think I'm taking advantage of you.

Demo: Can't take advantage of what's freely given, Paige.

Demo: You and the boys are a package deal. I get that. I support that. I WANT that. I would never pay for you and not the boys or vice versa. When we're out, all 4 of us or just the 2 of us, I'm paying. End of story.

Paige: You shouldn't have to. I should be able to pay for my own kids.

Demo: I don't view it as HAVING to. I view it as GETTING to.

Demo: Talk to me, beautiful. What's going through that pretty head of yours?

Paige: Pretty sure I'd be curled up in a fetal position with a tub of Rocky Road and a bottle of gin if I broke open that dam.

Paige: Sorry. That was a weird thing to say.

Paige: Demo?

> Paige: It's been about an hour. I understand. I warned you I'm a mess.

> Paige: Again, sorry. I hope you have a good night.

> Demo: Open your door.

* * *

PAIGE WAS SITTING on her couch with Nelly Bean resting on her lap while Mikey colored on the floor on his belly. Her oldest was shirtless with four glass cups suctioned along his spine. The faint trace of burnt cotton hung in the air.

She stared down at her phone wondering if she somehow misread the message. Nope, the instruction to open her door was still there.

Paige looked up and over at her front door, which she could just barely see from her position on the couch. She hadn't heard an engine outside, nor had she seen any headlights shine into her house like someone had pulled into her driveway.

Demo had been silent for over an hour prior to his last text message. What did he mean by open her door? Had he sent a food delivery?

The leftovers from the diner food he had delivered again to her clinic had been their dinner, which the boys appreciated. There was only so much boxed mac and cheese she could serve them before they started complaining.

Paige had been in the middle of texting Demo when Mikey had started coughing. His asthma was worse in the winter months and it didn't help that she had to keep the internal temperature of the house colder than she normally would to keep the electric bill down. The fancy house Richard had insisted on purchasing had electric fireplaces that provided no heat whatsoever and an HVAC system that controlled the entire house instead of sectioning off different areas. So she was forced to keep the house at a lower temperature than she personally preferred and lower than Mikey was supposed to have it long term. She absolutely hated that she couldn't afford to turn the temperature up any more. Even a couple of degrees could increase her bill exponentially because of the ridiculous square footage of their home.

As soon as he'd started coughing, she'd moved him onto a blanket in the living room, placing cushions and jackets around him. After removing his shirt, she applied the heated cups to his back along with eucalyptus oil to his feet.

Ding! Paige looked down at her phone to see another message come through.

> Demo: My balls are starting to shrivel up out here. Mind opening the door?

Not knowing what else to do, Paige stood. She repositioned Nelly Bean in her arms. Her baby was awake but resting after a day of running around with his brother and grandmother. She had a blanket swaddled around his little body. As much as she loved Cindy for her ability to watch her boys, Paige was tempted to take Steel up on his offer if the club opened a daycare center. Cindy wasn't getting any younger. Ronald was still recovering from his attack over a year ago when a deranged criminal had followed him down from Detroit and assaulted Ronald and Cindy in their home.

Peeking around the curtain, Paige wasn't sure why she was so surprised to see Demo shivering on the front porch.

Seeing her through the window, he reached into the plastic bag he was carrying around his left wrist and pulled out a carton of Rocky Road ice cream. He had an extremely cocky smile on his face.

Paige's jaw dropped, but she quickly unlocked her door and opened to allow him entrance. "What are you doing here?"

"You said you wanted ice cream and alcohol," he answered smoothly. "I came to deliver." He shuffled inside, kicking the thick wooden door with an intricate design closed using his snow covered boot.

Paige hadn't realized it had started snowing again. No wonder Mikey had an attack.

"*Brrr...*" Demo shuddered. "It's fricken cold out there!" He started to take his coat off, paused, and then put it back on. "It's fucking cold in here too!"

"Language," she hissed, indicating Nelly Bean in her arms. Her reaction was automatic. Richard had openly cursed around the boys and she'd always hated that.

"Oops." At least Demo had the decency to appear sheepish about his slip-up. "What's wrong with your heat? Why is it so cold in here?"

Her cheeks flamed as she admitted, "There's nothing wrong with it. There's just no reason to keep the house warm. We have sweaters and blankets. It's more environmentally friendly to preserve resources."

Demo stared at her for a solid second before he asked her, "Do you smell better when your nose grows longer?"

Her blush deepened.

Demo pushed past her into the foyer. "Where's your thermostat? There's absolutely no reason for your house to be this cold, Paige! You're going to get sick! The temperatures are supposed to drop into the teens tonight!"

She winced. She hadn't heard that. Then again, she no longer had a television to get the weather on and she rarely checked the app on her phone because she didn't want to waste her minimal data plan. She needed to save that for posting her foot fetish photos and videos as much as possible. Shame washed through her. She'd been riding high after nearly being booked up all week *and* having most appointment spots filled for the following week that she had turned down two special requests from the fetish site that day.

Only to do the math of what she'd earned this week versus what she owed this week and finding she would still be coming up short. *Stupid, foolish, arrogant...* If she had just done the degrading requests maybe she could afford to turn the heat up in her own home.

She heard the heat kick on and flinched.

Nelly Bean must have sensed her embarrassment. He burrowed closer to her and asked, "Mama okay?"

She squeezed him tighter to her chest, needing his contact for support. "Yeah, baby. I'll be fine."

She hated lying to her son. Would she ever be fine again? She had less than two months to pay back her stepfamily and she couldn't even afford to keep the heat on in her own home? She wasn't *fine*.

"Hey." Demo's voice was soft, soothing. She opened her eyes to see him standing right in front of her. She hadn't even heard him walk back up. "I'm sorry for snapping. I don't like the idea of you and the boys suffering needlessly."

It wasn't needlessly. She took the edge of the blanket wrapped around her Nelly Bean to wipe at her eyes. "You think I want to keep my house this cold? Look at Mikey," she snapped. "Keeping the house cold aggravates his lungs! But what else can I do? I have bills to pay and the amount of electricity this house uses is ridiculous! I can't afford..." Her voice cracked. Her chin wavered. "I can't afford *anything*," she settled on. "Every time I dig myself out just a little bit, another bill comes out of the woodwork. How can I possibly get ahead of it and keep my babies safe?"

Paige wasn't sure what sort of reaction she was expecting, but Demo stepping forward to embrace her with Nelly between them wasn't it. With his cut and jacket still on, Demo brought the two of them against his chest, squeezing his arms against her back. Paige buried her face in his warm chest as tears started to free-fall down her cheeks.

She had warned him how close her dam was to breaking... Well, it had officially broken.

Demo lifted her and Nelly Bean into his arms. Paige wanted to protest with his shoulder, but her fight seemed to have left her entirely. He never uttered a grunt of pain or seemed to struggle. At least, he only walked over to the couch to sit down. He arranged Paige on his lap with Nelly Bean still on hers.

Paige felt him shift under her as if he was stretching for something. Then he asked, "So, um, why does Mikey look like he was attacked by a giant octopus?"

Despite her tears, a laugh escaped her.

* * *

DEMO WAS UTTERLY and completely lost. He didn't know how to help Paige. He'd never been around a crying woman before like this and, frankly, he didn't like it much. He wasn't used to feeling so helpless.

Made him really wish Richard was still alive so he could kill him himself. Fucking Scar and his quick knives. At least he'd made the man suffer. Richard had not died a quick death. Scar had taken his cock and balls; Richard had died from blood loss. But seeing how Paige was suffering now? It wasn't enough.

He wanted Paige laughing and happy. Always. Never wanted to see another tear fall from her eyes unless they were happy ones. He could handle happy tears. Like...her standing at an altar before him...

Fuck, they'd only been dating a few days and he was imagining their *wedding*? What the fuck was wrong with him? Had her witchy magic done more than help his shoulder pain? What love spell had she put on him that he was entirely wrapped up in her so effortlessly?

He hadn't turned the heat up that much, not knowing if she liked her house on the cooler side or sweltering like a sauna. But there was no fucking way he was going to allow her to freeze tonight with the incoming weather. He'd pay for the damn bill himself and damn her pride before he allowed that to happen. Demo had hitched a ride with Pumpkin to the grocery store and then been dropped off here so Pumpkin could use his Bronco. It had better traction in bad weather than Pumpkin's four-wheel drive Camry. Thankfully, SJ had been asleep and Ranger, who had young nephews so he knew what he was doing, agreed to keep an eye on him. Pumpkin only needed formula, wanting to ensure he had SJ's brand in case the weather turned worse than predicted.

Demo looked over the back of the couch towards where he'd seen the kitchen entryway on his journey to the thermostat. Did Paige have enough supplies to last them if the storm continued into tomorrow? He'd only brought Rocky Road ice cream and a bottle of gin with him as a joke. Did this monstrosity of a house have a generator? Even if it did, was it gassed up for use?

Mikey eventually got up. He still had the cups on his back. Demo thought Paige was asleep against him until she instructed her son to turn around so she could release the suction cups. A slight whiff of burnt cotton reached Demo's nose with each *pop*. Then, to Demo's surprise, Mikey picked up all of the extra blankets and pillows from the floor and put them on the couch next to Demo. The kid burrowed and crawled his way into them before pressing his little body against Demo's side.

Demo froze. He had no idea what was going on or why this little boy was curling himself around Demo's left arm like he was a burrito shell.

Paige's hand reached over and touched the little boy's hair that was the same shade as his mother's but not as curly. "Kids have good instincts," she murmured softly. Her eyes were droopy, like her lids were too heavy to lift. "He knows you'll protect us."

Demo leaned down and pressed his lips to her forehead. "Always," he mouthed against her skin. She had an odd scent clinging to her that was different than her usual mixture of lavender, lemon, and peppermint. Almost like wintergreen or maybe rosemary? It wasn't a *bad* smell. In fact, after a couple of whiffs, he rather liked it. Whatever it was, it was earthy and he felt his sinuses open up more.

He didn't know if she heard him. Paige became dead weight on his lap, which he didn't mind in the least. Between the heat of the house rising, the body heat this spontaneous puppy pile was creating, and whatever that scent was that was clinging to Paige, Demo felt his eyes start to droop too.

Was this what it felt like to be in a family? To have a wife and kids so trusting of your love and protection that they could fall asleep so soundlessly in your arms? No wonder his club brothers had so easily given up their lives as bachelors. No wonder wars were fought and songs were written about this feeling.

It was new, like a pressure against his soul, but it was also all powerful and consuming. Demo knew he would do anything to ensure that *this*, right here with Paige and her boys, was his future.

Even if it meant burying the lies of her past so they never resurfaced.

* * *

THE SCENT of coffee roused her. She was warm. Sweltering to the point of discomfort. Paige cracked her eyes open to discover she was in her living room. Had she fallen asleep on her couch? Where were her boys?

For a moment, her sleep-filled brain thought the noises from the kitchen were coming from Richard and anger rose up at the idea that she had fallen asleep on the couch waiting up for him again and he hadn't bothered to wake her.

But then she started to blink away the haze of sleep, and realized it wasn't Richard in her kitchen but *Demo*.

Paige's eyes opened in shock, horror, and embarrassment as the memory of the night before returned. He'd brought her ice cream and alcohol—and she'd ended up ugly crying in his arms. What the hell must he think of her?

The source of the heat on her became obvious as she started to move. Mikey was sound asleep amongst the pile of blankets surrounding her. Where was Nelly Bean? Mouth open with little snores, she doubted even a marching band could wake Mikey. Still, she carefully eased herself out from under him and slid her way onto her knees by the couch. She'd sold most of their furniture, but kept the couch, kitchen table, and bedroom sets.

Gently, Paige rearranged the blankets around her son. She wondered if he was sleeping so soundly because he was warm or because he had gone to sleep reacting to her high emotional state. She didn't like the idea of the latter.

Closing her eyes, Paige bowed her head with a hand on his tummy. Prayer hadn't been a big part of her life for a while, but she needed it now. She needed *someone* to believe that she was a good mother, to acknowledge that she was doing her best and *trying*.

Paige forced herself to stand up. If she stayed as she was, she could very easily start to break down again. She needed to find Demo and apologize. It was early still, but she also needed to shower and get herself ready for work. If there were any private requests from the foot fetish site, she should probably grab it—regardless of how low the offered money was or what degrading action it asked of her. She needed to be able to pay for the heat being turned up the night before. Demo meant well, and she truly did appreciate the idea of what he'd done, but the reality was that she couldn't afford the heat to remain on like this. If it was propane-sourced like their old house, maybe. But electric heat was expensive.

God, she hated this fucking house. Maybe she should burn it down for the insurance money. Illegal, yes, but she'd be warm for a good amount of time.

Demo was in the kitchen, leaning over the expensive marble counter. At some point, he'd removed his cut, jacket, and boots. His long legs were encased in dark jeans that rode low on his lean waist. White socks covered his large feet that almost looked too big for his narrower frame. A black long sleeve shirt clung tightly to his toned torso and strong arms.

Richard's coffee cup advertising some damn country club he'd been so conceited about getting membership to was gripped in Demo's hand. When he brought the cup up to his mouth for a sip, it caused the hem of his black shirt to ride up to show the faintest hint of skin around his navel.

Asleep against his chest was a swaddled up Nelly Bean. Demo had his left arm under her son's butt with a blue sippy cup of milk gripped between his thumb and pinky finger of his left hand. Nelly Bean's little face was smooshed against Demo's chest like he'd fallen back to sleep mid-sip. His mouth was open and his nose looked uncomfortably molded upwards.

Paige thought her ovaries might explode at the sight. Which was completely ridiculous. She'd seen the man in his *underwear* during his treatment in her clinic. But there was absolutely nothing sexier than the image of him standing in her kitchen like it was *his* kitchen with her son asleep against his chest like he was *his* son. Above all, she should *not* be admiring his clothed body like he was a present wrapped just for her.

"You want any coffee?" he asked suddenly, making her jump. "Or are you planning on standing there ogling me all morning?" The playful smile he turned on her took out the arrogance of his question.

She was a bit impressed that her cheeks didn't flush at the

suggestiveness in his eyes. She squared her shoulders and walked into the kitchen. "Coffee."

He immediately put his mug down. One handed, he picked up an empty mug he must have taken out in anticipation of her arrival and poured her coffee for her. "I assume you take it black." He was keeping his voice low for Nelly Bean's sake, which made it seem deeper, with more of a rumble. Paige should *not* feel jealous that her son got to be pressed up against him so while she was only standing next to him. "I couldn't find any cream or sugar."

That she did feel her face heat at. Cream and sugar cost money. She didn't particularly like coffee without them, but she also couldn't justify the expense of them. Black coffee was just fine. She was growing accustomed to it, in fact. "I take it black," she said with as straight a face as she could.

Demo's raised eyebrows when he handed her the mug told her he didn't believe her, but he thankfully didn't call her on her lie as he had the night before.

She accepted the cup with a low, "Thank you."

From the strong smell, she could tell he'd used new grounds. She'd been trying to make the can of coffee last longer by reusing grounds over a couple of mornings. But she couldn't scold him for not knowing that or for using new grounds. Someone who wasn't counting every penny and trying to get a dime from a dollar wouldn't think to do something like that.

She took a sip of coffee. "I can take him." She gestured to her sleeping son.

Demo shook his head. "I got him. He's fine."

"Did he wake up when you did?"

"Actually, I woke up to him trying to get you up," Demo informed her. There was no accusation in his voice, just factual. "He needed to go to the bathroom and the house was dark." Paige's eyes went wide that she hadn't woken up when her son had needed her. Demo waved off her shock. "I got him up. We went to the bathroom and then came in here to get something to drink. He fell asleep soon after."

Shame and gratitude warred inside her. "Thank you," she pressed. "I can't believe I didn't wake up. I am so sorry about last night. I don't know what came over me."

"We need to talk, Paige." Demo walked over to the kitchen table and pulled out a chair, indicating for her to sit with the hand that wasn't holding her son.

The coffee nearly got stuck in her throat as she swallowed. Dread filled her gut. "Is this the part where you break up with me for being too much? I am so sorry I dumped all of..." Her voice trailed off. She hadn't actually *said* anything to him last night. She'd just cried on his shoulder while holding her son and then her oldest had joined them on the couch. She wasn't sure if that made what happened more or less awkward. "I *am* sorry, Demo."

Demo indicated to the chair again.

Her shoulders sagged as she walked over and took the offered seat. He sat down catty corner to her.

Demo plucked her mug of coffee out from between her hands, placed it a few inches to her left, and then reached forward to grip her hands in his big one. He moved carefully to not jostle Nelly Bean.

"Paige, please look at me." She hadn't realized she'd been laser focused on his hand on hers until he spoke. She lifted her gaze to meet his. "First, good morning. I hope you slept well."

Better than she had in a *very* long time. Longer than the two years since her husband had walked out on her. "I did," she assured him. "Um, and you?"

His smile held a promise, one she wasn't sure she understood yet. "I slept amazingly well. I can now see the appeal of puppy piles."

Her cheeks flushed. She opened her mouth to respond, but he cut her off.

"*Second*," he said with a stern gaze, "if you try to apologize again, I will turn you over my knee and spank your ass."

Heat flooded her...but for an entirely different reason. That statement should not have been *appealing*. She certainly would not have found it so if it had come from Richard.

A bit of cockiness touched his expression, like he knew the effect his statement had on her. "Another time," he vowed, dipping his chin down at her slumbering son on his arm. Paige was so taken aback by the offhandedness of his promise that she felt like she had gotten whiplash and had to concentrate to follow along to his next words. "Paige, I know you're going through a lot right now. It can't be easy thinking you were going to spend your life, your marriage, with someone and then to have them walk out on you. I can't imagine how hard that was for you." He squeezed her hands. "And I can see how much you're struggling. There's nothing to be ashamed of. Especially when the fault doesn't fall on you. I want to help you. I *need* to help you. Feelings for you aside, it's the right thing to do, but it's something I *have* to do because I have feelings for you."

Her breath hitched. Words got caught in her throat and she was unable to respond. Her pride wanted her to argue with his statement. But the fact that her situation had gotten so desperate that it was affecting Mikey's health stopped her. A tear escaped her eye, trailing down her cheek.

Demo reached up and brushed it away with his thumb. He cupped her face in his large hand and Paige found herself leaning into his comforting touch. The dam was breaking again.

"I understand that you might not want *my* help," he continued softly. "I don't know how else to say it except that I fucking *want* you, Paige. I want to be a part of your life. I'll be the first to admit I don't know a damn thing about kids." After a slight pause, he added, "The fact that I just cursed twice is probably evidence enough of that. But I want to learn. I want to get to know your boys. Not as Lucky's friend but as *yours*. Friend. Boyfriend." He leaned over the table and pressed his lips to her fingertips. "Lover." His voice was low, sultry. "I want more nights curled up on the couch with you and the boys. Mind, in my vision of that, there's a TV with a kids' movie playing"—she flushed—"but that just brings me back to my original point.

"If you don't want to accept my help, then let's call Harper and Lucky over. You can tell them everything if you're not comfortable talking to me about it. I *wish* you would," he emphasized, "but I can understand if you can't yet. But please, Paige, talk to *someone*. When I say I want to help, I'm not just talking about money. I got that message loud and clear." She met his smile with one of her own. "I'm an accountant. I don't have to *give* you money. I can look at what you're dealing with and see if we can devise a plan to help get you back on your feet."

Paige bit her lip, but before she could reply to him, his phone rang.

Her eyes landed on the clocks on her microwave and oven. It was around five in the morning. Who was calling him at this hour?

Demo must have thought the same thing, because he frowned and dug his phone out of his front pocket. "Yeah?" Whoever was on the other end of the phone said something short but it was enough to make Demo stand up suddenly. "The fuck?" he demanded. He handed Paige Nelly Bean a little rougher than he probably meant to, given his previous gentleness with her son. Paige quickly stood and took him. "Tell him to hurry the fuck up," Demo snapped and then ended the call.

He was partway out the kitchen before he paused and turned back towards her. Rushing over, he gave her a very quick but feverish kiss. "I have to go," he told her. "Stay here and keep the heat on. We'll finish this conversation when I get back."

Paige frowned after him. Something was wrong. She didn't know what or who had been on the phone. Demo looked angry, but also afraid. "Be careful," she pleaded, knowing he wasn't going to give her details even if she asked.

"Always," he promised. After another quick kiss, he ran out the kitchen and towards her front door.

Demo ran out her front door with his boots unlaced and clutching his jacket and cut in his right hand.

Yes, she reaffirmed to herself. Something was very, very wrong.

CHAPTER 7

*I*gnoring the bitter cold, Demo ran out of Paige's house and up her long driveway. His boots weren't even laced up, causing him to stumble along the way in the fresh snow. *Fuck*, he'd meant to shovel her driveway before leaving. Damnit! And based on the phone call he'd just had with Steel, he doubted there would be any free members or prospects to come over and help her.

He was tempted to tell her not to leave her house. At the very least, he knew she and the boys were safe and away from club property.

Headlights nearly blinded him as he saw his Bronco make the curve before the entrance of her driveway a little too fast. Thankfully, Pumpkin was an excellent driver, regardless of the road conditions.

The truck never came to a full stop. As soon as he was within arm's reach, Demo opened the passenger door and hopped inside. He nearly lost a boot in the process, but luckily didn't. Pumpkin executed a nail biting U-turn that had Demo grabbing the Oh Shit handle and then gunned the Bronco back towards the clubhouse.

"What the fuck is going on?" Demo demanded.

He put his foot up on the dashboard and started lacing up his boot. It had taken some time with an occupational therapist after the accident that had taken his three fingers to learn how to do certain tasks with only the use of his left thumb and pinky finger. On a bet, he'd once taped the pointer, middle, and ring fingers of several of his club brothers to their palms and then had them complete certain tasks they claimed should have been easy regardless of the number of fingers in use.

They'd all failed. Mind, most of them had also been a bit drunk, but Demo still liked to rub it in their faces that they'd lost the bet.

"Bones got up in the middle of the night to get something from his cage. Found a duffel bag lying between his cage and mine. When he opened it, he found a fucking *bomb*."

A fucking bomb. On club property. A cold sweat coated his skin. This was Demo's area of expertise, but he also hadn't been near a bomb since one took three of his fingers. "Timer?"

Pumpkin shook his head. "Not that Bones saw. He alerted Steel and Bulldog, then started working on evacuating the clubhouse."

"The women and kids?" Demo lowered his right boot and lifted his left.

"Back at the trailers with Frankie and the prospects. We weren't taking any chances there was more than one."

Demo agreed. "If there's no timer then it's remote activated. Does Keys have a signal jammer?" Demo had one in his equipment bag in his clubhouse apartment but couldn't call Keys to tell him that. Pumpkin and he were nearly to the club property gates.

"I don't know. I was sent to get you. Steel ordered everyone to turn off their cell phones after he called you and told the ol' ladies not to take theirs."

Well, that was something at least. Though Demo wished Steel hadn't called him himself and had Pumpkin a safe distance away while on the road. But Steel calling Demo did get him ready for pickup faster. He knew better than most that every second mattered when dealing with an explosive device.

"Can you tell me anything about the device?"

Pumpkin shook his head. "I threw SJ into Angel's arms and bolted to get you."

Demo caught the wavering in Pumpkin's usually steady voice and realized his friend was afraid. Pumpkin had always been a loner. Other than his mom, he didn't have family. There was no one Pumpkin had ever had to look after...until SJ. Demo could only imagine the fear his friend had felt when he'd been woken up to be told there was a bomb outside the clubhouse where he and his son slept. If Paige and the boys had been there... Christ.

They turned the corner and flew past the open gate to the club property. Demo saw Starbucks in the guardhouse and knew his brother was there to close and lock the gate once Pumpkin and Demo were through.

The drive down to the clubhouse was around three hundred feet. The former distillery had been popular enough to warrant the large parking lot area outside their main building before sales had started to decline. Demo had looked over the distillery's books before the club had purchased the property, though not as carefully as he would have if the club had been planning on continuing in the distillery business. It had been more to appease his own curiosity than anything.

Partway up the drive, two of the club's SUVs were placed nose-to-nose in a barricade formation. The headlights from his Bronco illuminated Steel, Bulldog, Lucky, Keys, Ghost, and Ranger. A look in his rearview showed Starbucks running down the drive after them. The bright lights surrounding the gate showed the shadow of the security arm blocking off entry to the club property.

Pumpkin slammed on the brakes. Demo leapt out of the

passenger door, grabbing his jacket and cut. He donned both of them as he approached.

"Pumpkin said there's no timer. Tell me you have a jammer," he said to Keys. He only gave a chin lift of greeting to the others. There was no time for niceties.

"I do, but the range isn't great. I also turned off the power source to the router." He turned a tablet around towards Demo. It showed a couple of quickly shot pictures of an open duffel bag. Demo could make out at least four wires of different colors, what looked like a white plastic bucket, and plastic explosive of some sort. C4 wasn't the only clay-like plastique on the market, but it was the one most widely known.

Unfortunately, the pictures on Keys' tablet did not get him the details he needed. He was going to have to get closer.

He handed the tablet back to Keys. "I don't suppose any of you grabbed my equipment bag from my room while you were fleeing for your lives?"

Pumpkin snorted. Steel did not look amused.

"No," Ghost answered. Demo saw the ginger's lips twitch at his dry humor. "Grumpy's on his way with his tools."

Now that Bulldog, Bear, Lucky, and Angel had built homes on club property, Grumpy, Jumper, and Pirate were the only ones who lived off property. Grumpy had a house outside of town while Jumper and Pirate shared a two-bedroom apartment with Jasmine in town. Demo had no idea if Jumper and Jazz had any plans for a house in their postnuptial future.

"He won't get here in time," Demo told them all. "Just because you don't see a timer, doesn't mean one isn't there. Only Hollywood and amateurs put timers on the top or in plain sight. Statistically, they hide them so you don't see it coming."

Demo looked at the SUVs placed between them and the bomb. The men might not be demolition specialists like Demo, but they knew enough from their various military experiences to know to place anything large and sturdy between themselves and the blast zone. Without knowing the range of the bomb or the impact, there was no way for Demo to know if the SUVs would accomplish that task.

"I need pliers at the very least." Demo reached into the inside of his jacket pocket. He kept a pocket knife there, but the worst time to learn it had fallen out would be when he was staring down at an active bomb.

Ranger opened the trunk of one of the SUVs and brought back a pair of needle nose pliers with bright yellow grips.

"Do we have any idea who—" Pumpkin started but Demo cut him off.

"Who put it there and why are later issues. Right now, we need to focus on disarming that bomb or detonating it somewhere safe."

"You want to move it?" Keys' eyes grew comically wide.

Demo shook his head. "I need to examine it first."

"I'll go with you," Pumpkin said.

"No," Steel snapped. "I will."

"None of you are going with me and we don't have time to argue," Demo interjected. "I do not need amateurs in my blast zone. Stay here and hunker down. I'll notify you once I know something."

"You have no protective gear—" Lucky started, but Demo ignored him. He was very aware he was heading towards a bomb with no protection.

Demo tucked the pliers into his jeans pocket and started down the snow covered lane. Every step felt like he had cement in his boots. His heart was pounding in his head. It had been nearly nine years since he'd last faced off with a bomb, but his training took over like it was only yesterday. The objective was to identify and disarm.

He needed to block out everything else. His club brothers, his father, his club nieces and nephews, his woman and her adorable sons... He pushed it all to the back of his mind. Laser focused on the duffel bag in front of him, Demo continued forward.

The last bomb had taken three of his fingers. He would not allow this one to take anything from him—especially his life.

* * *

THE BOMB ITSELF WAS CRUDE. After checking for tripwires, Demo used his pocket knife to cut away the duffel bag to give him an unobstructed view of the bomb. Red, blue, green, and white wires twisted around the explosive material in an intricate braid. The grayish plastic explosive was molded to a white bucket with a sealed lid, blocking Demo from seeing if the wires continued inside the bucket. Since he didn't see a power source outside the bucket, Demo could only assume they did.

Kneeling down in the snow covered driveway, Demo used Bones' cage to help protect him from the winter winds. The bright security lights outside the clubhouse blocked out the darkness of the predawn morning.

Demo wore no gloves. They would only impede the use of his fingers. He needed to feel as much as he needed to see.

With a gentle slide of his pointer finger, Demo checked the rim under the lid for tripwires. Though his heart was beating fast, his hand was steady. The rim seemed clean, but that didn't mean there wasn't something inside that would trigger when he lifted the lid.

Fuck, he wished he had his equipment bag. Hell, right now he would give his remaining left digits to have the portable x-ray machine his old unit used to use. It was more out of habit than anything for him to even have an equipment bag. Demo wasn't afraid to admit that it was a bit of a crutch and let him sleep better at night knowing he had it.

He never expected to actually need it.

Or for the first night in years that he slept away from the

clubhouse to be the night he would need it and wasn't sleeping next to it.

Demo shook off those thoughts. They did not help him. He would not get anywhere if he kept going over *what if* and *if only* thoughts in his head.

Movement out of the corner of his eye caught his attention. Demo turned his head to yell at Steel for disobeying him—and would probably die in the process of getting those words out—only to freeze when he saw who was standing over him.

Scar knelt down in the snow next to Demo. He handed out the black folded carrying bag that held all of Demo's tools.

Demo shook off his bewilderment that Scar was here *and* that Scar had gone into the clubhouse, not knowing what was going on with the bomb, to risk getting Demo's equipment bag for him. Demo took the equipment bag. With a quick pull on the strap, the folded canvas unraveled on the snow by Demo's right knee. He'd specifically gotten this bag to carry his tools and equipment in so he wasn't wasting time fiddling with a zipper.

"I'm not even going to ask where you came from or what you're doing here," Demo said dryly.

A quick glance at his former club brother showed that Scar had started to gain the weight back he'd lost when he'd first left the club. Nearly a year had gone by since Scar had gone rogue and slaughtered most of the offending members of the Heaven Haven Community, the cult that had held Abby captive for sixteen years. Bulldog had called for blood and Steel had stressed caution. They didn't have enough information for the full-scale attack Bulldog wanted. Per Bulldog, Scar knew that Bulldog was going to go with or without Steel's approval. Rather than have Bulldog risk his life, Scar had gone in his stead.

Demo still didn't know how Bulldog knew that. Maybe it was a guess, maybe it was fact. Bulldog was the only one in the club who knew Scar's past. Hell, Demo was pretty sure Bulldog was the only one who knew Scar's legal name *and* had ever heard him speak. Given their history together, Demo could only assume Scar had served in the Army, but no one knew for certain. Bulldog had always said that was Scar's story to tell...which, obviously, the silent man was not telling.

Bulldog still insisted that Scar *could* talk and chose not to.

After nearly six months of no contact, Steel, Jumper, Bulldog, and Ghost had run into Scar at a rival MC's clubhouse. Or, rather, Scar had randomly shown up exactly when they needed him to and covered their backs while they made their escape. Since then, Scar had been 'around', but he hadn't been reinstated into the MC or been to any of their meetings, club runs, or events. No one had seen him over the holidays, though he'd left every club kid a gift. Lucky also said the present Harper had left Scar under their Christmas tree had been gone Christmas morning.

Demo did not know how he would feel if he had a home and knew that Scar just spontaneously went in and out of it as he pleased. Per Scotty, Scar was a magician who could magically appear and disappear anywhere.

"Thanks, man," Demo said sincerely. "Now get out of here. You don't need to be risking your life too."

Scar stayed exactly where he was.

Not having the time to argue with him, Demo pulled out a small drill. It looked like a screwdriver but for the carbon steel hole saw bit at the end. Carefully, he placed his left hand on the lid to keep the bucket steady without applying pressure. With his right, he drilled a thirteen millimeter hole into the side of the bucket just under the lid.

His former commander would rip him a new asshole for drilling blind into an IED but Demo had little choice. He needed to see inside.

"If you're staying, you're going to be useful. Take this." Demo held out the drill. Scar took it, careful not to touch Demo's skin.

Demo pulled out a borescope camera. He secured the screen

to the inside of his left forearm with the attached Velcro straps. Carefully, he pressed the tip of the camera to the hole he'd created—and frowned.

Other than what looked like two batteries taped together with electrical tape, there was nothing inside the container. No screws, nails, shrapnel… Nothing to cause additional damage outside of the blast itself.

Not wanting to waste any more time looking at the device through the camera, Demo quickly turned it upwards to look at the underside of the lid. It was clear. No wires or pressure plates.

Demo withdrew the camera. "Something's not right," he told his former club brother. "This is a bomb to scare, not to create mayhem." With where it was by Bones' cage, it could have been placed there to destroy the vehicle. But Demo didn't think so. The duffel hadn't been *under* the cage.

Demo was still not convinced there wasn't a timer. If it was remote activated, how was the bomber to know when Bones had entered his cage. It was on the passenger side. Maybe it was meant for Pumpkin's cage on the other side?

Demo disconnected the scope from the screen attached to his arm. He didn't want to waste time playing with the Velcro again. He handed the scope to Scar next. "I'm opening the lid. Last chance to step back."

Scar stayed where he was.

The lid popped open as soon as Demo lifted the edge slightly. It wasn't a secure seal. What the hell was going on? The bomb was complex in its design but not in materials. He half-wondered if the explosive clay was even real plastique. Why wasn't the lid boobytrapped? Or even made to look like it? A simple hidden wire would have done the trick and easily created a time delay in opening the container.

Demo looked for thin wires as he lifted the lid barely an inch up. Grabbing a penlight with a push button, he shined the beam at various angles to ensure he hadn't missed something. There was nothing.

Straightening, Demo removed the lid fully. He placed it on the snow next to his left knee. What the hell?

A glance up at Scar showed the other man was just as perplexed as Demo was. Inside, just as the camera had shown, were two battery packs, maybe six inches long each, taped together in two places with black electrical tape. Small holes were drilled into the bottom of the bucket, much like Demo had just done, to feed various wires through to the batteries.

It reminded Demo of a spiderweb.

Any IED needed five basic components: a trigger, a power supply, an explosive material, a charge, and a containing unit. The rest was just showmanship.

This bomb had everything but a trigger. There was no timer, no remote switch, not even a manual detonation. If the wires were attached to the batteries, why hadn't the bomb gone off? What was containing the conduction?

Why hadn't it gone off already?

Demo stripped the coating from a wire and pulled out his multimeter. It came back with nothing. There was no voltage between the batteries and the wires, yet the wires were clearly attached to the batteries. Even old batteries could hold enough of a charge to spark an ignition. The batteries would have to be completely and utterly dead to not have gone off the moment the bomb maker touched the wires to the batteries.

Scar put the scope and drill down, bending closer to examine the device.

"You see it too?" Demo asked him, wanting to ensure he wasn't so out of practice that he was missing something.

Scar's eyebrows scrunched in a way that told Demo he was just as confused by the device as Demo was.

"What the fuck is going on?" He was not surprised when he got no answer. "Just to be safe, I want to disconnect these wires.

Can you start pulling off as much clay as you can without touching the wires?"

Scar gave a nod. He pulled a knife out and used the blade to scrape away the excess plastic explosive on the outside of the bucket. Taking a wire cutter out of his bag, Demo started to clip the wires. One of the first lessons he'd learned in basics was that "a wire was a wire was a wire". It meant that just because the rubber coating on the outside of a wire meant something specific to each country, it did not mean the wire underneath changed or had different functions.

It wasn't like in the movies when the hero automatically knew to "cut the yellow wire!" two seconds before the timer went off. Even electricians knew better than to trust the color coding system because amateurs did not always follow the National Electrical Code. Cutting a random wire senselessly was reckless and extremely dangerous.

But these were all dead wires. There was no electricity flowing through any of them. Still, Demo was careful and took nothing for granted. It could all be a trick.

Finally, he severed the last one. After checking for a pressure plate and finding none, Demo lifted the two batteries out of the bucket and away from the explosives.

His knees and lower pants were soaked through from the snow. He hadn't even noticed, concentrating solely on the bomb.

Demo called out, "All clear!" to the others at the SUVs.

Though the bomb appeared to have been a dud, Demo's shoulders sagged in relief. That could have ended very differently. He turned around to thank Scar for his assistance, only to find the other man was gone.

* * *

THE COLLECTIVE FEEL inside the clubhouse was anger mixed with confusion.

Pumpkin clasped Demo on the shoulder—thankfully his right —and laughed, "Good to see you didn't lose any more fingers!"

Now that the adrenaline was leaving Demo's system, many things became apparent. His left shoulder was throbbing relentlessly, he was freezing cold, and he needed to take a piss. Once the clubhouse and all of the homes had been swept to ensure there were no other devices, the patched members all entered the clubhouse. Most of them were still in pajamas of some sort. Demo hadn't noticed before, but Keys was wearing pajama bottoms with penguins wielding lightsabers on them. Most of the others were in sweatpants and hastily donned boots with their jackets.

As soon as the others noticed Keys' pants, they started to razz him about them.

"We leave the women and children where they are for now," Bulldog informed everyone in a loud voice. It immediately halted all the jokes and taunting at Keys.

"Jumper and Grumpy are on their way down the drive," Ghost told the SAA. "Jumper did not want to bring Jazz with him nor did he want to leave her alone so Pirate stayed behind."

As an officer, Jumper's presence was required. Pirate could be filled in on everything later.

Demo understood Jumper's reluctance to leave Jasmine alone. They lived off property. Then again, until this morning, Demo had believed the club's property was the safest place. If the bomb hadn't been a dud?

He shuddered at the thought—and then flinched as his shoulder protested.

"Contact Carlos," Steel told Bulldog. "We don't know what this is yet, but it might not be isolated." He looked between Keys and Demo. "Is the jammer off?"

Keys nodded. He had two tablets and his laptop set up in front of him on the front bar. "I am also running a trace for any external signals."

"No point," Demo told him. "There was no trigger. Even if someone had 'pressed the red button'," he said with air quotes using his right hand only, "nothing would have happened. They either forgot to add it or had no intention of adding it."

"What would that do?" Lucky demanded. "Why build a bomb but not add a trigger?"

Demo shrugged. "First time in my experience but any idiot has access to *Google* nowadays. Just be grateful the batteries had no charge left in them. At least, that's what I'm assuming the issue is."

Which Demo still found extremely odd. Most batteries had a reserve, which was how devices recognized being at low battery level. A controlled discharge was the best way to ensure draining the entire battery, like leaving a cellphone's flashlight on. Who was dumb enough to let the batteries they intended to use for a bomb be drained first?

Not satisfied with that train of thought, Demo walked over to where he'd placed the taped batteries on the bar. With his pocketknife, he removed the tape that held them together. He expected to find that the wires weren't even touching the terminals, but they *were*.

"Son of a bitch," he let out a nervous laugh. Others came over to take a look, but Demo spoke to Steel. "This bomber is either the luckiest or stupidest person I've ever not met. He used rubber glue to secure the wires to the terminals. Otherwise, he likely would have blown himself up. I'd bet my last dollar these batteries *are* fully charged. It's only the rubber that's keeping the connection from forming."

"Rubber glue?" Ranger questioned. He had his arms crossed over his broad chest. The edges of his Army Ranger tattoo peaked out from the black muscle shirt he was wearing. "Who the hell uses rubber glue?"

"Construction workers do," Cage said at the exact same time that Keys yelled out, "Son of a bitch!"

Everyone turned to Keys. He typed for another couple of seconds on his laptop and then turned the two tablets around to face the room. "Yelizaveta's husband came to pick her up yesterday evening. Guess what wasn't there when he came in and what was there when he pulled out."

"The duffel?" someone unhelpfully supplied as they all watched the security footage of a beat-up old pickup truck, the club's new housekeeper, Yelizaveta, and her son, Carter. Carter was one of Harper's students at the high school. He was high-functioning autistic and had been hanging out in the clubhouse after school while Yelizaveta finished working in the afternoons.

As the pickup pulled out of the parking spot, the duffel could be seen on the driver's side door of Pumpkin's cage. A few minutes later, Bones pulled into the same spot. With the duffel on the other side of the cage from him, Bones did not see the duffel before walking into the clubhouse. The video then sped forward through the dark of the night until Keys slowed it down in time to see Bones walking out to his cage in nothing but sweats and sneakers. Man wasn't even wearing a shirt in the freezing cold weather. As soon as Bones saw the duffel, he ducked out of sight to examine it. Then they saw him running back inside the clubhouse.

Everyone would have evacuated out of the back doors.

Something occurred to Demo then. They had two prisoners in the clubhouse. Nathan Moore, the child predator who had abducted and raped Bree when she was only twelve years old and held her for over two years, was below in the cellar. Angel owed the man a lot of pain for what he'd put Bree through. The other prisoner was a more unique situation. Veronica Banks was Aaron's biological mother and Cage's one-time high school lover. She was extremely religious and had arranged to have Aaron abducted to 'save his soul' after he'd come out as gay. Bree and Ollie had been with Aaron and been taken too, though that admittedly had not been her intention. Despite her religious zeal,

Aaron had pleaded her case and begged the club to spare her life. Steel's rather inventive alternative to execution was to lock her in an apartment in the clubhouse. She was allowed to leave at any time, but if she did, she would then forfeit her life. An added bonus to the woman's confinement was that her only source of entertainment was the gay porn playing nonstop on the secured television in her room.

Demo doubted Steel or Bulldog would have given the prisoners' safety a second thought during the evacuation. As Star unzipped his jacket, his cat poked its head out from its confinement. At least, the cat hadn't been left behind.

"Billy's an asshole," Cage snorted, "but you guys expect me to believe he built a bomb and left it here? Why? What's the cause? We employ his wife. His *son* hangs out here too."

"You work with him, right?" Bulldog asked Cage.

Cage nodded. "Yeah. Works for a plumbing company we contract with."

"I met him a few months ago when I was dropping Bree and Aaron off to spend the afternoon with Cage at the construction yard," Angel added. "Guy's got a total case of SDS going on."

"SDS?" Demo didn't know what that was either, but it was Steel who asked.

"Small Dick Syndrome," Angel explained with a sly smile.

Demo shifted uncomfortably. He didn't suffer from that, personally, but he also wasn't keen to look around and see if any of the other men in the room looked wary because *they* had SDS.

Cage rolled his eyes at his woman. "Like I said, the guy's a total asshole. But he also isn't smart enough to put two and two together."

"You saw the footage," Keys argued. "The duffel wasn't there before he pulled in and it was there when he left."

Steel looked to Bones. "You didn't see it when you pulled into the parking spot?"

Bones shifted his weight self-consciously. "No. I was...a bit distracted."

Bear's eyes narrowed as he picked up on what the other man wasn't saying faster than the rest of them were. "Your legs?"

Bones had only been a patched member for a little over a year. He'd survived a parachute accident that had broken most of the bones in his legs, resulting in him receiving a medical discharge from the Army. Though his legs were healed, he had several rods, bolts, and plates holding his legs together. He still went to therapy, but winters were hard for him. The cold weather made his bones ache and, at times, it hurt him to even walk.

Shamefaced, Bones nodded. "I shouldn't have been driving yesterday. It was stupid. Cage usually offers me a ride to work, but I had therapy so I declined. Afterwards, though, I..." He pointed to the tablets. "You saw me. I barely even made it inside. Only reason I went back out this morning was because I left my phone outside and didn't realize it until I got up to take a piss a little after five."

Demo glanced down at his watch. Somehow it was only six-thirty. Paige hopefully went back to sleep. He regretted not still being there. Helping her get the boys ready and then driving her to work. Hell, maybe he should suggest working at her reception desk to help her with patients and organizing between his own work.

Steel walked right up to Bones and slapped the patched member upside the head. "The *only* reason I am not doing more to you is because your *stupidity* alerted us to the danger far sooner than was clearly meant to. No doubt, that duffel was placed out there with the intent to get buried by the snow." Leaning in so the two men were nose-to-nose, Steel practically snarled, "How many fucking times do I have to tell you that you are not a burden? If you need help, *you fucking call!* That's what we're here for. Do I have to take away your rockers and demote you back to prospect to get that through your thick skull?"

Bones paled. "No, sir."

Steel nodded once, taking a step back. "Then this better be the last fucking time I hear about you not calling for help. In fact," Steel turned to Bulldog. "You have two new recruits coming soon?"

Bulldog nodded once. "Sara and Will are getting their patches at the end of the month. Viktor and Darrin should be arriving around that same time."

"Good." Steel turned back to Bones. "Pick one. He's going to be your bitch for the foreseeable future. He will drive you everywhere and you will even have to be his backpack on club runs."

Bones' eyes widened as his face flushed.

"That's right, tough guy. You just lost driving privileges until I say otherwise." Steel turned his back on Bones. "Until the new prospects arrive, Will, Mitch, or Sara will drive you around. If you're at work," Steel nodded his chin to Cage, "I expect you to help him out."

"Of course," Cage said easily. From the *I-told-you-so* expression on Cage's face, he'd had this conversation with Bones himself. Likely not so publicly.

Steel looked to Demo. "What can you tell us about the bomb maker?"

"He's crude, brilliant, and somehow a complete idiot," Demo told him. "The intricacies of the wire braiding were extensive. That took time and effort." Picking up the bucket that was sitting on the bar, Demo pointed to the plastique used. "Do you know where civilians find this stuff?"

"Specifically, no, but I know that explosives are common on the Black Market."

Demo shook his head. "This stuff isn't. It's homemade." He picked up a piece of the clay-like material and handed it to Steel. "This is known as a 'poor man's C4'. It's less powerful than Semtex or C4, but if you have a large enough batch, it'll definitely get the job done. Putting the bomb under a vehicle filled with gasoline certainly helps your cause."

Cage snorted. "Billy can't even pull his pants all the way up after taking a shit. You expect me to believe he can whip up a batch of C4 in his kitchen?"

"It would need to be in a chem lab," Demo corrected him dryly. "And I am not saying whether he did or he didn't. I am saying *that*," he pointed to the plastique in Steel's hand, "is not real C4."

Steel rolled the putty around in his hand, deep in thought. "Keys? Anything to add?"

"Other than Billy's internet searches since right around the time Yelizaveta started working for us have to do with bomb making?" Keys asked him with a measure of sarcasm. "No, nothing else to add."

Steel's nostrils flared. He rounded on Bulldog and Ghost. "Wait until Yelizaveta leaves with Carter for school this morning and then bring me Billy." To everyone else, he said, "The rest of you! Be alert, be mindful, but go about your lives like normal. Don't leave any of the women and children alone until we get some answers."

As the others started to disperse, Steel clasped Demo on his right shoulder. "Good job, brother. We couldn't see much from where we stood with the cages blocking our view of you, but it took ten years off my life to let you walk away like that."

Demo knew it took a lot for Steel to admit that. "Gotta say. Never thought I'd be facing off with a bomb again. Not after last time. There's a reason I got my accounting degree when I was discharged. Numbers don't blow up in your face."

"You seemed to handle it just fine."

Demo nodded. "It was nerve-wracking, I'll admit. Had a hard time concentrating at first. My mind kept thinking of Paige and the boys. My training told me to push it back but it wasn't as easy as I remember it being." After a moment, he added, "Having Scar there helped. That guy is sturdy under pressure. I swear, he never even blinked."

More than one patched member stopped and faced Demo. Shock and confusion covered their faces.

Demo looked to Steel. "What?"

"We didn't see Scar. Not even with the binoculars," Bulldog answered. He stepped forward. "You're telling me Scar was here?"

Demo nodded. "Gave me my equipment bag and then stayed to help. Why?"

Bulldog and Steel exchanged a look. Even Lucky, who was further away than the others with Bear, had a puzzled look on his face.

"Last we heard," Steel told Demo, "Scar and Ivy were going after a drug shipment in Texas. We haven't seen either of them in weeks and assumed they were still down there."

Demo blinked. "Well, I didn't see Ivy but I can guarantee you Scar is back."

Bulldog cursed. "He swore to me he'd stop doing that! I told him he can come and go as he pleases but he needs to check in with me! If only to let us know he's still alive."

"Well," Demo shrugged offhandedly, "the next time he comes to help assist me defuse a bomb, I will remind him of that. Until then, I really need to piss and take a shower."

He wanted to get back to Paige's house and shovel her driveway before she tried to take the boys out in this weather. They also needed to finish their talk.

CHAPTER 8

*W*ater dripped down Demo's chiseled chest as he stepped from his apartment shower. Steam hung in the air all around him. After wiping off his face and hair with a towel, he ran a hand over the condensation on his mirror to clear his view.

Even he wasn't blind to the pain on his face.

Shortly after entering his apartment with the intention of taking a piss, showering, and then getting back to Paige's, his shoulder began to throb unbearably. When slamming his shoulder against the door frame didn't work, he'd turned the shower on as hot as it could go and stayed under the pounding, burning water until the ache had begun to dull again. It still wasn't gone, but at least he wasn't imagining chopping off the arm himself just to make the pain go away.

His skin looked like he'd spent the day in the sun without any protection. He snorted, remembering a *TikTok* video about how women enjoy showers so hot, it could cook chicken. Guess, he was the chicken in this current scenario.

Demo heard his phone ring and looked around for where he'd

left it. Finally finding it in the pants he'd discarded on the floor, he smiled broadly when he saw it was Paige calling.

Unable to resist, Demo leaned back against the vanity and switched to a video call before answering. He held the phone back so she had a broader view of him.

Paige's jaw dropped when she appeared on his screen. Her eyes went wide as they roamed down his naked torso. He'd cut the image off just above his groin.

Demo's grin was full of lust and promise when her eyes finally made it back to his face. "You know," he drawled playfully, "if I didn't know any better, I'd think you were only with me for my body."

Her cheeks burned. "Until this moment, I would have argued otherwise. I—" Demo saw her eyes narrow and his grin dropped to a frown. She leaned closer to her screen. "What the hell is on your shoulder?"

Demo glanced down, saw the bruise developing from when he'd slammed his shoulder into the door frame, and cursed. "It's nothing," he said quickly, moving the view of the camera up so only his face now showed. Shit, this had turned not-so-sexy fast.

"Demo!" she snapped. She almost looked angry. "Let me see."

"I didn't call you for a medical consult, Doc."

Paige's eyes narrowed. "No, *I* called *you* to see if you were okay because I hadn't heard from you. Now show me your damn shoulder."

With a reluctant sigh, Demo dropped the phone down so she could see his left shoulder. He supposed he shouldn't be so annoyed that Paige had noticed the bruising, but he was a bit abashed that his finely toned abs hadn't distracted her very long. He'd worked hard to gain a body he was proud of. Most saw him and didn't think *accountant*, which always amused the hell out of Demo. Sure, Paige had stopped and stared. She definitely appreciated his form, he knew that. But she also hadn't gawked or turned into a bumbling bimbo at the sight of his nakedness.

Why was that so arousing to him? It certainly had a humbling effect.

"Demo, your shoulder has chronic pain. Your nerves respond to stimuli. *Please* tell me you did not try to increase your pain by slamming your shoulder against something to then decrease your pain?"

Demo brought the phone back up to his face. "What would you have me do, beautiful? I couldn't even get my shirt off. It was like my arm would only respond to pain."

"*You call me,*" she snapped. "Regardless of whatever else is going on between us, Demo, I am your doctor. You call me and let me help you." When he turned his head away from the screen, Paige scolded, "Do not make me go all legal name on you. Because I will. I will even call up Lucky right now to figure out what your middle name is because I don't have your chart in front of me."

Demo snorted. He turned back to the phone. "Lucky doesn't even know my middle name."

"Maybe not, but it got you to look at me." She gave him a sexy-as-fuck, sassy smile.

Demo grinned back. Fuck, he loved smart women. "You truly are beautiful. Don't ever doubt that, Paige."

A blush creeped across her cheeks. "I am getting ready to head out to the clinic. Are you able to meet me there? I can work on your shoulder before my first appointment comes in."

Demo glanced down at himself. "I might startle some old biddies into a heart attack on my way, but yeah I can head over that way."

Paige smiled widely. "They'll die happy. But *please* put on some clothes. I'd hate to have to treat certain areas for frostbite."

Demo flinched at the implication. "Fuck. Yeah, probably a good idea. I think I have a pair of gray sweatpants around here."

"Or come in the tightest jeans you own so I have to have you remove them."

Demo chuckled. "Not sure you know where the shoulder is, Doc, if you need me to remove my jeans to get to it."

Paige shrugged. There was enough mischievousness in her eyes to call her smile a smirk. "There is a method to my madness."

Demo saw her moving around by her front door. Remembering the snow on her driveway when he'd left earlier, he cursed. "I meant to shovel your drive before I left this morning, but obviously that didn't happen when I got called away." He started towards his bedroom. "Wait, there. I'm on my way."

"No, you don't need to," she told him. "Ronald came over this morning and took care of it."

Demo stopped in the middle of his studio apartment. His king bed and dresser were against the far wall, parallel to the little kitchenette he rarely used. Despite the fact that she'd used his name, Demo obviously knew she wasn't talking about him. "Ronald? As in, Hannigan?"

She blinked, as if trying to discern the sudden hostility in his voice. "Yes, my father-in-law. The boys' grandfather," she said pointedly.

As if he needed the reminder.

Demo put the phone upright on his dresser against the wall so he had his one good hand free. "He shouldn't have had to do that. It's my responsibility."

"Actually, it's mine," Paige reminded him. He wasn't looking at her, instead he was rifling through his drawers for a pair of boxer shorts, loose fitting sweats, and a long sleeve shirt. "I appreciated his help, though, because I can't leave the boys alone to go outside to shovel myself. Ronald knows this and he comes over to help when we've had bad weather. He took the boys back with him to his and Cindy's house for the day so I had a few child-free moments this morning."

Demo groaned as he hiked up his underwear. "And I wasn't even there for that! This morning just keeps getting better and better."

"You know, if you're going to tease me with a backwards striptease, the least you can do is step back so I can see what it is you're covering up."

Demo paused. He glanced up at the phone to see most of his body was covered by the dresser from the angle of the camera. He inclined his head to her and then took three big steps backwards so she could see his entire body in the frame. "Better?"

"No, you've already put your undies on."

Demo snorted. "I don't wear 'undies,'" he corrected. He put the sweats he'd been holding on the edge of the bed. Then he pushed his boxer briefs down and stepped out of them. Standing naked before the camera, he did a slow turn so she got to see his front *and* his back.

Paige licked her lips. "Yeah, I'm definitely seconding your frustration at being called away this morning."

Demo's cock twitched at her words. "Really? And what would you do to me if I was there and at your mercy?"

His hand dropped to his groin, stroking himself in lazy, long pulls.

"Come to the clinic and I'll tell you while I work on your shoulder."

Demo growled at being thwarted of the opportunity to have phone sex with her. "Really, Paige?"

She gave him a wide smile. "My first appointment isn't until nine-thirty. Just think of how much...*attention* I can give your shoulder in that time."

"If you think my shoulder is the area that needs your attention after this conversation, you might need to retake an anatomy class or two."

Paige chuckled. "Get your sexy ass to my clinic, Demo!"

"Fine! I'll pick up donuts and coffee along the way because I highly doubt you ate this morning after I left."

Her blush was answer enough, but she still said, "I wasn't that hungry."

"I'm going to ignore that lie and finish getting dressed. I'll see you at the clinic in half an hour."

"Wait!" she called when he moved to end the call. For a moment, Demo thought she still wanted to watch him get dressed. But that thought died pretty quickly. "What happened this morning? Why did you run out like that?"

Demo stood frozen for a moment. He hadn't yet explained that there were some things he wouldn't be able to tell her. Club business and all that. But...the other ol' ladies knew about the bomb threat. He wasn't sure how much they knew, but they had to know something from being evacuated out of their beds at five in the morning with their kids.

Despite his use of the word 'other' Paige was not his ol' lady. He hadn't officially claimed her, which meant that she didn't get the perks of being his woman. Right now, she fell into the 'club family' category. Like the club members' parents or in-laws, Paige was awarded the club's protection as well as an open invitation to their club events. Club businesses offered them discounts too.

An ol' lady was different. She would have the right to be told everything but the most secretive of details. Like the cellar beneath the clubhouse floor. No one but prospects and patched members knew about that floor plan detail. Other than Abby, Demo had to wonder how much *other* details their men gave the ol' ladies. Even if they weren't told something specifically, they had eyes and ears, probably picking up on a lot.

None of the women were stupid.

Demo and Paige's relationship was only days old. It was far, far too early to claim her as an ol' lady... Wasn't it? But fuck, that image returned to his head of Paige wearing his property cut... and, damn, how he wanted to make it a reality.

"Nothing major," he lied, feeling like his tongue was made of lead. "It was a small incident, but it's been handled. Only reason I had to be here was because I'm an officer." Clearing this throat,

Demo rushed out, "Let me finish getting ready. I'll see you at the clinic in a bit."

* * *

A LOT HAPPENED in the days following the bomb threat at the clubhouse. Yelizaveta came to Steel the day afterwards upset because her husband never came home from work. Steel called Carlos, who took the missing person's report from the couch in the clubhouse. Neither of them knew the man was only a few feet away in the hidden cellar beneath the floorboards.

The man was still there, naked and hanging from the ceiling by his wrists, next to Nathan Moore. Despite all the evidence against him, including that his fingerprints were found all over the pieces of the device and the duffel bag was his own gym bag with his DNA all over it, Billy Merrick continued to cling to his innocence. Steel thought prolonged time in the cellar might get him to change his mind.

Demo took apart the bomb with a fine-tooth comb. As he suspected, the batteries *were* at full charge. If Billy hadn't used rubber glue, he would have blown himself up building the damn thing. Demo wasn't sure that would have been a bad thing.

SJ was the only club kid living in the clubhouse, but that was still one kid too many that close to an explosive device. Based on the haphazard way the duffel was left between the cages, it was concluded that no specific member was the target. Plus, there was no way Billy could have guessed that Bones would be the one to take that exact spot. Pumpkin did not know Billy at all or Yelizaveta well enough to be a target.

"I gave her a ride home once," Pumpkin had told them all when asked. "But that was months ago, before SJ was born."

Keys even looked into the possibility that Billy had known Cheryl and the bomb was revenge for her execution but found no evidence there.

Paige and Demo were getting closer every day. She'd accepted his vague excuse of there being an 'incident at the clubhouse' and hadn't pried. Demo was beyond grateful for that, because he didn't want to be lying to her any more than he already was.

The Sunday following the bomb, Lucky, Harper, Demo, and Paige went out for brunch at the diner. Mikey and Nelly Bean were spending the day with their cousins Conner and Scotty under the supervision of Sissy and Sara, who had both taken on the title of 'aunt' to the boys. During which, Paige agreed to tell them everything:

"Richard was not the man you knew," she told Harper in a sorrowful tone. "I am so sorry to be the one to tell you this. He was horribly in debt. I don't know what he kept spending the money on, but it wasn't on me or the boys. I'm drowning in the debts he left me. Some I knew about, but others I only found out after he disappeared."

Both Demo and Lucky were sitting on the outside of the booth with their ladies against the wall. Demo sat with his back to the kitchen door so that Paige could hold his right hand while she talked. Lucky sat in such a way that a slight head tilt gave him a view of the rest of the diner. Kelly, the waitress, had already come and taken their orders, dropping off their waters and soda glasses when she did.

Demo squeezed Paige's hand reassuringly. He knew how much she'd been dreading this conversation. Though she had no idea just how informed Lucky and Demo already were about her situation.

"You know how much I hate my stepfamily. What I didn't find out until recently was that Richard had taken out a loan with my stepfather, Thad. They're demanding repayment and I don't have it."

A tear started to fall from her left eye, but Demo stretched his left hand across himself to catch it before it could.

Harper reached across the table and took Paige's other hand.

"How much does he owe them?" Demo was very grateful Harper phrased it that *Richard* owed the debt, not Paige. He'd been trying very hard to get her to stop calling Richard's debts *her* debts. "Maybe Lucky and I can help out."

Harper looked to Lucky for support. His answering, "Of course," was said without hinting to the fact that he knew they couldn't.

Paige let out a cynical laugh. "Not unless you won the lottery and didn't tell me. I have no proof that this is the actual number, because it's not like I ever saw a penny of it, but seven hundred..." Harper looked confused for a second until Paige added, "Thousand."

Harper's jaw dropped. "Holy fuck. And I thought three hundred thousand was bad!"

Lucky and Demo exchanged a quick look. As far as Keys could tell, Paige was not aware of Richard's association with Mateo Castillo or the fact that her husband had borrowed money from a cartel loan shark.

As much as Demo wanted Paige to seek out help, they were treading on thin ice. Demo wondered if Lucky had cautioned Harper not to mention some things about Richard's past or his connection to the club. Harper knew most of her brother's past after he'd abducted her. If Scar hadn't rescued her, there was still the question of what Richard's endgame would have been that day. According to Harper, he'd seemed a bit unhinged.

Paige's eyebrows drew down. "That's very specific. Why did you say 'three hundred thousand' like that?"

Harper bit her lip like she hadn't meant to say those words. "Look, I promised I wasn't going to say anything, but you have a right to know. I've always argued that. Keeping you in the dark was cruel, but they insisted on protecting you and the boys. If I hadn't found out as I had, I doubt they would have even told me." Her face scrunched up with anger. "No, I *know* they wouldn't have told me if I hadn't found out on my own."

"Who's 'they'?" Paige asked, her eyes flicking to Lucky but not Demo. She squeezed Demo's hand even harder.

"My parents," Harper said with a long sigh. "Moving to Mount Grove had always been the plan. You know that. Mom's got some land out this way that she inherited when her dad passed. When Mount Grove offered Dad the position as sheriff, he wasn't going to accept. In fact, he'd already turned down an offer from the town council. But then Richard came to them. He..." Harper picked at the napkin in front of her. "He was in deep with a loan shark and he'd been threatened. You all had."

Paige's jaw dropped. "A loan shark? A *loan shark*? What? Why?"

Harper glanced to Lucky. He wrapped his arm around her shoulder reassuringly and pressed a kiss to her temple. Harper leaned into her husband for a moment before she turned back to Paige. "Richard had a gambling problem, Paige."

Paige's face blanched. "*Gambling*? No, he's an accountant."

Demo refrained from pointing out that *he* was an accountant too. Paige didn't know about his extracurricular activities with the club, though none of that included gambling.

Harper nodded sadly. "He was in deep too. One-hundred and fifty thousand, according to my dad. It was all of their savings, but Dad gave Richard the money to pay off the loan shark. Unfortunately, Richard decided to take that money and gamble it. But he lost and doubled his debt."

"Three hundred thousand," Paige muttered disbelievingly under her breath. "I can't... There's no way I can..." Tears free fall down her cheeks. "There's no way I can pay that back too." Demo reached for her, turning her in the booth to face him. Paige's eyes were wide with fear and dismay. She looked at him frantically. "A million dollars. I don't have a million dollars."

"You don't need a million dollars," he told her as sternly as he could.

She nodded her head like a bobblehead. "Richard owes money

to a *loan shark*, Demo. If they don't get their money back, they come after the person and their family. They—" Paige's eyes went suddenly wide and she rounded on Harper across the table. "Ronald and Cindy's attack? Ronald said that it was a criminal from Detroit, someone Ronald had arrested in the past who wanted revenge?"

Shame washed over Harper's face. "He lied. The loan shark came down to Mount Grove to demand his money. When he couldn't find Richard, he went to my parents."

Paige dropped Demo's hand to clasp her cheeks in both of hers. "I can't... My God... Why didn't you guys *tell* me?"

"I wanted to," Harper defended herself. "I never thought it was right that they kept you in the dark. They made me swear not to tell you. They were convinced that you didn't need to deal with Richard's sins after he walked out on you. They wanted you to concentrate on the boys and healing."

"*Healing?*" She slapped her palms down on the table. "How the hell am I supposed to do that when a loan shark could come after me or my boys any day for money I don't have and never had any part of?" Paige demanded harshly.

Harper looked like she was going to start crying. Kelly walked up with their food right then. Seeming to sense the tension at the table, she passed around their food, quickly asked if they needed anything else, and then left them.

No one touched their plates.

Harper looked frantically at Lucky for help.

Lucky ran his hand through his ol' lady's long, raven hair before he turned his attention to Paige. "The club stumbled upon the attack at the former sheriff's house. We intervened. Hannigan covered up the fact of *who* had been at his house to protect his son's reputation but also to protect us. We killed the loan shark to protect Cindy and Hannigan."

It didn't happen *exactly* like that but it was close enough.

Paige blinked. "The club was involved?"

"Briefly," Lucky emphasized. "If Harper hadn't wanted to go visit her parents that day, the outcome would have been very different. Bear and I were with her and we rescued the Hannigans. As you know, one of our prospects lost his life that day protecting Harper."

"Conner," Paige breathed out his name. She turned to Demo. "You knew? You knew about Richard's gambling problems." Her voice was accusatory.

Demo nodded. "I didn't know that *you* didn't know until recently. I didn't even know *you* until recently, Paige."

"Why didn't you tell me?" she demanded.

"And how would that conversation have gone?" he asked her in return. "'Hey, pretty lady, wanna go out with me? Oh, and by the way, are you aware your husband is a gambling addict?'"

Paige's cheeks flushed. "You could have still told me," she insisted.

"And how was I to know what you did and didn't know?" he asked in return.

Paige didn't seem to have an answer for that. She looked back to Lucky. "You killed the loan shark. Is that... I mean, it's over then? I don't have to worry about paying back that money too?"

Demo bit his tongue against saying she didn't have to pay back the other money to her stepfamily either.

"We were able to get ahold of the loan shark's brother," Lucky told her gently. "Richard's debt with them was cleared. Hannigan can verify this if needed."

Paige was silent for a moment as she tried to process all of this.

Demo saw Lucky nudge Harper, but Paige's eyes were cast downward towards her uneaten food and wouldn't have seen it.

"Paige, will you tell me about your stepfamily?" Harper prompted.

She quickly wiped at her eyes. "You mean other than they're a bunch of money-hungry bastards who are threatening to take away my boys if I don't pay them back every penny your brother borrowed from them?"

There was a great level of contempt in Paige's voice.

Harper flinched. "They are threatening to take away your boys?"

Rather than answer her sister-in-law, Paige turned in the booth to face Demo again. "You knew about that too," she accused. "Steel came to me and told me that Ronald told him about their threat. He gave me the club's lawyer's card. Told me to tell her everything and to get a restraining order against the Barringtons."

"Did you?" Demo asked her in lieu of answering her own question.

"She's looking into it," Paige told him. Her eyes were still narrowed. "You knew about the threat though?"

Demo slowly nodded.

Shame washed over her like a wave. Demo reached for her, not wanting Paige to ever feel ashamed for circumstances outside of her control.

"Let me out," she demanded.

Demo blinked. "What?"

"Let. Me. Out," Paige snapped, louder this time. "You lied to me. You... I let you into my life! I... I was falling..." She wiped harshly at her wet cheeks. "I trusted you. Are all accountants liars?"

"Paige, I didn't lie—"

"A lie of omission is still a lie, Demo!" Her voice was loud enough that patrons started to look their way. Paige pushed against his chest. "How could you? You knew Richard is a gambling addict. You knew about my stepfamily's threat to take my boys away. Did you know about my debts? When you encouraged me to come here and spill my secrets, did you already know them too?"

With each question, Paige slammed her palms against his

187

chest. Demo didn't want to let her go until he explained—he had no idea what it was he was going to explain, but he knew he didn't want to let her leave angry—but he also didn't want her to hurt her hands by pushing on him so.

Demo scooted to the side and got up. Paige grabbed for her purse and looped it up to her shoulder. She nearly tripped as she got out of the booth. Demo reached out to steady her, but she threw off his hand.

"You lied to me!" she shouted, not caring who saw or heard. "Was it all some sick game to you? Watch the poor single mom struggle to pay her bills and then swoop in like some hero to save her? The computer equipment, the internet, fuck—my heating bill? Is my life some sick joke to you?"

Demo got right up into her face. "How dare you ask me that? I *never* would play games with you like that. Did I know some extra things about your past that you probably didn't want a stranger to know? Yes. But I *never* would play with your feelings or the boys' like that."

Demo had been spending more time with the boys since the night of their puppy pile on Paige's couch. They didn't seem to have a problem with him and Demo found he really enjoyed being around them. Even if all they did was color on the floor while Mikey received his asthma cupping treatment.

He hated leaving the family each night, but he also wanted to give Paige space. For now, they were taking Bulldog's advice and building on their friendship before they added sex into the mix. There had been a lot of sexy times—like the video phone call the other morning—and plenty of heavy make out sessions that had left Demo hard and Paige soaked, but they had not had sex yet.

Paige's chin trembled as she looked away from him. "I was already in one relationship where I couldn't trust my partner, Demo. I can't handle another one. I'm sorry but lying is a hard limit for me." She glanced over her shoulder. "I'm sorry, Harper. I need some time. I'll call you when I'm ready to talk again."

With that, Paige started walking towards the diner's front door.

Fuck. Watching her go was worse than getting shot had been. There were no words to describe it, no expression to quantify the agony of watching her walk away from him. If he let her go, if she walked out that door... Demo was pretty sure he would shatter into a thousand pieces. Paige Hannigan had somehow burrowed her way under his skin in less than a week.

Six days, actually.

He couldn't let her go. It wasn't possible. Each step she took was like a knife to his soul. She was tearing him up inside.

Demo couldn't fault her. He *had* lied to her. He had omitted the truth. There were many things that he hadn't told her and even more that he could never tell her. But there was one thing he'd always been honest about.

"I never lied about loving you!"

The entire diner fell silent at his shouted words. Paige froze, only steps away from the front door. Hell, she could probably stretch her arm in front of her and touch the metal bar.

Seconds ticked by. No one moved.

Then, slowly, Paige turned around to face him. Her eyes flicked to their still audience before returning to him. "What did you say?"

Demo completely ignored their audience. The building could have been on fire and he wouldn't have noticed. Every molecule of his being was focused only on her. "You said you were falling for me? Well, I've already fallen. I am aware that I messed up withholding some facts from you, but this is my first relationship. I have no idea what I'm doing—and I certainly didn't expect to fall for you.

"I should have. You're beautiful, Paige. And, fuck, you're so smart. You're witty and you love your boys so much that you'll sacrifice your own health and safety for them. I'm very aware that I'll be third on your list if you do decide you can love me back and I'm completely okay with that. Third time's the charm and all that. And that's the way it should be. I can only hope that one day you'll be third on my list too. Maybe even fourth if I'm lucky enough that you'll give me another kid.

"But *please*, Paige, *please* don't walk out on me. I'm not sure I could survive it."

Tears streamed down her cheeks. Her chin trembled.

Her purse hit the linoleum floor with a loud *thunk*. Something inside jingled like coins colliding together. She took a step forward.

Demo's heart leapt. He'd just—very publicly—laid his heart bare to her. And she wasn't walking away.

Paige let out a loud sob before she bolted down the aisle between filled booths and tables towards him. Demo opened up his arms and Paige leapt into them.

Their lips collided as she wrapped her legs around his waist. He gripped her tightly, vowing there and then to never let her go.

Their audience burst into cheers and applause. Parents covered their kids' eyes. A burst of tears next to them informed Demo of Harper's approving reaction.

Paige gripped his cut like he was her lifeline.

When they finally broke apart for some air, Paige rested her forehead against his. "I fell too," she whispered. "I fell so hard. I'm sorry I got so angry."

Demo tilted his chin up to touch his lips to her nose. "No need to apologize." Really taking in their audience for the first time, Demo glanced around her ear to see the entire diner still had their attention on them. "Wanna get out of here?"

She nodded against his forehead, closing her eyes to block out the gazes of their fellow patrons.

Demo headed towards the door, Paige still in his arms. He threw over his shoulder at Lucky, "Box that to go! I'll pay you back later."

Lucky's amused snort was his only response. Or at least, the only one Demo heard.

Kelly helpfully picked up Paige's purse at the door and looped it over Demo's elbow. He nodded to her in thanks.

"You got your keys on you?" Demo asked Paige when he stepped out into the cold.

She nodded, ducking her face down into the crook of his neck against the wind. The only good thing about her having been walking out on him was that she was already wearing her jacket and he didn't have to stop to help her get it on.

Demo carried her down Main Street in the direction of her clinic. It was closed—and Demo had a fantasy of bending her over those damn massage tables to fulfill.

CHAPTER 9

*T*hey laughed and fumbled their way into the clinic. Paige was grateful Demo had the wherewithal to lock them back inside. She was too lust-drunk to remember to do anything so practical. They both slipped off their jackets and shoes in the lobby, throwing them on or under the waiting chairs.

Paige circled her arms around Demo's neck and leapt back up. He caught her easily, as if anticipating the move. They kissed feverishly—or, at least, it was feverishly until Demo started chuckling against her lips.

Paige pulled back. Not concerned, but curious as to what he'd been thinking that would cause him to laugh like that. "What?"

She was slightly taller than him when he held her so. She liked how balanced he felt even though he was supporting her weight entirely.

"We didn't even make it a week."

Paige cocked her head to the right. "A week? What do you mean?"

She caught him fiddling with her thermostat on their way past as he carried her to the first therapy room. She'd turned the heat down again with the clinic being closed on Sundays. For once, she didn't balk at the idea of increasing her electricity bill. Demo knew about her money troubles, and moreover, he knew they weren't her own doing.

With the increase in her clinical appointments, plus the three higher paying requests through the foot fetish site this week, Paige might actually be able to come out on top this month. She still couldn't believe someone was willing to pay six hundred dollars to see her clip her toenails, file them, and then paint them baby pink. She'd removed the polish right after finishing the live video.

Demo placed her butt on the massage table. He reached behind her and flipped on the heat lamp, ensuring it was facing her back. She appreciated the gesture, because the vinyl under her butt was *cold*. "Five days ago, Bulldog advised me about making sure our foundation was secure before we had sex." He leaned over and kissed her lips. "I have every intention of not even making it a week."

Paige chuckled, understanding his humor. "Me too."

"Thank fuck!" He went to kiss her again but Paige put her hand up between them, making his lips press against her palm instead of her lips. His eyes flew back open but he didn't pull back. "What's wrong?" he said against her palm.

Paige smirked and pushed him back with her hand. He only moved to put some space between their faces but kept his place standing over her with his hands on the massage bed by her hips. "Nothing's wrong, but I do want to reiterate something."

He raised an eyebrow but didn't speak.

"Trust is a dealbreaker for me, Demo. I need to be able to trust you. I *need* that more than I need your love, if that makes sense. *Please*, I am begging you, don't ever make me lose or question your trust."

Demo didn't reply for a long moment, making Paige's heart

beat erratically in her chest. She hoped that wasn't an issue for him. She didn't think it sounded unreasonable. What sort of relationship could they have anyway if they couldn't trust each other? Because trust was a two-way street. He needed—or should want to—trust her too.

Slowly, he sank to his knees before her. Both he and the massage bed were tall enough that the action placed his chin by her knees.

Demo took hold of both of her hands and brought the tips to his mouth. He held her hands against the scruff on his cheek, staring up at her. "Paige, there will be some things that I can never tell you. It's for your protection. The club, well, we call it 'club business' when we have to keep something from our families or significant others. As my ol' lady, you'll be able to know a lot more than anyone else, but there will still be things you can't know. You have to trust that I am doing what is in the best interest of you, our family, and the club and I have to be able to trust that you won't reveal what secrets I *can* tell you. Trust is a dealbreaker for me too."

Paige swallowed hard. "Ol' lady?" she repeated. Her pulse picked up speed for a different reason.

Demo nodded. "I understand if you don't want my cut right away. Consider this your open ended offer, Paige. Whenever you're ready, be it now or a year from now, it'll be yours."

"It's been less than a week," she reminded him. What they'd only been joking about minutes ago seemed far more serious now.

"Do you love me, Paige?" His sea green eyes bore into hers. "Forget everything else. Forget your troubles and the fact that you're still legally married. The only stipulation I'll accept is if it affects the boys. Do you love me?"

She nodded, no longer able to deny it despite their little time together. Demo was smart, funny, and honorable. He *cared*. She doubted there was another man in the world like him that could make her heart dance and her blood sing. "I do. I love you."

"Then that's all that matters. We'll figure the rest out. You," he brought her hands to his lips, "are more important to me than I ever thought possible. You're in my every thought, my every dream. I go to bed at night longing to be in yours next to you, even if it's fully clothed. As much as I want us to make love right now, if you asked me to wait, I would. I've *never* wanted to be with a woman as I do you. It's like you're fundamental to my very existence. I'll never make fun of Bulldog not being able to let Abby out of his sight because I know *exactly* how he feels. Anytime I have to leave you, it's like you're calling me back. I love you, Paige Hannigan. I'm no longer asking if it's too soon or if it's too fast. I just want *you.*"

"And the boys," she reminded him. "Package deal."

"Oh, I'm very aware. We'll figure out what sort of relationship you want me to have with them as we go on. I've never *wanted* to be a dad before," he smirked at her, "but I am definitely starting to see the appeal."

"How about you just be their friend for now?" she offered. "I don't want to move too fast where *they're* concerned."

Demo nodded. "Completely reasonable."

"Is there anything else you have to tell me?" she asked him softly. "Or," she corrected, "that you are *allowed* to tell me?"

"That's a longer conversation when my cock isn't trying to rip its way out of my jeans." Demo gave her a wicked smile. "If you want to talk now, then we'll talk. But, honestly, all my blood is not exactly stimulating my brain right now."

She laughed. "You know that's a myth, right? You actually have increased blood flow to both areas during sex."

He blinked. "Really? I don't think I knew that."

Paige grinned at him. "The average erection only holds four-point-four ounces of blood." Glancing down at the bulge in his pants, Paige added, "Though in your case, you might be higher than average."

Demo stood up. "Have I told you that I love smart women?"

"*Women?*" she questioned. "Have I mentioned that cheating is another hard limit of mine?"

"Me too," he answered immediately. Leaning in, he nipped at her ear. Paige shivered at the sharp contact. "I will *kill* any man who dares touch you, Paige Hannigan. You're mine."

Breathless, Paige managed to say, "I had a controlling husband, Demo. I'm not interested in being a trophy on a shelf."

He pulled back enough to meet her eyes. "I'm possessive, not controlling. Unless it pertains to your safety, then I reserve the right to control the hell out of you."

Despite herself, Paige snorted. "Is that so?"

"So," he told her sternly. "I can't lose you, Paige. I don't think I could bear it. Please, when it comes to you and the boys' safety, don't question me on it. If I ever tell you to run, even if it means leaving me behind, I need you to do it."

There was such depth of emotion behind his eyes, they truly did remind her of the ocean. It was the concern there, though, and the fear that had her nodding her head. She couldn't imagine ever actually doing that—running and letting him face whatever anticipated danger he feared—but she agreed to appease him. It seemed like something he needed from her.

He gave her an appreciative smile and leaned in to kiss her.

"Can I ask you something?" she asked when he pulled back.

"Anything."

"You claim that I'm yours. You want me to wear a cut that says that I'm your property. Does..." she hesitated. "Does that mean you'd be mine too?"

"Fuck yes, it does. I will walk across the street and get your name tattooed on my chest in big bold letters right now if that's what you need."

Paige laughed but then stopped when she saw the seriousness on his face. "Wait. Are you serious?"

He nodded.

She looked his clothed body up and down, trying to remember. "Do you *have* any tattoos?"

He nodded. "You probably didn't notice in the video call because you were too busy staring at my ass."

Paige snorted. She reached to untuck his shirt from his belted jeans. "Show me. I want to see."

Demo reached behind his back and pulled his long sleeve shirt up and over his head in one swift movement. His well-formed pecs and abs immediately drew her attention. Paige licked her lips appreciatively.

"You know," she touched the ridge between his six-pack, "the first time I saw you without your shirt on, my very first thought was *damn, I want to lick that man all over.*" Paige leaned in, her tongue out as if she was going to follow through on her words. Then she abruptly sat up and looked exaggeratingly around his naked torso. "I don't see any tattoos!"

"Tease," he grumbled. "Don't promise me a good licking session without following through, minx. My heart breaks easily."

Paige smiled innocently up at him. "I never tease, he-man. I just want to see your tattoos before I lick you…*everywhere.*"

He let out a groan and then turned his back to her. She had only seen his bare back on the video call as he'd been on his back during his treatments. Above his right shoulder blade was the club's insignia. Underneath was the single word *Treasurer.*

"Just the one?" she asked.

He shook his head. "There's two."

Paige put her hands on his hips. Staying seated on the table, she started moving him every which way to try to find the other tattoo. She was pretty sure he didn't have anything under his arms but checked there to be sure. She even checked around his belly button.

"Is it in your pants?" she asked.

"This is your exploration," he laughed.

Paige turned Demo around to face her. She undid his belt, then the button and zipper of his jeans. He played with her unruly curls as she pushed his pants down over his hips. His black boxer shorts went with them. "I don't feel like getting up, so step out of them for me please. Socks too."

Chuckling, Demo stepped back and did as ordered. Naked as the day he was born, he did another slow circle like he'd done the day of the video call. His toned ass was ink-free. As were his thighs and calves. She was well-acquainted with his feet from his treatments so she knew he didn't have any there.

Her eyes widened when she saw the length of his half-hard cock. Like him, it didn't have much width, but the length was impressive. Something flashed in the overhead lights. She tilted her head, watching his cock rise up the rest of the way.

It was long enough that the piercing on the underside of the mushroomed head of his cut cock touched the skin above his belly button.

Paige swallowed. Hard. She'd heard of guys getting their dicks pierced but had never met a man with one.

She licked her lips. "Did it hurt?"

Demo circled his fingers around the base of his cock. He followed the length up to the head and then rolled his palm over the pierced tip. "The initial piercing did. Now? It just feels amazing."

Paige dropped to her knees before him. Demo quickly grabbed his discarded shirt and laid it out on the cold floor before his feet. She maneuvered it beneath her, grateful for the barrier between her knees and the cold floor.

She reached forward. When Demo made no move to stop her, she touched the tip of her finger to the top bell. The silver bar went through his urethra and out the bottom, behind his glans, to complete a circle. Two silver balls decorated the bar.

"It's called a Prince Albert," he explained. Paige looked up to see him staring down at her with an intense heat in his eyes. It was obvious he liked seeing her before him so.

Without breaking their eye contact, Paige leaned forward and kissed the rounded tip of his cock. The metal felt cool against her lips.

A sense of power rose up within her when that small act elicited a long groan from him. She felt triumphant, even though she was the one on her knees. Running her tongue down the underside of his heavy erection.

"No tattoos here," she mused. "Perhaps I should look elsewhere?"

"I think you need to look harder." His voice didn't sound normal, like he was speaking through gritted teeth.

Inside, Paige chuckled. "Oh, am I close?" She moved her head to the other side and repeated her tongue's investigation.

"No, but I am," she heard him mumble.

Stroking and licking, she continued to play with him in her impractical attempt to find a tattoo she knew was not where she was looking.

Demo bunched her long curls up on top of her head and used it as a grip to help guild her endeavors. "Fuck, Paige, you're going to make me come."

Her mouth came off the end of his cock with an audible *pop*. She smiled sassily up at him. "I found your piercing, but not your tattoo."

"My piercing is enjoying your search a little too much. As much as I would *love* to come in that delectable mouth of yours, there's only one place I plan on coming today and that's not it."

Paige feigned a pout. "Fine, if I must."

Demo let out a mixture of a groan and a chuckle as he helped her back onto her feet.

Paige pursed her lips. "Is your other tattoo inside your mouth?"

"How many tongue exams have you done on me?" he retorted. Leaning close, he bent over her again. "But, by all means, do another."

Demo kissed her, his tongue delving into her mouth as if on an exploratory mission of his own. Paige opened up, allowing him entry. She squirmed under his attention, though his hands never touched her. Fuck, the things he could do with that tongue. She was very much looking forward to putting it to use again… elsewhere.

Both of them pulling back, Paige managed to gasp out. "Nope, didn't see any tattoos in there."

Demo laughed. "Do you really want to know?"

She nodded. He picked her up by her hips and placed her back on the massage table. Then Demo knelt between her legs again. Only this time, he turned his back on her. He tilted his head to the right and then bent his earlobe down so she could see the skin behind it.

Paige bent down for a closer look. At a distance, it could have been mistaken for an oddly shaped mole. But upon a deeper inspection, she realized it was a music note with the initials *LBS* along the tie.

"LBS?" she questioned, thinking maybe it was a band she had never heard of before.

"Laurel Bethany Snyder." Demo released his ear, looking at her over his shoulder. "My mother."

"Your mother?" She couldn't recall Demo saying anything about his parents. Honestly, she'd avoided asking him, not wanting him to ask about hers.

"She died when I was five. They say sound is the first memory to go when you lose someone. But I never have to worry about that. My mom was an opera singer. I have thousands of record-ings of her singing voice. But it was the times when she would hold me close in my bed and whisper how much she loved me that I never want to forget. I put the tattoo there as a reminder to always listen for her."

Paige felt her heart clench. She reached for him, her goal comfort rather than lust this time. "I'm so sorry, Demo."

He kissed her palm. "Took the guys a long time to find that tattoo too. I was nearly stripped naked one night by them because they were convinced I didn't have a second tattoo."

Paige laughed despite the sorrow she still felt for him. She had been too young when her birth father had died for her to remember anything about him. "Did they finally find it or your piercing?"

"Yes to the tattoo, no to the piercing." He smiled broadly up at her. "Wanna hear something hilarious? Your first secret as my ol' lady."

Though Paige hadn't accepted being his ol' lady yet, she still nodded. Because she loved to see him smile so mischievously as he was.

"Pumpkin has one too. Exactly where mine is."

She blinked, not understanding the joke. "A Prince Albert?"

"God no!" he said loudly, eyes wide. He chuckled, "I meant the tattoo! But his is a pumpkin. He got drunk one night about four years ago. Angel tattooed a little pumpkin behind his ear. We all waited the next morning for him to say something or notice the pain and take a look..." Demo shook his head. "But he didn't. As far as we know, he still doesn't know about it!"

Paige gasped as her own eyes widened. "You tattooed him without permission?"

Demo nodded. "They got the idea from how well mine was hidden. We were drunk, but we were cognizant enough not to put it somewhere that would impede his day-to-day life. Like his forehead."

Paige shook her head, covering her mouth with her hand. "That is so mean! I don't know if I should laugh or cry for him."

Demo shrugged. "Pumpkin had it coming. We're still not convinced the girl he claims he slept with the night of his patch-in party exists. It's a constant reminder for him to find her to prove she does."

"Harper told me about his name. He woke up the morning after cuddling a pumpkin instead of the woman he claims he slept with, right?"

Demo nodded, his lips fighting a smile. "We're not as wild or careless anymore. Not when a good number of the guys have kids and women around now, but we still like to party and have a good time." His eyes lowered to her chest. "Speaking of which, I am completely naked while you are entirely clothed. I don't think that's fair." He pulled at the top button of her V-neck button up, taking a peek at her cleavage. "Maybe I need to explore your body for tattoos."

Paige could have very easily saved him the trouble and told him that she didn't have any. Instead, she said, "You're welcome to search. I had a few wild nights in college myself. There might be a tattoo or two that I don't know about."

Demo smiled widely. Standing up, he claimed her lips. "I'll be sure to do a *very thorough* search."

"Mmm…" Paige moaned against him. "Be sure to check every inch."

"Yes, ma'am."

* * *

DEMO MADE quick work of Paige's clothes. The heat hadn't kicked on fully so he made sure the heat lamp was still facing towards the massage table. He knew she had pillows in one of the cabinet drawers to help patients who needed the extra support. Grabbing out two of those, he placed them over the head of the table where the face hole was.

Paige laid back, her curls fanning out around her head on the white linen. "Are you sure you're okay on top? What about your shoulder?"

"Fuck, Paige, you're far too gorgeous splayed out for me to even notice my shoulder. One of these days, I'm going to bend you over this table and fuck you." He gave his long cock a slow stroke. "But not today. I want to, believe me, I do, but now I find myself wanting to savor you."

Paige gave him a look full of longing. "I feel like I'm on fire for you. I don't know if this is stupid or foolish. Legally, I'm still a married woman. But I want you, Demo. I can honestly say I've never wanted anyone the way I want you. Right or wrong, this is where we are." She held a hand out to him. "Are you here with me?"

Demo placed a knee on the table between hers. It was so narrow that their positions would be limited. Crawling over her body, he settled himself so they were chest to chest, hip to hip. Paige widened her legs to create a cradle for him.

Demo cupped her face with his left hand, using his right to hold him up. "I'm here. Always. You are mine and I am yours. This is the start of our forever, Paige."

Promises of tattoo exploration forgotten, Demo kissed her. In their enthusiasm and haste, their teeth clanked together, but soon they found their rhythm. Naked, his pierced dick pressed insistently between her thighs, but did not enter her. The friction of him running it back and forth over her clit coupled with the guttural moan she released nearly had him blowing his load all over her belly like a virgin teenager.

Demo refused to come first. She'd been stuck in a marriage with an extremely selfish husband. He had many doubts that they had a satisfactory sex life—not that he wanted to think about that. But she did have two sons. Obviously, she'd had intimate relations with her husband, the fucking bastard. Demo wanted—no, *needed*—to ensure that Paige's experience of any of their times together was amazing and mind-blowing. Beyond wanting to ensure she enjoyed herself, Demo wanted to express the depths of his feelings for her in the most intimate of ways. She deserved to be worshiped, hand and foot...and mouth.

His hands went to her breasts. Though full-sized, she had small areolas and nipples. The idea of her breastfeeding her sons came to the forefront of his mind. Why was that image so arousing and, at the same time, heartbreaking? He shouldn't be jealous of the fact that she'd had children with another man. The fact that he hadn't seen her pregnant, hadn't been there for the births, or helped her afterwards...

Demo couldn't change the past. But he could ensure that she and her sons never wanted for anything in the future. He would be there for her, no matter what.

Paige arched her back, pressing her breasts into his hands. Unable to pinch her right nipple as he could her left, Demo dropped his head down to take the taut peak into his mouth. Paige whispered his name in reverence.

Demo sucked harder.

"Oh God!" she moaned, throwing her head back on the pillow. She squirmed against the onslaught of his mouth, hand, and cock.

"Come for me, beautiful," he encouraged around her nipple. He ground his hips against hers, increasing the pressure against her clit.

She was teetering on the edge. Demo could feel it. Fuck, and he wasn't going to last very long once he got inside her.

Demo reached down with his left hand, hiked her right leg up, linking her knee with his elbow, and increased the speed of his thrusts against her.

Paige cried out with the force of her orgasm, shaking violently beneath him. "Demo! Holy shit!"

He sat up, shoving his knees beneath her legs. Paige was splayed out as if on display—and there had never been a sexier sight in all the world. Her nipples were red and swollen from his onslaught. Her hair disheveled from both his hands and her own.

Her chest rose and fell with her heavy breathing. Her eyes were glazed over. Her pussy shimmering with the evidence of her arousal.

Demo couldn't resist reaching down and stroking his cock. "Are you on birth control, Paige?"

She blinked, as if not following his question. It took her a second before she shook her head. "I had my period the week before I met you. I'm probably ovulating."

Demo swallowed hard. The concept of sinking deep into her fertile body was a captivating one. As desire driven as he was right then, even he knew that now was not the time to get pregnant. *If* they decided to have that conversation, it would be in the future while they were both fully clothed and prepared to have a long pros and cons discussion.

Glancing to his pants on the floor, he wished he'd thought to grab a condom out of his wallet before climbing up on the table. He looked down at Paige. "You know, it would be really helpful right now if you were a witch and I didn't have to move from this spot with this amazing view of your naked body. But," he snapped, hopping off the table, "because you *claim* you're not a witch, I have to get up and move around like a muggle."

Paige laughed so hard, her hands clenched around her middle. "I'm not a witch!" she exclaimed again.

Demo bent and pulled his wallet out of his back pocket of his jeans. "Are you sure? Because you certainly put a spell on me."

Paige rolled her eyes but did not lose her smile. "I'm sure. There'd be a lot I'd change about my life if I was."

Curious, Demo asked, "Oh yeah? Like what?" as he pulled a condom out of the billfold.

Paige blinked for a moment. "Actually, other than my stepfamily, I can't think of anything right now. Maybe you're the witch," she pointed out as he moved around to the foot of the table. "Magically making my life better."

Demo grinned down at her. "I'll take you dancing in the moonlight next time I go."

"Naked?"

"That's a given." Then Demo grabbed her by her hips and dragged her down to the edge of the table. He knelt on the linoleum floor. "Now hold on tight, beautiful. I'm going on a tattoo hunt of my own and I'm starting in the most heavenly of places." Then he buried his face between her legs.

* * *

PAIGE LET out a long groan as Demo's tongue slid between her wet lips. Teasing her hole and coming oh-so close to her clit. Hot breath entered her core as he made love to her with his mouth. His tongue probed deep within her, causing Paige to squirm.

Hiking her legs over his shoulders, Demo replaced his tongue with a long finger. He moved his mouth up to her clit as one finger, then two, thrust in and out of her. Paige writhed, her hips bucking up against him. She could feel the bristle of his beard scruff against the most sensitive of places and knew she never wanted him to shave fully.

Demo sucked her clit into his mouth, licking and teasing the tight nub between his teeth. Paige scrambled for purchase and ended up gripping the wooden frame beneath the sides of the mattress.

Her muscles contracted around his fingers. For the second time that morning, she found herself crying out in orgasm. Wave upon wave of pleasure rocked through her body. She cried out, back bowing off of the table.

She heard and felt Demo move. Somehow, she found herself back up on the table with her head on the pillow and Demo hovering over her.

He did not give her time to recover. Mouth and chin glistening with her juices, Demo kissed her fiercely and thrust his pierced cock inside her in one quick motion.

"Fuck, Paige," he groaned against her. "You're fucking perfect. You're so tight you're squeezing my cock."

It wasn't until later that his words made more sense to her. Though long, his cock did not have the girth most men boasted about. The 'wide as a beer can' porn star cocks that broke hearts as well as pussies. Demo had a very long, narrow penis that likely didn't grow in length much upon getting an erection. Paige was sure that this had its advantages and disadvantages.

One of the advantages *she* foresaw was a lot of quickies in their future as foreplay probably wasn't needed to prep her.

At that moment in time, though, all Paige felt was bliss. Even through the condom, she could feel his piercing. It was new and wondrous. As he claimed with her, *he* was perfect just as he was. He was perfect *for her*.

There was no need to compare Demo to Richard or vice versa because there was no comparison. Each was his own man. Demo was just a *better* man.

"Demo," she moaned. "God, I love you. Please…"

He took her mouth again. "Fuck, Paige, you have no idea how amazing it is to hear you say those words." He grabbed her hips and slammed into her. "I fucking love you too."

Paige cried out at the shock of his body hitting hers with such force. The table shook with the power of his thrusts, the speed and momentum. Paige felt the pillow beneath her head slide out from under her and hit the floor.

He kept going.

She urged him on.

Paige wrapped her legs over his hips and ass, locking her ankles as if she could hold him inside her forever. The new angle let him in deeper.

Over and over again, Demo fucked her with his long cock. His grip on her hips was so hard, it would probably bruise, but Paige didn't care. Her fingernails dug into his back. What had started out as slow sensuous lovemaking had turned into a down and dirty fuck—and neither was complaining.

All it took was a flick of her oversensitive clit and Paige was coming for the third time. She watched a wave of emotions cross Demo's face before he took her lips, moaning into her mouth as he released into the condom.

Paige barely had a chance to savor the bliss of their shared passion before there was a loud groan of protesting wood followed by an ear-piercing *crack* as the massage table beneath them collapsed.

CHAPTER 10

*S*udden weightlessness was immediately followed by extreme gravity. There was no time or space for heroic actions. With her arms and legs still wrapped around him and Demo still inside her, there was little Demo could have done anyway. In her surprise and fear, Paige let out a shriek and locked her limbs around him tighter. This action was their only saving grace.

On instinct, Demo stiffened his arms and bent his knees up under her butt. All he could do was brace for impact. Though the massage table had a mattress, it was still a jarring landing. The broken wood beneath created an uneven surface that the mattress barely padded.

Demo's hands and knees hit the floor. Hard.

There was a solid, heart stopping second following their descent in which Demo's mind processed what had just happened—and then his left shoulder buckled out from under him.

Demo rolled to the left, once more hitting his shoulder with his body weight. His cock slipped free from Paige's body as they rolled. She let out a squeal at their next sudden movement. Her arms and legs were still wrapped around him like a koala.

Demo had to bite back a shout of pain. His entire arm, shoulder, and the left side of his neck felt like it was on fire. Muscles twitched uncontrollably and he wasn't even sure his fingers had survived the impact.

Still, his priority was the woman at his chest. His arm could fall off for all he cared. Using his right hand, he moved her unruly curls out of her face so he could see her properly.

"Fuck, Paige, are you okay?" he gasped out.

Shaken, Paige nodded. "I think so." She clutched him tighter for a second before releasing her hold and scooting back from him. Doing so took her weight off of his left arm and caused a new wave of pain to radiate out from his shoulder.

The broken frame of the massage table made a makeshift boat for them. They were in a divot on the mattress with pieces of wood stuck up around them on all sides. As far as Demo could feel, none of the sharp and splinted edges penetrated the mattress.

Paige could only move back a few inches from him. Her eyes went wide as she looked at the mess around and under them. Her body started to shake and it wasn't until he saw the suppressed smile on her face that he realized her body was shaking from laughter, not shock. "Oh God!" she burst out, arms around her middle as if she was trying to keep her laughter in. "Are *you* okay?"

"Peachy," he growled out. He couldn't fault her for laughing. The whole thing *was* pretty funny, but he had a hard time joining her when his shoulder felt like it was being held over an open flame.

"I'm sorry," she tried to stifle her amusement. Her eyes were concerned as she gave him a once over. "Is it your shoulder?"

Reluctantly, he nodded. This was *not* how he wanted the first time they made love to have ended. Though no one could claim it wouldn't be memorable.

Paige moved to her knees, seeming unaware or unconcerned with her nudity. Despite the pain coursing through him, Demo took in his fill of her lovely body. "I'm not laughing at you, I promise," she assured him.

"Careful," he cautioned as she moved around. Just because no larger pieces hadn't penetrated the mattress and impaled them like a shish kebab didn't mean there weren't smaller splinters or shards around. He didn't want Paige to get stuck and injure herself.

She ignored his warning. "Can you sit up? Do I need to call for help?"

Fuck. No.

Since there was no other alternative, Demo gritted his teeth and used his right hand to balance himself as he rose. The pain was immense but survivable. He just needed to remember how to breathe, dammit. What would *not* be survivable would be having Paige call for help and have either his brothers or an ambulance witness him splayed out on the floor in a virtual cradle of the broken massage table with a used condom still hanging off of his dick.

Knowing his brothers, pictures would be taken before any help would be administered.

Demo was *not* having them see Paige naked either. He didn't care if he trusted them with his life or hers. There were some things that were for his eyes only.

With Paige's guiding hand, Demo was able to shift his weight and hips enough to sit up. One of the table legs was still mostly upright. He had no idea if it was sturdy enough, but he needed the support.

Paige shifted around to his left side and started to examine his arm. Demo tried to hold in the grunts of pain, but every uncontrollable twitch felt like a hot poker being jammed into his joint.

"You know," she said drily as she ran her witchy fingers over his skin, "if you wanted free treatments, you could have just asked. Seducing me seems a bit extreme."

Demo grunted out a snort. "Seemed like a good idea at the time."

He glanced at her. Paige was holding his arm out, pressing it back against her chest as she carefully and expertly rotated his shoulder joint.

There was a pause in which one could have heard a pin drop —and then both of them started laughing.

* * *

IT TOOK SOME TIME, but eventually they were able to get themselves up and dressed. The table itself was a complete goner. If it wasn't for his injured shoulder, Demo was pretty sure Paige would have smacked his arm when he suggested they take a selfie in front of it to memorialize the first time they'd had sex.

"Men!" she scoffed before heading off to the back room to find a broom.

Demo pulled out his phone and summoned two prospects to bring a truck. The club could use the frame for tinder during their bonfires. It wasn't like Paige would be able to glue it back together.

When she reentered the room with a broom, dustpan, and some *Terry* rags—for reasons Demo had no clue—he turned his phone around to show her a massage table he found online. "Is this like what you had?"

Her eyes narrowed on the phone. "I don't need you to buy me a replacement table. It would be a business expense anyway—"

Demo raised an eyebrow and stopped himself from informing her that he was *very* aware of what did and did not count as a business expense. "I'm not asking if this is what you need as a replacement. I'm asking if this is like what you had."

Suspicious, she looked closer at the phone. "Thereabouts. Obviously mine didn't have a stainless steel frame. That one," she nodded at the phone, "is a little wider too."

"Excellent." Demo turned the phone back around. He was only able to use his right hand at the moment. Paige had a heating pad currently attached to his left shoulder and some minty cream. In an hour, she planned on using her needles of witchcraft to relieve some of the tension but wanted to apply heat first. "And...ordered."

Paige rounded on him from where she'd started sweeping up splinters. "Demo! I told you, I don't need you to buy me a replacement table!"

"I didn't," he said in all innocence. "I learned my lesson about buying you things without talking to you first."

"Then why did you just buy me a new massage table? The stainless steel ones are a lot more expensive."

"Yeah. Some of those mechanical ones were like fifteen hundred!" he exclaimed. "Thankfully, the one I got was only around four hundred and is even foldable. It'll be at your house in a few days."

"What—" Paige paused. "My house? Why would you have a new massage table go to my house?"

"Well," he put his phone back in his front jeans pocket, "I assume you're going to be buying a replacement table similar to the one we just destroyed for here. There is no way in *hell* we are never doing this," he pointed between the two of them, "again. Fuck no. I don't know about you, but that was the best sex of my life."

Her rosy cheeks answered that rhetorical question for her, to which Demo felt a surge of masculine pride. Fuck, he loved making her blush.

"So I got us a massage table for your house. One that's a lot sturdier and can handle all the pounding I plan on us doing on it."

Paige's expression was a mixture of lust and aghast. "I feel like

I should scold you for the audacity of ordering us a *sex* table," she emphasized the change of category, "or being so turned on that I suggest we go into the other therapy room and test out the sturdiness of *that* table."

Demo gave a full belly laugh. He snagged her around her waist and brought her to his chest. "Fuck, Paige Hannigan, where have you been all my life? How could you have been right under my nose this whole time? I feel so blind and stupid for having not realized how utterly perfect you are."

"I'm not perfect," she corrected with a note of sadness in her voice. "But I *am* pretty awesome."

"Fuck yeah, you are," he agreed before bending to claim her lips.

Pounding on the clinic's front door interrupted them before he could deepen it. Demo's head shot up with a scowl.

Paige giggled, patted his chest, and then headed to answer the door.

* * *

AFTER PAIGE WORKED her witchy magic, his shoulder felt *better* but not great. News of their romantic moment in the diner had spread through the club like wildfire. All of the ol' ladies kept asking Demo to "describe the moment" to them and then looked utterly disappointed when all he would say was "we made out like teenagers before fucking like rabbits". Despite his crude words, Paige laughed anytime she heard them and then would take over the story. Somehow, she always seemed to add more detail than Demo remembered.

Demo's club brothers would not let the broken massage table go and Demo couldn't help the surge of pride whenever it was mentioned. He may or may not have exaggerated the stability of the table prior to its breakage.

The two had created a routine of sorts over the next week or so. Paige was not yet comfortable with Demo sleeping over at her house with the boys. Demo understood it but wasn't happy about it. However, he would never overstep or pressure Paige into doing something she wasn't ready to do or didn't feel the boys were ready for. That did not stop them from taking advantage of their new massage table during the boys' naptime or in the small gap of time they had from when they arrived at Paige's house to when the boys were going to be dropped off by their grandparents. It just meant that their time was more limited and Demo had to drive back to the clubhouse each night before rising early to meet them for breakfast.

It was Demo's hope that the more he was around the boys, the more Paige and they would get comfortable with his new presence in their lives. Declarations of love aside, he could still see the hesitation in Paige's eyes. They'd only been dating for two weeks. It was going to take time to get her to trust him with more than just her body.

Demo was fine with that. He could handle late-nights and early-mornings with lots of extra driving if it got her to finally believe he wasn't going anywhere. He'd come to realize that Richard had abandoned Paige in their marriage long before the club had captured and killed him.

After purchasing the required car seats, Demo had started chauffeuring Paige and the boys around too. First, because taking her to and from work and the boys to and from Cindy's house gave them all extra time together. But also because Demo wanted to contribute in a small way to her financial situation. Him driving meant she didn't need to pay for gas and it was less wear and tear on her cage. He already felt guilty enough for keeping the fact that he was paying for her electric bill a secret. Mind, when he'd done it, he hadn't been in love with her and had thought nothing of having Keys intercept her call to the electric company to discover she had a credit instead of an overdue amount.

Susan Black had also gotten Paige in touch with a lawyer who claimed to take her case on *pro bono* when, in fact, Demo was paying the bill. He made it *very* clear that she was the client and he was just the money. All decisions were Paige's and Paige's alone.

Based on Thad's and Clifton's threatening voicemails, Paige was able to secure a restraining order against her stepfather and her stepbrother. Once the order was approved by a judge, it would be served within the week and included virtual contact.

Demo encouraged her not to give a dime to her stepfamily unless they could provide a contract that stated the money they had given Richard was a loan and not a gift. He made sure she understood that, unless *she* had signed the contract, she was not liable for Richard's debt regardless of marital status.

Since she was currently in the process of serving a restraining order against her stepfamily, it wasn't like Paige could call them to ask for such a contract. She told him her fear was, if there was a contract, that Richard had forged her signature as she'd discovered he'd done on other occasions. Like their second mortgage that had not been done through a reputable bank.

As the Barringtons were currently facing an investigation for embezzlement that Keys promised he had *not* fabricated but *may have* clued the authorities in on, they had more pressing matters than coming after Paige for Richard's debt. Her stepfather could be facing up to twenty years in jail if found guilty. While they might still try to get Paige to pay Richard's debt to help them with legal fees or to keep up with their lifestyle, the threat of having her boys taken away was now just empty words. They had nothing to hold over her.

Once Paige learned of this, she would be able to take the money she'd been putting aside to pay back her stepfamily and apply it towards her current financial needs. It wouldn't fix everything, but it was certainly a start.

The acupuncture clinic, with its new massage table, was

holding steady thanks to its new clientele and increased appointments. To the point where Paige was no longer able to keep running it on her own. After discovering that her former receptionist had understandably already taken another job, Abby stepped up and offered to help out.

Bulldog was both thrilled and concerned about her decision, but never uttered a word of his reservations to Abby. There was no doubt in Demo's mind that she still knew about them though. Those two were always on the same brain wave.

Abby was starting out slow on a part-time basis. She would help with organizing files, answering the phone, and greeting patients as they came and went. With no work experience, Abby was having to learn certain things from scratch. But she was a fast learner and wanted to expand her circle outside of the club.

And since Abby was working, Paige's clinic got a new bodyguard in the form of a very overprotective, hovering Bulldog. Demo certainly was okay with that.

IT AMAZED her how seamlessly Demo had inserted himself into their lives. After the wreck that had been her marriage, Paige would have thought it would take longer. But it was like he was the missing piece of her family. He hadn't molded himself or changed her to fit the puzzle. He just *fit*. All on his own.

Demo didn't hold it against her that she had two boys from a failed marriage. From what she could see, he loved being around them. He'd even hinted at maybe having more kids one day. Paige wasn't sure she was up for that. Not that she didn't want to have a larger family. The idea of having kids with Demo was tempting, but she wouldn't be able to do so until she had her finances back under control.

If she could just pay off her debts, maybe she could sell this damn house. Even if she took a small loss or just broke even, she'd consider it a win.

Paige didn't know where she would move to. She knew Jasmine lived in an apartment complex in town. Maybe there would be availability there for her and the boys. Demo lived in the clubhouse, so it wasn't like they could move in with him.

This ridiculous house didn't even have a backyard for the boys to play in. It was all driveway and fancy porches.

Tires on the drive caught her attention as she was washing the dishes after putting the boys to bed. Paige frowned, wondering if Demo had forgotten something. He'd left for the night about a half hour ago.

The first time Demo had come over in the morning to drive the boys to Cindy's and her to work, he'd been angry that she'd unlocked her front door prior to him arriving. He'd texted he was on his way and Paige had figured that was the courteous thing to do since she might be busy with the boys when he arrived. But she'd learned quickly that it was not the *safest* thing to do, and Demo was all about her safety.

She'd offered him a spare key, but he'd refused that too. Somehow, he'd instinctively known she wasn't a hundred-percent comfortable with the idea and had only been offering because she thought it was the polite thing to do. Feelings and sex aside, Paige was not ready to move their relationship along any faster. For both her and the boys' sakes, she liked how things were for now. Maybe in a few months, she would reconsider.

Hell, maybe in a few months there would be a For Sale sign on her front lawn.

Therefore, Demo sometimes had to wait for her to get to the door after arriving. He claimed he didn't mind, as it kept her and the boys safe and gave her peace of mind. Still, on some of the days that it took her longer to get to the door, she felt a bit guilty.

After drying her hands, Paige headed to the front door to wait as he parked and then headed up the porch steps. Demo didn't ring the doorbell or knock. He always sent her a text when he had arrived in case the boys were still sleeping, as they were now.

Without waiting for a text, Paige opened the door—and then froze. It wasn't Demo standing on her front porch.

* * *

DEMO PARKED outside the clubhouse and strode inside. It was only nine-ish at night. He would have loved to stay at Paige's but could tell she was exhausted. He tried to get her to sit down so he could wash the dishes, but she flat-out refused. Stubborn woman. Demo figured the least he could do was leave so she could get to bed earlier. He loved their sensual late nights together, but not at the cost of her getting a good night's sleep.

He wanted his presence in her life to make things *easier* on her, not harder.

There wasn't much going on in the clubhouse these days after dark. The members with kids were already in their individual homes and the singles were at *Demon's*. Demo wasn't sure he liked a quiet clubhouse. He didn't miss the partying itself, but maybe the atmosphere. He wasn't really sure.

Wandering down the hall to the apartments, he spotted Pumpkin pacing with SJ in his arms. Demo approached his friend.

Pumpkin gave him a chin lift but did not stop his pacing or jostling. When Demo peered over his crooked arm to see if SJ was asleep, Pumpkin said, "You can talk. Kid can sleep through anything once he's *actually* asleep. Unfortunately, he doesn't seem to want to sleep in his crib right now. Cries every time I put him down but goes right to sleep when I hold him."

Demo frowned. "So how are *you* supposed to get to sleep?"

"No clue. When I figure it out, I'll let you know," Pumpkin answered dryly. "If he keeps it up, though, I might have to go to the ladies. I can't keep working the heavy machinery at the shop on only a couple hours sleep."

Pumpkin worked at Grumpy's auto garage. He was a CDL driver and drove their tow trucks or flat beds as needed.

Demo leaned back against the wall next to his apartment door frame. "Do you miss it?"

Pumpkin raised an eyebrow. "Sleep? Fuck, yes."

Demo snorted. "I meant being single. This time last year, this place would have had a party raging all night. Now it's empty and quiet, and it's not even ten o'clock yet!"

Pumpkin continued his pacing. "I miss some of it," he said carefully. "Hell, you saw me those first few days after Bear told me I was going to be a dad. I did *not* take the news well."

That was an understatement if he ever heard one. If Angel hadn't talked Pumpkin off the ledge, Demo wasn't sure what Pumpkin might have done.

"But," Pumpkin went on, "more than missing how it was, what I don't like the most is how it feels like the club's divided right now. The singles versus the couples. We all have different priorities now. It's not all fun and games anymore."

"Not necessarily a bad thing," Demo commented, thinking about Paige and the boys.

"It's not," Pumpkin agreed. "It's just different. The club's expanding and we're hitting some growing pains right now until we figure out what our new normal is."

He had a fair enough point. Hell, a month ago, Demo would have never dreamed or considered that he was going to be counted amongst 'the couples'.

"Why do you ask?" Pumpkin inquired, still pacing. Demo saw his eyes narrow. "Why are you back so early? Is everything okay with Paige?"

"Everything's fine," Demo insisted with a wave of his hand. "She was exhausted and I felt bad about keeping her up so late all the time when she has work in the mornings. I was just thinking as I walked into the clubhouse that it was too quiet."

Pumpkin nodded. "I do miss the noise. You know how people make soundtracks of city noises when they move out to the country? Maybe I should make a recording of a good party and—"

Usher's *Yeah!* interrupted Pumpkin's grand plan. It took Demo a minute to realize that the noise was coming from his pocket. He pulled out his phone to see that Paige was calling him.

"Scotty get ahold of your phone?" Pumpkin chuckled.

No doubt. The goofy teen was always changing the club members' ringtones on them. He used to only do it to Lucky's and Sissy's phones but had expanded to the other club members since teaming up with Lila.

Clearing his throat, Demo answered the phone in a sultry voice, "What are you wearing, beautiful?" There was a long pause. Long enough for Demo to pull the phone back from his ear to see if the call was still connected. It was. Demo put it back to his ear, asking, "Paige?"

A little voice came over the line. "Is this Demo?"

Demo's blood ran cold at the fear in Mikey's voice. "It's me, Mikey. What's wrong?" He caught Pumpkin's eye and mouthed for him to call Bulldog. As soon as he got Pumpkin's nod, Demo started running for the front doors.

"A scary man is here."

Fury ran through him. He'd left them less than an hour ago! What the fuck?! Demo jumped behind the wheel of his Bronco. "Mikey, where's Nelly Bean?"

"Asleep. We're in our room."

Thank God for small favors. "Mikey, I need you to take the chair that's in the corner of your room. I know it's heavy so you're going to have to be really strong for me. I need you to push it in front of the door. Can you do that?"

There was a small, "Ah-huh."

"Where's your mom?"

"Downstairs with the scary man." Demo could hear the faint huffing and puffing of the boy trying to push the chair across the carpet to the door.

"Did you recognize him?" Demo pulled onto the main drive and immediately gunned it. Unlike some of his other club members, Demo didn't normally carry a weapon on him in a hip or shoulder holster. But he did have a gun in a lockbox under his seat just in case.

"No," Mikey whined, like he was in trouble.

"That's fine," Demo assured him. The scary man was dead regardless, but Demo wasn't going to tell the boy that. He caught sight of headlights behind him and recognized Angel's white Traverse. "Mikey, you're doing really well. I need you to do me two big favors. Can you do that?"

"Yeah!"

"I need you to place the phone as close to the door as possible. Leave the call connected and put it on speaker. Just put it by the crack under the door and leave it there. After that," Demo added quickly, "I need you to get Nelly Bean and hide both of you in the closet. Can you do that for me, Mikey? Can you put the phone down and then go hide?"

Mikey's fearful voice cracked as he answered, "I think so."

"Good boy. You're doing great! I am so proud of you."

"Are you going to save my mom?"

Fuck, yes, I am. "Absolutely. I'm almost there."

"Okay. I'm putting the phone down now."

"Put it on speaker," Demo reminded him. "And, Mikey, you were very brave to call me. You did good."

"Thanks, Demo," he muttered. Then Demo heard the scraping sounds of the phone being put down and the pitter-patter of small feet walking away.

Voices carried over the line. Nothing intelligible, but two very distinct voices. One male, one female. Paige was still alive.

Demo had been concentrating so hard on Mikey and keeping *him* calm that he hadn't allowed himself to consider the possibility of what was happening to Paige at that moment. There were fates worse than death, but Demo would never allow it to come to that. No matter what happened, Paige would survive and he would love her nonetheless.

Any alternative was unthinkable.

He made a sharp turn into Paige's driveway. He saw the porch light was still on and her front door was partly open. Through the shades on the living room windows, he saw two adult silhouettes standing very close to the other.

Demo pulled his wheel sharply to the left, blocking in the *Mercedes* parked in her driveway. Angel's Traverse pulled up behind him, but it was Bulldog and Bear who jumped out. Demo didn't pause to ask why they were in Angel's cage. He grabbed out his SIG M17 from the lockbox below his seat and ran for Paige's house.

CHAPTER 11

"*B*ack door," Bulldog ordered to Bear. The Road Captain nodded and ran off into the snow. "How many?"

"One," Demo said as he pounded up the stairs. He was not caring about a stealth entrance. Their headlights would have given them away.

The front door was already ajar. Demo shouldered his way inside. Not knowing where Paige was in the room, Demo kept the muzzle of his gun lowered and his finger off of the trigger.

A man in a disheveled suit stood in the living room. It took Demo a moment to see around the days-old beard and the stains for him to place Clifton Barrington. The once pristine, clean cut man from Keys' pictures was *not* looking his best.

Paige stood on the far side of the living room. She had tears streaked down her cheeks and red-rimmed eyes, but otherwise looked unharmed. Demo could not afford to spare her a longer look.

"Who the fuck are you?" Clifton demanded haughtily. As he shifted his body, Demo saw the small snub nosed revolver in his right hand.

Demo raised his gun, gripping it steadily with both hands. "Drop the weapon!" A sharp pain entered his shoulder at the quick movement, but Demo ignored it.

Clifton went to step forward. His arm twisted as if he was debating on raising it, but then spotted Bulldog behind Demo and thought better of it. Movement from the other side of the living room showed Bear entering with his Glock raised. Demo's club brother moved to stand directly in front of Paige.

Demo could not let himself outwardly show his relief. Not while her stepbrother was still armed.

"Who the fuck are you?" Clifton repeated.

"The man telling you to drop your weapon or I will fire mine." Demo might have been trained with a firearm, same as the others, but unlike his fellow club brothers, Demo had never fired his before.

He would do so now without hesitation if it meant keeping Paige safe.

Clifton glanced between Demo and Bear, whose large body completely hid Paige from sight. Slowly, he squatted down and tossed the revolver onto the beige carpeting of Paige's living room. It hit with a muffled *clunk*. Once he stood straight again, Clifton backed away from the weapon with his hands raised.

"Sit," Demo ordered shortly.

Clifton parked his ass on the couch.

Bulldog stepped to the side of Demo to pick up the snubby. As soon as Bulldog had possession of the weapon, Demo flipped the safety on his M17. He tucked it into his jeans at the small of his back as he rushed across the living room to get to Paige.

Bear stepped out of the way.

The fear Demo had been trying his damndest to suppress rose to the forefront as Paige came into view. She was shaking, her beautiful face coated in rivers of tears.

Demo wrapped her up in his arms, not caring in the slightest that the movement caused fire to burn through his shoulder and up the side of his neck. He'd burn for real for this woman and her two kids.

He clutched her tightly to his front, one arm around her shoulders and upper back with the other arm wrapped around her head. His fingers and face were buried in her thick brunette locks. Her scent of lavender, lemon, and peppermint permeated his nose...and he just breathed her in.

"Longest fucking ride of my life," he murmured into her hair.

She had her arms locked tightly around his back. Her entire body shook as she cried into his chest. It took him a moment to realize she was asking about her boys.

Demo raised his head enough to look over his shoulder at Bear and Bulldog. "The boys. Upstairs, second door on the left. Mikey was trying to move a chair in front of the door."

Bear nodded once and then left the room. Demo could hear his big boots pounding up the stairs. Mikey and Nelly Bean knew both Bear and Bulldog from playing with their kids.

Just then Steel and Lucky came bursting into the house with their guns drawn. As soon as they saw the living room, they immediately lowered and holstered their weapons.

"Upstairs," Demo told Lucky. They knew Bear, but they would be more comfortable with their uncle.

Lucky went running up the stairs after Bear.

Steel turned his icy gaze down on Clifton as he stepped up beside Bulldog. The man flinched and looked away.

Demo carefully lifted Paige's head up. She was a mess with red blotches on her cheeks, puffy eyes, tears, and snot. It made his heart hurt to see her so wrecked, yet it did nothing to diminish her beauty or strength in his eyes.

"Are you hurt?" he asked gently. He should have asked that first, but his priority had been getting to her.

She shook her head. "He just scared me. I thought it was you at the door."

Demo scowled. "I told you, I will always text you first. You should never answer your door without knowing who's on the other side."

Anger replaced her fear in an instant. "You think I don't know that?" she snapped. "I made a mistake, Demo. You don't need to treat me like I'm a child—"

He stopped her with a gentle kiss. Raising his head, Demo started to use his sleeves to gently wipe her face. "I know. I'm sorry. I didn't mean it like that. I've just never been so goddamn scared in my life."

She snorted. "You used to face down bombs for a living."

Demo gripped her face between his hands, forcing her to look up at him. "Never been so goddamn scared in my life," he repeated.

Paige turned her cheek into his right palm. "How did you know?"

"Mikey called me on your phone," he told her. "Said there was a 'scary man' in your house."

Paige glared at Clifton sitting docilely on the couch with Bulldog and Steel standing over him. "More like a fucking coward!" she sneered.

She made to step forward, but Demo kept her back. They still hadn't checked Clifton for any more weapons he could have hidden on his person.

Finishing wiping her face, Demo moved her curls away from her eyes. "Why don't you go check on the boys?" he asked her gently.

"Lucky's with them," she argued. "I want to watch you beat the crap out of Clifton the Coward."

Clifton blanched at her words and looked ready to bolt. A quick and terrified look between Bulldog and Steel had him changing his mind. He slumped further into the couch cushions.

Demo raised an eyebrow. Out of the corner of his eye, he saw Bulldog and Steel exchange a look.

"Oh, please," Paige pushed her way past Demo. "I might not be in your 'inner circle' but I've been around you guys enough to know you take security and family very seriously. You're not going to let him just walk out of here without at least a few broken fingers. Not when he entered my house with a gun."

Demo had no idea what to even say to her. Did he confirm her words? He wasn't sure what the others told their women. "Umm…"

Just then Bear came down the stairs holding a bundled up Nelly Bean in his arms. Demo saw the second Paige's priorities changed from bloodlust to maternal instinct. She rushed across the living room to meet Bear in the hallway. Demo couldn't help the sigh of relief that came out of his mouth as his shoulders slumped. He had *no idea* what he would have said to Paige if Bear hadn't come down the stairs with her son.

Looking up, he caught Steel's eye. Shifting uncomfortably, feeling like a little boy being caught cheating on a test by his teacher, Demo gave an awkward shrug. It wasn't like he'd *told* Paige anything. He couldn't help that she was so smart and observant.

As Paige took Nelly Bean from Bear's big arms, Lucky came down with Mikey on his shoulders. The five-year-old was holding onto his uncle's head tightly with his little hands but sitting up tall like a king. He even had his chest puffed out. Lucky had a good grip on the boy's ankles over his shoulders.

"Hi, Mommy!" he shouted loudly. "I did good, right? I called Demo to save you from the scary man!"

Paige reached up to touch his back from his added height on Lucky's shoulders. "Baby, you did really good. You were so smart to call Demo."

"Uncle Lucky said I was brave too!"

Paige wasn't the only adult who chuckled at the boy's not-so-subtle attempt for additional praise. "You were extremely brave," she told her son with true admiration. "I am very proud of you."

The little boy beamed from atop his uncle's shoulders. "Can I have a cookie?"

Demo had gone grocery shopping with Paige and the boys a couple of days ago. Paige had scowled at him for throwing in cookies, snacks, and some of the more expensive produce into the cart. He claimed he wasn't buying them for *her* but for *him* when he was over at her house. He just happened to let the boys know that the food was in the kitchen and they were welcome to it any time their mom said it was okay. Paige was not the sort of mom to allow her pride to stand between her boys and a good meal.

"Yes, baby," Paige said with a small laugh. "I think you've earned it."

"Nelly Bean too!" Mikey shouted down to her as Lucky carried him into the kitchen. Both Mikey and Lucky had to duck down so he could squeeze under the door frame, making the little boy laugh. "He was really good, Mama! He didn't cry or anything!"

"I think Nelly Bean fell back asleep," Paige said as she followed Lucky through the kitchen door while holding her youngest. "Why don't you save him a cookie for tomorrow after lunch?"

Demo heard Mikey's voice but not his words. He tuned out the conversation from the kitchen as he rounded on Clifton.

The man was ten years his senior but looked twenty. There was a grayish pallor to his skin and Demo had to wonder when the last time the man showered. In all the pictures Demo had seen of the man, he was always polished and well kept. His white dress shirt had food stains down his front, his tie was loose and not professionally knotted, and his pants had drying wet marks around his ankles and calves, making Demo think he'd walked through high snow at some point in his loafers and suit.

Demo didn't see a jacket or trench coat anywhere and wondered if the man left it in his cage.

"So how many fingers do you want to break?" Bulldog asked Demo. His voice was low so it didn't carry into the kitchen, but there was no masking the amusement in it. Good, at least his SAA wasn't pissed about Paige's comments.

"Who says I'm just going to break them?" Demo retorted.

"The fuck?!" Clifton shouted. He tried to sit up, to look important and powerful. But it was all a façade. "Do you have any idea who I am?"

"I know exactly who you are," Demo answered darkly, "and I don't give a fuck." He looked between his club President and SAA. "Do you have anything we can tie him up with? I don't want to do this here."

Which was code for, *I want him in the cellar.*

"Yeah, Angel should have something in her cage—" Bulldog started but then a pair of flex cuffs flew over their heads to land on Clifton's lap.

Clifton let out a shout as if someone had just dropped a grenade on him.

Bulldog let out a growl as menacing as his namesake was capable of. "Scar, you son of a bitch!" He rounded to face the former enforcer, who was standing behind them as if he'd been there all along.

On Scar's chest was a vest worthy of Batman. The club used to joke it was Scar's Bat Vest. It used to be hidden under Scar's club cut, but now he wore it openly. The vest consisted of many pockets that held things, like flex cuffs, in addition to the number of knives, daggers, and throwing stars in sheaths all along it.

"Outside, now!" Bulldog shouted, pointing an accusing finger at the scarred man. If Scar were anyone else, Demo was fairly certain Bulldog would have scruffed him to force him outside. Thankfully Scar followed Bulldog without argument—or vanishing into thin air like a fricken ninja to avoid whatever confrontation was about to take place between the two friends.

Demo wasn't sure if he could even classify Scar and Bulldog as *friends*. The word seemed too casual and familial. He knew the rumors around the club were that Bulldog and Scar had served together prior to the club. That made the most sense since Bulldog had chosen Scar to be his enforcer before Scar had left the club. But Angel had served under Bulldog's command and she claimed that she'd never seen Scar before she joined the club. Therefore, the history between Bulldog and Scar remained a mystery.

Unfortunately, the two seemed more at odds than any other pair of friends Demo had ever seen before. Demo knew that Bulldog trusted Scar *and* Scar had given up his place in the club for Bulldog. But Demo had to wonder what sort of conversation was going to happen outside in Paige's driveway. Besides a one-sided one, that is…

Clifton tried to scramble away but Steel threw him to the floor and held him there with a knee to his back. With ease, Steel cuffed the man's hands behind his back.

Demo helped Steel raise Clifton up onto his knees. "What was your plan, tough guy? To scare a woman and her two little boys into giving you money she doesn't have?"

"The bitch turned us over to the FTC! If it wasn't for her, my dad wouldn't have gotten arrested—"

Demo threw a punch at the man's chin to shut him up. Clifton's head snapped back with a sickening crunch. "That was for calling Paige a bitch," Demo sneered. "I would choose your words more carefully in the future," he warned. "Though, where you're going, it's not going to matter much."

* * *

PAIGE TOOK Demo up on his offer to stay the night. She was honestly grateful for it, not sure she could have gone to sleep otherwise. Demo told her he would sleep on the couch downstairs, but Paige took his hand and led up up the stairs to her bedroom. He took what was usually her side of the bed, the one closest to the door, while Paige slept on what used to be Richard's side. The boys slept between them.

Steel, Bear, and Lucky said they were taking Clifton to the sheriff's station. Paige couldn't help but wonder if there were going to be any pit stops between her home and dropping him off to the police. She hadn't been kidding when she'd told Demo she'd picked up on how the club handled some things. She hadn't seen anything herself, but she'd heard some of the ol' ladies' vague words, and more importantly, seen some of their pointed looks between each other. As if to warn one of them to not say anything incriminating or too openly. The men of the club were not the sort to let something like breaking into her house with a gun slide.

She wondered if she was going to need to go down to the station in the morning to make a statement, but Demo told her that it wasn't pressing.

As she fell asleep with her boys cuddled between her and Demo, Paige's hatred for her house increased. She couldn't wait until she was financially stable enough to move out of it. She hated everything about it—including her bed. She hated that she couldn't even afford to replace the mattress Richard had once slept on with her.

Maybe someday, Demo and she would go mattress shopping for a bed of their own. That was a nice dream to hold onto.

After he spent the entire next day with her and the boys, Paige was sorry to see him go. She tried to contain her sadness as she walked him to the front door.

"I wish I could stay," he whispered against her lips. "You have no idea how much, but I need to get back. Steel's called a meeting for the officers. I'm already running late."

Paige nodded solemnly. "Is it childish of me to say that I understand but I don't like it?"

Demo chuckled. "Not at all."

"You know…" Paige started and then bit her lip.

Demo used his left hand to raise her chin up. "I know a lot of things, beautiful, but I don't have the ability to read your mind. Just tell me."

Eased by his attempt at humor, Paige went on. "I was just thinking that maybe you'd like to come back here after your meeting."

Demo was silent for a moment. "It might be late."

"I can give you a spare key."

"It would mean remaining here all night."

"I was hoping it would."

He studied her face carefully. "Are you sure? As much as I want to say 'yes', I want to make sure you're really okay with that."

"I am." When he said nothing, Paige shifted uncomfortably. "Maybe I hope I am. I want you to spend the night, Demo. I just…" She shook her head. "Never mind. It was a stupid idea. Forget I asked."

"No." He used his left hand to move her face back towards him when she tried to move it away. "I won't forget, because I love that you asked." He leaned down and kissed her. "But my answer is also 'no'. I respect you too much to push you too soon, Paige. Last night was an exception, I get that. As much as I want to spend tonight too, I won't until you can ask me with confidence." He touched his lips to hers again. "Because, I'll be frank with you, I won't be able to leave your bed once I'm in it for real —as in, without two little boys between us. So make sure that's the move you're ready for us and I'll jump into it so fast I might break that one too."

She chuckled. "You better not."

"I make no promises." He kissed her forehead. "I really do have to go."

Paige nodded sadly. "Thank you." At his raised eyebrow, she explained, "For seeing I wasn't ready, even though it's what we both want."

"Your safety and wellbeing will always come first, Paige," he vowed. After one final kiss, Demo left her house.

Paige quickly threw the deadbolt and lock. Walking back to her bedroom, she peeked in on the boys first. Both were sound asleep. Paige was a bit jealous of that ability to sleep so soundlessly after what had happened the night before.

Deciding to get some work done on her finances, Paige headed to her room. She spent the next few hours going through her accounts. Over the last week, Demo had been helping her get everything organized. He knew about the insurance checks and how Paige had been putting the money aside to help pay off her stepfamily. Though Demo was confident that she did not have to pay back Richard's debt to them, Paige was not willing to risk touching that money until the restraining order was finalized. Demo advised that she pay current debts first and worry about future debts later. So her goal for tonight was to figure out which debts were most immediate and what to pay off first with the money she'd been putting aside.

They had also discussed her declaring bankruptcy. That was a scary thought in and of itself, but mostly because of the stigma surrounding such an endeavor. Paige needed to do more research on it and speak with a bankruptcy lawyer to figure out if that was a better option for her. Demo mentioned that he didn't know enough about it to advise her with specifics. However, he did know that it was generally better to file for divorce first and then declare bankruptcy.

Paige hadn't heard anything from Steel about what his PI found regarding Richard's whereabouts. Next time she saw him, hopefully he would have answers. If not, she would ask.

Ding!

Paige glanced at her phone and was instantly disappointed when she saw it wasn't Demo sending her a message. It was a notification from the foot fetish site.

Since going out with Demo, she'd only done a handful of requests to help make ends meet and none since they'd started sleeping together. It hadn't felt right. Not like she was cheating, per se, but close to it. It felt dishonest if anything. She'd told him about her debts and the financials for the clinic...but she hadn't told him about this.

Paige was about to swipe left to ignore the notification, but her finger paused when she saw the message. Her eyes nearly bugged out of her head. The request was for two thousand dollars!

She'd never had a request that high before. She was honestly surprised no one else had grabbed it up by now. This wasn't the first time some of the requests had sat there longer than she would have expected. But two thousand dollars? That should have been grabbed up faster than a winning lottery ticket.

More curious than anything, Paige opened the app. As tempting as that dangled carrot was, she had no intention of accepting the request.

> PRIVATE REQUEST: PLACE DONUTS (BIG OR SMALL) ON YOUR TOES. SMEAR THEM IN TOPPINGS OF YOUR CHOICE. THEN EAT THEM. I WANT TO HEAR YOU MOAN. BE NAKED.

Paige gagged. Eating donuts off of her toes? No, thank you. As much as two thousand dollars would help her, she had her limits. Plus, she didn't have any donuts in the house and she couldn't leave the boys to go get them...

Or did she? Demo had brought them donuts the day before for breakfast. Were there any left over? He always bought too much, saying he wasn't sure how much the boys would eat. Paige knew it was bullshit, but she didn't call him out on his generosity.

He was being sweet while also respecting her wish for him not to swoop in and save the day with money and objects. In all honesty, he'd found the one loophole she couldn't refuse: feeding her boys.

There potentially was a partial box of donuts in her fridge downstairs.

Paige put her phone down, shaking her head. No, this was crazy. She was *not* going to accept a private request to eat donuts off her toes. Even for two thousand dollars.

Her eyes landed on the Past Due notice for her clinic. Business had picked up so much that Abby had been coming in on a part-time basis to help her out. But she still was past due on her rent. Her landlord could pull her lease at any time and then where would she be?

She was still seventeen hundred dollars short on her notice. The request would cover that. Even with the fees taken out by the site, she would have some leftover to replenish some of her dwindling supplies.

Paige stood up. Leaving her phone where it was, she decided just to check her fridge. *If* she had donuts left and *if* the request was still there when she got back, then *maybe* she would answer it.

One last video.

* * *

"WHERE IS HE?" Demo demanded as soon as the Chapel's doors closed.

"In the cellar," Bulldog answered him. "Carlos made it look like he made bail and left town."

Demo raised an eyebrow. There was a time when Carlos wanted nothing to do with the club's grayer side of their lifestyle. "I hope that didn't cause an issue between you and him."

Bulldog shook his head. "The man threatened Paige with a

loaded gun with her boys upstairs. Trust me, no persuasion was necessary." Bulldog turned to Steel. "He did specifically ask that he knows no more about where Barrington is, though, or his fate."

Steel inclined his head in agreement. "Carlos doesn't know about the cellar and the latter is club business. Barrington hurt and threatened Paige and her boys. She's one of us and will likely become an ol' lady—"

"More than likely," Demo interjected. Looking around the table of his fellow officers, he declared, "She's mine. She might not wear my cut yet, but she's mine."

Steel's hard expression did not change, but Demo saw the approval in the older man's eyes. "I take any threat against an ol' lady and club kids very seriously. Demo has the right to choose Barrington's fate."

Demo didn't have to think about that answer. "Because of him and his father, Paige has been drowning in debt for months. So much so, she hasn't been putting the heat on fully in her house because she couldn't afford the electric bill. I plan to drown him just as slowly."

"Don't use the pond," Lucky warned him. He was sitting on Demo's left. "Our kids ice skate on it during the winter and swim in it during the summer. Breaking the ice on it could weaken it even if it freezes back over."

"I hadn't considered the pond," Demo said honestly. "I plan on having the prospects bring a bathtub down to the cellar and running a line below. Strap him down with weights. Some days I'll bring it up high enough to make him think he's going to drown while others I'll let him be."

"Diabolical," Ghost said with a vicious smile. He offered Demo a fist bump. "Love the symbolism too."

Demo was feeling a stroke of genius for it, even if he didn't say so himself. "Eventually, I just won't turn the water back off and he'll drown."

"It'll be more complicated than that," Bear said from across the table. "Human skin starts to breakdown from prolonged submersion in water. He'll get sores and fungal infections. The pressure of the constant water on him will also decrease circulation. Depending on how long you plan on dragging that out, he'll likely suffocate without even being fully submerged."

Demo shrugged. "End result is the same as far as I'm concerned."

Bear didn't argue with any of Demo's points. "Just be prepared for the smell."

"Barrington's fate has been decided then." Steel pulled everyone's attention back to him. "But Merrick's hasn't been yet. Given the evidence collected, I plan to call for a vote."

"He's seen our faces," Bulldog reminded Steel. There was a slight warning in his voice. "He knows who we are, even if he doesn't know where he is."

"I will not execute an innocent man," Steel argued back. "If we believe he's been framed then we deal with it. I will not risk punishing the wrong man and allow the actual culprit to plan another attack on us unawares."

Ghost leaned forward. "It's been two weeks. There's been no evidence of a second attack or anything else happening to indicate that he was working with another."

"We've condemned others with less evidence," Bulldog pointed out. "But," he added pointedly, "Cage is still holding strong that Merrick is not smart enough to have created that bomb."

Steel nodded slowly. "Barrington's fate is Demo's, but I won't make the call about Merrick's on my own. Not with the club at odds about his innocence. We'll meet with the others tomorrow." Steel turned to Bulldog. "I'm giving you until then. Any means necessary. Either get a confession or we figure something else out. Clearly, we are all too undecided amongst ourselves to take a vote."

Bulldog nodded solemnly. "I'll head down once we're done here." He looked across the table at Demo. "You coming with me?"

Demo had never been down to the cellar before. There'd been no point—and, frankly, the place creeped him out. But to exact his revenge on Barrington for his treatment of Paige and daring to enter her house with a loaded weapon?

"Fuck yeah," he seethed without hesitation. It was time to get his hands dirty.

* * *

THERE WERE donuts in her fridge. Paige begrudgingly carried the half-filled large box back to her room.

Crap. She was not looking forward to this. But it wasn't like the request would still be there. Someone else would have grabbed it up for two thousand dollars.

Paige looked at her phone and felt her eyebrows shoot up. The request was still there. Fuck.

Feeling sick to her stomach, Paige hit the Accept button. *It's not cheating... It's not cheating...* If she did this—and it was no longer an *if* because she'd already accepted the request—then this was it. Her last video ever.

Getting her camera setup out of her closet, Paige looked at the request once more. She had up to fifteen minutes to start the video. She needed the toppings it requested. Christ, she hadn't even checked her kitchen for 'toppings'. She had no idea what she had or what 'toppings' went on a donut other than sprinkles.

Down in her kitchen, she found a jar of jelly, some peanut butter, a bottle of syrup, and a can of frosting. The frosting was expired, but she had no intention of actually eating the donuts off of her toes. *Gag.* Since her face was not required to be on camera, she could bring her foot off camera, take the donut off of her toe *with her fingers*, and then just make chewing and moaning sounds that the request asked for.

Ugh. This was probably the most disgusting video she'd ever done. It was a good thing it was going to be her last. She was done with this. Utterly and completely done.

Demo could never know. If he ever did find out, she didn't know what she would do. Die of humiliation? But he would understand. Right? He was a reasonable person. He commended her for the sacrifices she made for her boys. He would understand that she did what she needed to do to survive.

God, what if Demo had a foot fetish?

Arms full of the requested toppings, Paige paused partway up the stairs to her bedroom. Demo had never indicated he had a foot fetish. After these past months and the number of requests she'd done, Paige was pretty sure she had the *opposite* of a foot fetish. If Demo ever tried to touch her feet, she might just vomit.

God, she hoped she would never find out if that was true.

Knowing time was running out, Paige hurried to her bedroom. She quickly stripped out of her pants, leaving her panties on. The request had said *naked* but there was no way in hell she was abiding by that.

Realizing just how much of a mess she was going to be making, Paige hurried to the boys' bathroom. She removed the clear shower curtain as quickly as she could while also trying not to make noise that would wake Mikey or Nelly Bean.

Once back in her room, she laid out the curtain to protect her carpet. If she ever did get a chance to sell this ridiculous house, she did not want to have to spend money on replacing the carpeting because of jelly stains.

Sitting back, Paige checked the angle of the camera to ensure nothing personal was in the shot. Then she placed a donut over her big toe like the world's largest toe ring. The cooked dough was too big and squished between her toes.

Paige hoped to God she was able to fake the necessary eating and moaning sounds. If she didn't do a good enough job convincing the payer, he could refuse that he was satisfied. The moment she'd hit Accept, the money went into an escrow account. If he—and Paige was using 'he' as a generic gender—refused to pay, she could appeal. Then someone from the fetish site would review the video and choose if the money would go to her or back to the payer. The result from the appeal could mean either she or he would have their account suspended or removed from the site.

Not that Paige would care about her account being removed as this was her last video, but she did want to get paid.

Taking a deep breath to calm herself, Paige pressed the button to start the live video. She picked up the squeeze bottle of grape jelly and poured it all over the donut, her toes, and her midfoot.

* * *

THE STENCH OF STALE, acrid air wafted up from the cellar upon Bulldog pulling the hidden latch. Demo stared down the rickety, wood stairs, but not with trepidation as he thought he would. In the past, when other officers had gone below, he'd stayed above. One reason had been Jumper, so he would not be the only officer not going below with the others. He could even argue the lack of space and his presence not being required. But the truth of the matter was that the cellar always wigged Demo out.

Bulldog clasp Demo on the shoulder. "Ready to pop your cherry?"

Demo snorted. "Other than the smell, it's not as daunting as I thought it would be."

"Yeah, it can get pretty rank down here. We send the prospects down to wash it, but I think the smell of fear has seeped into the walls. Kinda leaves a permanent pungent stench, you know." Bulldog reached into his pocket and pulled out a small jar. "Menthol rub, if it gets too bad. Just dab some under your nose."

Demo accepted the jar. "Is it usually this quiet?"

Bulldog started down the stairs first. Demo followed, pulling the hatch closed behind them. Even though it was late, they couldn't risk someone walking into the clubhouse that should not know the cellar existed. "Nah. Cowards are just hoping if we can't hear them then we can't see them either."

The dim lighting below only added to the eerie atmosphere. Demo knew that four sets of chains had been drilled into the ceiling by Cage when he'd added the soundproofing. A single drain in the middle of the concrete floor allowed for easy cleanup. Since the cellar was below ground and not part of the above HVAC system, it could get extremely hot or cold depending on the time of year. A small space heater was in the room, but it didn't really break the brisk chill of the room.

Chains rattled from the two hanging on the far right. Neither clothed, Billy Merrick and Clifton Barrington hung by their wrists. Even in the low lighting, Demo could make out the bluish tint to the men's lips and fingertips. Demo was sure Bear was monitoring the room to ensure the occupants didn't die of hypothermia. But being cold only added to their torment.

Nathan Moore was not hanging from the ceiling. The child rapist was currently nailed to a wooden chair, slumped over. If it wasn't for the puffs of visible air coming from him, Demo would have thought the man was dead. He recalled seeing Moore the day Ivy had dropped him off at the clubhouse as a 'gift' from Scar. Nearly seven months of constant, daily torture had turned the man into a skeleton. Flesh hung off of his emaciated form. He had no fingernails, toenails, or teeth from when Angel had removed them. His long hair was matted, greasy, and falling out in clumps. Demo couldn't see from where he stood, but he was pretty sure Angel had removed the man's eyelashes too. Either that or was planning on it soon.

All three men faced the wall where torture devices had been hung up neatly. Demo thought that was a nice touch. To always remind them of what was coming.

Demo walked over to where Barrington hung. The man was barely tall enough to be able to stand with his toes touching the floor. Blood coated his arms from where the manacles were digging into his wrists from trying to relieve his legs and letting his body weight hang from his wrists. Under his nose and mouth were still splattered with blood from when Demo had socked him at Paige's house.

"What the fuck did you think you were going to accomplish by going to Paige's house?" Demo asked him, getting up in the man's face. "Do you think she has millions just hidden away in her house?"

The man's teeth rattled as he answered, "Wanted to make her pay…"

"Your failures are not her fault," Demo snapped. "You made a deadly mistake by going to her house. If you'd gone there only to talk to her, I may have just broken some fingers and let you on your way. But you brought a *gun* into her home. You *scared* her little boy—your nephew! That I cannot and will not let go."

Demo gripped Barrington's chin and forced him to look over in the corner of the room where Moore sat, naked and nailed to a wooden chair. "Your *only* saving grace is that you did not harm Paige or her boys—or you would be nailed to a chair right next to him. I won't make your death last quite so long."

Tears started streaming down the man's face. A new stench rose up as Paige's stepbrother lost control of his bladder and bowels. Demo stepped away to not get anything on his boots. He might need that menthol after all.

Bulldog's expression was a mixture of disgust and amusement. "Made a man shit and piss himself. Not bad for your first time."

Demo chuckled. "Man's too much of a coward. A butterfly

would probably have had the same effect on him. Not sure it really counts."

"Take the win," Bulldog offered. He went over to the wall of devices. "Besides, it'll take a day or two for the prospects to get the bathtub down here. He can enjoy the scenery while he waits." Bulldog picked up a pair of brass knuckles. "Merrick, here, is a different story. His time has come to an end. Whether he tells me what I want to know or not." Turning over his shoulder so he was speaking directly at Merrick, Bulldog added, "Telling me what I want to know only makes the end more painless."

Merrick, dirty and cold, tried to hock a loogie at Bulldog but was too dehydrated. Demo was pretty sure he said something along the lines of "fucking moron".

Demo leaned up against the table that was against the wall of torture devices. There were no chairs in the cellar—except for the one Moore occupied. He crossed his arms over his chest. "Got anything to take off fingers?"

Bulldog handed him a pair of pruning shears.

Demo accepted them, but didn't approach Barrington. Being in the cellar reminded Demo that the wall of torture devices hadn't been set up for Bulldog, but for Scar. The line of daggers and throwing stars were all the former enforcer's. Demo carefully turned the shears over in his hands. "Can I ask you something?"

Bulldog threw a punch against Merrick's jaw. The man's head snapped back. "Of course." Bulldog used the fist with the brass knuckles to deliver a blow to the man's right kidney.

"What's up with you and Scar right now? You always seem angry at him."

Bulldog took his right hand to cover Merrick's mouth and nose, depriving the man of air. He held on tightly. Despite the man's struggles beneath his grip, Bulldog's voice was even. "I'm not angry with him. I'm concerned for him."

The concept seemed so weird to Demo. "But...it's *Scar*. He'll be fine."

"And you think he was 'fine' when he got that scar across his face? How about the ones on his neck, arms, torso, and the rest of him?"

Demo shifted uncomfortably. He'd never known Scar without those markings, but he could admit that Bulldog had a point. It wasn't as if Scar had been born with that scar on his face. "I guess he just gives off this air of confidence that it makes him seem infallible." Demo looked down at his left hand with its missing fingers. "I of all people should have been more sympathetic. I mean, none of us walked away completely unscathed."

"Some more than others," Bulldog added. As Merrick's struggles started to lessen as he suffocated, Bulldog waited another few seconds before letting the man's face go. Merrick sagged from his chains, unable to hold up his own weight as he gasped for breath. "Why do you ask?" Bulldog turned his back on Merrick to look at Demo.

Demo shrugged. "The few times he's been back, you always seem pissed at him."

Bulldog waited a heartbeat before saying, "I didn't ask him to go rogue. I didn't want him to. I brought him to the club so he would have a sense of family, a *home*, after what he'd gone through. For him to just throw it away?" Bulldog shook his head. "And for *me*? I'll never forgive myself for that."

"You didn't ask him to," Demo reminded him softly, remembering the Church meeting when Scar had turned over his cut to Steel. "I know both you and Steel feel guilty about him leaving, but it was his choice."

"I know that," Bulldog admitted. "But he was supposed to find peace here. Not going off hunting child predators and human traffickers."

"Is that what he's been doing?" Demo asked. "I mean, I knew he was going after certain people," he tipped his chin towards

Moore, "but I wasn't sure if he was still doing it. He just randomly pops up places, so I figured he was hanging around town."

"From what I can gather, yeah. He and Ivy are working on a list."

Demo hesitated before asking, "Look, you can tell me to go fuck off, but I've got to know: does he talk to you? I mean, he *can* talk, right? I always figured he could and stayed silent for the creep factor."

Bulldog raised an eyebrow. "The creep factor?"

Demo shrugged, slightly apologetic, but didn't say anything. Bulldog couldn't be blind to how some of the club were freaked out by Scar's silence.

Bulldog turned back towards Merrick. Without a word to Demo, he started on the suspected bomber like he was a living punching bag. Bulldog even circled around him, delivering heavy blows to the man's back.

Merrick gagged, grunted, and heaved, but nothing came up. Demo doubted there was anything in the man's stomach *to* come up.

When Bulldog took a breather, Demo threw him a towel from the basket on the table next to him for Bulldog to wipe himself with. Bulldog caught the cloth with ease.

"I think the rest of you take for granted how easily you walked away from your tours. Even Jumper with his torments..." Bulldog shook his head. "I'm not even sure he would understand. Scar wasn't just *injured* while out on patrol. He was captured for weeks. Tortured by the Taliban and watched as his teammates were slaughtered in front of him. Those scars you see on his neck?" Bulldog pointed up at the manacles around Merrick's and Barrington's bloody wrists. "I wonder if any of you have even pieced together how he got them."

Demo's eyes went to the prisoners' wrists. Where blood seeped out from them trying to relieve just a little bit of pressure off of their legs. He swallowed sharply, finally understanding Bulldog's meaning. The marks on Scar's throat... They were put there by something tight around his neck.

"I didn't know he was captured," Demo said softly.

"For weeks," Bulldog repeated.

Demo looked down at the shears in his hands. "That sucks." Which was probably the understatement of the century. He wasn't sure what else to say at the revelation.

"Scar's silence isn't a 'creep factor' or something he does to give him an air of mystery," Bulldog admonished. He took the now soiled towel and threw it on the table next to Demo. "I wanted him to find peace here with the club. Instead, I sent him down an even darker path. You asked if I was angry with him? I'm not. I'm *terrified* for him. There's so little of my friend that walked out of those Afghani caves that I'm utterly terrified that soon I'll lose him entirely—and I know that there's nothing I'll be able to do to bring him back again."

The two men were silent for so long that Moore regained consciousness for a minute before passing out again.

Finally, Demo said, "I don't think I ever realized... I don't think any of us ever did. We took Scar for granted without seeing his torment. He was always just...*there*." Looking up at Bulldog, Demo vowed, "I'll do better. We all will. I'll talk to the others. The next time one of us sees Scar, we'll do more to encourage him to stay."

Slowly, Bulldog nodded his head. "I appreciate it, but I fear it won't be enough. Scar has it in his head that he's better off away from us but I don't know why."

"Has Ivy said anything?" Demo wasn't sure what Ivy and Scar's relationship was, though he was fairly certain that it was more of a tenuous partnership than anything else. He had a hard time imagining it being physical, with how anti-touch Scar was.

Bulldog shrugged. "I think she knows less than I do."

"That's not good."

"No, it's not."

"I meant what I said," Demo told him. "If I see Scar again, I'll try to encourage him to stay. I know you don't think it'll do much, but maybe if he hears it from more than just you, it'll finally sink in."

"Thanks, man." Bulldog pointed to the shears in Demo's hand. "Need some help with that?"

Demo looked over to Barrington and stood up off of the table. "Nah. I got it."

CHAPTER 12

here was a heavy air to Church the next day. No matter what Bulldog did to the man, Billy Merrick was still clinging to his innocence. He shouted obscenities and called them names, but he never once indicated that he was responsible for the bomb found on club property. Despite the evidence, Billy should have cracked by now. From the way Cage described the man, he wasn't the sharpest tool in the shed. There was no reason many of them could see for Billy to still claim he was innocent unless he *was* innocent.

Steel slammed his gavel down on the table. Everyone went immediately quiet. "When we first discovered the cellar, I never thought it would be put to use in the way it has been in the past two years. Additionally, I never thought we'd turn into executioners. Don't get me wrong: I have no regrets. The men, and women," he added begrudgingly, "who have died by our hands have all deserved it. Whether they threatened us, this town, or the innocent, they all deserved to meet their fates. Some," Steel said pointedly with an inclination of his head towards Demo, "died too quickly as later crimes have been discovered. Regardless, we cannot raise the dead.

"I have never been conflicted about someone in our cellar before. I know what the evidence states, but I also know what my gut says. And I am questioning Billy Merrick's guilt. He's been in the cellar for nearly two weeks. Bigger and stronger men have not lasted half as long."

"The evidence is solid," Keys argued. "Everyone saw the video. Unless we believe that somehow *Yelizaveta* framed her husband and built that bomb, which I don't see how she could have because she was on the other side of their truck at the time it was planted?"

"I hate to ask this," Grumpy leaned forward, "but what sort of background check did we do on her? She's Russian and I know she got a green card into the country when she married Merrick. Does she have any connection to the Bratva or any other syndicate?"

Keys shook his head. "I did a *very* thorough background check on her. No connections whatsoever. She calls her aunt in Russia weekly. Beyond that, she has no other family. They were all either executed or imprisoned years ago when she was a child."

"How did she come to America?" Angel asked.

Keys shifted uncomfortably. "Merrick paid a mail-order bride service. Yelizaveta was *barely* legal at the time."

Other than the officers who already knew this fact about Yelizaveta's history from the time when they'd hired her, every-one's jaws dropped.

"Wait, so Yelizaveta is an honest-to-God Russian mail-order bride?" Pirate asked with awe.

Steel's gavel hit the table with an echoing *thwack*. "Yelizaveta is to be treated with respect at all times!" he admonished. "She is a hardworking employee who deserves no less. Her marriage and the circumstances of how she obtained sanctuary in this country is no one's business but her own."

Pirate nodded. "I meant no disrespect," he said sincerely. "I just didn't know that was still a thing outside of porn."

"Yelizaveta has been in this country for nearly twenty years and still struggles with everyday English," Bulldog pointed out. "That should tell all of you how little her husband pays attention to her. He hasn't even tried to acclimate her to this country."

Cage cleared his throat. "I've heard him call her 'the bitch' to some of the other guys on a jobsite. More than once. I've never put up with that shit, even before I knew who Yelizaveta was. He's careful not to say it around me anymore after I threatened to knock his teeth out last summer."

"He calls her 'Elizabeth'," Angel added. "He doesn't even use her real name."

"We can all agree that the man's an asshole," Steel interjected. "Unfortunately, if that was the stipulation we used for entry into the cellar, we'd need to build a rotating door into it."

"And a bigger cellar," Lucky stated dryly.

"He's more angry than scared," Angel added. She was running her fingers along the edge of the MC's insignia carved into the long conference table. "I even offered Moore a free day if he got Merrick to talk, but Merrick proclaimed he was innocent and that we were fucking idiots."

"*He* is a fucking idiot," Cage emphasized again. "I don't think you guys are comprehending just how stupid this man is. I am not saying anything against those mentally challenged," Cage quickly added towards Lucky. "I am saying that Merrick is just plain dumb. He is the worst plumber on the team. *No one* wants to work with him because they know they'll have to go behind him and fix everything he just did. I once saw him apply duct tape to a fitting because he couldn't figure out it was on backwards and that was why the threads weren't matching up." Cage shook his head. "There's no way he built that bomb. You'll never have me believing so."

"Any idiot with *Google* can build a bomb," Demo argued. "Hell, most supplies needed are in people's kitchens and they just don't realize it. Who here knows that sugar can be used to make an explosive more powerful than dynamite?"

Some faces looked more shocked than others.

Demo turned his attention back to Cage. "Only a really stupid person would use *rubber glue* to fuse wires to battery packs *and* forget to add a trigger."

"Or someone really smart," Jumper added softly.

Everyone turned towards the quiet man. As a general rule, Jumper didn't talk during Church. He preferred to listen. More than once, Demo had heard him tell Bulldog or Lucky that it helps to keep him in the present. Aerial was lying peacefully at his feet. Jumper was always careful of the wheelie chairs around her.

"You think he's being set up?" Steel questioned the other officer.

Jumper shrugged. "You have a man of questionable intelligence being accused of making a sophisticated explosive device that required making a homemade plastique. That in and of itself is difficult, regardless of one's search histories. The smallest mistake could make the plastic explosive useless or too volatile."

"He's right," Demo agreed. "We used to call it the Goldilocks Effect. The recipe has to be *just right.*"

"Yet he makes the one mistake that rendered his creation utterly useless?" Jumper inquired of the table as a whole.

"*He* put the bomb in the parking lot," Keys reminded them all, again.

Jumper shrugged, "Maybe. But who says he knew what was in the duffel?"

"You can't honestly believe someone was able to trick the man into leaving a *bomb* in a duffel on our property?" Cage scoffed.

"According to you, he's a dumbass."

"Even *he's* not *that* dumb."

Steel wrapped his knuckles on the wood table. "The bomb

took time to create. Regardless of the fact that it was a dud, it took purpose and intent. Merrick lacks motive."

"He hates us," Pumpkin put in. "Yelizaveta has lent me a hand a few times with SJ. I've asked her how she likes working here. She says she loves it but her husband doesn't. He wants her to quit."

"Her broken English is difficult to understand at times," Lucky said gently. "I've tried to talk to her but it's hard. How did you get so much from her?"

Pumpkin shrugged. "My deadbeat of a dad was Ukrainian and spoke Russian. I grew up bilingual before he left us for his secretary. Took a bit to remember some things, but we muddle through. While I can't guarantee a perfect translation, it's enough for us to hold a conversation when she helps out."

"Why is she working here if her husband doesn't want her to?" Everyone turned to Grumpy.

Angel's eyebrows flew up. "Because a wife needs her husband's permission to work somewhere?"

Grumpy did not take the bait, though his perpetual scowl did deepen slightly. "Of course not. I meant, given her history and what seems to be the uneven dynamic of their marriage. Merrick seems like the type of man who is misogynistic by nature."

"She knew of the job opening from Harper," Lucky said from the other side of the table. Yelizaveta's son, Carter, was one of Harper's students. "Steel and I interviewed her. She likes cleaning and has always wanted a job but she can't leave Carter home alone. Harper assured her before she came in to interview that Carter was welcome here whether she was on the clock or not."

"Merrick not approving or wanting Yelizaveta to work here still isn't a motive to plant a *bomb*," Bones piped up from beside Pirate. Demo knew he'd been quiet for most of the meeting because he was trying not to draw Steel's attention to him. Steel was still pissed about Bones not calling for help following his therapy session two weeks ago. Since then, Will had been at Bones' beck and call per Steel's order.

"And around and around we go," Bulldog scoffed. "I am fairly certain we could argue this all damn day."

Steel hit his gavel against the table. "Which is why I am calling for a closed vote now. Normally we openly vote," Steel explained, "but given how divided we are, I am willing to do a closed vote should anyone here wish it."

Demo flipped the top sheet on his legal pad to a blank page as Lucky said loudly, "All in favor of a closed vote?"

No one spoke up.

Lucky turned to Steel. "Open vote it is."

Steel looked to Demo. "Ready?"

Demo nodded.

"Those who believe Billy Merrick is guilty of planting the bomb at the clubhouse with the intention of having it explode to wound and/or kill many of us, raise your hand."

Out of sixteen patched members, eleven raised their hand. Bear, Angel, Cage, Bones, and Jumper did not. Though an officer, Bear, as Road Captain, did not get a vote unless it was to be the tiebreaker. Since there were sixteen in the room, removing Bear from the voting members gave them an odd number so there couldn't be a tie. If someone was absent or wished to transfer their vote to Bear, then he would become the tiebreaker.

Clearly, more than half of the club believed in Merrick's guilt.

"That settles it then," Steel said. He turned to Bulldog. "Merrick is yours."

Bulldog looked to Ghost. "I'm taking Abby out on a date tonight. I worked him over good yesterday. Take him his last meal tonight and let him say his prayers. I'll take care of him in the morning and then the prospects can clean up the mess."

Ghost nodded.

"Which brings me to our last topic of discussion before we

adjourn," Steel said, "we need to vote on patching in Sara and Will—"

Loud laughter rose from the other end of the table. Demo was one of the few around the table who looked confused. Bear looked like he was torn between amusement and nausea while Lucky let out a long groan and laid his head down on the table.

"Kill me now." His voice was muffled by his arms and the wood table, but Demo was close enough to hear him where others probably couldn't.

"What's going on?" Demo asked Ghost, who was keeled over laughing.

Steel smacked his gavel down on the table numerous times. "What the fuck is wrong with you? If something happened that would prevent either Sara or Will from being patched in, I need to know about it."

The table quieted down, but most of the members were looking at Lucky expectantly.

"Lucky?" Steel demanded. "Is something going on with Sara?"

The question was a reasonable one. At Christmas, Lucky's daughter, Sissy, had come out to the club as bisexual and was dating Sara, the club's female prospect. Rumor had it that Lucky had not handled this revelation well. Not because of his daughter's sexuality but because Sara had not come to him to ask permission to date his daughter. After whatever family confrontation had taken place, Lucky had pronounced to the club that he supported and approved of their relationship. No one had said a word about it since. It just was.

Like the action pained him, Lucky sat up. He did look a little green in the face. "Scotty was really excited by the news that Sara's going to be patched in soon." He spoke as if he had something sour in his mouth. "He asked Sara if he could give her her road name like he did with Grumpy and Pirate."

Snickers came from around the table again but were silenced by Steel's intense glare.

255

Lucky tried to speak but failed. Demo seriously wondered if he was going to throw up. Finally, he was able to get out, "Apparently, Scotty overheard Sissy and Sara talking about...scissoring and," he winced, "how *great* Sara is at...scissoring..." Lucky swallowed hard. "So he wants to give Sara the road name of 'Scissors' and then asked Sara to see her scissor collection."

There was a collective silence before the entire room, aside from Lucky and Steel, burst out into uncontrollable roars of laughter.

* * *

Once everyone calmed down enough for the votes to be cast, it was unanimously decided that Will and Sara would receive their patches the following week. Viktor and Darrin, the club's newest prospects, would be arriving around the same time. Mitch's vote wouldn't be until mid-March.

Lucky got outvoted as to whether Sara would be named 'Scissors'. Since no one had a specific name for Will, he got to choose his own. Once Demo had his road name, he would be able to order the rockers and patches necessary for their new cuts.

Demo also planned to ask Sara, or Scissors, if she wanted him to order her a property cut for Sissy. Once Sara was patched in, she could claim Sissy as her ol' lady. Demo didn't want to presume but he was ordering a property cut for Paige and denim cuts for her boys for when she was ready. Dare he hope by the first club run of the year?

The clubhouse was crowded as the patched members descended the stairs. Before heading to Church earlier, Demo had dropped Paige, Mikey, and Nelly Bean off at Harper and Lucky's house. The four of them were heading to Johnstown after the meeting to spend the afternoon at a trampoline park that had a toddlers' foam pit.

The sight of Paige and her boys mixed in amongst the ol'

ladies and club kids did something to Demo's insides. It settled a part of him that he hadn't even realized had been unsettled within him. The only other time he had ever felt something like it was his first time returning to American soil after his deployment. Like walking off a ship you hadn't realized was rocking until you stepped back onto solid land.

He walked right up to her, sidestepping where the boys were playing on a rug with Caleb, Abby and Bulldog's boy, and leaned over where she was sitting on the couch to kiss her.

He felt her lips curve into a smile against his. "Hi," she let out in a chuckled breath.

"Hey," Demo said.

A tugging on his pants had him looking down to see Mikey had seated himself on Demo's right foot and was holding himself to his calf. Realizing this, Nelly Bean followed suit with the other foot. Looking disheartened that Demo didn't have a third leg—the immature boy that resided in Demo's head let out a snort at the unintended innuendo—Caleb started to pout.

Unable to resist, Demo dropped his right arm down so the toddler could leap onto it and swing like Tarzan on a vine.

"If you'll excuse me," Demo said down to a smiling Paige, "I have to go walk over there," he pointed randomly over his left shoulder with his thumb, "for no apparent reason whatsoever."

"Of course," she answered while also taking out her phone. "Don't let me stop you. That's a very important reason to head in that random direction."

Weighed down by three giggling munchkins, Demo hobbled his way around the clubhouse. The parasites currently attached to his legs and arm laughed and giggled as he took exaggerated steps and swung his arm needlessly. Demo waved to his club brothers and even stopped at the bar to have a very animated conversation with Ranger behind it. Then he made his way back over to Paige on the couch.

The adoring smile she gave him was totally worth it.

"Good thing I wore a belt today," he commented as he sat down on the opposite side of the couch from her. He turned on his butt, swinging legs and children up onto her lap. He brought Caleb up onto his chest.

Paige grabbed up her boys as they scrambled to hug her. "Probably not the time or place to lose your pants."

Demo chuckled. He took exaggerated breaths to make Caleb rise and fall on his chest. The two-year-old toddler held on to his hands tight like he was on an exhilarating roller coaster ride.

"The boys and I just had lunch with the others," Paige told him. "We're ready to go when you are."

"Good. Why don't you take the boys to the bathroom? I snacked a little upstairs but I want to make a sandwich or something for the road. Coffee?" he asked her.

"Please. My water bottle's in my purse at the door. Can you fill that and the boys' travel cups?"

"Of course. Let me see if I can find any takers for this one." It wasn't like Abby or Bulldog were hiding.

Demo swung Caleb up over his shoulder and lugged him off, calling out playfully that he had a kid for sale. Unfortunately, the boy's parents claimed him before Demo could make any money off of him.

* * *

THE BOYS HAD a blast at the trampoline park. Demo even went into the foam pit with Nelly Bean because he was too short and would have gotten lost in the foam blocks. Paige loved how taken the boys were with Demo. Despite her reservations about jumping into a relationship with him so quickly, she hoped it was a good sign for their future.

They both fell asleep on the car ride home, so Paige was extremely grateful for Demo's help in getting them all into her house before leaving for the night.

The house was quiet as she started breakfast—*not donuts!*—and the coffee machine the next morning. Demo had been appalled when he'd discovered she was reusing coffee grounds. The next day, a delivery box came to her door with probably a year's worth of coffee. The company, *Grounds and Hounds*, used a portion of their profits to support animal rescue organizations for dogs. Damn him for finding another loophole, because there was no way she could have returned that coffee knowing the funds from his purchase were going to such a good cause.

Demo was still denying having any part in the fact that cream and sugar had mysteriously shown up in her fridge and cabinet that day too. Paige shook her head, fighting the amusement she should not feel every time she saw that damn cardboard box of coffee bags in her pantry.

Tires on her drive had Paige looking out her window. She smiled at the sight of the Bronco. Though she'd learned her lesson about opening the door without checking who it was, she didn't wait for his text message. Paige watched Demo exit his car and walk up her steps. He paused there to pull out his phone.

Before he could message her, Paige unlocked and opened the front door. She held out his mug of coffee, grinning at the surprise on his face.

"Fuck, I need that." He took the coffee from her hand and stepped inside. After closing and locking the door, he placed the mug on the little shelf built into the wall by the door. It was supposed to be for keys but Paige always kept hers in her purse. Therefore the space was empty for him to put the mug in.

Then he took her by her shoulders, spun her around until her back was to the front door, and he kissed her. "Need you more," he moaned into her mouth.

As sleep and caffeine deprived as Demo was that morning, there was nothing like the feel and taste of Paige to get his body and mind moving. She was a wonder and he loved seeing that wicked smile on her face when she'd surprised him at the door. The lack of noise in the house confirmed that the boys still weren't up yet.

Good. Demo needed more of Paige. So much more.

Pinning her to the door, he took his fill of her mouth. She tasted like coffee and toast. He would need to get her a more substantial breakfast after this. She could insist she wasn't a 'breakfast person' all she wanted, but he was still going to make her eat more. If they could wear the boys out again this morning and early afternoon, there could be adult time later during their nap time.

Careful not to be too rough, Demo spun her around until her front pressed against the thick wood of the door. He rubbed his own wood against her spandex encased ass. Paige moaned, pushing back against his hard cock. Demo made quick work of her lounge pants. He loved how her ass looked in them, but right now they were in his way. He dropped them and her panties down to her knees.

Winter clothing was so overrated. If it was warmer out, she might be in a summer dress that required only a quick flip of her skirt to get to her sex. Fuck, he couldn't wait. The idea of stealing some quickies with her in some not-so-private places held some serious appeal.

Demo would never allow another man to see her naked. Her body was for his eyes only. But hearing her moans? Knowing that *he* was the one giving her pleasure? Fuck yeah. If Paige was all for it, so was he.

He kicked her legs as wide as her pants would allow her to go. A quick check with his fingers confirmed she was soaked between her thighs.

Demo removed the condom pack he kept in the front pocket

of his jeans for occasions just like this. He lowered his zipper, freed his straining cock, and sheathed it in the latex. Paige's tight little ass tempted him like no other, but that would take more time and prep than they had at the moment.

"Wet already?" he murmured into her ear. His teeth scraped along her lobe. "You dirty, dirty girl."

"Only for you," she moaned, tilting her head to give him better access to her ear and neck.

Demo's chuckle was low and heady. "Damn straight, only for me." He nipped at her exposed neck, though not hard enough to break the skin or leave a mark. As much as he wanted to, Paige could not go to work the next day with a hickey on her neck. "You're mine, Paige Hannigan. Only mine." He rubbed his cock between the gap of her thighs. "Say it. Tell me who you belong to."

He worked his right hand under her shirt and into the cup of her breast.

"You!" she gasped as he pinched a nipple. "I belong to you, Demo!" Before he could respond, Paige reached behind herself and grabbed his cock. "But you belong to me too!"

Paige backed herself up, sliding his cock inside her tight, wet pussy.

Demo groaned, relishing every inch that he sank into her. "Fuck yes!" He leaned down and kissed the back of her neck. Paige dropped her hand as his pelvis ground against her ass, his cock inside her as far as it could go.

Paige braced both hands against the front door. Demo had his left hand on her hip to help guide her and his right continued to play with her nipple. Her back pressed against his chest, their hearts thundering against each other.

He fucked her slow at first, letting her adjust. Eventually, though, he simply couldn't stop himself. He increased his speed, pounding into her again and again. Her moans grew louder with each thrust. Aware they were out in the open where small people could come walking in on them at any moment, Demo brought his left palm up to her mouth to help muffle her cries of pleasure.

Dropping his right hand down, he rubbed ruthlessly against her engorged clit.

Paige cried out as she came around his cock, his palm blocking the sound.

The feel of her inner walls fluttering around him had Demo coming too. He pressed his mouth to the back of her head, burying his face in her thick curls to dampen his own noises.

They fell against each other, Paige's arms giving out until they were both using the door to stay upright. Demo held her close, savoring the smell and feel that was Paige.

"How did I get so lucky as to find you?" he muttered against her hair.

"Pretty sure you had no choice." Her voice was breathless from their shared passion, but humor rang loudly. "Steel threatened to drag you to me by the ear, if you recall."

Demo chuckled. "Remind me to send him a Thank You card."

* * *

SINCE THE BOYS had gone to bed without a bath the night before, Demo and Paige spent most of the morning in the bathroom with them trying to contain the water to the limits of the porcelain tub. Demo didn't have a spare change of clothes with him, so he removed his sweater—much to Paige's appreciation.

It was very domestic, the act of giving two giggling and squirming boys a bath. It certainly hadn't been on the list of things Demo expected to be doing with them that day. But there was a simplicity to it that brought joy to him.

Both Mikey and Nelly were big enough that they could sit up on their own and only needed assistance with the actual bathing part. Paige had a couple of water toys for them. Demo didn't know much about kids or their needs, but he couldn't help feeling like the number of toys was limited. It wouldn't shock him in the slightest if he learned that Paige had to sell some, or most, of their toys. He'd picked up early on that they didn't have electronics in the house other than Paige's phone.

He wished he could do more. He wasn't rich by any stretch of the imagination, but he lived comfortably. He didn't pay rent or utilities living at the clubhouse. He owned his Bronco and hog outright. With limited expenses, he'd been able to save a good chunk of change.

He'd spend every last quarter on Paige and these wiggly, soaked boys if she'd let him. All he would ask for in return would be a kiss. He would never demand sex or even the promise of a life with him in exchange for helping her. That wouldn't be right, nor would it be honorable. All he needed was her happiness.

Some *Disney* soundtrack was playing on his phone. He knew Paige had a cheaper, limited-data phone plan so he offered to stream the music from his account. Christ, it would be so simple to add her to his phone line if she would let him.

Richard Wagner's *Ride of the Valkyries* interrupted a song about not talking about some guy named Bruno.

Paige's eyebrows flew up in confusion as Demo dried his hands off with the towel that had been covering his lap.

"Scotty likes to change our ringtones," Demo said in way of explaining the song choice. "Lila's been helping him to expand his song choices."

"Is that why Bulldog's ringtone was *I'm Sexy and I Know It* the other day?"

Demo laughed as he reached for his phone that was sitting up on the bathroom vanity, safely out of the splash zone. Unlike him. He'd had to move a towel to his lap to save his jeans or risk needing to take those off too.

Paige might be comfortable with him helping to bathe the boys, but he was pretty sure that would change if he started stripping down to his birthday suit too.

"No doubt," he answered Paige as he slid his thumb across the screen. "Steel, what's up?"

"Are you with Paige?" his President asked without preamble.

"Yes," Demo answered honestly. Paige and he were sitting close enough on the tiled floor beside the tub that there was a chance she could hear Steel's voice without Demo having to put his phone on speaker. To warn Steel that she was near without being obvious, Demo said, "We're giving the boys a bath. What's up?"

Steel got the message. "Are you able to come to the clubhouse when you're done? There's no rush. It's not going to change what we discovered."

Demo's eyes flew to Paige. She stiffened, having heard. He raised an eyebrow at her. Steel hadn't phrased his statement like a question for Demo's benefit. "Did you hear him?"

Paige nodded rigidly. "Just tell me." Even her voice sounded stilted. Demo tilted the phone more towards her. The boys were playing obliviously beside them. "Just tell me, Steel. Please."

Steel didn't say anything for a moment and then his gruff voice changed her life forever. "He's dead, sweetheart. I'm sorry."

Paige let out a mix between a sob and a whimper. She closed her eyes, turning her face into her right shoulder.

Demo transferred his phone to his left hand and brought it to his ear. "We'll be there as soon as we can," he told Steel as he placed his right hand on Paige's shoulder.

"We'll be waiting," Steel said shortly before hanging up the phone.

Demo knew this was coming. It was the cleanest way to break Paige of her marriage without Keys having to fake a divorce. Paige might get suspicious if she never spoke directly to or saw Richard during the entire process. Richard *was* dead. Telling her was the right thing to do—even if the club fudged some of the details surrounding his death.

Demo didn't know what Steel had planned. It was decided to keep him in the dark so his reactions were a bit more genuine. Another thing Demo hated about the entire situation. If it was only his fate in her hands, Demo would sit her down and tell her everything. From start to finish.

But it wasn't just him.

It wasn't a lack of faith in her either. Demo believed in the club and the good they were doing. There had to be a path where Demo could not betray his club but still be honest with Paige. This was the closest he could think of.

By telling her Richard was dead, not only would Paige get closure but so would Harper and her parents. Demo could care less about Ronald Hannigan's feelings, but he liked Cindy. She deserved to be able to officially grieve her son. To know once and for all that he wasn't coming back. Harper suspected, but like the Hannigans, she didn't know Richard's actual fate.

Perhaps in doing it this way, they could all move on. The Hannigans and the club. Richard had brought a blight to Mount Grove, but he'd also brought Harper, Paige, his sons, and Cindy. Demo couldn't entirely fault the man. In a twisted way, he owed him.

Demo let Paige have a minute. He knew better than to ask her if she was okay. She'd openly told him that she didn't love Richard anymore. That it had been years since she had and was only sticking out her marriage for the sake of her sons.

But Richard was a part of her life whether Demo liked it or not. It chafed, knowing the bastard had her first, but Demo couldn't change the past. He could only move forward and help her do so too.

When Paige sat up again, Demo saw that there were no tears in her eyes or on her cheeks. She was shaking slightly, but there was almost a look of anger on her face where he expected to see grief.

"What do you need?" he asked softly. "Steel said to take our time. It won't change anything he has to say whether it's in an hour or in five hours. What do you need, Paige? The choice is yours."

She shook her head. "I need a bottle of gin and a pillow I can scream into."

"Done," he said automatically. "What else?"

She gave him a side-eye. "Really? I have to go deal with even more sh—" Paige cut her word short with a glance down at her boys. "*Stuff*," she amended. "All the *stuff* Richard now left behind. Can't do all of that drunk."

"Don't care," Demo shrugged. "If that's what you need, then that's what you need. I'll call Steel back and tell him that we aren't going to make it. Today, tomorrow, next week… It's not going to change anything, Paige."

"But it changes certain things," she argued. "I need to figure out what it means for me, the boys… Oh God!" Her eyes went wide. "Cindy and Ronald! I need to call them. And Harper."

"Stop!" Demo ordered. "You do what *you* need to do for *you*," he emphasized. "I am here to help you and take care of the boys. If you need to get drunk and shout or cry into a pillow, then that's what you do."

Paige shook her head, scoffing. "Bastard doesn't deserve my tears." She stood up, taking the towel that had been on her lap to dry off her hands and arms. "I just… I need a minute. Can you…?" She gestured to her sons.

He nodded. "Of course. Water's getting cold anyway. I'll get them cleaned up, dried off, and we'll meet you in your room. Okay?"

Paige nodded solemnly. "Thank you." She headed towards the door and then paused. Turning around, she said, "I'm not sad he's gone. I'm angry. Confused. Maybe even hurt. But I'm not sad. Is that wrong of me? *Shouldn't* I be sad?"

"You're asking the wrong man," Demo told her honestly. "You have a right to how you feel. After all he's put you through, I'm not surprised anger is your first reaction. Maybe sadness will come later."

She turned to go again. Only to pause. Over her shoulder, she said softly, "Thank you for being here."

"Of course. We'll be out in a few."

* * *

THE BASTARD WAS DEAD. Paige was a *widow*.

In a haze as if she was drunk, Paige wandered into her bedroom. The room she'd shared with Richard. Who was now dead. The bastard.

She stood for a long moment in the doorway. There was no trace of Richard left in this room. She'd sold all of his belongings for every scrap of money she could, including his large mahogany dresser. Hell, there wasn't a trace of Richard left in this house after two years. Unless one counted the gaudiness of the actual house.

Christ, Paige hated this house. She hated everything about it. A family of four did not need a five bedroom monstrosity. It had a three car garage and so many electric 'smart' utilities that sometimes she wondered if it qualified as a robot more than it did a house.

Her eyes landed on her closed closet door where her camera equipment was. If Demo thought that it was strange the boys' bathtub didn't have a shower curtain on it, he hadn't said anything. She hadn't returned it after posting the donut video.

Shame washed through her—followed quickly by anger. The fucking bastard had left her and their two toddler children to fend for themselves with a mountain of debt, a house too big for them, and no resources. She'd starved herself, limited the heat in her home during the dead of winter, and had to sell her sons' *toys* to help make ends meet. And the fucking bastard had been *dead*? Had he been dead the entire time? Had the loan shark caught up to him before coming to Mount Grove and attacking Ronald and Cindy?

She didn't know and wouldn't know until she spoke with Steel's PI.

That seemed like so much energy. Did she even have that in her?

Paige didn't think so. It was too much. It was all too much.

She didn't remember laying down on her bed. That hadn't been a conscious decision. At some point, Demo came in with her boys. Their hair was wet but they were clean and dressed. From their milk mustaches, she knew Demo had taken them to the kitchen before joining her in her room. Her boys' innocent laughter gave her the spark she needed to sit up.

Paige leaned her back against the headboard and pulled her sons onto her lap. Then she spluttered out a laugh when she saw Demo had a matching milk mustache.

He pursed his lips like a duck as if modeling a new fashion trend.

Paige shook her head at his ridiculousness but was also grateful for it. She crooked a finger at him around Mikey's back to indicate for him to come closer. Demo bent over her. When she tried to kiss him though, he backed away.

"You'll ruin my mustache!" he exclaimed with feigned protectiveness.

"Where's my mustache?" she demanded. "I feel like the odd woman out here."

Demo brought his hand out from behind his back and held out a glass of milk for her. The boyish expression of excitement on his face was *exactly* what Paige needed to snap the rest of the way out of her funk.

She might be a widow, but she wasn't alone. That mattered more than she could express.

* * *

CINDY AND RONALD sat on the couch next to Jenna, who was present for moral support. Lucky held his pregnant wife on his lap in one of the lounge chairs. Though morning sickness had passed after Harper entered her second trimester, she had woken up feeling extremely nauseous—and that was before she'd gotten the news that there was an update on her brother's whereabouts. She was currently sucking on a honey lollipop while Lucky rubbed her round belly soothingly.

Demo had brought over two barstools for Paige and him to sit on. Paige had a death grip on his left hand that she held between her two on her lap.

Steel and Carlos stood in the background. Word had been spread for everyone to stay out of the clubhouse for the time being. The last thing Harper and Paige needed was spectators, even if they meant well. Mikey and Nelly Bean were playing with their cousins in the Pentagon backyard. There was a snowman building contest going on that should keep them entertained for a long while. Both were too young to understand what was happening. Though Richard was their father, neither remembered him.

Perhaps that was Paige's fault. Nelly wouldn't have remembered Richard regardless, but Mikey might have. While Paige made an effort never to say anything negative about Richard in front of them, she also did not make an effort to speak about Richard to them. She didn't mention their father at all.

Standing front and center was a police detective from Atlanta, Georgia. Paige hadn't been paying much attention when she'd introduced herself. She looked vaguely familiar, but Paige couldn't place why.

"He's been listed as a John Doe for nearly fourteen months. The city cremated him." Her southern drawl accentuated her words. She had her dirty blonde hair pulled back in an intricate French braid that started at the front of her hairline and went all the way down to between her shoulder blades. "The City of Atlanta will be shipping the remains up to you as soon as I get some information from all of you. Now that they know who Mr. Hannigan is, they will continue the case."

The detective turned towards Paige. "I understand you and Mr. Hannigan were married at the time of his disappearance. Were divorce proceedings started?"

Paige shook her head. "He just didn't come home one day. Things were really crazy around town. I still wasn't very familiar with everyone and the town itself."

"Did you report his absence?"

"I called Rona—um, Sheriff Hannigan." She looked towards her father-in-law.

"You were sheriff here at the time?" the detective inquired of Ronald.

"Interim, but yes."

Carlos stepped forward. "I brought our file on Mr. Hannigan's missing person's case."

The Atlanta detective took the offered manila file folder. Paige wasn't sure why it surprised her it was so thin.

"Not much here," the detective mussed. She looked at Ronald. "Your own son goes missing and this is all you have?"

Ronald shifted uncomfortably in his seat. "The first few days that he was missing, I...I didn't know what to think. There was also an arson investigation that was happening at that same time. My son... He had his problems, Detective. I'd warned him prior to us moving to Mount Grove that I was no longer going to dig him out of any more financial holes he got himself into."

"Are you referring to the financial troubles he had with one Mateo Castillo?"

Paige felt Demo stiffen beside her but was concentrating on Ronald's reaction.

Her father-in-law flinched at the name and then nodded.

"This would be the same Mateo Castillo who attacked you and your wife in your own home the following August?"

"Yes," Ronald answered gruffly.

Mateo Castillo must be the name of Richard's loan shark then. Ronald's reaction to the man was understandable. He'd tortured Ronald and threatened Cindy. Who knows what would have become of them if the club hadn't stumbled upon them?

The detective turned back to Paige. "I understand you've had some financial troubles of late." She indicated between Paige and Demo. "How long have you been involved with Mr. Snyder?"

Paige swallowed hard, not liking the implications behind the question. She'd been a widow for over fourteen months, but she hadn't known that when she'd started sleeping with Demo. For all intents and purposes, she *had* been unfaithful to her marriage because *she* didn't know she was no longer married.

"Less than a month," Demo supplied honestly.

"And did you ever meet Mr. Hannigan?"

Demo shook his head, "Never."

"It would be helpful to our investigation if you gave us access to both of your phone records," the detective prompted.

"Whatever you need," Demo told her. "Neither of us have anything to hide. Paige was not even aware of the extent of Mr. Hannigan's debts until creditors started contacting her a few months ago."

"Is this true, Mrs. Hannigan?"

Before Paige could answer, her phone rang from inside her purse. It was sitting on the bar across the way. Everyone looked in that direction. Paige sighed as she got up with a muttered, "Excuse me," to the detective. The only reason she was going to answer it was in case it was Abby or Bulldog regarding her boys.

When she saw the caller ID was her mom, Paige hit ignore

and threw the phone back inside her purse. She was *not* dealing with her mother right now. The woman had the worst timing ever and, frankly, Paige did not want to hear her mother bitch and complain about Paige taking a restraining order out on her husband.

There was enough drama going on in Paige's life right now that she did not need to add her mother's to it too.

"Sorry about that," Paige said as she retook her seat. "What was your question?"

Before the detective could voice it, her phone rang again. Paige scowled at her purse. She stomped over to the bar, pulled her phone out, ignored the call, and then put her phone on silent. She would deal with her mom later. Like, in five years.

Paige retook her seat.

"Are you sure you don't need to get that?" the detective asked with a raised eyebrow.

"No," Paige said shortly. To Demo's inquiring look, she whispered, "My mother."

He nodded his understanding.

"Mrs. Hannigan, other than contacting the police," the detective looked pointedly at Ronald and then Carlos, "what efforts did you make to find your husband?"

Paige wished she could correct her and claim Richard was her *ex*-husband. As morbid as the thought was, Paige was grateful that she didn't have to fight her way through a messy divorce. At least Richard's death would give her that.

But the fact that that thought even crossed her mind made her feel guilty, even after all he'd done to her and the mess he'd left in his wake.

"To be honest, not much. I inquired with the police often, but nothing beyond that. I had two small children at home that required my full attention and I needed to get my business up and running. Richard running off with his latest floozy wasn't exactly a high priority." Glancing at Cindy, Paige added, "Sorry."

Cindy waved her harsh words off. "It's taken me a long time, but I've come to terms with my son's faults. I know he had many and I'm sorry you got involved in them at all." She dabbed under her eyes with a tissue.

The detective gave them a moment before continuing, "So your husband was having an affair?"

Paige let out a long sigh. "I suspected for a long time that he was. I can't give you a name or names. I never saw actual evidence of such. There was a time, just before we came here, that Richard came home crying. He said he'd had a hard day at work. He brought me flowers and this expensive jewelry set. It was diamond earrings, a bracelet, and a necklace. I never knew why he was so upset, but I suspected. I always got gifts after he was away on business trips and I found more than one piece of clothing with lipstick stains or missing buttons."

Demo took her hand again. She squeezed it tightly. Her suspicions regarding Richard's behavior was one of the reasons she had such a hard time accepting gifts from Demo.

With her eyes on the detective, Paige missed the exchanged looks between Demo, Steel, and Lucky. She did notice Ronald's flinch, though, and suspected it was difficult for the man to add *infidelity* to his son's long list of sins.

Harried footsteps came barreling down the stairs to the main room. Paige had never been upstairs in the clubhouse. She knew the club called the large conference room their Chapel and it was where they held their meetings they called Church. Demo attended an officers-only meeting there on Fridays and then a meeting for all patched members on Saturdays. Even Harper said she'd only been up there once and that was because she'd followed Jasmine inside after the other ol' lady had barged into a meeting to tell them something she'd remembered.

Keys leaped down to the main floor, skipping over the last three or four stairs. He came running up to them, a frantic look in his eyes.

Lucky and Demo stood. There was a change in their posture and expressions that made Paige want to immediately find her boys and ensure their safety. Steel even moved closer to Jenna, though his attention was on Keys.

Both Carlos and the detective looked around as if for danger, their hands on the holsters guns at their hips.

"You need to see this," Keys said through gasped breaths. He handed Steel a large tablet. From her seat, Paige could only see a paused newscaster standing outside of a gated lawn.

Carlos, Demo, and Lucky moved closer to also see the tablet as Steel pressed Play.

"...outside the home of Detroit Philanthropist and Entrepreneur, Thaddeus Barrington. At this time, the Barringtons are not making a statement regarding this latest blow to their, up until recently, flawless reputations.

"For those of you just tuning in, in the early hours this morning, a popular adult website, Fan Feet Fun, *servicing clientele with a proclivity towards feet was hacked. The names, addresses, billing information,* and *fantasy requests of both the clients and the models have now been released to the public. On that list, is Thaddeus Barrington's stepdaughter. Married to* Barrington Holdings' *former CFO, Richard Hannigan, Paige Hannigan has been revealed as one of the models. She currently resides in Mount Grove, a small town in southern Pennsylvania with her husband and two sons.*

"The Barringtons, who have always claimed to uphold Christian-American values and strong family ties, have chosen not to comment on this latest scandal, one that has not been seen on such a global scale since the Ashley Madison *scandal in 2015. Politicians, city officials, and even members of the clergy are being named alongside average citizens. Unlike with* Ashley Madison, *no one is taking responsibility or laying out demands. Officials cannot confirm or deny if the once proclaimed* Impact Team *is involved again.*

"Unlike other adult sites that will accept fake names, profiles, and email addresses, Fan Feet Fun *requires all who subscribe to prove their*

identities before they can model or purchase products. *They do this with a picture of themselves holding up their country's driver's license or passport with a codeword the site provides to prove the picture was not forged or AI generated. The* Fan Feet Fun *company claims this is for the safety of all involved. Their earlier statement regarding this hack did not show any remorse for what their site has to offer, but rather apologizing to those on the list whose lives will never be the same. Back to you, Norm..."*

CHAPTER 13

There was a paused shock followed by all present turning towards Paige. This couldn't be happening. *This couldn't be happening!* No wonder her mother, who hadn't called her in years, had been trying to get ahold of her.

This day, which was already shitty from the news that her *runaway* husband was actually her *dead* husband, had just gotten worse. So, so much worse.

They had her name. She wasn't just some anonymous poster anymore. They had her name. The *whole world* had her name. They'd linked her to her stepfamily and were using her involvement in the foot fetish site to drag the Barrington name even further through the mud. Paige didn't know what other scandal or ridicule her stepfamily was currently facing, and she didn't care.

What she cared about was that *her name* was now linked to their immoral behavior. Was she proud of being a foot fetish model? Hell no. But she'd done it to survive. She'd done it for her sons. And she would never be ashamed of *that*. She'd done nothing illegal. Unorthodox, certainly, but it wasn't like she'd robbed a bank.

There wasn't much she would put past her stepfamily if it meant keeping their wealth and social status.

Paige wasn't able to look at any of them. Not her in-laws, Harper, Lucky, Jenna, Steel, Keys, Carlos, the detective... And not Demo. Especially not Demo. She never planned to tell him about the foot fetish modeling, but if she had to, she would have wanted it on her own terms. In her own words. In her own time. Not where others saw her humiliation, heard someone *else's* perspective.

Tears flowed down her cheeks. She swayed on her barstool. Suddenly strong arms were around her, pressing her side into his sculpted chest.

Paige slammed her eyes closed. She clung to him, unsure if this was the last time she would get to do so. What must he think of her?

* * *

"WHAT DO YOU KNOW, KEYS?" Steel demanded. There was a murderous look in his eyes that Demo knew echoed in his own.

Ivy Benson, former SWAT member of the Atlanta Police Department, looked just as furious. She'd been playing the role as detective as a favor to Steel. Demo wasn't sure what the plan was to explain her random presence around the clubhouse when she decided to stop in but figured Steel had planned an explanation for that too.

Nearly all of Paige's body weight was pressed against his chest. Demo held her tightly, one arm around her chest and the other clutching to the side of her head. He pressed his lips against her hair, which she'd left loose. Demo loved seeing her hair down, and not just because he'd learned Richard and her stepfamily had always been on her about taming her unruly curls. He loved it down because he got to play with her hair more easily. But he also loved counting the number of pens and writing utensils she managed to unconsciously store in her hair throughout the day. Bottom line, he loved her hair, up or down.

Fuck, his chest hurt. Whoever the fuck had done this was dead. Dead! He didn't know what sort of person had the skillset to do something like this and would leave that part up to Keys. But the actual *person*? Take away their computer and they bled just like anyone else.

That reporter had also just added his name to Demo's shit list. How *dare* he name Paige like that? Her name, her hometown, her life, her *sons*? The boys were far too young to understand anything about this, but there would be a time when they were older that they would.

Paige trembled against him, sobs wracking her body. Demo was helpless to do anything but hold her.

"Not much," Keys answered Steel. He had his tablet back in hand and was typing one handed on it. "It came to my attention only because I monitor anything that has to do with one of our names. Paige's name flagged during the report. As difficult as it is to believe, this sort of thing happens all the time. More often than people care to believe. They think their information is secure but there's always someone like me out there. Average encryptions are breached all the time. I'm not talking National Security level encryptions, but the ones used to protect your phones, devices, even banks and internet sites. Someone hacks in and the company pays their demands so it doesn't go public. That's generally how a situation like this goes. For the hacker to publicly post the information without any demands... I'd have to dig deeper but my money would be on that this was personal."

"Track them down," Steel ordered him. "Can you take down the list?"

Keys shook his head. "Even I'm not that good. The damage is already done. Do you know how many copies are out there by now? Copies of the copies? Pictures and hardcopies? The first thing someone does when they see something like this is take a screenshot, so they still have the evidence when it gets taken down. There's no way for me to track all of that."

"Are you saying there's nothing you can do?" Demo demanded over Paige's head.

"To take down the list? No. To find the hacker or hackers?" He smiled mischievously. "*That* I can and will do."

"What do you need from us?" Steel asked him.

"Nothing. Everything's in my room. Just don't be surprised if you don't see me for a couple of days."

Keys went to leave, hesitated, and then turned to Paige. "I'm sorry this happened to you, Paige. I'll try to make it right."

Paige hiccuped against Demo's chest but didn't respond. Keys looked up worriedly at Demo, who waved him off. It was understandable that Paige would not want to talk to Keys. Demo tightened his hold on her.

"We'll leave too." Harper stood up. She waved her parents onward. "Paige, I'm so sorry. We'll keep the boys tonight if you need us to. Just take care of you. This is a lot, and today of all days. Just let me know what you need."

Demo felt Paige's mouth move against his pec but couldn't hear what she said. Harper ushered her parents out of the clubhouse. Jenna followed after a quick goodbye to Steel. They all paused at the double doors to don their jackets, hats, and gloves before heading outside.

Lucky and Carlos stayed. With a jerk of his chin from Steel, Ivy left too.

Demo lowered his ear down to try and catch what Paige was muttering over and over again against his chest.

"...I'm sorry...I'm sorry...I'm sorry..."

"The fuck!" he roared when he finally heard. He released his hold around her, took her by her shoulders, and moved around so they were face to face. She still leaned heavily against him, like her bones had turned to rubber. "What the fuck are you sorry for, Paige? You have *nothing* to be sorry for!"

Her cheeks and shirt were saturated with her tears and snot was running freely from her nose. Her chocolate eyes bore such despair that it nearly broke Demo's own heart. She couldn't even look at him.

"I didn't..." Her chin was shaking so hard, her teeth were chattering together. "I wasn't..."

Demo leaned forward and pressed his lips against her forehead. "I know, beautiful, I know. You did it for your boys."

Paige's breath caught. His words seemed to knock her free of her shock. Slowly, she turned her body more to face him and met his eyes. "You know?"

Ignoring the slight accusation that reminded him of that day in the diner, Demo nodded easily. "That you became a foot fetish model to help keep a roof over your head and food in your sons' bellies? Yeah, I know. Or I guessed. Everything you do is for them, Paige. It's one of the things I love about you." When she gasped, he chuckled humorlessly. "I'll admit, my first reaction was wondering why you didn't tell me you had a foot fetish. We haven't been sleeping together that long, but I was still shocked it wasn't something you had told me. I even briefly considered whether it was something I would be interested in sharing with you."

At her disgusted face, Demo assured her, "It's not."

Now that she was sitting up more fully and under her own weight, Demo moved his hands from her shoulders to cup her face. "Paige, you are an amazing mom. Everything you do is for those boys. There's not a selfish bone in your body. Once the initial shock wore off and I saw your reaction, I knew that your involvement was monetary, not sexual."

She let out a pathetic little sob that was entirely unsexy but somehow completely endearing. Demo used the sleeve of his sweater to start wiping up her face.

"I didn't think I'd actually get any money from it, but I started to get all these personal requests. That's what the site calls it when someone has a private request. If you accept, you have to do as they ask. The money was too good to turn down. I owed so much to so many people and I couldn't risk being homeless or that my stepfamily would take away my boys."

"Did you…" Demo hesitated. He really had no right to ask, but he also wanted to know. "Did you post anything since we started dating?" At her quick intake of breath, Demo hastened to add, "I don't blame you if you did, Paige. I'm just curious."

Stiffly, she nodded. "Once. Last week. It was for two thousand dollars, Demo! I could pay off my back rent with it! I don't even understand why it was still there. For two thousand dollars, it should have been snatched up by someone else."

Demo leaned in and kissed her on the lips. "We'll figure out who did this, Paige. Keys is the best there is. The Navy were fools the day they lost him."

"What am I supposed to do until then?"

"Go on as normal," Demo encouraged. "There's nothing else for you to do."

"Go on like I wasn't just outed on national television for being a foot fetish model?" Paige scoffed.

"People have enough of their own shit to worry about," Steel interjected from behind Demo. "If they truly have an issue with you then they have an issue with us. And believe me," his tone turned dark, "they won't like having an issue with us."

* * *

PAIGE SAT at the reception desk at her acupuncture clinic with her elbows on the table, her hands gripping the hair at her temples, and tears falling down onto the piece of paper in front of her. It had nearly been a week since the hack on the foot fetish site. To say that it had been a good week would be a flat out lie.

It had been an awful week.

The fact that she'd discovered she was a widow at the beginning of the week wasn't even the worst part of it. The worst part wasn't even seeing all the cancellations on her appointment calendar or the spray painted foot on her clinic's front door. It wasn't even when she'd been in the grocery store and the cashier put a Closed sign on her lane when Paige had approached. Having the word *foot whore* texted to her anonymously didn't even reach the top ten.

No, the worst part—the absolutely *worst* part—was seeing the notice from her landlord, whom she'd paid in full, deliver her an eviction notice. He didn't care how many times Paige tried to explain that she was not using her clinic to *rape* her client's feet. The man wanted her out and was giving her two weeks to do it.

The bell above her door chimed. Paige looked up, hoping to see Demo, but wasn't entirely disappointed to see Abby. It seemed the only people in this town who hadn't turned on her had ties to the club. Kelly, the waitress, had been just as sweet as ever but her mom had refused to bring her products over to the clinic on Monday like they'd planned. Kelly apologized profusely, but Paige wasn't about to blame her for her mom's actions or behavior.

As it turned out, it would have been pointless for Jody to bring over her candles and soaps anyway since Paige had no clients and soon she wouldn't even have a clinic.

Abby was bundled up in a cute little faux fur hat that looked extremely white against her red hair. Her black coat was also lined in white fur and she had a white hand muff. "Brr!" she exclaimed with a smile. "It is cold outside!"

Despite having no clients other than VDMC members and families, Abby had still insisted on coming in for her shifts like normal.

After shaking slush and snow off of her boots, Abby looked and her eyes widened at what Paige could only imagine her face looked like. Bulldog came in then too. He was never far behind

Abby. Abby had to jump out of the way so her husband's large body could fit inside and the door would close.

Bulldog picked up on Paige's misery faster than Abby had. "What's wrong? What happened?" His eyes danced around, looking for danger.

Not having the energy or the words to tell them, Paige held up the eviction letter. Bulldog hurried forward to take the paper from her.

Bulldog took a moment to read the notice and then snarled out, "That son of a bitch! I'll kill him!"

From the rage on Bulldog's face, Paige wasn't entirely sure that was an expression.

Abby put a gentle hand on Bulldog's large arm. It was like her touch instantly calmed him. His face gentled and he looked down at her with nothing but love in his eyes. He handed her the letter so she could read it too.

Abby gasped, her hand flying to her mouth. "Oh, Paige. I am so sorry, honey. Is there any way to fight it?"

Paige shook her head. "He doesn't say it there, but he thinks I'm *raping* my clients. Using their feet during my treatments to get myself off or something sick and twisted like that." Abby's face paled. Paige suddenly gasped, realizing what she'd said. "Oh, God! Abby, I'm so sorry."

Abby waved off her concern. "It's fine. I'm fine." She struggled to swallow. "It's just a word. It can't hurt me."

As soon as Abby reacted to Paige's words, Bulldog pulled her against him, wrapping his large body around her like a shield against the world.

Paige moved around the reception desk. "I am so sorry, Abs. Please. Come sit."

Bulldog helped Abby remove her coat and hat. He unnecessarily brushed his fingers through her hair like he was getting snow off of her. Paige figured the man was taking any excuse to touch her.

Abby shakily took her seat at the reception desk. After hanging up her coat, Bulldog came around. He knelt beside her.

"I'm fine," Abby told him with much more conviction than she had a minute ago. "I promise, my José." She looked up at Paige, who was now standing on the other side of the reception desk. "What are you going to do about the letter?"

"What can I do?" Paige repeated. "He owns the building. He has a right to evict me and sever my lease. He had the right to do so the moment I fell behind on my rent payments."

"But you said you paid him?"

"I did!" Paige insisted. "But it only covered the back rent and the late fees. I still owe this month's rent, which I thought I'd be able to do *today* after having another week full of appointments. Which obviously didn't happen."

"This is ridiculous!" Bulldog snapped. "I'm not even sure this is legal."

"Say I fight it?" Paige argued. "What then? Clearly the people of Mount Grove have made up their minds about me. How am I supposed to make rent or buy supplies or pay Abby without any clients? I'm back at Square One."

Bulldog took the letter from Abby. He read it over again. "Does Demo know about this?"

Paige shook her head. "My landlord left about twenty minutes before you guys came in. I was still... I haven't even processed it myself yet."

"He's down at the dealership today. We're expecting a shipment in." Bulldog pulled out his phone and started to text one handed. "I need to call Susan Black. There has to be a way to fight it."

"And again I ask you what the point would be?" Paige nearly shouted. "Why fight it? People now think I abuse my patients. I can't stay in business with that sort of reputation."

"My Abby is happy here," Bulldog snapped without looking at her. "I'll pay the damn rent myself if I have to."

Bulldog did not see Abby roll her eyes over his bent head, but there was no contempt in the action. If anything, the cartoon hearts in Abby's eyes just grew three sizes.

Paige, though, was not blinded by love. "Bulldog, that is completely ridiculous and unnecessary. Not to mention unrealistic. I'll figure something else out."

Bulldog read something on his phone and then pocketed the device. "I am going to go meet Demo at Susan's office. Are the two of you okay here for about an hour?"

Paige opened her arms to show off her empty clinic. "I think somehow we'll be able to manage the crowd."

Bulldog said nothing to her. He bent over Abby and kissed her as if the two of them were the only people left in the world. Paige actually had to look away, the moment seemed too intimate to witness. "Be back soon, Red," she heard him promise. "Angel is right across the street if you need anything."

As he passed by Paige, he vowed, "We'll get this sorted, I swear."

Paige crossed her arms over her chest. "Clearly you're not going to listen to me on this." She waved him towards the door. "Go! Just make sure you mansplain in a way that my delicate womanly ears can understand when you get back."

His eyes narrowed on her. "You know damn well this has nothing to do with you being a woman."

"Yes, I'm aware," Paige snipped. "Abby's happiness is your top and only priority."

Bulldog gave her a stern look and then headed out the clinic's door.

Paige rounded on Abby. "How do you *stand* that? He's so overbearing. Normally, I look up to the two of you as far as romance goes, but damn. That was a bit over the top."

Abby looked adoringly after her husband. "He means well. There's something fundamental about knowing he'll do anything for me."

285

Paige could understand that. To a point. She knew that Demo would do the same for her. The difference was, she would fight him tooth and nail to do it herself first and *then* accept his help. Paige needed to know that she could stand on her own two feet. She didn't look down on Abby for needing such support from Bulldog. In a way, she admired her for it. But it just wasn't the sort of relationship *she* wanted and she loved that Demo respected that.

"What do you want to do today?" Abby asked her.

Paige shrugged. "I guess we can start on the back room. I was able to cancel the supply order I placed on Monday, but I mean to stay open until I'm forced to close my doors. I need to make sure I have enough supplies for the appointments I know are still going to come in."

Abby nodded and pulled the clipboard out of the bottom drawer of the desk. "Lead the way, boss!"

Paige shook her head but also couldn't fight the smile from touching her lips.

* * *

THE CHIME of the door caught their attention not even ten minutes later. Paige and Abby looked up, a bit confused since the eleven o'clock appointment had cancelled.

"One of the guys?" Paige asked.

Abby shrugged. She was on the floor with a box of cotton ball bags in front of her. "Probably Angel checking in on us."

Paige would not be surprised if it was. Bulldog would not want to leave Abby alone for too long. She got up from her spot on the floor. "Be right back."

Heading out down the hall, she tried to catch a peek as to who was out in the lobby but didn't see anyone. "Hello?"

Paige just barely stepped out from the doorway when a hard

body slammed into her. She lost her balance and toppled into the hallway. Her head collided with the edge of the frame. Immense weight landed on top of her, forcing out all of the air from her lungs.

She heard a muffled shriek of "Paige!" before she felt something wet draw a path up the side of her cheek. Hot breath touched her ear as a menacing voice snarled, "My goddess, I found you!"

Then a large hand tightened around her throat.

* * *

PAIGE CAME TO SLOWLY. Her throat and head hurt, making her wonder if she was coming down with something. She hoped not, because that meant the boys would likely get sick too.

Something grunted to her right. Her mouth was dry, but Paige found an obstruction when she tried to lick her lips. What the hell was in her mouth? When she went to move her hands to find out, she found they wouldn't budge.

Paige forced her eyes open. The bright lights above her hurt her retinas, but she needed to figure out what was going on.

Her eyes looked towards the muffled grunting sound and widened in shock when she saw Abby was sitting on her rolling stool. They were inside one of her therapy rooms. The rooms were nearly identical, but Paige could tell them apart. They were in the first one.

Abby had a cloth gag in her mouth, tied behind the back of her head. Her hands were zip tied at the wrists in front of her. She was pushed into the front left corner upon entering the room with her legs drawn up against her chest. Fear radiated off of the poor woman. She was trembling so badly that the wheels kept shimming beneath her.

Paige made to move to get to her but was once again stopped.

She turned her head to figure out why. In the mirror on the wall across from her, she saw her reflection—and blanched.

Paige was tied to the massage table on her back. Her arms were bound to each other by a long rope linking them underneath the wood of the table. There was a white cloth gag in her mouth, just like Abby. Rope bound her hips to the table as well as her shins. Her ankles were bound together.

Her shoes and socks had been removed, but otherwise she was still clothed.

Paige screamed! What the hell was this!? What the hell was going on!? And Abby! Poor Abby. She'd been through enough in her life. Who the hell could do this to her? Never mind herself. Paige could care less about herself. She needed to get Abby out of here!

The gag muffled her cries to where they were barely audible to her own ears. She knew that the volume she was hearing was more of an echo of her own vocal cords inside her body. There was no way she was projecting any volume.

But she still had to try.

A shadow moved in the doorway.

Both Abby and Paige froze at the new presence. The best way to describe the man was *mousy*. He was small, probably five-six at best, with a very lean and frail looking physique. It was no wonder he had to tackle Paige the way he did. She probably weighed more than he did soaking wet. He had short blonde hair, glasses, blue eyes, and the biggest ears Paige had ever seen on a man his size. They reminded her of Dumbo.

The man stood hunched over. He was fiddling with something in his hands as he entered the room. He was wearing a pair of jeans and a reddish turtleneck sweater. He had such a long neck that there was still a good gap of skin below his chin. The man was so pale, it was obvious he didn't get out into the sunlight much.

Paige had no idea how long she'd been unconscious. It could have been five minutes, it could have been fifty. Bulldog had said he'd be back in an hour. That wasn't an exact deadline, but it was probably pretty close given it had come from Bulldog.

The man walked to the bottom of the massage table by Paige's bare feet. Her stomach dropped as she saw him stare at them rather than her.

"I finally found you, my goddess." Even his voice was mousy. It had a high-pitched squeak to it. Paige recalled him speaking to her before she'd passed out and wondered if she'd imagined the malice in his voice or if he'd specifically spoken like that.

Paige grunted through her gag. She tried to maneuver her body but the bindings held her tight.

Was this man going to kill her? Abby? Oh God. What would happen to her boys if she died? She didn't even have a will naming Ronald and Cindy as their guardians. Demo wasn't their biological father or anything to them. No court would ever let him have the boys, not when there was blood family that they could go to.

And Abby? Paige couldn't imagine a world where Bulldog existed and Abby didn't or vice versa. Was it possible that their love and connection was so strong that Bulldog would take his last breath the moment Abby did?

It was scary how right that notion felt. Morbid and sad, but it fit them. There was no *one* without the other. They were two halves of a whole.

Was Paige about to die on the replacement massage table she'd had to buy after she and Demo had destroyed the first one with their lovemaking? God, she hoped not. Their relationship was new, but it *felt* solid, right. She loved him as if he was a missing piece of her soul.

There had to be a way out of this...whatever *this* was.

The man leaned down as he trailed a finger over Paige's right metatarsals. She flinched, not only at his touch but his cold finger.

"As soon as I saw you, I knew you belonged to me. I've," he leaned down and inhaled her toes deeply, "waited so long. I had to find you. I had to make you mine."

Paige had a sick feeling he was talking to her *feet* when he used the word 'you' and not *her* as a person. He had yet to actually look at her.

He knelt on the linoleum floor. He was so short that Paige could barely see his head over her feet. But she could see him in the mirror.

Horror suffused her as she watched in utter helplessness as the man pressed his clean shaven face into the sole of her foot. Paige tried to kick him off of her, but the bindings were too tight. She could do little more than wiggle her toes at him.

Unfortunately that only seemed to encourage him. He moved in ecstasy and raised up to take Paige's big toe into his mouth.

Paige heaved against her gag. It was only the knowledge that if she threw up, she would only have to swallow it back down that kept her stomach from retching back up the breakfast Demo had brought her and the boys that morning.

The man licked and moaned as he sucked on her big toe like he was a starving man devouring his favorite meal.

Paige tried to keep her head clear. The assault currently taking place had to do with the fetish site, that was *very* obvious. He'd seen her photos online and then must have tracked her down after the hack released her information.

Keys had been able to track the hack to an activist group known for taking down corrupt corporations and blackmailing politicians. Unfortunately, he also said it wasn't like they all lived in the same town and were working out of the same location. The hackers lived all over the world. But the self-proclaimed leader of the hacktivist group claimed they had nothing to do with the foot fetish site being taken down.

The last Paige had heard, Keys was still investigating. Paige was not computer savvy enough to know what that meant.

"Oh my goddess!" the man moaned as he moved over to her other foot. Worshiping it like he had her right foot.

Paige was barely able to swallow back the bile that rose up her throat.

"All the times we spent together... All the videos..." he groaned. Paige couldn't see where his left hand was but did not like where it looked like it was from her view in the mirror. "I was so hurt when you stopped accepting my requests. I knew I had to find you..." He licked the underside of her left foot from heel to toe.

Paige was beyond grateful that she did not have sensitive or ticklish feet. She did not want to feel *anything* even remotely funny about her situation. Even if it was an uncontrollable reflex.

Movement in the mirror drew her attention up from the man, who was now licking his rough tongue between her toes like they were weave poles.

Abby was carefully moving the rolling chair along the wall. As soon as she realized she had Paige's attention, she paused. Lifting her bound wrists, Abby held up the pointer finger and thumb of her right hand. She indicated her chin towards the man and then lowered her thumb multiple times like it was a trigger.

Fear replaced disgust. Abby was telling her the man had a gun. That must have been how he was able to subdue Abby without having to knock her out as he had done Paige.

Paige nodded her understanding. After glancing down at the man again, she moved her eyes to the open doorway. The man didn't seem to even notice Paige, other than her feet. It was doubtful he even remembered Abby was in the room. If Abby could go get help... Angel was right across the street.

Her legs weren't bound. As soon as she was out of the room, she could make a run for it. Paige had no idea where their phones were. Hers might still be in the backroom where she left it while they were counting inventory.

The look Abby gave her was full of sympathy, like she didn't want to leave Paige alone. Paige's was full of encouragement. If she didn't go get help, there was no doubt in Paige's mind that she wasn't making it out of here alive. She imagined being killed off and then the man cutting off her feet and having them taxidermized like some sick, fucked up sex toy for him to take out and play with.

Abby made it to just before the door. She paused, checking to see if the man had noticed her movements.

He didn't.

Abby gave Paige one last look that seemed to say *good luck*, stood, and tiptoed from the room. As much as Paige wished she would run, to get help faster, she knew Abby was trying to be as silent as possible.

A horrible thought occurred to Paige when she remembered the buzzer Keys had set up at her front door. Had the man locked them inside? Would Abby be able to silence the buzzer before making her escape?

Paige feared the man going after Abby with his gun.

Ding-dong!

Paige stiffened, her eyes going wide as the man jumped to his feet. She waited for him to go after Abby, but his eyes were solely transfixed on her feet. Had he even registered the chime of the door? If he did, he was clearly ignoring it.

How long would it take for Abby to run across the street to get Angel? A minute? Two minutes, tops?

Horror gripped Paige as the man moved just enough to realize he had his cock out of his pants. The organ was erect, but not overly large. Three inches at most. Vaginal rape had not occurred to her with his fixation on her feet.

Hurry, Abby! Paige shouted in her mind.

The man, though, made no move to undress Paige or get to

her sex. Instead, he kicked over the stepstool some of her shorter patients used to get up onto the massage table. He climbed atop it, so his hips were just above the table.

Eyes closed, his face tipped up towards the ceiling with a look of elation across his features, the man started to masturbate over her feet.

CHAPTER 14

Rise of the Valkyrie interrupted their goodbye and show of appreciation to Susan Black. She'd confirmed Bulldog's suspicion that the landlord to Paige's building had no cause to terminate her lease now that she was paid up and current. And even if he did, he had to give her a thirty-day notice and bring her before the magisterial district court with probable cause.

Demo frowned when he saw the caller was Angel. "Angel, hey, we're—"

"Get to the clinic! Get to the clinic now!" From the sound of wind in the background, Demo deduced Angel was running.

Demo wasn't sure which one of them hung up the call first. "We need to go!"

Bulldog did not waste time arguing. He was already uneasy being away from Abby as he was. They raced out of Susan's offices. The clinic was down Main Street, on the other side of the traffic light. Demo hated it, but driving would be faster than running with the snow and ice obstacles.

They didn't fight over who was driving. Demo's Bronco was closer. "Something's happening at the clinic," he told his SAA. "Angel was running."

Fury crossed over Bulldog's features. He did not need to tell Demo to get them there fast. Nor did he press Demo for more information. He knew Demo would have given it if he had it. Demo sped out of the parking spot and shot down Main Street. He didn't even check if the traffic light was green before he crossed it, paying attention only to ensure the crossing was clear.

He hit the brakes hard outside the clinic. Not bothering to park properly, Demo only brought the vehicle to a complete stop before throwing the gearshift. He ran out and into the clinic.

The expectant *ding-dong!* of the bell was covered by the blast of a gunshot. *Bam!*

"Abby!" Bulldog roared, pushing past Demo. The fear in his voice was palpable.

Demo's own heart was thundering as he followed on Bulldog's heel to the first therapy room. A room Demo had come to think of as his and Paige's quickie room. It was all they had done in there since the first time when they'd broken the massage table.

Bulldog and Demo came to a halt in the doorway. The room itself looked as it always had, immaculate due to Paige's need to clean so thoroughly... Except now there was a splattering of blood along the back wall.

"Paige!" Demo yelled when his eyes landed on her bound to her own massage table. Fear radiated off of her. Tears streamed down her face from wide eyes. Her mouth was gagged with some sort of cloth that knotted at the back of her head.

He rushed forward, pulling his pocketknife from his pocket. He cut loose her right wrist, the one closest to him, which released her left he discovered. The rope must have bound them together under the table.

The moment he removed her gag from between her teeth, Paige let out the most heart-wrenching, ear-piercing scream. She threw her arms around his neck as Demo pulled her equally as tight against him. She cried and sobbed against his sweater.

"Where's Abby?" he heard Bulldog demand.

"Studio," Angel said. Demo had done a piss poor job of clearing the room before entering. All he'd seen was Paige in distress.

He shifted slightly, still holding onto Paige, so he could see the rest of the room. Bulldog left the doorway, presumably to go find his wife.

Angel stood opposite of Demo by the tall cabinet where Paige kept most of her supplies. The doors were currently open and no supplies were inside, making Demo wonder where it all was. He knew Paige and Abby had been working on inventorying.

On the floor at her feet was a...boy? No, a man. He was dead, given the bullet wound between his eyes. Angel was a former sniper and didn't miss her targets. Demo's blood nearly boiled when he saw the man's cock was sticking out the zipper of his jeans.

"What happened?" he asked Angel through gritted teeth. Paige was in no condition to answer. His heart seized at the idea that he could have lost her.

"I don't entirely know." Though the man was dead, Angel still stood guard over him and did not put away her gun. "Abby came running into the tattoo studio. Her hands were zip tied and she had managed to wiggle her gag out of her mouth enough to tell me that a man held Paige hostage here. I left her with Cage, ran and called you." She indicated to the man with the barrel of her gun. "You know the rest."

Demo looked down at Paige to see her feet were bare. There was a sheen to them, like something clear was lathered on them, in addition to blood splatter.

Had the man...? Why would...?

Angel answered his unspoken questions. Her voice was soft as if she was worried about upsetting Paige more. "He was masturbating over her feet."

Paige shot up so fast she nearly clipped Demo under the chin.

"He *licked* and *sucked* on my toes. He kept calling my feet 'my goddess'! He never even looked at me. I don't even think he knew I was here once he tied me down."

Fury seethed from her.

Demo felt himself stiffen. He was not a violent man by nature, but damn he wished Angel had not killed the man so quickly. That was far too quick a death.

Suddenly, Paige gasped. "He has a gun!"

Neither Demo nor Angel corrected Paige on her use of the present tense. The man *had* nothing now.

Angel bent and patted the man's pockets. She reached under his back and pulled out a silver pistol. One look at it, though, and Demo knew it wasn't real.

As if to demonstrate, Angel pointed the gun at the wall and shot the stream of water from it. "Water pistol. Looks real but isn't."

"He knocked me out. I heard the bell and thought one of you had come back since I didn't have any appointments on the schedule. He tackled me and I hit my head." She touched the back of her head and winced.

"Let me see," Demo said gently. He moved Paige's thick locks around until he found the goose egg on the back of her head. "No blood, but you got a good bump." He carefully pressed his lips to her head next to it.

"I didn't know he had a gun until Abby told me. I think that's how he tied her up. Threatened to shoot her."

"Abby's a fighter," Demo told Paige with confidence. "She knows how to act to make someone think she's complying while her mind is working on escape."

Paige looked doubtful by this knowledge, but the club knew it to be true. Abby had spent years in captivity and faced unimaginable horrors. But she never stopped fighting her captors and trying to break free to get back to Bulldog. It might have taken sixteen years, but she finally succeeded.

Whatever Abby had been thinking, Demo owed her for being able to get away and get to Angel.

The clinic door burst open and heavy footfalls echoed into the hallway. Carlos came through the door, followed closely by Steel and Lucky.

"Abby?" Demo inquired.

"Safe," Carlos and Steel answered in unison. "Bulldog insisted on calling an ambulance for her," Carlos continued. "One's on the way for you too, Paige."

"Thank you," Demo answered as Paige said, "That's not necessary."

"The fuck it isn't," Demo snapped. "You could have a concussion. You're getting checked out."

Paige lowered her voice as she confessed, "I don't have insurance."

"You think I give a damn?" Demo asked, harsher than intended. "You're going to the hospital, you're going to get checked out, and I'll pay any goddamn overpriced bill that comes our way."

Then he was figuring out how to get her and the boys on the club's insurance plan. How the fuck did he not know she didn't have health insurance? While no longer penalized, it was not a good idea to not have coverage. Sure, it was expensive, but what if she got hurt?

Like now!

Demo seethed. He wanted to punch Richard. Maybe he needed to look into necromancy to see if there was a way to raise the bastard from the dead so he could kill him again.

Steel approached the massage bed. He carefully unbound her legs from the table. "Get her out of here. We'll take care of this."

There wasn't much for the club to 'take care of'. For once, this was a legitimate and legal shooting that they did not have to cover up. Get answers about? Absolutely, but Angel had been within her rights to shoot to kill.

298

Though Demo did wish Angel was a slightly worse shot, he appreciated her protecting Paige.

Demo picked Paige up and carried her out of the therapy room. Maybe it was a good thing her landlord was evicting her, even if the eviction wasn't valid. He doubted Paige would want to stay working here after this anyway.

As he carried her from the clinic, he pressed a kiss to her temple. "I love you," he reminded her.

She tightened her arms around his neck, pressing her nose against the warmth of his skin. "I love you too."

* * *

Two Months **Later**

In the cool March afternoon, Paige stood next to Demo at the gravesite of Richard Hannigan. She held Mikey while Demo held Nelly Bean. Though neither one understood what the service was for, Paige felt that they had a right to be at their father's funeral. She wasn't sure exactly why she felt like she needed to have this service. She certainly didn't owe it to Richard. Her therapist, Dr. Rutenberg, reminded her that funerals were for the living, not the dead. In a way, Paige supposed she was laying to rest the part of her life that she'd shared with Richard by having a service to honor his life.

Harper and Lucky stood at Demo's right. They had not brought Conner, as the weather for the day was brisk at best. Paige had not wanted to wait longer and had chosen to bury Richard as soon as the graveyard said the ground was thawed enough to dig.

Ronald and Cindy stood at Paige's left. They were both solemn, mourning the son they had raised and not the man he had become. With everything else that had happened the day Paige had been told about Richard's death, it hadn't occurred to her until later that neither Ronald nor Cindy had looked surprised by the news. When she'd asked them about it, Cindy had confessed that she'd suspected Richard was dead after so long of no contact. She hadn't voiced it to Paige because it would have made it too real.

Demo was her rock and her salvation. He hadn't even blinked when she told him that she wanted to have a funeral for Richard. All he'd asked was when and if she wanted him to be there.

Of course, she had. While some might consider it awkward for Demo to be present at his lover's late husband's funeral, Demo didn't. And, bottom line, Paige needed him. She wouldn't have survived the day without him.

Neither Paige nor Abby had any lasting physical injuries from the attack at the clinic. Paige had a minor concussion and some abrasions from the ropes used to bind her. But both had taken a while to get through what had happened mentally. Paige knew that Abby's night terrors, which she'd been over a year since her last episode, had returned. Paige felt horrible about that, though neither Abby nor Bulldog blamed her.

The mystery behind the foot fetish site's hack was finally solved as soon as Paige's attacker was identified. Jeromy Copley was a twenty-one year old hacker who resided in Beaming, Missouri. He'd joined forces with the hacktivist group over three years ago but still did some side jobs on his own. He used the group's signature code to infiltrate the foot fetish's site.

Keys was able to find evidence that Jeromy had been following Paige's postings on the site nearly from the beginning. Something about her feet called to him, because there were numerous printouts of her pictures as well as stills from her videos in his basement bedroom at his parents' house.

What Paige hadn't known was that a user could request a specific model for their personal requests. All of those video requests that she'd been receiving where she thought it was odd no other model had taken the job were not open to the entire community. Jeromy had requested her specific screen name for those videos and had been upping the amount he would pay per live video when she'd stopped posting.

Something about her last video with the donuts had triggered Jeromy into finding Paige, so he hacked the site. To hide his motives, he laid a trail to the hacktivist group and posted the client list to the public. While they would never know what had happened to make him act the way he did, Paige secretly wondered if perhaps Jeromy had somehow been able to tell that she hadn't actually been eating the donuts as he'd instructed.

With his death, it would forever be a mystery.

Her stepfamily had ceased their harassment with no proof of the debt they claimed was owed to them. Paige was also able to file a restraining order following a very nasty voicemail her own mother had left her the morning the foot fetish site had been hacked. No one had heard from Clifton since his arrest for breaking into her house. Paige could honestly say she was not surprised by that news.

After filing for Richard's death certificate, Paige was finally able to make some headway on her outstanding debts. The credit cards that Richard had in his name alone, Paige learned she did not need to pay back after his death. Though technically that money should have come out of his estate before any inheritance was given. Since Richard hadn't left an inheritance behind, those credit card companies were just out that money. Paige did feel sorry about that, but still took the legal out.

She was not going to be filing for bankruptcy. After a long look at her finances, along with getting the remaining payout of Richard's insurance policy, she was able to put her house up for sale. So long as the house sold for at least four hundred and fifty thousand, she would be able to break even. The remainder of her credit cards would be paid off in time.

Paige did give up her clinic. Firstly, because she did not want to pay a man rent who thought she would have any part in sexually assaulting her clients, and secondly, because she had a hard time entering her clinic following her assault.

While it did feel a bit cowardly, she just couldn't do it. She'd been talking to Dr. Rutenberg, who was also Jumper's therapist, to work through some of her trauma too as well as her grief and anger regarding Richard.

After she walked away from his grave today, she would never think of Richard again. Demo was her future and she planned on making it a good one with him.

* * *

SARA—NOW Scissors—and Will—now Jigsaw—were officially patched in at the end of January. At their party, Scissors had proposed to Sissy. Down on one knee in front of everyone, she'd waited for Sissy's answer.

Of course, she'd said yes.

Sissy had officially joined the rank of ol' ladies, with her father's blessing, and ditched her club kid denim cut for one that said *Property of Scissors*. She and Paige, who wore her *Property of Demo* cut just as proudly, had come up with the idea of Paige utilizing some of the empty rooms in the clubhouse as her new clinic.

Paige was now the club's acupuncturist and massage therapist. Until the town settled down about Paige being a foot fetish model—which Demo still did not understand the big deal of— Paige did not feel comfortable opening another clinic in town. Tessa had gone a step further and asked Steel for a medical clinic as well. Cage had the plans drawn up and would be starting construction soon. Pumpkin and SJ were going to be moving into the trailer next to Frankie while construction took place as Pumpkin did not want the dust and noise around SJ.

Once her house sold, Paige would be moving into the same

apartment complex as Jumper, Jasmine, and Pirate. Demo would be remaining at the clubhouse. It wouldn't be forever and, as much as he wanted to move in together, he understood Paige's need to keep a small bit of distance between them. Independence was important to her.

Demo was looking forward to the day when Paige wore his ring as well as his cut.

The scare of Clifton's break-in and then her assault at the clinic had prompted Paige to have a very serious conversation with Demo regarding the boys' future. Should something happen to Paige, what should happen to the boys?

After assuring her over and over again that he wouldn't allow anything to happen to her, Demo had told her he would be honored if she entrusted her most precious creations to him. He did, however, understand if she felt they should go to Ronald and Cindy or Harper and Lucky. It wouldn't change how he felt about them or the hand he planned to have in raising them.

Following her release from the hospital, Paige had a will drawn up naming Demo as the boys' guardian should anything happen to Paige. Both Demo and Paige also signed paperwork to become the other's medical and financial Power of Attorney.

Come spring, Demo was breaking ground on the club's newest housing area. This one would be known as the Square, because it only had four plots. The design would be the same, though, and have a communal backyard between the four houses.

While no other takers had claimed the other three plots, bets were flying. Pumpkin was the top contender with SJ but he seemed adamant about staying in the clubhouse.

Demo wanted Paige to have a hand in everything going into his new house. He wanted her to feel welcome for when she was ready for them to start having sleepovers, as well as eventually move in. Be it in a month or in a year.

Everyone was gearing up for Jasmine and Jumper's April

wedding. It was not a rare sight to see Pirate and Sophia, as Best Man and Maid of Honor, at each other's throats regarding one detail or another. There were also bets taking place for how long before the two either came to blows or started fucking. Demo was betting on the latter, mainly because he knew Pirate would never actually hit Sophia—no matter how often the club brother looked like he wanted to strangle the sassy minx.

Every day Paige worked her witchy magic on him a little bit more. Just when he didn't think it was possible to love her any more than he already did, she would do something to prove him wrong.

Following her assault, their sex life had taken an understandable hiatus. She hadn't felt *clean* and it had taken some time before Paige had felt comfortable with the two of them engaging in any sexual activity. It was rare for Demo to see Paige insecure, but old wounds had shown themselves when Paige had asked him if he wanted to take a break from dating her while she got her head on straight.

When he'd asked why, she replied nervously, "So you don't feel guilty about wanting to seek out other sexual partners."

Demo nearly busted a lung laughing so hard. "You do recall when I said 'I love you' right? That wasn't contingent on you being willing or able to put out, Paige. I could care less if we ever have sex again. Okay," he amended, "I *do* care, sue me. But there's no need to rush things. You take care of you and I'll take care of you."

"Then who takes care of you?" she asked in return.

"My right hand," he said while wiggling the digits in front of her face. "Paige, you never have to wonder or worry about me being faithful. You own me, heart, body, and soul. That includes my cock and lips, last I checked. I'm yours, regardless of when you're ready to have sex again."

A few weeks later, he'd surprised her with two new tattoos. In true Demo fashion, he'd gotten several lines to Austin Giorgio's *You Put a Spell on Me* down his back. The only change or addition he made to the lyrics was adding *Paige* with a comma before the first line. Then he got a tattoo below his bellybutton that read *Property of Paige* with an arrow pointed down at his groin.

Paige laughed so hard that she'd nearly toppled off of her bed.

Standing at the gravesite of Richard Hannigan, Demo felt good about facing their future. He'd found his woman and she'd given him two adorable little boys that he would one day get to call his own.

And it helped that his woman had magic needles that helped him manage his shoulder pain.

Demo even made peace with his dad. It had taken a shouting match over the phone for his father to hop on a plane and finally make it out to Pennsylvania. It would take time for father and son to mend bridges entirely, but his father's heartfelt apology was a very good start. He was even considering moving to Mount Grove to spend more time with Demo, as well as get to know Paige, Mikey, and Nelly Bean better. The idea of being a grandpa had brought a smile to his father's face that Demo had never seen before.

Time would tell. Demo was willing to let bygones lie so long as his father did.

Taking her hand, Demo led Paige away from her late husband's gravesite. Their present was just as important as planning for their future—and Demo knew there was an ice cream bar waiting for them back at the clubhouse.

Paige was his miracle and proof that magic did exist in this dark world. Demo would do anything and everything necessary to ensure her happiness. As he'd told Paige before, there was no rush. They had time. There was no relationship checklist and monitor verifying they completed certain milestones by a certain date. Paige would move in with him and wear his ring when *she* was ready and not a moment before—because Demo wouldn't let her.

Their future was theirs and theirs alone. Filled with laughter, love, lots of witchy magic, and the promise of dancing naked in the moonlight.

NATIONAL DOWN SYNDROME SOCIETY

NDSS empowers individuals with Down syndrome and their families by driving policy change, providing resources, engaging with location communities, and shifting public perceptions.

To Donate or to learn more about the NDSS go to https://ndss.org

MORE BOOKS BY ELISE

Books in the VDMC Series

1. Lucky
2. Bear
3. Bulldog
4. Jumper
5. Angel
6. Demo
7. Pirate (February 2025)

VDMC Novellas

- Carlos-Part 1
- Carlos-Part 2
- Carlos-Part 3
- Scotty's Halloween Adventure
- A VDMC Holiday Special
- Louisa's Valentine (February 7, 2025)
- Lucky's Lucky St. Paddy's Day (February 21, 2025)

Books in Mountain Mutineers Series

1. Mountain Refuge
2. Mountain Revenge (Release: 2025)

FOLLOW ME

**Follow me on Social Media for Updates, Promos, and
Announcements!**
@elisegedickeauthor
www.elisegedickeauthor.com
elisegedickeauthor@gmail.com

Made in the USA
Columbia, SC
14 April 2025

56567336R00178